EMPIRE RISING

ALSO BY RICK CAMPBELL

The Trident Deception

EMPIRE RISING

RICK CAMPBELL

ST. MARTIN'S PRESS ⌇ NEW YORK

EMPIRE RISING. Copyright © 2015 by Rick Campbell. All rights reserved. Printed in the United States of America. For information, address St. Martin's Press, 175 Fifth Avenue, New York, NY 10010.

www.stmartins.com

Designed by Steven Seighman

The Library of Congress Cataloging-in-Publication Data is available upon request.

ISBN 978-1-250-04046-6 (hardcover)
ISBN 978-1-4668-3580-1 (e-book)

St. Martin's Press books may be purchased for educational, business, or promotional use. For information on bulk purchases, please contact the Macmillan Corporate and Premium Sales Department at 1-800-221-7945, extension 5442, or write to specialmarkets@macmillan.com.

First Edition: February 2015

10 9 8 7 6 5 4 3 2 1

To mom and dad—I wish you were still here.

ACKNOWLEDGMENTS

Many thanks are due to those who helped me write and publish this novel:

First and foremost, to my editor, Keith Kahla, for his exceptional insight and fantastic recommendations on how to make *Empire Rising* better. To others at St. Martin's Press—Hannah Braaten and Justin Velella—who helped me in numerous ways while I wrote and revised *Empire Rising*. And finally, thanks again to Sally Richardson and George Witte for making this book possible.

To those who helped me get the details in *Empire Rising* right: to U.S. Navy captains and former SSN and SSGN commanding officers Steve Harrison and Murray Gero for reviewing the submarine chapters and helping me with the SSGN scenes, to Navy Captain and former commander of Strike Fighter Wing Atlantic—Craig "Spot" Yager for assisting with the air combat scenarios, to Commander Rob Kurz for the aircraft carrier chapters, Commander Mike Wheeldreyer for the cruiser scenes, former Navy SEALs Matt Maasdam and Brandon Webb for the SEAL scenes, and to Lieutenant Colonel Billy Dubose and Major Joshua Roberts for imparting a basic understanding of Marine Expeditionary Force operations. Thanks also to Lisa Brackmann and Cindy Pon for helping with the scenes in China and the nuances of naming Chinese characters.

To my writer friends in Purgatory and The Pit, thank you for your support on this long journey and for your inspiration while writing *Empire Rising*.

And finally, to the men and women who have served in our armed services. My heart and thoughts will always be with you.

I hope you enjoy *Empire Rising*!

PRINCIPAL CHARACTERS

(A COMPLETE CAST OF CHARACTERS IS PROVIDED IN ADDENDUM.)

UNITED STATES ADMINISTRATION
KEVIN HARDISON, chief of staff
CHRISTINE O'CONNOR, national security advisor
NELSON JENNINGS, secretary of defense
STEVE BRACKMAN (Captain), senior military aide

PEOPLE'S REPUBLIC OF CHINA ADMINISTRATION
XIANG CHENGLEI, president of China and general secretary of the Party
HUAN ZHIXIN, chairman, Central Military Commission
BAI TAO, prime minister
SHEN YI, Politburo member
YANG MINSHENG, head of President Xiang's security detail

UNITED STATES JOINT CHIEFS OF STAFF
MARK HODSON (General), Chairman, Joint Chiefs of Staff
MEL GARRISON (General), Chief of Staff, Air Force
GRANT HEALEY (Admiral), Chief of Naval Operations
ELY WILLIAMS (General), Commandant of the Marine Corps

UNITES STATES MAJOR MILITARY COMMANDS
VANCE GARBIN (Admiral), Commander, Pacific Command
CARL KRAE (Major General), Commander, Cyber Warfare Command

MICHAEL WALKER (Rear Admiral), Commander, Naval Special Warfare Command

TIM MOSS (Rear Admiral), Program Executive Officer (Submarines)

USS *MICHIGAN* (GUIDED MISSILE SUBMARINE)

MURRAY WILSON (Captain), Commanding Officer

PAUL GREENWOOD (Lieutenant Commander), Executive Officer

KASEY FAUCHER (Lieutenant Commander), Engineering Officer

KELLY HAAS (Lieutenant Commander), Supply Officer

KARL STEWART (Lieutenant), Weapons Officer

STEVE CORDERO (Lieutenant), Junior Officer

KRIS HERNDON (Lieutenant), Junior Officer

JOE ALEO (Commander), Medical Officer

JEFF WALKUP (Chief Electronics Technician), Radioman

SAM WALSH (Machinist Mate Second Class), Torpedoman

BILL COATES (Electronics Technician Second Class), Quartermaster

USS *NIMITZ* (AIRCRAFT CARRIER)

ALEX HARROW (Captain), Commanding Officer

HELEN CORCORAN (Captain), Air Wing Commander

SUE LAYBOURN (Captain), Combat Direction Center (CDC) Operations Officer

MICHAEL BERESFORD (Lieutenant Commander), Officer of the Deck

NATHAN REYNOLDS (Lieutenant), Conning Officer

USS *RONALD REAGAN* (AIRCRAFT CARRIER)

CHARLES "CJ" BERGER (Captain), Commanding Officer

EMIL JONES (Captain), Air Wing Commander

TIM POWERS (Captain), Executive Officer

DEBBIE KENT (Captain), Combat Direction Center (CDC) Operations Officer

ANDREW FELLOWS (Commander), Chief Engineer

USS *ANNAPOLIS* (LOS ANGELES CLASS FAST ATTACK SUBMARINE)

RAMSEY HOOTMAN (Commander), Commanding Officer
TED WINSOR (Lieutenant Commander), Executive Officer
DON MILLER (Lieutenant), Weapons Officer
MIKE LAND (Lieutenant), Junior Officer
ARMANDO HOGARTH (Lieutenant), Junior Officer

USS *JACKSONVILLE* (LOS ANGELES CLASS FAST ATTACK SUBMARINE)

RANDY BAUGHMAN (Commander), Commanding Officer
BECK BURRELL (Lieutenant), Officer of the Deck

USS *TEXAS* (VIRGINIA CLASS FAST ATTACK SUBMARINE)

JIM LATHAM (Commander), Commanding Officer
JOHN MILLIGAN (Lieutenant Commander), Executive Officer
COLBY MARSHALL (Petty Officer First Class), Fire Control Technician

NAVY SEALS

JOHN MCNEIL (Commander), SEAL Team Commander
JAKE HARRISON (Lieutenant), SEAL Platoon Officer in Charge (OIC)
DAN O'HARA (Chief Special Warfare Operator), SEAL Platoon Chief
DREW GARRETSON (Special Warfare Operator First Class), Communicator
TRACEY MARTIN (Special Warfare Operator Second Class), Breacher
KELLY ANDREWS (Special Warfare Operator Second Class), Rappeler

CHINESE MILITARY

TSOU DESHI (Fleet Admiral), Commander, People's Liberation Army (PLA) Navy
GUO JIAN (Admiral), Commander, East Sea Fleet
CAO FENG (General), Commander, Fourth Department
ZHANG ANGUO (General), Commander, Nanjing Military Region

ZHOU PENGFEI (Captain), Commander, 34th *Hong Niao* Missile Battery

CHENG BO (Captain), Officer-in-Charge, East Sea Fleet Command Center

ZENG YONG (Commander), Commanding Officer, submarine CNS *Chang Cheng*

ZHAO WEI (Commander), Commanding Officer, submarine CNS *Jiaolong*

EMPIRE
RISING

BEIJING, CHINA

IT WOULD HAVE BEEN PERFECT.

Bai Jiao's pulse raced as she stood stiffly under the bright lights, her cold hands gripping the bouquet of flowers as tightly as the white gown squeezed her waist. The veil across her eyes partially obscured her vision, but she could see enough to make out the cavernous Grand Ballroom of the Pangu Hotel, an immense chandelier suspended from the center of the thirty-foot-high ceiling. The white carpet runway beneath her feet, passing by row after row of guests, stretched to infinity.

Feeling a nudge on her right arm, Jiao remembered she wasn't standing alone; she felt her father's arm intertwined with hers. Turning her head, she sought his wizened face. Tao was looking down at her. He smiled, and for a moment she was a little girl again, sitting in her father's lap as he imparted words of wisdom to his precious *qianjin*. He patted her arm, conveying his love and support. She knew that, even now, she could call it off. Even though the arrangements had cost over two million yuan, Tao would not think twice about the loss. The shame he would endure, however, if his daughter backed out on her wedding day . . .

It was just nerves, after all. She loved Huang, and was ready to begin their life together. She forced a weak smile and nodded her head.

Slowly, in rhythm to the music that began with her first step, Jiao and her father proceeded down the center aisle of the ballroom, passing the four hundred guests turned out in tuxedos freshly pressed and formal evening gowns sparkling under the ballroom lights. Jiao kept her eyes focused at the end of the long white carpet where Huang waited, standing at attention in his maroon and pine-green military uniform.

Along the perimeter of the room, men in black suits, with a coiled cord hanging from one ear and tucked inside the collar of their jackets, cast a watchful eye over every entrance to the ballroom as well as the guests. For as long as Jiao could remember, men like these had guarded her family. It wasn't until her teenage years that she gained an appreciation for the power her father wielded as one of the Party's nine Politburo members and now as China's prime minister.

As China's economic czar, Tao was charged with infusing capitalistic traits into the country's socialist economy, so Jiao was not surprised when her father requested her wedding be a blend of Western and traditional Chinese ceremonies. As Jiao proceeded down the aisle in her white wedding gown, she looked forward to the Tea Ceremony that would follow in the adjacent ballroom. She would change into the traditional *qi pao* dress, its red color symbolizing good luck, warding off evil spirits.

At the end of the white runway, her father released her arm. Jiao stepped up to the altar, turning toward Huang. As she looked into his eyes, a warm glow spread through her body, chasing away the nervous chill. The day she had dreamt of as a young girl had finally arrived. She knew with certainty they would spend the rest of their lives together. Nothing could tear them apart.

As Huang lifted the veil from her face, a flash of movement distracted her. Men in black suits were sprinting down the sides of the ballroom, headed behind a beige curtain that hung from the ceiling, forming the backdrop of the altar. Over Huang's shoulder, she spotted Feng Dai, her personal body-guard since she was a child, racing toward her. A commotion penetrated the curtain, accompanied by a mosaic of dark shapes shifting behind the sheer fabric. She turned back toward Huang, and as she met his questioning eyes, there was a deafening boom.

Jiao was buffeted by a blast of hot air and she had the odd sensation she was flying through the air. Her vision clouded in an orange, blossoming haze, and white-hot pain stabbed into her body as her limbs bent in directions they weren't designed for. There was a vague feeling of her back hitting something hard and sharp, the pain piercing through her stomach. Her vision slowly cleared and a thousand yellow lights came into focus, swaying above her.

She was lying on the floor somewhere, gazing at beautiful lights swirling above. It was peacefully quiet at first, but then faint sounds greeted her ears, growing gradually louder until they coalesced into a dissonance of high-pitched screams of terror mingled with low moans of pain. As if responding to the sound, her mind was reminded of the sensations slicing through her body. The slightest attempt to move—breathe, even—magnified the excruciating pain.

Jiao turned her head slowly to the side. She was surrounded by a nightmarish collage of sight and smell. Bodies strewn across a red-streaked floor. Bloodied hands reaching toward heaven, splayed fingers clawing the air. Men and women wreathed in fire were dancing under the ballroom lights, collapsing onto the floor, their charred features shrouded in an orange, flickering haze. The scent assailing her nostrils was foreign but unmistakable: the stench of burning flesh.

A few feet away, Jiao's father lay on his back, his neck at an awkward angle, his eyes frozen open. Just out of reach, Huang was facedown, a dark stain spreading out from under him across the white carpet. Jiao felt warmth ooze across her stomach, moving up her chest and down her legs as liquid saturated her wedding gown. She looked down at her tattered garment, and as her thoughts faded into darkness, Jiao wondered when she had changed into her red dress.

OPENING MOVES

1

WASHINGTON, D.C.

A light rain was falling from a gray, overcast sky as a black Lincoln Town Car merged onto the 14th Street Bridge, fighting its way north across three lanes of early morning traffic. In the back of the sedan, Christine O'Connor gazed through rain-streaked windows at the Potomac River flowing lazily east toward the Chesapeake Bay. She ignored the rhythmic thump of the sedan's windshield wipers, focused instead on the radio tuned to a local AM news station. As she listened to the morning's headlines, she wasn't surprised the most important news of the day was absent from the broadcast.

As the president's national security advisor, Christine was briefed daily on events occurring around the world with the potential to affect the safety of American citizens. This morning, she was returning from the Pentagon after her weekly intelligence brief with Secretary of Defense Nelson Jennings. Near the end of the meeting, the discussion had turned to yesterday's assassination of China's prime minister. There would be instability within China's Politburo Standing Committee as its eight remaining members determined the replacement for the second most powerful person in China. Concern was voiced about the loss of Bai Tao, a staunch opponent to using military force to resolve China's conflicts. Considering what the United States was contemplating signing, that was not an insignificant issue.

The MAER Accord—the Mutual Access to Environmental Resources Accord—was the exact opposite of what it purported to be. Christine opened the manila folder in her lap, revealing the one-inch-thick document on the right side and her notes on the left, and began reviewing them one final time before her meeting with the president. Upon reading its title, one would think the accord ensured equal access to the world's supply of natural resources, which were straining to meet the demands of the industrialized and developing countries. Oil and natural gas production were simply not keeping pace, and within three years, there would not be enough to go around.

Instead of ensuring every country would receive their fair share, the MAER Accord included complicated price calculations that favored the United States and its allies. Less fortunate countries, including China, would be forced to pay much higher prices. Additionally, it included a military defense assurance between the United States and the Pacific Rim nations, who were fearful of an aggressive China, which had been rattling its sword and staking claim to many of the region's natural resources. The future lay in vast Asian offshore oil fields, and the half-century-long MAER Accord assured America and its allies would have access to the resources their economies would require for the next fifty years. In return, America would respond to any attempt by another country to claim the natural resources of another.

Christine's Town Car turned right on West Executive Avenue, bringing her closer to the White House and her final meeting on the accord with the president and Kevin Hardison. The mere thought of the president's chief of staff threatened to bring on a migraine. They were once close friends, working together on Congressman Tim Johnson's staff twenty years ago, when Hardison, ten years her senior, had been her mentor. But all that changed once she became the president's national security advisor, when she surprised Hardison with a mind of her own, refusing to subordinate herself to his orders.

Unlike most administrations, the president preferred to have counsel from both political parties. Unfortunately, Christine was the outsider, which meant she had the burden of fighting the uphill battles. Still, she had won a surprisingly large percentage of them, which was probably one of the reasons for the animosity between her and Hardison. Their disdain for each other wouldn't help in a few minutes when they met in the Oval Office, with one last opportunity to convince the president of the dangerous repercussions of signing the MAER Accord.

The Lincoln Town Car pulled to a stop under the north portico, next to two Marines in Dress Blues guarding the formal entrance to the West Wing. Standing between the two Marines—almost a head taller—was a Navy Captain wearing the Navy's version of its Dress Blues, with four gold stripes on each sleeve. Steve Brackman was the president's senior military aide, with whom she had forged a close working relationship. Christine had called ahead and asked him to meet her when she returned to the White House. As she prepared for battle with the president's powerful chief of staff, she preferred to have the military on her side.

Brackman greeted her as she stepped from the sedan, polite as always. "Good morning, Miss O'Connor."

Christine returned the Captain's greeting, and Brackman followed her to her corner office. She entered and dropped off her leather briefcase, but Brackman stopped at the entrance to her office. Christine returned to the doorway.

"I'm sorry, Miss O'Connor. Mr. Hardison requested I meet with him in a few minutes. Is there something quick I can help you with?"

Christine frowned. Hardison apparently had the same battle plan she had. She answered, "The president is going to make his decision on the MAER Accord today. Hardison is pushing the president to sign it while I'm advising against it. I wanted to spend a few minutes with you, so you fully understood my concerns."

"I think I understand both sides of the argument," Brackman replied.

Christine pressed her lips together. As the president's senior military aide, Brackman could tip the scales. "And your recommendation will be . . . ?"

Brackman's eyes searched hers for a moment, and it seemed he was about to answer, but he checked his watch instead. "If you'll excuse me."

As Brackman turned to leave, Christine grabbed his arm. "Don't let him persuade you. I'm counting on your support."

Brackman hesitated before replying. "I know, Miss O'Connor." He eased his arm from her grip, then turned and headed toward Hardison's office.

Christine watched him disappear down the hallway, then decided to wait where she could keep an eye on the Oval Office's doors. She headed down the seventy-foot-long hallway, turning left into the Roosevelt Room. While she waited, she took the opportunity to admire the two oil paintings hanging on opposing walls: Alfred Jonniaux's portrait of Franklin Delano Roosevelt seated behind his desk, and Tade Styka's equestrian portrait of Theodore Roosevelt titled *Rough Rider*. In accordance with tradition, the incoming administration had reversed the two portraits, placing the image of FDR over the fireplace and Theodore Roosevelt to Christine's right, on the south wall.

As Christine examined the portrait of Theodore Roosevelt, she reflected on his famous slogan—*Speak softly and carry a big stick*. If the president signed the MAER Accord and China responded as she predicted, the United States was going to need a big stick, indeed.

There was a knock on the Roosevelt Room's open door, and Christine turned to spot chief of staff Kevin Hardison, who tapped his watch. "The president's waiting."

Christine followed Hardison into the Oval Office. Captain Brackman also joined them, and Christine took her seat in the middle of three chairs opposite the president's desk, with Hardison and Brackman flanking her.

The president addressed Christine. "Any details on the assassination of China's prime minister?"

Christine answered, "Our Intel agencies have narrowed the potential motives down to the two most probable. The first is a terrorist attack by one of the separatist organizations from the Xinjiang region in northwest China. The second is internal strife within the Politburo, with one of the junior members taking matters into his own hands. In that case, Shen Yi is the leading suspect. He's the longest serving Politburo member, yet sits third in the power structure behind Xiang Chenglei, the general secretary of the Party and president of China, and Xiang's protégé, Bai Tao, the prime minister. Shen is getting up in years, and the death of Bai Tao is fortunate from his perspective, making him the leading candidate to replace Xiang when he steps down." Christine paused for a moment. "Or if something happens to Xiang."

The specter of Politburo strife plunging China's leadership into chaos couldn't have come at a worse time. The instability would make an accurate prediction of China's response to the MAER Accord impossible. In concert with Christine's thoughts, Hardison changed the subject.

"We need to discuss the accord, sir. The terms expire at the end of this week, so you need to sign it before you leave this afternoon for Camp David."

"What are the current projections?" the president asked.

Hardison replied, "Without price constraints, world demand for oil will increase by eight percent per year, with oil production increasing by only one percent. To reduce oil consumption to within production capacity, the price of oil will double over the next three years. We crafted the accord to prevent skyrocketing prices, and the terms we negotiated are more than fair, restricting each country to an appropriate percentage of the world's oil supply."

"The terms are *not* fair," Christine replied. "The method used to calculate each country's fair share is flawed, and you know it. The accord will strangle China's economy."

Hardison shrugged as he turned toward Christine. "And that's a bad thing? They had their chance to negotiate a better deal, and failed."

"They failed because we bribed our way to favorable terms, offering over a hundred billion dollars in military grants."

"We negotiated," Hardison jabbed. *"Negotiated."*

Christine folded her arms across her chest. "Bribed."

Hardison leveled a malevolent gaze at Christine before turning back to the president. "Gasoline prices have doubled since you took office and will double again before the reelection if you don't sign the accord. If you want another term in office, you don't have a choice."

"I don't recommend it," Christine interjected. "The main question is whether China will use its military to obtain the resources it needs. They won't be able to buy the oil and natural gas they require, and they might use their military to obtain it by force. It'll be Japan and Pearl Harbor all over again. In 1941, the United States placed an embargo on oil and gasoline exports to Japan, cutting off eighty percent of their oil supply. Japan did in 1941 what China will likely do today—they moved south to secure the natural resources they required.

"The Pacific Rim contains several billion barrels of oil, plus nine hundred trillion cubic feet of natural gas. China has already staked claim to the Spratly Island Archipelago and the Senkaku Islands. The Spratly Islands alone are under the control of six different nations, and if China decides to enforce its claim to these islands and their offshore natural resources, it's going to put the United States in a bind. Per the MAER Accord, we'll have to come to the defense of these countries. We'll be at war with China. Is that what you want? Because that's exactly what you'll get if you sign the accord."

"China wouldn't dare start a war," Hardison replied. "They know we'd come to the aid of anyone they attacked. And another thing to consider, Mr. President," he cast a derisive glance in Christine's direction, "is that Christine has a track record of being wrong, so I recommend you factor that into your decision."

Christine leveled an icy stare at the chief of staff. She hadn't kept tally, but was pretty sure it was Hardison who was wrong most of the time. His long list of flaws apparently included a short memory.

While Christine glared at Hardison, the president reflected on the relationship between the man and woman sitting across from him. Aside from a temporary truce following the *Kentucky* incident, Christine and Hardison got along like oil and vinegar, and didn't realize what a great team they made. He had selected Hardison as his chief of staff primarily for his experience, and secondarily for his ruthlessness, an essential trait of an effective chief of staff. But he also recognized Hardison's zeal would intimidate many of the men and women on his staff and in his Cabinet.

He had wanted a strong national security advisor, someone with the necessary background and keen insight. But—just as important—he needed someone who wouldn't wither under Hardison's overbearing demeanor, and he had known after his interview with Christine that she was the right woman for the job. She told him his proposed policies would ruin the country's ability to defend itself. She spoke her mind and pulled no punches.

Christine was the right woman for the job, and it didn't hurt that she was attractive. He noticed how his two teenage sons popped out of the woodwork whenever Christine dropped by the Executive Residence. Their eyes followed her every movement, surveying her attractive face—sparkling blue eyes framed by auburn hair—and her lean, yet womanly curves. After Christine departed, the two boys would vanish as quickly as they appeared.

The president clearing his throat brought Christine's attention back to the commander-in-chief. He looked toward Brackman. "What's your assessment? If China uses its military, can we defeat them?"

Brackman didn't immediately respond, and the president's question hung in the air as Brackman cast a sideways glance at Christine before focusing on the president.

"If China starts a war over oil," Brackman answered, "we can defend any country they attack. Although they've significantly modernized their military over the last decade, they're still no match for our Pacific Fleet. With five carrier strike groups off China's shore, along with our Marine Expeditionary Forces—two Marine divisions and their air wings—any attempt to seize oil reserves in the region will be defeated."

Christine gave Brackman a frosty glare as the president absorbed the Captain's words, his eyes canvassing each of the individuals seated in front of him. Christine felt a deepening uneasiness as the president moved toward his decision.

Finally, he spoke. "I'll sign the accord."

A smile broke across Hardison's face. "I'll have Sikes inform the press. How about a signing in the Rose Garden at noon?"

The president nodded. "That's fine." His gaze swept across the three individuals on the other side of his desk. "Anything else?" After all three offered negative shakes of their heads, the president added, "I'll see you at noon."

Christine stood, leading the way from the Oval Office. Brackman turned right as he exited while Christine and Hardison turned left, headed toward their diametrically opposed corner offices in the West Wing. Christine looked up at Hardison as he joined her at her side.

"You better be right," she said.

Hardison offered a smug, condescending smile. "I always am."

No other words were exchanged. As the chief of staff entered his office while Christine turned right, toward hers, her instinct told her signing the accord was a serious mistake.

2

FUJIAN PROVINCE, CHINA

As the sun slipped behind the Wuyi Mountains, shadows crept east from the red sandstone slopes, sinking into the lush green gorges of the Jiuqu Xi River before encroaching on the Pacific Ocean. Not far from the coast, a lone figure ascended a narrow trail toward a grassy plateau overlooking the East China Sea, its frothy white waves crashing into the rocky shore six hundred feet below. With a steady gait, the elderly man moved toward a circular stone building flanked by a curving thicket of magnolia trees.

After climbing a half-dozen cracked stone steps, Xiang Chenglei entered the Mazu temple, stopping before the altar to kneel on the cold granite floor. In the four corners of the building, torches flickered in the fading light, bathing the goddess of the sea and her two dragon guardians in dancing hues of amber and burnt orange. Carved from the metamorphic mountain rock, Mazu sat upon her throne holding a ceremonial tablet in her right hand, a staff in the other. On her left coiled the fierce dragon *Thousand Miles Eye*, the red paint peeling from the two-horned guardian, while on her right reclined the fading green *With-the-Wind Ear*, the dragon's single horn broken near its tip.

For tonight's prayer, Xiang knew he could have chosen a more decorative temple, with Mazu and her guardians fabricated from precious metals and jewels instead of simple stone and paint, but it was fitting that he knelt before this unadorned goddess just as his mother had done countless times when Xiang was a child. As he knelt beside her in silence, the moisture collecting in her eyes, he wondered what she prayed for; she clasped her hands so tightly her fingers turned white. It was not until Xiang became an adult that his father explained, the revelation igniting his hatred. Tonight, forty years after learning his mother's dark secret, personal and political aspirations had unexpectedly converged. Lijuan and China would finally have justice.

Xiang prayed tonight for the protection that would enable that justice, requesting Mazu watch over the thousands of men who would soon journey upon the seas. As he finished his appeal to the patron saint of fishermen and sailors, a warm, moist wind blew in from the ocean, carrying the scent of childhood memories. He had grown into a man in the small fishing village at the bottom of the winding path he had just climbed. The only son of Bohai and Lijuan Xiang, he was no stranger to hard work; the life of a fisherman was arduous at best. Although he had planned to follow in his father's footsteps, the older man had a grander vision, explaining that the hands of a fisherman could take him only so far. The mind of a scholar, however, could take him anywhere. But not even his father could have imagined the path his son would follow.

After completing his prayer, Xiang rose to his feet, the stiffness in his knees reminding him of his sixty-five years. Exiting the temple, he strolled to the edge of the plateau, looking down at the small fishing village nestled along the shore. He knew the six men at the base of the narrow trail would be nervous by now. The men from the Central Guard Bureau's Cadre Department had objected when he instructed them to stay behind, but he wanted to visit the temple of his childhood, filled with strong memories of his mother, alone. He ought to head back now; he guessed he had only twenty minutes before dusk succumbed to night, the dying light of day supplanted by the pale glow of a full moon. But there was another building of stone and mortar he desired to visit, not far down the sloping cliffs overlooking the Taiwan Strait.

Xiang carefully descended another trail, winding his way down the steep slope until he came to a smooth outcropping of rock. Upon close examination, he spotted a rectangular seam in the side of the protrusion and knocked firmly on the heavy metal door. A few seconds later, a cover over a small window in the door slid away, revealing the face of a young soldier, the green epaulets on his uniform proclaiming him a Private First Class in the People's Liberation Army.

Even in the dim light of dusk, Xiang could see the blood drain from the young man's face when he recognized the man standing outside. The Private stuttered an unintelligible greeting, then slammed the cover shut with more force than required. Xiang waited patiently as the soldier's footsteps raced away from the door, returning a moment later at a more measured pace, another pair of footsteps joining his. The lock mechanisms rotated, and the door swung inward. Standing next to the Private was a Captain who saluted crisply, as did the Private a split second later.

Tension was evident in the stiff posture of both men, and Xiang attempted to put them at ease by issuing the formal greeting to his troops, a time-honored custom since the words were first uttered by Zhu De in 1949.

"Greetings, comrades."

"Greetings, leader!" both men replied in unison.

The two men stood rigidly at attention, awaiting Xiang's next words. He offered a warm smile instead, and the Captain and Private dropped their salutes.

"There has been much progress since your last review," the Captain said, accurately assessing the purpose of Xiang's visit. "We are now fully operational, and have many new men who will be proud you have visited us."

Leaving the Private behind, the Captain turned and headed down a long hallway. As Xiang followed Captain Zhou Pengfei down the narrow passageway, his thoughts returned to the path he had traversed since leaving the sandy shore of his village almost fifty years ago. After excelling in elementary and high school, he gained entrance to Beijing's Tsinghua University, where he earned a degree in mechanical engineering. While in college, he joined the Communist Party of China during the Cultural Revolution, quickly concluding Mao Zedong's socialist reforms were crippling the country, stagnating sorely needed economic growth. During those formative years, Xiang developed the yearning to lead China to prosperity. All he lacked was the opportunity.

That opportunity emerged when the repression of the Cultural Revolution ended. China's new leader, Deng Xiaoping, implemented the "Four Transformations," promoting foreign investment and entrepreneurship, infusing Party leadership with men who were younger, more knowledgeable, and more revolutionary. Xiang was promoted quickly up the Party ranks and just before his fiftieth birthday became the youngest member ever of the powerful nine-member Politburo Standing Committee, China's supreme ruling body. Now, as both general secretary of the Communist Party and president of the country, there was no one more influential in all of China.

Yet his vast power had proved insufficient to sustain China on its path to prosperity.

Less than twenty-four hours ago, barricades had come crashing down. The United States and its allies had negotiated preferential access to the world's oil supply. Xiang had reviewed the projections of his economic ministers— the exorbitant oil prices they'd be forced to pay would plunge China's economy into a death spiral, unraveling the last forty years of progress.

Xiang and Captain Zhou reached the end of the long corridor and turned left, delving deeper into the mountainside. The opening led to a twenty-by-twenty-foot room crammed with electronic consoles, the blue glow from the displays illuminating the faces of the soldiers seated behind them. The Captain called out as Xiang entered and the eight men snapped to attention, awe evident in their expressions as they stood in the presence of China's supreme leader. After Zhou ordered them To Rest, the men settled uneasily into their chairs, exchanging glances as Xiang and the Captain stopped behind one of the consoles.

"I believe it is dark enough to bring the battery on-line," Zhou said. It was more a question than a statement, and Xiang answered with a nod of his head.

Zhou turned and issued orders to the enlisted man seated at the console. The soldier acknowledged, and as his fingers flicked across the glass surface of the touch-screen display, Xiang knew that above them, radars were being raised from recesses in the mountain's surface, beginning their rhythmic back-and-forth sweeps. A three-dimensional image of an island appeared in the center of the display, separated from the mainland by a two-hundred-mile-wide swath of the Pacific Ocean.

"With our new *Hong Niao* missiles," Zhou proudly announced, "we have complete coverage of the Strait. Nothing can enter without our permission."

Xiang nodded again. China had spent the last decade developing advanced anti-ship cruise missiles, deploying them along the coast in forty concealed bunkers like this one. The People's Liberation Army had done their task well, camouflaging their construction from American satellites in orbit. The United States had no idea what awaited them.

The Captain added, "Each man controls one of the eight launchers, selecting the desired target. Come, the launchers have been installed since your last visit."

Zhou led Xiang out of the control room, crossing the hallway. They entered a second room containing eight quad-missile launchers, the fifteen-foot-long missiles pointing toward a closed portal measuring four feet high by sixty feet wide. The Captain tapped a control near the room's entrance, and a twelve-inch-thick section retracted slowly upward, revealing the Pacific Ocean, providing a flight path for the thirty-two missiles.

As Xiang stared through the portal of the casemated bunker, the horizon melting into the darkness, he recalled the times he stood on the plateau above them in his youth, straining to see the distant shore of Taipei, the island referred to by the West as Taiwan. It was to Taiwan that Chiang Kai-shek's forces, defeated in China's civil war, retreated in 1949. If the Politburo Standing Committee approved the People's Liberation Army's plan tomorrow, there would be many benefits, one of them being the long overdue unification of the two Chinas.

Zhou interrupted Xiang's rumination. "It is an honor you have visited us again."

"The honor is mine, Captain. It is the dedication of men like you, who serve the people, that keeps our country safe and prosperous."

Upon uttering those words, Xiang's thoughts returned to the MAER Accord. The United States had restricted China's access to vital oil supplies, strangling its economy. Although America's aggression hadn't been formally approved by Congress, its proclamation was just as clear.

America had declared war.

3

BEIJING, CHINA

In the center of Beijing, on the western edge of Tiananmen Square, is China's Great Hall of the People, its gray marble colonnades rising above a thin ringlet of cypresses and pines. China's parliament building covers almost two million square feet, containing over three hundred meeting halls, the largest of which—the Great Auditorium—seats over ten thousand. Affixed to the center of the Great Auditorium's ceiling is an immense ruby-red star, the symbol of the Party, surrounded by the People—represented by a sparkling galaxy of lights embedded within four concentric rings, their scalloped, wavering edges illuminated in a diffuse, white light.

Along the eastern facade of the Great Hall, with the early morning sun slanting through tall rectangular windows, Huan Zhixin moved briskly down a corridor lined with marble statues honoring the Heroes of the People. Mao Zedong's statue rose a foot taller than the others, but Huan's attention was drawn instead to the resemblance of Zhou Enlai, China's first prime minister. The assassination of Bai Tao, China's current prime minister, was fresh in Huan's mind, and he could sense the anger in the man beside him.

On Huan's right walked Xiang Chenglei. His appointment as general secretary and president ten years ago wasn't without concessions. Xiang and his rival had been deadlocked, and Shen Yi, the most senior Politburo member, would cast the deciding vote. Shen's endorsement of Xiang was contingent on accepting his nephew Huan as chairman of the Central Military Commission—head of the People's Liberation Army, and Xiang had agreed.

As head of the People's Liberation Army, Huan had meticulously reviewed the PLA's plan, and was confident they would prevail. However, as the Politburo cast the most important vote in four millennia of China's history, a majority would not be sufficient. Huan's proposal required unanimous approval.

At the end of the long hallway, Huan pushed against two heavy ten-by-twenty-foot wooden doors. Each of the mammoth doors swung silently inward, revealing a twenty-by-thirty-foot chamber. Seated around an oval table were the seven junior Politburo Standing Committee members, grim expressions on their faces. Xiang took his seat at the head of the table while Huan settled into a chair along the room's perimeter. The empty chair at the table weighed heavily on Huan, and while Bai Tao's death was unfortunate, it was also fortuitous. Tao had been staunchly opposed to Huan's proposal.

Huan turned his attention to the front of the conference room. Standing beside a large plasma screen was Admiral Tsou Deshi, the highest-ranking Admiral in the PLA Navy. The Admiral wore a disapproving frown. The conservative officer had never been enamored with the objective of his assignment, but he had crafted a superb plan. But before Admiral Tsou began his brief, Huan decided to prime the Politburo members.

He stood, addressing the men seated around the table. "As you are aware, we face the most severe crisis in the history of our country. For the last four decades, we have compromised our principles and endorsed capitalism, convinced the prosperity of our people is more important than the purity of our ideology. That sacrifice has been wise—China has become a formidable economic power and will soon overtake the United States. As our economy has grown, so has our influence around the world. America fears what we have become and is frightened even more by our potential. So they are trying to cripple us, depriving us of the oil our economy needs to thrive.

"If we do nothing, everything we have sacrificed over the last four decades will be for naught. So I ask you—do we sit by and let America destroy us?" Huan paused as the eight men shook their heads solemnly. "Or do we take action?"

Huan could tell his message was resonating, so he moved quickly toward his proposal. "America believes we are cornered, outmaneuvered politically, and without the military might to challenge them. However, they are mistaken. We have significantly improved the capabilities of the PLA, and we now have the ability to defeat the United States' Pacific Fleet. We can obtain the resources we need, ensuring China's continued prosperity. All that stands in the way, is your vote."

Huan paused momentarily before addressing the one critical element. "I understand your reservations. We cannot embark on this path without the assurance of success. Admiral Tsou is here to brief us on the PLA's plan, to convince you we will defeat America." Huan turned his attention to the Admiral, standing stiffly at the front of the conference room.

Admiral Tsou's gaze swept across the conference room, his eyes surveying the eight Politburo members, coming to rest on the chairman of the Central Military Commission. Huan was a visionary. A decade earlier he had predicted China would find itself in this situation. When Huan approached him years ago, Tsou was convinced the objective was a bridge too far. The Chinese navy lacked the sophisticated command and control and advanced weapons of the American Fleet. But Huan had promised him that gap would be closed, and he had delivered. Now, it was his turn.

Tsou pressed a remote control in his hand and turned to the side as the monitor behind him energized, displaying a map of the Western Pacific Ocean. To the east of China lay the island of Taipei, the bait for their trap.

"The PLA has been tasked with securing the natural resources we require, located primarily along the Pacific Rim. Standing between our country and those resources is the United States Navy. Thus, the first step we must take is the neutralization of America's Pacific Fleet.

"In the open ocean, we are no match for the American Navy. So we must engage their Navy in the littorals, where our missile batteries along the coast will eliminate the American advantage. Additionally, we must engage the United States in a campaign where we can predict their strategy and tactics. To do this, we must invade Taipei."

Admiral Tsou paused. There was no visible reaction from the men seated at the table. He continued, "The Americans believe they are the guardians of democracy, and will surge their Navy to Taipei's defense, which is exactly what we want. We have spent the last decade developing the missiles and submarines required to defeat the Americans, and we are finally ready."

Tsou spent the next thirty minutes detailing how the United States Pacific Fleet would be drawn toward its demise. It was a delicate chess match, and in most cases China's pieces on the board were inferior to America's. In addition, a sacrifice would have to be made, further weakening China's position. But Tsou was confident the gambit would succeed.

At the end of his brief, Tsou pressed the remote in his hand and the display fell dark. Silence descended upon the conference room.

Finally, Xiang asked the only question that mattered. "Are you sure we can defeat the United States?"

Tsou thought carefully before replying. He had supervised every detail of their military buildup, simulated the American response countless times with endless variations, and the PLA was now consistently victorious. There was no doubt in his mind.

"We will prevail."

Huan waited patiently as additional questions followed. He had chosen well, promoting Tsou to Fleet Admiral ten years earlier. He had superbly guided the PLA Navy, and a decade of preparation had come down to this moment.

When the questions ended, Huan addressed the Politburo. "Admiral Tsou has outlined our new path to prosperity. But before we proceed, you must vote. We cannot commence offensive military action without unanimous approval." Huan turned to the most junior committee member.

After a moment of reflection, fifty-five-year-old Deng Chung spoke. "I am uncomfortable with the use of military force. The loss of life will be great, and I fear that even if we obtain the natural resources we need, our economy will be crippled by international sanctions." Deng paused, surveying the other Politburo members before returning his attention to Huan. "We should continue diplomatic efforts, not resort to war."

Huan considered Deng's words. Like Deng, Huan had initially misunderstood the role of war. But Mao Zedong had not.

"We *are* continuing diplomatic efforts," Huan replied. "It was Chairman

Mao himself who stated—'*War is the continuation of politics by other means. When politics develops to a stage beyond which it cannot proceed by the usual means, war breaks out to sweep the obstacles from the way.*'"

Huan continued, "We failed to negotiate access to the natural resources we need. It is time to employ a more effective method of diplomacy. It is time for war.

"Once the American Pacific Fleet is destroyed, America and the world will eagerly accept our terms—the unification of the two Chinas, access to the natural resources we require, and termination of any economic sanctions imposed. The war will be short, and it will help us *negotiate* the terms we desire but have failed to achieve by peaceful methods."

There was silence in the conference room as the Politburo members digested Huan's assessment. Finally, Deng nodded his consent. "I concur with the plan."

One by one, each member of the committee approved until only Huan's uncle, Shen, and Xiang remained. Huan already knew how his uncle would vote, and he did not disappoint.

"I concur," Shen said.

Huan's eyes moved to Xiang. The older man was silent, reflecting on the information presented. As Huan waited for Xiang's vote, China's future—as well as Huan's—lay in the balance. Huan needed to persuade him. Perhaps he could motivate Xiang to approve the plan for personal, rather than political reasons. However, it was risky to bring the topic up. He had no idea how Xiang would react.

"There are many benefits to my plan," Huan began. "Benefits your mother would surely approve of."

Xiang's eyes narrowed. "What happened to my mother will *not* be discussed here." He clenched his teeth, glaring at Huan before replying. "My personal prejudice will not affect my assessment of what is best for China." There was an uneasy silence as the two men remained locked in each other's stare.

Xiang finally broke contact, his eyes roving across the faces of the other committee members as he spoke. "Huan is right. America fears what we have become, and our potential even more. They are cowards, attempting to castrate our economy. China requires a new path to prosperity, one that places our fate in our own hands, not in corrupt negotiators courting even more corrupt oil suppliers." Xiang's eyes settled on Huan. "I concur with your plan."

Huan nodded his appreciation, then turned to Admiral Tsou. "How long until you are ready?"

"Seven days."

4

WESTERN MARYLAND

The beat of the helicopter's four-bladed rotor filled the humid morning air as the VH-60N White Hawk skimmed low over the thick forest canopy, climbing the gentle slope of the Catoctin Mountains. Although it could carry eleven passengers, there were only two aboard the presidential helicopter for the half-hour trip from the White House to the compound originally called Shangri-La by President Franklin Roosevelt, renamed Camp David by President Eisenhower in honor of his grandson. Christine O'Connor and the president's senior military aide, Captain Steve Brackman, were approaching the end of their seventy-mile journey, and in a few minutes, Christine would deliver the unwelcome news.

A change in the rotor's tempo and the feeling of her seat falling away announced the helicopter's arrival at Camp David. Peering out the starboard window, Christine watched their steady descent toward a small clearing in the dark green forest. A moment later, the White Hawk's landing wheels touched down onto the concrete tarmac with a gentle bump. Stepping out of the helicopter, Christine and Brackman hurried across the pavement and slipped into the backseat of a waiting black Suburban.

After passing the camp commander's cabin, the Suburban turned right onto a steep secondary road, immediately pulling to a halt at a security checkpoint. The Marine guard checked the IDs of the driver and both passengers, then waved the Suburban through, and the SUV began winding its way through the heavily wooded 120-acre compound. A few minutes later, Aspen Lodge came into view, sitting atop a three-acre clearing lined with cattails and irises, sloping down to a copse of maple, hickory, and oak trees. Calling the president's residence a lodge was misleading at best. The four-bedroom ranch-style cabin, constructed with natural oak wall panel-ing and exposed ceiling beams, was cozy but certainly not elegant.

The Suburban ground to a stop on a narrow gravel driveway and the Marine sentry standing guard near the front door saluted as Christine and Brackman stepped from the SUV, with Brackman returning the salute. After knocking on the door and hearing the president's acknowledgment, Brackman opened the door for Christine, then followed her into the cabin's small living room, stopping beside a stone fireplace as the president rose from a couch against the far wall. Through the window behind the president, the late morning sun reflected off the surface of the swimming pool behind the cabin, the bright sparkle contrasting with the president's dark eyes.

The president waited for Christine to begin.

"Mr. President, China is mobilizing the People's Liberation Army. Lib-erty for all military personnel has been canceled and two army groups are being moved toward the coast across from Taiwan. Every warship is being loaded with a full weapon complement, with most of the activity occurring at night."

"Do they have any war games scheduled?" the president asked.

"Not to our knowledge."

The president reflected on Christine's words before replying. "China's relationship with Taiwan has never been better."

"The timing points more toward the MAER Accord than their desire to unify the two Chinas. Their mobilization began almost a week ago, right after you signed the accord."

"Perhaps China is just rattling its sword," the president offered, "mobi-lizing their military to pressure us into modifying the accord."

"Perhaps, Mr. President, but we can't be sure."

The president didn't immediately reply. Finally, he asked, "How do we respond?"

"SecDef recommends we increase Pacific Command's readiness one level and cancel leave for all warship crews, putting Pacific Fleet on a twenty-four-hour leash. He also recommends we reroute all combatants on deployment in the Western Pacific toward Taiwan, just in case."

The president nodded his agreement. "I'll give Jennings the order." He paused for a moment before continuing. "We need to find out what's going on and diffuse the situation. I'd send Ross, but she's on a flight to Moscow for a meeting with her secretary of state counterpart. I don't want to cancel the meeting and divert her to China, nor do I want to wait another week to address this issue. That means I send someone else."

He stared at Christine for a moment, then asked, "How's your Mandarin?"

5

GUIDED MISSILE SUBMARINE
USS *MICHIGAN*

"Raising Number Two scope."

Standing on the Conn in the submarine's Control Room, Lieutenant Steve Cordero lifted both hands in the darkness, grabbing the periscope ring above his head, rotating it clockwise. Although he couldn't see the scope as it slid silently up from its well, he knew the handles would emerge in three seconds. Dropping his hands, he held them out near his waist on each side of the scope until the top of the periscope handles hit his palms. He snapped the handles down and pressed his face against the eyepiece as the scope finished its ascent, checking the periscope settings. He twisted his right hand forward, verifying the periscope was set on low power. With a flick of his left wrist, he rotated the handle backward, tilting the scope optics skyward. But there was only darkness.

Cordero called out to the microphone in the overhead, "All stations, Conn. Proceeding to periscope depth." Sonar, Radio, and the Quartermaster acknowledged the Officer of the Deck's order, then Cordero followed up, "Dive, make your depth eight-zero feet."

The Diving Officer repeated Cordero's order, then directed the two watchstanders in front of him, "Ten up. Full rise fairwater planes."

The watchstander on the left pulled his yoke back, and five hundred feet behind them, the control surfaces on the submarine's stern rotated, pushing the stern down until the ship was tilted upward at a ten-degree angle. To the Dive's right, the Helm also pulled the yoke back, pitching the control surfaces on the submarine's conning tower, or sail as it was commonly called, to full rise.

"Passing one-five-zero feet," the Dive called out. USS *Michigan* was rising toward the surface.

Years ago, Cordero would have rotated on the periscope during the ascent. But protocols had changed. Peering into the periscope eyepiece, he looked straight ahead, up into the dark water, scanning for evidence of ships above, their navigation lights reflecting on the ocean's surface.

As *Michigan* ascended through the black water, aside from the Dive's reports, it was silent in Control. There would be no conversation until the periscope broke the surface and the Officer of the Deck called out *No close contacts* or *Emergency Deep*. Like the rest of the watchstanders in Control, Cordero knew their submarine was vulnerable during its ascent to periscope depth. A few years earlier, transiting these same waters, USS *Hartford* had collided with USS *New Orleans* during the submarine's ascent to periscope depth, almost ripping the sail from the top of the submarine.

With a submerged displacement of eighteen thousand tons, *Michigan* was less maneuverable than the nimble fast attacks. The former ballistic missile submarine was almost two football fields long, seven stories tall, and wide as a three-lane highway. Converted into a guided missile submarine, *Michigan* was now capable of carrying 154 Tomahawk cruise missiles, loaded in twenty-two of its twenty-four missile tubes, with the remaining two tubes converted into access hatches to two Dry Deck Shelters attached to the submarine's Missile Deck. Within each DDS rested a SEAL Delivery Vehicle—a mini-sub capable of transporting Navy SEALs miles underwater for clandestine operations. Aboard *Michigan*, in berthing installed in the Missile Compartment during its conversion, slept four platoons of Navy SEALs, ready should their services be required.

Their services wouldn't be necessary tonight. This was just a routine journey to periscope depth. As *Michigan* rose toward the surface, Cordero couldn't see the submarine's Commanding Officer, Captain Murray Wilson, in the darkness, but he felt his presence. Sitting on the starboard side of the Conn in the Captain's chair, Wilson monitored his submarine's ascent. There was heavy traffic in the narrow Strait of Hormuz tonight as the ship began its long transit home to Bangor, Washington, in the Pacific Northwest.

It was from Delta Pier in Hood Canal that Captain Wilson had cast off lines three months ago, leading *Michigan* west. This was Wilson's first deployment aboard *Michigan*. Cordero and the rest of the officers in the Wardroom had been surprised when Wilson had been assigned as their new Commanding Officer. Captain Murray Wilson, the most senior captain in the Submarine Force, had already commanded the fast attack submarine USS *Buffalo* and had just completed an assignment as the senior Submarine Command Course instructor, preparing officers for command. Rumor held he played a pivotal role in the *Kentucky* incident, selected for Rear Admiral as a result. But he had supposedly turned down flag rank, choosing to end his career at sea.

It didn't take long for Cordero and the rest of the crew aboard *Michigan* to appreciate the breadth and depth of the Captain's experience. However, they were perplexed when he ordered an indirect path for their journey to the Persian Gulf, forcing them to transit at a higher than desirable speed. The crew soon realized the deviation was made with the sole purpose of passing through a specific point on the chart. When they reached the prescribed spot, Wilson ordered the Quartermaster to activate their Fathomer, sending one ping down toward the ocean bottom. As Captain Wilson sat in the shadows on the submarine's Conn, Cordero could see the moisture glistening in the older man's eyes as they passed over the watery grave of HMAS *Collins*.

That was three months ago and they were now headed home, ascending to periscope depth to download the radio broadcast. As Cordero peered up through the black water, a small wavering disc of light appeared in the distance, growing slowly larger; the moon's blue-white reflection on the ocean's surface. The Dive called out the submarine's depth in ten-foot increments, and Cordero gradually rotated his left wrist back to its original position, tilting the scope optics down toward the horizon. As the Dive called out *eight-zero feet*, the scope broke the surface of the water and Cordero began his circular sweeps, searching for nearby contacts—quiet warships or deep-draft merchants bearing down on them as *Michigan* glided slowly at periscope depth.

After assessing the half-dozen white lights on the horizon, Cordero called out the report everyone in Control was hoping for.

"No close contacts!"

Conversation in control resumed, with the Dive and Chief of the Watch adjusting the submarine's buoyancy to keep it a tad heavy, so the passing ocean swells wouldn't suck the submarine up to the surface.

Radio's report over the 27-MC communication system broke the subdued conversations in Control. "Conn, Radio. In sync with the broadcast. Receiving message traffic."

The Quartermaster followed with his expected report, "GPS fix received."

Cordero acknowledged Radio and the Quartermaster, then after the usual two-minute wait, Radio confirmed *Michigan* had received the latest round of naval messages. "Conn, Radio. Download complete."

They had accomplished the two objectives for their trip to periscope depth, so Cordero ordered *Michigan* back to the safety of the ocean depths. "All stations, Conn. Going deep. Helm, ahead two-thirds. Dive, make your depth two hundred feet."

Each station acknowledged and *Michigan* tilted downward, leaving periscope depth behind. "Scope's under," Cordero announced, then turned the periscope until it looked forward and snapped the handles back to their folded positions. Reaching up, he rotated the periscope ring counterclockwise, lowering the scope into its well.

The lights in Control flicked on, shifting from Rig-for-Black to Gray, allowing everyone's eyes to adjust, then shifted to White a moment later. As *Michigan* leveled off at two hundred feet, a Radioman entered Control, message board in hand, delivering the clipboard to the submarine's Commanding Officer. Captain Wilson reviewed the messages, then handed the board to Cordero.

"Change in plans," Wilson said. "We're taking a detour on the way home."

Wilson surveyed the men in Control before adding, "Come down to five hundred feet. Increase speed to ahead flank."

6

SHANGHAI, CHINA

It was a twelve-story building off Datong Road in a mixed-use area of Pudong. To United States satellites in orbit, the building's electromagnetic signature appeared no different than the surrounding commercial buildings. The complex, however, housed China's Unit 61398, the premier unit of the PLA's Fourth Department, responsible for cyber warfare. On the twelfth floor, Admiral Tsou Deshi and General Cao Feng, Commander of the Fourth Department, supervised the most critical element of Admiral Tsou's plan: the dismantling of Unit 61398.

"Everything must be moved to underground bunkers before hostilities commence, Admiral," General Cao commented. Tsou looked around as the thirty men and women busily packed away computers, displays, computer servers and their racks, power supplies, and cables. It was like watching a vacuum operate in slow motion—an entire hi-tech complex disappearing into hundreds of cardboard boxes.

"There will be a temporary disruption in ability," Cao added, "but we are doing this in stages, and this is the last unit to be moved. All units will be fully operational by morning."

Tsou nodded as General Cao continued, "We are a decade ahead of our American counterparts in cyber warfare, but they are catching up fast. They have finally realized the predicament they are in, and have established their own cyber warfare command. Fortunately for us, they have no idea of the inroads we have made.

"They will realize all too soon what we have done, and will attempt to respond in kind. But we have thoroughly prepared, Admiral. Their communication networks are vulnerable, while our nodes our impervious to cyber counterattacks.

"However, while our command and control networks are protected from cyber attacks, we cannot underestimate America's ability to harm us via conventional methods. Our critical communication nodes must be moved to hardened underground bunkers, along with our cyber warfare units. We cannot risk the possibility America will discover their existence and eliminate them with Tomahawk missiles or Air Force strikes. You know better than anyone that your plan hinges on their capabilities."

Admiral Tsou could not argue with the General's words. Cyber warfare was the one area where China had superiority over the United States, and Cao was taking every measure to ensure America could not destroy that advantage during the conflict.

The last of the computers were placed into cardboard boxes and sealed, then loaded onto dollies and wheeled toward nearby elevators. A few minutes later, the Admiral and General stood alone on a desolate floor, with loose papers and dust balls littering an otherwise deserted office space. The two men headed toward the elevators in silence. The General would join Unit 61398 in one of the underground command bunkers, while Tsou would accompany his aide, waiting in the car below, for the long trip to Ningbo, headquarters of the East Sea Fleet.

THE GAMBIT

7

NINGBO, CHINA

On the first floor of a four-story concrete, windowless building, Fleet Admiral Tsou Deshi stood in the shadows with his aide, off to the side of a large auditorium. Gathered in the headquarters of the PLA Navy's East Sea Fleet this morning, fifty-four admirals sat in their dark blue uniforms, arranged neatly in sections representing the three fleets—the North Sea Fleet based in Qingdao, the East Sea Fleet headquartered in Ningbo, and the South Sea Fleet sortieing from Zhanjiang. All together, the three fleets fielded an impressive arsenal of ships, consisting of twenty-five destroyers, forty-seven frigates, fifty-eight diesel and nuclear-powered submarines, plus eighty-three amphibious warfare ships and over five hundred landing craft.

The PLA Navy was a formidable force indeed, except when compared to the American Pacific Fleet. But Tsou had toiled diligently to level the playing field and make America pay dearly for its righteous superiority and willingness to employ it. After years of honing carefully guarded plans, it was time to reveal them.

Tsou took a deep breath, then nodded, and his aide strode onto the stage, announcing "Attention on Deck" as he emerged. Conversation in the auditorium ceased as the admirals surged to their feet, standing at attention as Tsou followed his aide to the front of the auditorium. The aide departed, leaving Tsou standing in front of a twenty-by-forty-foot view screen towering above him, which would display every facet of the plan as it unfolded.

"At ease," Tsou announced. "Be seated."

Fleet Admiral Tsou surveyed the men assembled before him as they took their seats. Their mood was somber; they knew the upcoming battle would be difficult. In a few minutes, they would understand just how difficult.

"Good morning," Tsou said. "Many of you have guessed why we are here today. The preparations made over the last week have no doubt indicated our intent, and I am sure you are confident in our ability. But there is more to our plan than meets the eye. The invasion of Taipei is merely bait, drawing our enemy close. For us to be victorious, not only must we defend our amphibious assault from the United States Navy, we must go one step further. Our real goal is to destroy the United States Pacific Fleet."

Tsou listened to murmurings throughout the auditorium. Until this moment, the obvious goal of their assault had been the unification of the two Chinas. Now, with the true intent of their plan revealed, astonished expressions spread across the room. Admiral Tsou continued as the murmuring died down, "It won't be easy, but this is how we're going to do it." Tsou paused for a moment before beginning the two-hour operations brief.

After explaining the last element of his plan, Admiral Tsou turned from the view screen and faced his admirals, waiting for the expected reaction. He wasn't the only one who understood the Herculean task they'd been assigned. As the murmuring began throughout the auditorium again, a Vice Admiral stood to address Admiral Tsou. His ships were assigned the most difficult—and seemingly impossible—task.

He began by identifying himself and his command. "Vice Admiral Shao, Commander, 10th Submarine Flotilla, East Sea Fleet."

Admiral Tsou acknowledged the flotilla commander. "Proceed."

"Pardon me for being a skeptic, but after years of studying the American Navy's capability, I have a different assessment of the outcome."

Tsou had seen this coming from the moment the plan was conceived. "And your *opinion* is . . . ?"

"My *opinion*," Admiral Shao replied, "is that this plan is ludicrous! We cannot defeat the American Pacific Fleet!"

Shouting broke out throughout the auditorium, as some admirals echoed Admiral Shao's sentiment, while others admonished him for both the disrespectful manner with which he voiced his disagreement and his lack of faith. Yet everyone in the room knew there was a kernel of truth in the Vice Admiral's assertion.

Fleet Admiral Tsou stood with his hands clasped behind his back, waiting patiently for the fervor to die out. Finally, he replied, "Well stated, Admiral."

Tsou's response took everyone by surprise; they had expected him to defend the battle plan vehemently. Instead, he agreed his plan had no chance to succeed. Tsou continued, "Under normal circumstances, you would be correct in your assessment."

Admiral Tsou cast a glance across the auditorium. For the plan to succeed, his admirals must *believe* it can. The PLA's new capabilities had been kept secret long enough. It was time to reveal them. It was time to reveal *everything*.

It was only a few minutes later when Admiral Tsou finished. Heads nodded throughout the auditorium, confidence radiating from the men within. They now believed they could defeat the American Pacific Fleet. And that, of course, was the most important ingredient.

With the operations brief complete, it was time to send his men on their way so they could make final preparations for tonight's attack. Admiral Tsou stood at attention, and for today's farewell, he decided to follow an American Submarine Force tradition. The PLA Navy's new submarines, after all, would play a crucial role. His eyes scanned his men as they drew themselves to attention in response, then he uttered the time-honored farewell.

"Good hunting!"

8

BEIJING

Night was settling over the city, neon café signs illuminating pedestrians strolling the sidewalks as two black 7 Series BMWs, their armored frames riding low to the ground, wound their way through the center of Beijing. Joining Christine O'Connor in the back of the lead sedan was the United States ambassador to China, Michael Richardson, flipping through an appointment calendar on his lap. Christine could see the reflection of the sedan behind them in the security glass, which was raised between the front and rear seats, offering privacy for her discussion with Richardson.

Eighteen hours earlier, Christine had boarded an Air Force Boeing 747 waiting at Joint Base Andrews, the combined Navy and Air Force base southeast of D.C., landing at Beijing's Nanyuan Airport. As she descended the staircase onto the tarmac, Ambassador Richardson, leaning against the black government sedan, had stepped forward to greet her.

The news he delivered was unexpected. There had been a change to her itinerary. Instead of heading to her hotel near the American Embassy, they would proceed to the Great Hall of the People. Tomorrow's meeting had been moved up to tonight. No reason had been given for the change other than "schedule considerations dictate an immediate meeting." Even more perplexing, the planned meeting with her Chinese counterpart, Vice Premier Wang Qui, had been replaced with a meeting with China's president, Xiang Chenglei.

Richardson closed the appointment book as he looked up at Christine. "Nothing. I can't figure out why they want to meet tonight, or why you're meeting with the president instead of the vice premier."

Christine had an inkling. "If China has decided to attack Taiwan, tonight's meeting might include a formal request the United States refrain from interfering. Of course, they'd be just going through the motions, knowing we'll come to Taiwan's aid regardless."

An astonished look spread across the ambassador's face. "That would mean hostilities are imminent."

"That's what I'm worried about," Christine replied. "I hope they're still in the consideration phase and can be reasoned with."

The sedan ground to a halt beside the Great Hall of the People, the entrance to the building framed by massive gray marble colonnades illuminated by bright white perimeter lighting. Standing at the base of stone steps leading to the entrance were five men—four in a single line, while a fifth man, taller than the rest, stood behind them. The two men in the center were dressed in charcoal gray suits, while the other three men wore black suits. Christine figured the men in black were from the Central Guard Bureau's Cadre Department—the Chinese equivalent of the Secret Service—their wary eyes surveying the two cars that pulled to a stop.

Christine and Ambassador Richardson stepped from their sedan as two U.S. Diplomatic Security Service agents exited the second car, flanking Christine and the ambassador.

One of the men wearing a charcoal gray suit extended his hand. "Welcome to Beijing, Miss O'Connor. I am Huan Zhixin, chairman of the Central Military Commission."

Christine shook the hand of the man in charge of China's military, responding in Mandarin. "Jiǔyǎng." She had memorized a few Mandarin phrases for her meeting with Wang Qui, and decided to try the standard Chinese greeting between professionals, hoping her pronunciation was correct.

Huan smiled warmly. "It is a pleasure to meet you as well." He turned sideways toward the man behind them. "I'd like to introduce Yang Minsheng, head of President Xiang's security detail." Yang merely nodded as Huan continued, gesturing to the man beside him. "And this is Xie Hai, the president's executive assistant, who will keep Ambassador Richardson occupied while you meet with the president."

Christine exchanged a concerned glance with Richardson. "The ambassador won't be joining us?"

"I'm afraid not, Miss O'Connor," Huan replied. "We have several issues we would like to discuss with the ambassador tonight."

"And the DSS agents?" Christine asked.

"They may accompany you to the conference room, but they'll have to disarm at the security checkpoint."

As Christine talked with Huan, Yang stared at her, completely ignoring Ambassador Richardson. Christine was an attractive woman and was accustomed to stares and glances from the opposite sex, but there was something odd about the way he studied her.

Huan turned and led the four Americans up the steps into the Great Hall of the People, where Xie Hai peeled Ambassador Richardson from the group. Christine and the two DSS agents continued on to a security checkpoint, consisting of a metal detector and baggage X-ray machine, where the two DSS agents disarmed.

After passing through the detector, Christine joined Huan at his side as they strode down a brightly lit corridor, their footsteps echoing off marble walls. Following closely behind were the two DSS agents, and behind them, Yang and the two Cadre Department bodyguards. Huan offered no further conversation. As they approached a pair of large mahogany doors, Huan pushed the heavy wooden doors inward.

The doors swung open to reveal a large circular chamber, just over one hundred feet in diameter. The Politburo Diplomatic Reception Hall was similar in design to the other thirty-three halls named after China's provinces and regions, each chamber decorated according to the local style of the province it represented. Although the Diplomatic Reception Hall was frequently furnished with up to fifty chairs arranged in a semicircle, tonight it contained only two, positioned at the far end of the chamber beneath an imposing twenty-by-thirty-foot oil painting of the Great Wall of China, winding its way atop the mountainous region north of Beijing.

Sitting in one of the two chairs was Xiang Chenglei, with two additional Cadre Department bodyguards standing rigidly behind him, hands at their sides. Xiang rose to his feet as Christine entered with Huan, followed by the contingent of American and Chinese security agents.

Christine moved across the plush red carpet toward the most powerful man in China, extending her hand with a smile on her face in feigned exuberance. The unexpected change in itinerary, combined with an odd tension exuded by the two Cadre Department bodyguards behind the president, told Christine something was brewing.

"Good evening, Mr. President." Christine greeted Xiang in Mandarin, as she had done with Huan.

"Aaah, nicely done, Miss O'Connor," Xiang said in English as he shook Christine's hand firmly. "Welcome to China. I hope you had a pleasant trip?" Xiang's accent was strong, but his grammar impeccable.

"I did, Mr. President."

"Call me Chenglei. May I address you as Christine?"

"Absolutely."

Xiang gestured to the second chair. "Please, have a seat."

Christine and Xiang settled into their chairs, and as Christine smoothed the skirt of her business suit, it was Xiang who spoke first.

"I apologize for the last-minute change to your schedule, Christine, but considering the topic of your meeting with Wang Qui, I thought it best we had a conversation tonight, while there is still time."

"Time for what?" Christine asked.

"Time to reconsider." Xiang smiled, but Christine sensed the frustration— even anger—boiling behind his pleasant facade. "That you are here tonight tells me America is aware, at least to some extent, of our preparations. Let's be direct, shall we?"

Christine nodded and Xiang continued. "The United States has—how do you say it—painted us into a corner. Of course, we have plans we can implement to deal with the accord. But I am hopeful you bring news that will make those plans unnecessary."

"Actually, Chenglei, that's why I'm here. Any issues you have with the MAER Accord can be addressed peacefully. There is no need for military action."

"There is no need for military action only if America agrees to modify the accord, granting China affordable access to the resources we require. Do you come here with that news?"

"I'm afraid not, Chenglei. It took over a year to forge terms acceptable to all parties—"

"The terms are not acceptable!" Anger flashed in Xiang's eyes. "America deliberately negotiated terms that would harm my country. I will not stand by while forty years of progress are destroyed." Xiang paused, gathering his thoughts. "I ask you again, Christine. Will the United States dissolve or modify the accord?"

Christine shook her head. "No, Mr. President."

Xiang stared at Christine for a long moment, then looked up at Yang and nodded.

Yang barked out a command and the Cadre Department bodyguards pulled their firearms. Two of the Cadre bodyguards stepped behind the DSS agents, pressing a pistol into each man's back. The two Americans raised their hands, surprise and consternation on their faces.

Christine stood, looking down at Xiang in his chair. "What is the meaning of this?"

"It's unfortunate," Xiang replied as he pushed himself to his feet, "but you will be detained. Relations between our countries are about to take a turn for the worse."

"What do you mean?"

Xiang's face hardened as he answered, "We are taking matters into our own hands and will obtain the resources we need by force. That begins tonight with the unification of the two Chinas."

Christine's thoughts began to swirl. China was launching an assault against Taiwan and America would respond. China and the United States would be at war. She wondered if she could talk Xiang out of his madness.

"We're well aware of your preparations, Chenglei, mobilizing your military. Our military readiness has been increased in response, and I assure you any attempt to invade Taiwan will be defeated. The only thing you will accomplish is the murder of thousands of men and women, not to mention initiating scores of international economic sanctions."

"I have no doubt your military is ready, Christine, but so is ours. As for economic sanctions, you have effectively invoked them by crafting the MAER Accord. You left us with no choice. So let us be clear on who is to blame for what is about to happen. The United States is the aggressor, and not China, who merely defends her right to prosperity."

Christine pursed her lips together as she considered his words. Xiang had a point, and it appeared he and China were committed. There was nothing she could say to dissuade them.

"What now?" she asked.

"You will be detained until we decide what to do with you. Hopefully when this . . . issue is resolved, you will be released. Until then, you will enjoy the hospitality of the People's Republic of China. He turned to Yang. "Take her away."

Yang gave an order to one of the Cadre bodyguards, who motioned Christine toward the Reception Hall exit with a wave of his pistol.

9

USS *JACKSONVILLE*

In the darkened Control Room, Lieutenant Beck Burrell placed his right eye against the periscope, giving the Junior Officer of the Deck a break from the monotonous, circular sweeps. Burrell slowed each rotation as he passed the Chinese coast, scouring the dark shoreline in search of warships heading to sea. Two days earlier, as *Jacksonville* cruised the Taiwan Strait, the fast attack had received new orders. They were now operating just north of Taiwan, within visual distance of Zhoushan, one of the East Sea Fleet's three major ports. Zhoushan was eerily quiet.

Two days and not a single warship heading to sea. Yet Burrell's sixth sense told him something was brewing. The 7th Fleet Intel reports detailed an overall increase in China's military readiness while the PLA Navy moved in the opposite direction, like a tidal wave gathering at sea, the water receding from the beach before the massive wave broke upon the shore. Burrell paused again on another circular sweep. He shifted to high power and kicked in the doubler, increasing the periscope magnification to twenty-four times normal, searching for the navigation lights of outbound warships.

Nothing.

Burrell continued his circular sweeps, planning to give the Junior Officer of the Deck a five-minute break. After almost six months at sea, they could all use a break. Fortunately, in another week *Jacksonville* would be surging east, toward family and friends waiting on the pier, waving excitedly as the submarine returned from its six-month West Pac deployment. This was Burrell's last West Pac, and a month after returning to port, it was off to well-deserved shore duty on COMSUBPAC staff and time with his family.

Lieutenant Burrell shifted to high power as the scope swung around toward the coast. There were no stars or moon tonight, hidden behind an invisible cloak of clouds; the only illumination came from distant lights dotting the shoreline. He paused on the bearing to the main channel.

Still nothing.

He was about to continue to his right when something unusual caught his eye. Actually, it wasn't what he saw—it was what he *didn't* see. On a bearing of 260, the yellow lights along the shore that had been present every sweep were gone. Either the lights had been extinguished or something was blocking them. Burrell steadied on the bearing, and a moment later the lights reappeared.

With his eye still pressed against the periscope, he called out, "Sonar, Conn. Report any contacts on a bearing of two-six-zero."

The Sonar Supervisor repeated back the order, "Conn, Sonar. Report contacts on a bearing of two-six-zero, aye, wait."

Burrell waited patiently as another set of lights disappeared and then reappeared. An object was moving swiftly down the coastline. It wasn't surprising he had picked up the contact before Sonar had. The noise coming from the electrical generators in the nearby power station ashore would mask quiet ships. But now that he had focused Sonar's efforts, they should be able to pull the contact from the noise.

A moment later, Burrell's assessment was confirmed. "Conn, Sonar. Hold a new contact, bearing two-five-eight, designated Sierra four-three. Analyzing."

Burrell shifted left two degrees as another set of lights disappeared, reappearing a few seconds later. A ship was underway without navigation lights, attempting to slip out to sea undetected, its silhouette blocking the lights along the shore in the process. But what type of ship? A few minutes later, Sonar answered that question.

"Conn, Sonar. Sierra four-three is classified warship. Shang class nuclear fast attack submarine."

With his eyes still pressed to the periscope, Burrell reached out in the darkness, retrieving the Captain's Phone from its holder, pressing one of the buttons next to it, buzzing the CO's stateroom. "Captain, Officer of the Deck. Hold a new contact, Shang class submarine, designated Sierra four-three, outbound from Zhoushan on a southern course paralleling the shore."

The Captain acknowledged and entered Control a moment later, stepping onto the Conn. "Let me take a look."

Burrell stepped back, handing control of the periscope to Commander Randy Baughman, who placed his eye against the scope. After a moment, Baughman spoke as he tweaked the periscope left in two-degree increments. "What do we have for a solution?"

Burrell glanced at the nearest combat control console. "Contact bears two-four-eight, range eight thousand yards, course one-eight-zero, speed fifteen."

The Lieutenant's answer was followed up by another report over the 27-MC. "Conn, Sonar. Hold a new contact, designated Sierra four-four, bearing two-six-zero, classified warship."

Commander Baughman swung the scope around until the glowing red numbers on the periscope bearing display steadied up on 260. After a long pause, he announced, "Sierra four-four is also paralleling the coast, headed north instead of south."

A moment later, Sonar followed up. "Sierra four-four is also classified Shang class nuclear submarine." There was a slight pause before Sonar reported again. "Conn, Sonar. Hold a new contact, designated Sierra four-five, bearing two-six-zero, also classified Shang class submarine."

Burrell was attempting to assimilate the data when Sonar called out again. "Conn, Sonar. Sierra four-three and four-four have zigged, both contacts turning toward us. Sierra four-five remains steady on outbound course."

The hair on the back of Burrell's neck stood up. All three Chinese submarines were headed toward them now, one directly at them and one on each side, sweeping the entrance to the port. *Jacksonville* was at periscope depth, at five knots only a few thousand yards away, and there was no way they could evade all three submarines. No matter which way *Jacksonville* turned, she would be caught between two of the outbound submarines.

Lieutenant Burrell's thoughts were disrupted by another report from Sonar. "Conn, Sonar. Receiving Main Ballast Tank venting sounds from each contact. All three submarines are submerging."

Commander Baughman stepped back from the scope, reaching up and twisting the periscope locking ring. The scope slid silently down into its well as he spoke. "Come down to one-five-zero feet and head east at ahead standard. Let's buy some time while we figure out how to slip between them on their way out."

Burrell relayed the Captain's order to the Dive and Helm, and *Jacksonville* tilted downward, sinking to 150 feet, increasing speed as the submarine turned to an outboard course of 090. The lights in Control shifted to Gray, then White, now that they were no longer at periscope depth, and as Burrell stood next to the Captain, he assessed the solutions to the contacts with concern. The three submarines had increased speed and were slowly closing. They would detect *Jacksonville* unless she also increased speed. Unfortunately, any speed above standard would create cavitation on the propeller's surface, giving away their presence.

That was their choice—kick it in the ass and get the hell out of Dodge, or take their chances passing between two of the Shang class submarines, the most capable variant in the Chinese fleet, undetected.

"Attention in Control," Commander Baughman announced. "I intend to slow and let the Chinese submarines pass on either side of us, then return to monitoring Zhoushan. Carry on." He ordered Burrell to slow to five knots, reducing the noise from their main engines and propeller, then spoke toward the microphone in the overhead. "Radio, Captain. Have the Communicator draft a message to CTF 74 concerning the three outbound contacts."

Radio acknowledged over the 27-MC as Burrell analyzed the track of the nearest two Chinese submarines, determining the optimal course so *Jacksonville* would pass exactly halfway between them. Burrell was about to issue new orders to the Helm when he heard a powerful sonar ping echo through the hull.

The Sonar Supervisor's voice came across the 27-MC a second later. "Conn, Sonar. Sierra four-five has gone active."

Burrell turned his attention to the combat control displays. The center of the three Chinese submarines had just sent a ping into the water, searching the ocean for other submarines. Had they picked up *Jacksonville* on her passive sonar and were pinging to determine range?

A second sonar ping echoed through Control.

"Conn, Sonar. Another ping from Sierra four-five."

"Dammit," Commander Baughman muttered. "They'll detect us for sure at this range. We can't hang around here with three Shangs on our tail. We need to get out of here and come back once we've lost them." Baughman shook his head. "This is going to be embarrassing when we get back—"

Baughman was cut off by the Sonar Supervisor's voice, blaring over the 27-MC. "Torpedo launch transients, bearing two-six-zero! Sierra four-five is shooting at us!"

Lieutenant Burrell's first reaction was disbelief.

Sonar must've gotten it wrong. There was no way the Chinese submarine had launched a torpedo at them. They must be blowing auxiliary tanks or operating other machinery—something that *sounded* like a torpedo launch. If *Jacksonville* initiated torpedo evasion maneuvers on a false alarm, they'd be detected for sure. But if it really was a torpedo, they'd better act fast.

Sonar followed up with another report. "Torpedo in the water! Bearing two-six-zero!"

Burrell swung around, staring at the sonar monitor on the Conn. A bright white trace at a bearing of two-six-zero was burning into the display.

Commander Baughman responded immediately. "Ahead flank! Left full rudder, steady course north! Launch countermeasure. Man Battle Stations!"

The watchstanders in Control sprang into action: the Helm twisted the rudder yoke to left full as he rang up ahead flank on the Engine Order Telegraph, sending the signal to the Throttleman in the Engine Room. The Chief of the Watch, seated at the Ballast Control Panel, ordered the crew to Battle Stations over the 1-MC, then activated the General Alarm. The loud *bong, bong, bong* reverberated throughout the ship as the Junior Officer of the Deck leapt to the Countermeasure Control Panel, launching a torpedo decoy into the water.

Commander Baughman followed up, "Quick Reaction Firing, Sierra four-five, Tube One! Flood down and open outer doors, all tubes!"

Men began streaming into Control, manning dormant consoles as red bearing lines to the torpedo appeared on the nearest combat control console every ten seconds. The torpedo was closing rapidly. Burrell did the mental calculations—they had less than two minutes before impact. Under normal circumstances with the crew at Battle Stations, that would be more than enough time to shoot back. But with the crew starting in a normal watch section and the torpedo tube outer doors still shut and weapons powered down . . .

It didn't look good.

Even worse, the odds of them evading the incoming torpedo were slim to none. They'd been fired at from almost point-blank range. Even if their torpedo decoy was effective, the incoming torpedo would pass by it before it turned around, and in the process would likely lock on to the much bigger submarine speeding away. *Jacksonville* was a fast attack, but not fast enough.

"Torpedo bears two-five-zero, range one thousand yards!"

One minute left.

Sonar's report echoed in the surprisingly quiet Control Room as the crew donned their sound-powered phone headsets and energized the dormant consoles. Maybe, if they were lucky and the incoming torpedo missed, they'd be able to take out one or more of the Chinese submarines. *Jacksonville* was an old 688 class submarine, but she was still superior to anything in the Chinese arsenal.

"Five hundred yards!"

Thirty seconds left.

Burrell's eyes shifted nervously between the sonar display and the Weapon Launch Console. The Weapons Control Coordinator had finished assigning presets to the torpedo in Tube One, and was waiting for the torpedo tube to finish flooding down and the Torpedomen to open the outer door.

Nearby, the submarine's Executive Officer was directing the three men on the combat control consoles, assigning each man to one of the three Chinese submarines, determining their course, speed, and range. Commander Baughman, standing on the edge of the Conn, monitored the progress of weapon preparation, contact solution generation, and the bearing of the incoming torpedo.

Both Baughman and Burrell's eyes were glued to the Sonar display, trying to discern if they had fooled the torpedo and it was now passing harmlessly behind them.

The Sonar Supervisor's report over the 27-MC answered that question. "Torpedo is homing!"

Sonar had detected a change in the torpedo's ping pattern, signaling the torpedo had detected them and was refining its target solution.

Baughman responded immediately, "Helm, right hard rudder, steady course zero-nine-zero!"

Jacksonville kicked around hard to starboard, steadying up quickly on her new course. Everyone in Control waited tensely for Sonar's report, wondering if the torpedo had detected *Jacksonville*'s turn to the east.

"Torpedo bears two-five zero. Range two hundred yards! Still homing!"

Ten seconds.

Their fate was sealed.

With ten seconds left, there was nothing they could do.

As Burrell counted down the seconds, the faint pings of the incoming torpedo echoed through the submarine's steel hull. He had heard the sound many times from exercise torpedoes. The frequency of these pings were a bit higher, but unmistakable nonetheless.

When Burrell reached zero in his mental countdown, *Jacksonville* jolted violently forward, throwing him back against the starboard periscope. The wail of the flooding alarm filled his ears and the lights in Control fluttered, then went dark momentarily before the emergency lights kicked on. The Chief of the Watch initiated an Emergency Blow upon the Captain's order, but the submarine soon slowed and its stern began to squat from the weight of the ocean flooding the Engine Room. As Lieutenant Burrell watched the red numbers on the digital depth detector swiftly increase, he knew *Jacksonville* would never surface again.

10

BEIJING

Beneath the Great Hall of the People, Christine walked down a narrow corridor lit by incandescent light fixtures spaced every twenty feet, bathing gray concrete walls in weak, yellow light. Behind her followed one of the Cadre Department bodyguards. She could sense the presence of his drawn pistol pointed at her back. As her mind raced, wondering what lay ahead, she hoped Ambassador Richardson and the two DSS agents would be treated well.

The bodyguard directed Christine down a narrow stairwell into the sublevels of the Great Hall, then down a musty corridor until they reached a metal security door with a twelve-by-twelve-inch plasma display located shoulder height on the right side of the door.

The bodyguard spoke in English, with a heavy accent. "Step aside."

Christine complied, moving against the corridor wall. The man approached the plasma display and began to place his hand on the panel when he pulled up short, his hand going to his ear instead. He turned and faced Christine as he listened to the receiver in his ear, finally speaking into his jacket sleeve in Chinese.

He dropped his arm, addressing Christine. "We wait."

Several minutes passed while Christine and the bodyguard waited in the dimly lit hallway, the silence finally broken by the sound of approaching footsteps. Christine looked down the corridor the way they had come, spotting Yang Minsheng, head of Xiang's security detail.

Yang eyed Christine again as he approached, but said nothing as he passed both the bodyguard and Christine, stopping at the security door where he placed his right palm on the plasma display. The display lit up upon his touch, and a bright, vertical red light scanned his palm from left to right. After the scan was complete, the metal door slid open, revealing an identical corridor to the one they were in, except for several dozen doors spaced ten feet apart, lining the left wall.

Detention cells, no doubt.

Yang passed through the doorway, and the other bodyguard motioned for Christine to follow. Christine stopped when she reached the doorway, her anxiety increasing. Yang turned, and noticing her hesitation, gave a command to the other guard. A second later, Christine felt a firm hand on her back, shoving her forward.

She stumbled into Yang and he grabbed her, holding her against his body longer than was necessary, the musky scent of his cologne assailing her. She looked up, his eyes probing hers for a moment, then he shoved her against the wall with one hand. His hand remained on her chest, his palm between her breasts, his fingers touching her bare skin where her blouse parted. Then he ripped her blouse open, exposing the top of her breasts and her white lace bra.

He stepped back and spoke to the Cadre Department bodyguard. The guard retrieved a set of keys from his pants and unlocked the nearest door.

As the door opened, Yang pulled Christine away from the wall by her arm and shoved her inside the darkened room. The lights flicked on a second later and Christine took in the Spartan accommodations—a small cot against one wall and a toilet along the other. The door closed, leaving Christine inside the cell with the two men. Yang spoke to the other man, nodding in Christine's direction.

There was no doubt what was about to happen. But she wasn't going to take this lying down, so to speak. Even against two men, she could inflict a reasonable amount of pain. She knew she'd be on the losing end of a physical confrontation, but she really didn't have much choice.

Yang spoke again, but the guard hesitated. Christine could see the reservation in his eyes and hope set in. Perhaps she could leverage his concern into a way out of her predicament. But then Yang leaned toward him and whispered into his ear, and the restraint melted from the guard's eyes. He licked his lips as his eyes devoured her body, his leering gaze undressing her. He took off his jacket and handed it to Yang, along with his pistol and holster. Christine's eyes went to Yang as the man handed him his jacket. Yang was watching the other guard with a sly smile. If she survived this ordeal, she would find a way to hunt Yang down and kill him.

Her eyes shifted back to the other man, and her thoughts returned to defending herself from the pending assault. Christine's pulse began to race, her heart pounding as she backed up, pressing her body against the cold, concrete wall, putting as much distance between her and the two men in a futile effort to delay the inevitable.

The man dropped his hands to his waist, loosening his belt, and Christine's panic crested and then broke, the fear flowing past her. She took a defiant step forward with her left foot, balancing her weight on the balls of her feet as she raised both hands in front of her in a defensive posture. She wasn't going down without a fight. The man pulled the belt from his waist, wrapping it around his fist, the buckle tight along the outside of his knuckles.

Yang raised his pistol and pointed it at Christine. In clear, unaccented English, he said, "Let's not make this more difficult than it needs to be, Ms. O'Connor. I have no desire to hurt you."

Christine almost laughed at the absurdity of his comment. "I suppose rape doesn't hurt?"

Yang stared at her with dark eyes for a moment, then swung the pistol toward the other guard's head. He pulled the trigger and a red puff exited the opposite side of the man's head, the moisture splattering against the far wall of the cell. The Cadre Department bodyguard crumpled to the floor.

She stared in stunned silence as Yang stuffed the pistol inside the waistband of his trousers. He opened the cell door, then stepped into the corridor, turning back toward Christine. "Hurry. We don't have much time."

Christine stood frozen at the back of the cell, staring at the pool of blood spreading across the gray concrete floor, trying to make sense of what had happened.

"Come, Christine!" Yang called from the hallway.

The sound of his voice spurred her into action. Stepping over the corpse, Christine entered the corridor as she rebuttoned her shirt. Yang was busy at the security door, typing something into a touch-screen plasma display, identical to the one on the other side of the door. Christine stopped next to him, glancing alternately between his face and the plasma display, attempting to discern what he was doing and why he had murdered the Cadre Department bodyguard.

Yang finished tapping the display. "Give me your right hand."

"What for?"

"There are other security doors you must pass through to escape. I cannot accompany you so I'm entering you into the security system."

"Why are you doing this?"

"I work for your country," Yang said quickly, followed by something in Chinese. Christine sensed a reservation in his voice. Yang followed up in English, "One heart, one soul. One mind, one goal," as if that explained everything.

Yang slipped his left hand into his pants pocket, retrieving what looked like a USB flash drive. "This flash drive contains the details of China's military offensive. Without this, the United States has no chance of defeating the PLA.

"Now give me your hand," he added.

Christine offered her right hand and Yang placed her palm on the plasma screen. A bright red light scanned across the display. After the scan was complete, Christine pulled her hand back and a menu screen appeared. Yang tapped several of the Chinese characters, stopping when the display blinked green. He tapped three more buttons, and the schematics of the Great Hall appeared. With two taps and sideways slide across the glass panel with two fingers, he shifted the schematics to their current location.

"We're here," he said, "and you need to travel this path." Yang traced his index finger along several corridors, pointing to a set of stairs she needed to ascend two levels. "There's a security camera above the exit door, which I've disabled. They'll eventually figure out which exit you departed from, but it will gain you valuable time. You must move fast once you are outside the Great Hall, but not so fast that you attract attention. Understand?"

Christine nodded as Yang continued. "There's a CIA safe house not far from here. After you exit the Great Hall, cross the street into Tiananmen Square, then head south through Zhengyang Gate onto Qianmen Street. Go three blocks and turn left into the first alley after Dajiang Hutong. Follow the alley and someone will find you."

Yang placed the flash drive into the palm of her left hand and the dead bodyguard's pistol into her right.

"When I learned of your meeting with the president, I planned to slip this flash drive to you after the meeting. The PLA will not discover the drive is missing until their inventory Friday afternoon. Until then, they will simply be searching for America's national security advisor. You and this drive must be out of the city by Friday afternoon. If not, I fear you will not leave Beijing alive."

"What about you?" Christine asked. "What are they going to do to you when they find out what you've done?"

"They will not find out," Yang said. "The dead bodyguard is the only one who knew I came down here." Yang folded Christine's fingers into a fist, wrapping them securely around the flash drive in her hand. He offered her a warm smile before he added, "You don't have much time. The security patrols outside will be heading past this part of the Great Hall in ten minutes. You must pass through the ringlet of trees and into Tiananmen Square before then. Go now."

Things were moving too fast. A minute ago she was a prisoner in the Great Hall of the People, and now her escape was being orchestrated by the head of President Xiang's security detail.

"Dajiang Hutong. Hurry!" Yang began entering commands into the plasma screen.

Christine's mind and body were numb, processing what had happened in the last fifteen minutes. She turned slowly, then took a step forward, followed by another, willing her body into motion. It wasn't long before she was jogging, then sprinting down the desolate corridor.

11

BAISHAWAN BEACH, TAIWAN

Her bare feet left deep imprints in the soft white sand, barely visible in the fading light before they were washed away by gentle waves breaking upon the shore. As day transitioned to night, Peng Weijie could barely make out the silhouette of volcanic cliffs rising a few hundred yards inland. Weijie enjoyed her walks along the sandy shore each day, and the scenery even more. On the northern tip of Taiwan, just forty minutes from Taipei City, Baishawan Beach offered spectacular views of both the east and west. In the early morning hours, the approaching dawn illuminated the horizon in an inspiring fusion of pink and orange hues, and in the evening, the crimson sun set upon her country, stolen by the communists.

Weijie was only five when her family fled the mainland. She could still recall the image clearly—peering over the rusty railing of an aging fishing trawler at the disappearing shoreline, clinging to her mother's leg as they fled to Taiwan with Chiang Kai-shek and what remained of his supporters. As the trawler pitched in the rough seas, fighting its way across the Strait, the loss was almost unbearable. Their father had been killed by the Red Army in the waning days of China's bloody civil war.

That was over sixty years ago, and Weijie remained proudly defiant. Her people would never succumb to their larger and more powerful neighbor. She feared the communists would eventually attempt to take their small refuge by force, but they would not be easily conquered. She cast a reassuring glance at the volcanic cliffs. The plateau was populated with dozens of early-warning radars and missile batteries, defending what remained of her homeland. Beneath her fierce defiance, however, Weijie harbored a glimmer of hope that their two countries would indeed be united, her children and grandchildren inhabiting a single, democratic China.

As Weijie's thoughts turned to her family, she looked forward to tomorrow's visit by her daughter and granddaughter. She and her daughter would swing Xiaotien between them as they walked along the beach, dipping the child's feet into the ocean. Weijie's rumination ended when she stepped on something hard in the soft sand. Stooping to examine the object, she unearthed a mollusk shell, its striated colors shimmering even in the dim light of dusk. Xiaotien would be thrilled to add it to her collection.

Weijie stood, brushing off the remaining sand, and was about to put the shell into her pocket when an unusual sound coming from the west captured her attention. As the sound grew louder, Weijie watched as hundreds of tiny, bright red lights streaked overhead. Seconds later, explosions rocked the peaceful shore, illuminating the plateau in a splattering of fire while hundreds of bright red dots continued inland. After a fearful glance at the darkening west, Weijie turned and ran toward home, dropping the shell onto the soft white sand. To the east, the horizon was alight in an orange glow.

12

BEIJING

A blood-red moon hung low over the city as Christine burst into the cool night air, her breath condensing into a white mist. Behind her, the security door swung slowly shut, clicking into place next to a plasma display matching the one on the other side of the door. Christine paused for a moment to catch her breath as she examined her surroundings, barely visible in the weak moonlight. As Yang mentioned, there was a camera mounted above the door, and the small LED light beneath the lens was dark. Surrounded by ten-foot-high granite walls, she stood in a small C-shaped alcove with the fourth side open. The night sounds around her were a strange contradiction; the high-pitched chirping of nearby crickets, almost masked by the sound of cars traversing a busy street not far away.

Christine was carrying an object in each hand: a flash drive in one and a semiautomatic pistol in the other. She searched for a place to hide both items. The flash drive slid into a slim pocket in her slacks, but there was no easy way to hide the pistol. Thankfully, she was wearing a business suit, and she folded her arms across her chest as if warding off the evening chill, tucking the pistol inside her jacket.

The events of the last few minutes jumbled though her mind as she stood in the small alcove, but there was only one item of relevance at the moment: the security guards who would sweep past this part of the Great Hall in a few minutes. There was no time to lose. She moved cautiously to the alcove exit, which opened to a twenty-foot-wide swath of concrete encircling the Great Hall, bordered by a ringlet of trees. Beyond that was the busy Guang Chang Boulevard and Tiananmen Square.

After verifying that no one was within sight, Christine hurried across the concrete path, slipping into the cypress and pine trees. She picked her way through the uneven terrain, reaching the far edge of the trees a minute later. Tiananmen Square was across the street. She hoped she could reach the CIA safe house without drawing attention. She was a Caucasian with auburn hair, but it was dark and if she kept her face down, perhaps she could blend in.

Standing a few feet inside the tree line, she scanned the busy street, searching for the best place to cross, spotting a crosswalk fifty feet to her right. She waited for a break in the pedestrian traffic, then stepped onto the sidewalk unnoticed. As she approached the crosswalk, the electronic crossing sign turned from a red stick figure to a green one, and Christine fell in a few feet behind a man and a woman engaged in conversation. After crossing the street and entering the west edge of Tiananmen Square, the couple turned left while Christine continued straight ahead, her eyes scanning the sparsely populated square.

There was a cluster of boisterous young men in the northeast corner of the square, with a few dozen other people traversing the concrete expanse, some meandering hand in hand while others hurried across. Directly ahead of Christine rose the Monument to the People's Heroes, a 120-foot-tall granite obelisk bathed in bright white light. As she approached the lower of two tiers of white marble railing surrounding the monument, she turned right and headed toward the south exit of Tiananmen Square.

Between her and the exit was the two-tiered Mausoleum of Chairman Mao Zedong, surrounded by a thin strip of trees. The mausoleum was closed at this time of day, and there were only a few people milling around the perimeter of the square building; tourists by the look of things, taking pictures of the exterior. Christine hugged the edge of the green foliage as she passed by, proceeding toward Zhengyang Gate looming directly ahead. The gate and the Menjianlou behind it, both built during the Ming Dynasty in the fifteenth century, comprised the only gate complex in Beijing whose Gate and Arrow Towers were still intact, each tower traversed via a fifty-foot arched tunnel in its base.

Pedestrian traffic was sparse as Christine approached the four-story-tall Zhengyang Gate, passing peddlers at the entrance to the tunnel, their wares laid out on blankets spread at their feet. She eyed Mao lighters, DVDs, and socks of every color as she entered the tunnel, her footsteps echoing off stone walls until she emerged onto the sidewalk of a busy boulevard running between the Zhengyang Gate and Arrow Tower. Christine waited for a break in traffic, then crossed the street and entered another arched tunnel, this one passing beneath the Arrow Tower. After another fifty-foot trek, she exited the empty tunnel and pulled to a stop. Qianmen Street was teeming with people. Locals and tourists packed the busy pedestrian and streetcar thoroughfare.

Christine abandoned the idea of avoiding others on the way to the safe house. This was better—she would melt into the sea of tourists patronizing the upscale stores and famous restaurants lining Qianmen Street. She continued on, passing under a decorated archway painted in vibrant colors, marking the entrance to the district. Six wooden pillars supported the archway, each pillar framed by two stone lions facing opposite directions.

The buildings in the shopping district imitated the architecture of the Qing Dynasty. Along both sides of the street, pagoda-style roofs sat atop two-story buildings constructed of green tile and red pillars. Streetcars moved up and down the sixty-foot-wide boulevard, passing by artists performing acrobatics and vendors peddling candied haws on sticks, filling the air with their distinctive, sweet aroma.

Threading her way down the middle of Qianmen Street, Christine dodged the occasional streetcar, distancing herself from waiters standing outside the restaurants, men dressed in the robed attire of the Qing Dynasty who greeted passersby, bowing with their hands folded across their waist. As she moved down the boulevard, the buildings gradually transitioned from the decorative Qing architecture to boxy brick buildings more representative of modern Chinese design. Christine's eyes flicked to the birdcage street lanterns lining the boulevard, wondering if they contained security cameras feeding images to government officials. She wondered if they were already searching for her.

Christine checked the street sign at each intersection, searching for Dajiang Hutong. Finally, rising above the mass of pedestrians, gold letters glittered atop a black background. After passing Dajiang Hutong, she turned left at the next alley, entering a twenty-foot-wide hutong. Following the hutong as it curved to the right, Christine increased her pace, passing narrow red-brick residences interspersed between storefronts constructed of cement blocks faced with white tile.

As the sounds of the busy shopping district faded behind her, so did the lights. The street was soon draped in shadows, lit only by storefront lanterns hanging near their entrances. Christine peered into one of the stores as she passed by—a hole-in-the-wall restaurant serving a different clientele than the upscale restaurants along Qianmen Street. Men seated in plastic chairs gathered around square metal tables. Construction workers by the look of things, their tanned and burnt faces tilted over their food, paying no attention to the woman passing by.

Christine returned her focus to the street as she approached a cluster of men; teenagers arguing loudly outside an abandoned storefront. One of them noticed Christine and the conversation ceased as every head turned in her direction. Christine moved to the opposite side of the street as she prepared to pass by, but that only spurred the group into action. In unison, the young men sauntered across the road at a pace that would intersect Christine's path as she headed into the darkest section of the street. Christine slowed, evaluating her options.

She could turn around and go back up the alley toward Qianmen Street. But that was no guarantee the teenagers would leave her alone—and if they chased her, she doubted she could outrun them. Additionally, Yang had told her to keep going once she turned into the alley, and someone would find her. Christine decided she would have to go past these men.

As the teenagers approached, the group spread into a line that arched into a semicircle. Christine stopped near a street lamp hanging outside what looked like the entrance to an apartment complex—she had only a few seconds before she was surrounded. She moved to the side of the street, pressing her back against a redbrick wall rising four stories above her as the men completed their encirclement, stopping ten feet away.

Christine assessed her predicament. If the men's intentions were nefarious, she had a pistol but didn't dare use it—the gunfire would draw attention she could ill afford. But perhaps brandishing the weapon would frighten the men away, or at least generate enough respect to allow her to pass without harassment. After a moment of indecision, she pulled the pistol from underneath her jacket, letting her hand fall by her side.

The sight of the semiautomatic generated a reaction, but not the one she had hoped for. Conversation rippled through the teenagers, accompanied by derisive laughter.

As Christine faced the twelve young men, she wondered how many rounds were in the pistol's magazine. But even if she had enough bullets, if the men rushed her, there was no way she could shoot them all.

A man in the middle of the semicircle spoke. "Where are you headed, lady? And why do you have a gun?" He seemed the oldest of the men, nineteen maybe, while the others appeared to range from sixteen to eighteen. He was five-feet, ten-inches tall, a Uyghur from western China by the look of things—brown hair, hazel eyes, and a broad face with high cheekbones, with a thin scar running down the right side of his face. Christine mentally tagged him as *Scarface*. His English was surprisingly good. Good enough to understand her response.

"None of your business."

There was an assortment of catcalls and laughter from the men, accompanied by a few elbows to the ribs. Apparently they understood English and considered her response humorous. Perhaps she needed to clarify her answer.

"Clear a path for me, or I'll clear one myself."

Scarface took a step toward her. "There's no need to be rude, lady. We just want to know how we can help." His statement was accompanied by another round of jeers and catcalls, and it didn't take much for Christine to imagine the kind of help these men had in mind.

"I don't need your help."

The man smiled, revealing crooked yellow teeth, then spoke harshly in Chinese. From the periphery of Christine's vision, she spotted men at each edge of the semicircle working their way toward her, the ring of men slowly contracting. Gripping the pistol with both hands, she raised it toward Scarface. "Tell everyone to freeze or I'll put a bullet in your chest."

The man lifted his hands out to his sides, palms facing Christine as he glanced at the other eleven men, who froze instinctively, waiting for direction. "We mean you no harm," Scarface replied. "We are only looking for entertainment tonight, and we could not let an attractive foreigner pass by without . . ." his smile widened as he continued, "engaging in conversation."

"We've talked enough. Now clear a path."

Scarface stared at the weapon in Christine's hands before replying. "There is a price for your passage. You hold a Type 92 Norinco, carried only by special units in the People's Liberation Army or government. That you have this weapon means you are a special woman, so we will let you pass without further harassment. However, you must first give me your pistol."

Christine considered the man's proposal for a second before rejecting it. There was no way to know if he was telling the truth—once the pistol was handed over there was no guarantee she'd be allowed to pass unharmed. The odds of safe passage were better, she figured, as long as the pistol remained in her possession.

"No deal. And I'm running out of patience."

The man's smile faded. "I doubt you would shoot unarmed men." He paused a moment before adding, "Tell me I'm wrong."

As he spoke, the man on Christine's right moved toward her again. He was dangerously close now—only three arm lengths away. She had to do something. She swung the pistol toward the advancing man and squeezed the trigger. As the shot echoed down the hutong, the man collapsed to the ground, clutching his thigh as blood oozed between his fingers.

Christine swiveled back toward Scarface, leveling the pistol at his head. "Now, *how* wrong do *you* want to be?"

The man uttered a harsh command in Chinese. The men withdrew to their original semicircle, with one man remaining behind to assist the injured teenager, stripping off his shirt and applying it as a tourniquet around his friend's leg. Christine waited in silence as the injured man was pulled to his feet, his arm draped around the other man's neck. Slowly, the two men limped back, joining the others.

Christine was about to demand passage again when the faint wailing of a police siren greeted her ears. Red and blue flashing lights reflected off white-tiled storefronts as the siren grew louder. Christine sucked in a sharp breath as she searched the hutong for someplace to hide.

Scarface pointed to the darkness on her left. "Into the shadows. Hide in a doorway."

He turned to the other men and shouted in Chinese, and a path was cleared for Christine. After she passed through the gap, the men closed ranks and turned toward the street, forming a motley group with the injured man hidden behind them, standing now without the aid of his friend. Christine slid into the shadows just as a police sedan appeared around the curve. Feeling her way along the damp wall, she found a doorway. She stepped back into the one-foot-deep recess, pressing her body against the cold wooden door as the white sedan ground to a halt in front of the men.

An officer wearing a dark blue uniform stepped from the passenger side while the driver remained inside, eyeing the group of young men suspiciously. The officer standing outside the vehicle asked a question. Several of the young men offered short answers while others shook their heads. The officer repeated the same question, met again with negative responses. The alley fell silent as he scanned the faces of the twelve teenagers, eventually directing his gaze up and down each side of the hutong. His eyes stopped moving as they focused on the darkness where Christine was hiding, his eyes probing, staring directly at her.

Christine's grip on her pistol tightened, wondering if the officer had spotted her. As his eyes probed the darkness where she stood, her pulse raced.

The officer's gaze shifted back to the young men and he shouted a command, waving down the hutong in the direction Christine had come. The young men offered curt responses, then turned and shuffled down the hutong toward Qianmen Street. As the teenagers trudged off into the distance, the officer slipped back into the sedan. A moment later, the flashing lights atop the police car went dark and the vehicle did a slow U-turn, then sped down the street in the direction it had come.

Christine let out a deep breath. A minute after the sedan disappeared from view, she stepped from the shadows, moving down the desolate street in the same direction the sedan had headed. The hutong continued curving to the right and pedestrians began to appear along the sidewalks, the establishments lining the street growing brighter and louder.

As Christine hurried down the street, she had no idea how to determine when she had reached her destination. As she scanned both sides of the road, she spotted a black BMW 7 series sedan with tinted windows moving slowly toward her, the angel-eye headlamps illuminating the sidewalks.

Christine scanned the storefronts nearby, searching for a place she could slip inside to avoid detection. Up ahead, she spotted a red and blue neon sign marking the Matrix Game Parlor, occupying the ground floor of a six-story building faced with white and orange tiles. But it was a hundred feet away and the sedan was closing fast. Increasing her pace as quickly as possible, she traversed the hundred feet, slipping into the Matrix as the sedan's headlights illuminated her profile.

Pausing near the entrance, she scanned her surroundings. The Matrix was a maze of arcade games and computer terminals, packed with teenagers clustered around game consoles, laughing and yelling over arcade game explosions and synthesized music. Smoking in public establishments in China was illegal, yet almost everyone was smoking. A multicolor haze drifted upward, illuminated by flickering arcade screens and strobe lights swiveling from the ceiling. Christine turned and peered out the entrance at the passing sedan, just in time to see it coast to a halt. A second later, the driver and passenger doors opened and two men in black suits stepped from the vehicle.

Christine pushed her way through the throng of teenagers, pausing at the end of the first aisle of arcade games, turning back toward the entrance just in time to spot the two men entering. Christine turned and ran deeper into the Matrix, searching for a back exit, bumping into boisterous teens as she weaved between the arcade aisles. Finally, Christine spotted what she was looking for: at the back of the parlor, above a metal door, was the Chinese symbol for *Exit*.

She hit the exit door's metal release bar at a full sprint. It flung open and Christine stumbled into a dark alley lined with overflowing garbage cans. The only light came from the pale moon reflecting off dank, brick walls rising high above her. The alley curved in both directions, each end disappearing into the darkness. She decided to head left, continuing in the direction she'd been headed before entering the parlor.

Christine took off at a brisk run, the exit door disappearing in the darkness. Behind her, the door opened again, the sound of the metal door slamming against the brick wall echoing down the alley. She pulled to a halt and removed her shoes—she could run only so fast in heels, plus the sound clattering down the alley would be a dead giveaway. With her shoes in one hand and the pistol in the other, she sprinted down the dimly lit alley. To her dismay, the alley began to narrow. A hundred feet later, it was barely four feet wide. It continued to shrink and her shoulders began to brush against both walls.

Christine pushed on, gulping the cool night air as footsteps raced down the alley after her. The alley narrowed to barely two feet wide, forcing her to angle sideways until she burst into a large courtyard. She paused for a second, assessing her new surroundings. In the center of the square courtyard, lit by a small yellow lantern, was a garden encircling a six-foot-tall stone statue of a Mahāyāna Buddha. Along the perimeter of the courtyard were four exits—one on each side of the square. As she tried to determine which exit to take, a hand clasped around her mouth and an arm wrapped around her waist.

A man whispered in her ear as he dragged her toward the perimeter of the courtyard, deeper into the darkness. "I am here to help you. Do not resist."

Christine decided it was wise to do as she was told.

As she melted into the darkness, two men rushed into the courtyard—the same men who had entered the arcade. She was fairly certain they were Cadre Department bodyguards, who would either kill her on sight or return her to the Great Hall.

She'd take her chances with the man holding her.

Christine felt his grip tighten as the two men scoured the courtyard, their eyes sweeping past the darkness where they stood. There was a quick exchange between the two men and then they split up, one heading out the exit to Christine's left, the other departing via the opening on the opposite end of the courtyard.

As the two men disappeared from view, the man's grip loosened and he whispered in Christine's ear. "As I said, I am here to help you, Miss O'Connor. Do you understand?" Christine nodded slowly and she was released. She turned toward her abductor, his silhouette barely visible in the darkness. "Follow me," he said, stepping back toward the alley she had emerged from.

Christine followed behind as he entered the narrow alley. He was maybe five-feet, eight-inches tall, with a wiry build; Chinese. She followed him only a few hundred feet before he disappeared. Christine slowed, approaching the spot where he had vanished, when a hand grabbed her arm and pulled her into a small side alley four feet wide. The man retained a grip on her arm as they worked their way slowly up the dank alley, eventually slowing to a halt. A moment later, a vertical seam of light appeared as a door opened. The man stepped inside, dragging Christine into the light.

13

BAISHAWAN BEACH, TAIWAN

Under a cloudless night sky, Jiang Qui gripped his assault rifle with both hands as he stood shoulder to shoulder in the cramped amphibious landing craft. The ocean spray, whipped over the front of the vessel by blustery winds, rained down on him and the other men in his platoon, soaking their dark green uniforms. Jiang heard a dull roar overhead and looked up. Fighter jets streaked toward shore, their white-hot afterburners illuminating the darkness; bright red plumes leapt from the jets toward their targets. Over the edge of the landing craft ramp, the black sky pulsed with orange glows, and muffled explosions grew louder and clearer with each passing minute.

Time crept slowly as the landing craft sped toward shore. As Jiang waited for the vessel to grind to a halt on the sandy beach, he thought about the dilemma he faced a year ago and the decision that had changed his life. Before joining the People's Liberation Army, he had spent his entire eighteen years in a small village nestled below terraced rice paddies in the foothills of the Xuefeng Mountains, working his father's farm. He had never held a rifle, never been at sea.

After turning eighteen, he had asked for Xiulan's hand in marriage. Her father, wanting more for his daughter than a meager life toiling farmland, had refused. Only a man of sufficient station would be allowed to marry beautiful Xiulan, a stature Jiang could never hope to attain. Desperate, Jiang latched on to a brilliant plan. He would join the People's Liberation Army, and with enough commendations, gain entrance to the Party. With Party membership came an urban registration permit. He would bring Xiulan to the city with him, away from the hardship of life in rural China.

Xiulan's father agreed it was a good plan and gave Jiang three years. As Jiang prepared to enlist, he talked his best friend Feng into joining him on his adventure. Feng had accompanied him each step of the journey and was even now standing next to him in the landing craft. Up to this point, Jiang's decision to join the PLA had been a wise one. Even as a Lie Bing, the most junior private in the PLA, he made twice what his family made working their small farm. He sent his money home each month, less a modest allowance for personal items and one night out each month with Feng and the other men in his platoon.

The landing craft began to rock between the ocean swells, peaking as they approached the shore. The tension combined with the pitching seas was too much for Feng. Bending forward, he retched noisily, his vomit splattering against the steel ramp. Jiang steadied Feng with a firm grip on his arm as the landing craft crested another swell, tilting forward and picking up speed as it rode the wave toward shore.

The amphibious landing craft ground to a halt and the ramp fell away, plunging into the dark water. Jiang was supposed to charge ashore immediately—it had been drilled into every soldier on the landing craft. Each second wasted before reaching the cover of the shoreline was a second in the open, exposed to strafing gunfire. But Jiang stood there instead, taking it all in.

Dark cliffs rising from the shore were illuminated in fiery red explosions. Missiles overhead streaked inland toward their targets while hundreds of red tracer trails streamed out from the shoreline, sweeping across the ocean. One of the red trails cut across his landing craft, and Jiang heard high-pitched zings accompanied by soft thuds. The side of his face was splattered with warm liquid. Feng lurched against him, crumpling to the deck a second later. A quick glance down told Jiang his best friend was dead.

The explosions along the shore provided enough light to see the fear illuminated in the faces of the men alongside him; to observe the Second Lieutenant in charge of Jiang's platoon screaming at them. Jiang couldn't hear his Lieutenant over the deafening explosions rocking the coast, the waves breaking upon the beach, and the bullets churning the water around them, but the sight of the officer pointing toward shore spurred him into action.

Jiang lifted his rifle above his head to protect it from the water, and after taking a deep, shaky breath, he leapt into the madness.

14

WASHINGTON, D.C.

In the basement of the West Wing, the air was cold and the tension thick as Captain Steve Brackman preceded the president into the Situation Room. Seated on one side of the polished mahogany conference table was Secretary of Defense Nelson Jennings, followed by three members of the Joint Chiefs of Staff—the chairman and two of the four service chiefs. On the opposite side of the table were Vice President Bob Tompkins, chief of staff Kevin Hardison, and Secretary of State Lindsay Ross. As the president took his seat at the head of the conference table, Brackman slid into the last seat.

The situation couldn't have been worse. Four hours ago, Chinese missiles had swarmed Taiwan, destroying defense batteries along the coast and military command centers inland. An hour later, the first Chinese troops began landing on the shore of Taiwan. The United States had well-formulated war plans to defend Taiwan, but it would take time to generate the forces required to repel the Chinese invasion. Time they might not have. The speed and ferocity of the Chinese assault were startling.

"What's the status?" the president asked, looking toward his secretary of defense.

Jennings answered, "China has landed two army groups along the western shore of Taiwan, pushing inland from six beachheads. Taiwan's navy and air force have been destroyed, along with the bulk of their anti-air batteries, so China has uncontested control of the sky. With the PLA Air Force providing ground support, the outcome is inevitable unless we intervene."

"How long do we have?"

"Our best estimate is the last Republic of China pocket will collapse in ten days. We'll have to land Marines or cut off the Chinese supply lines from the mainland before then."

"What's our obligation to intervene? Are we committed or do we have a choice?"

"Technically, we have a choice, Mr. President. Under the former Sino-U.S. Mutual Defense Treaty, we were obligated to defend Taiwan from Chinese aggression. But when we recognized the People's Republic of China in 1979 and terminated formal relations with Taiwan, the Mutual Defense Treaty was replaced with the Taiwan Relations Act. The wording is purposefully ambiguous as to what our obligations are, but Congress's intent, as well as the position of every administration up to ours, has been clear. The United States will defend Taiwan.

"However, not only has China invaded Taiwan, it appears they have also attacked the United States. We had three fast attack submarines stationed off the Chinese coast, monitoring each of the PLA Navy's three fleets, and all three of our submarines have likely been sunk. Our SOSUS arrays detected three underwater explosions off the coast where our submarines were stationed, and all three fast attacks have failed to report in."

The president's eyes clouded in anger. "How do we respond?"

Jennings answered, "I'd like to refer your question to the chairman, who will outline the current status of the Chinese offensive, then to General Williams and Admiral Healey, who will detail our response."

After a nod from the president, four-star Army General Mark Hodson, chairman of the Joint Chiefs of Staff, seated next to SecDef Jennings, picked up a remote control on the conference table, energizing an eight-by-ten-foot monitor on the far wall, displaying a map of Taiwan overlaid with red and blue icons. "China has committed two army groups, represented by the red squares with Xs through them, to the invasion of Taiwan, landing over one hundred thousand men so far. Opposing them, represented by blue icons, are seventy thousand ROC combat troops. Chinese forces have made substantial progress, completely encircling Taipei City, with China controlling fifteen percent of Taiwan as of 10 A.M. this morning." Red borders appeared on the screen, outlining the progress of China's invasion.

"On the naval front," General Hodson added, "China has sortied seventy-two surface combatants and fifty-eight submarines to sea, with several hundred landing craft ferrying troops across the Strait. In response, we have five carrier strike groups at our disposal in the Pacific—*George Washington* based in Japan, the *Nimitz* Strike Group currently eight hundred miles east of

Taiwan, with the LANT carrier *Lincoln* in the Persian Gulf. *Vinson* and *Stennis* are departing from their homeports of San Diego and Bremerton. Additionally, every available submarine in the Pacific is heading toward Taiwan."

Hodson handed the remote control to the Marine Corps four-star General to his left. "General Ely Williams will discuss our amphibious response."

General Williams pointed the remote at the back wall, and the monitor shifted to a map of the Pacific Ocean. "We have two Marine Expeditionary Forces in the Pacific, ONE MEF based in California and THREE MEF in Okinawa. THREE MEF is loading aboard their amphibious assault ships and should be underway by tonight. ONE MEF will be headed across the Pacific by tomorrow."

Williams pressed the remote again, and the display zoomed in on the island of Taiwan. "To avoid significant losses to our MEFs as they land, it's imperative the Republic of China retain control of at least one beachhead." Eight beachheads on the eastern side of the island illuminated in green. "To ensure Taiwan holds out long enough, we need to provide air support, slowing the Chinese advance. We also need to clear Chinese submarines from the approach lanes to the beachheads. Admiral Grant Healey is responsible for both of those efforts."

General Williams handed the remote to the four-star Admiral seated next to him, who zoomed the display back out to the entire Pacific Ocean. Another click and red and blue icons appeared, with Chinese units indicated in red and American naval forces represented by blue.

"Our initial goal is to provide air support to ROC ground forces," Admiral Healey began, "and we'll do that with Air Force fighter jets from Kadena Air Base on Okinawa, plus the *Nimitz* and *George Washington* Carrier Strike Groups operating east of Taiwan. Unfortunately, that places both carriers within range of the Chinese DF-21 ballistic missile, which can disable an aircraft carrier with a single hit. To protect our carriers against the DF-21, Admiral Vance Garbin at Pacific Command has decided to wait until the *Nimitz* Strike Group joins *George Washington*, so we have enough Aegis cruisers and destroyers, with their SM-3 missiles, to provide an adequate ballistic missile defense. Of course, their success will depend on the density of the incoming missile barrage.

"As far as submarines go," Admiral Healey continued, "we have thirty-two fast attacks in the Pacific, but with two in deep maintenance and another three sunk, that leaves us with twenty-seven fast attacks to counter fifty-eight Chinese submarines. The first three fast attacks—*Texas,* which was already on her way to the Persian Gulf, plus two more submarines surging from Guam, will support *George Washington* and *Nimitz*, with the remaining submarines arriving with the other three carrier strike groups. Our submarines will clear a path to Taiwan for the Marine Expeditionary Forces while the carriers provide air cover—and once the MEFs have landed, our strike groups will sweep inside the Strait, cutting off supplies streaming across from the mainland. Without resupply, it will be only a matter of time before the Chinese ground forces are defeated."

There was a long silence as the president considered the military's plans. Before he spoke, Captain Brackman broke in. "Sir, there's one wild card in play."

The president looked down the table toward Brackman. "What's that?"

"Christine was detained after a meeting with President Xiang, but escaped to a CIA safe house in Beijing with the assistance of a CIA agent in the Central Guard Bureau's Cadre Department. In the process, the CIA agent gave her a flash drive we hope contains information about China's military offensive. We haven't been able to access the information on the drive, so we're going to transport it out of Beijing to a facility with the ability to extract the information. We're hoping we can use that information to our advantage."

The president said nothing for a moment, reflecting on the detainment and subsequent escape of his national security advisor. "How are we going to get Christine out and obtain the flash drive?"

"One of our guided missile submarines, *Michigan,* is on its way to Taiwan. She'll insert a SEAL team into the coastal city of Tianjin while the CIA escorts Christine to the port, where she'll meet the SEAL team and be brought aboard *Michigan*. Hopefully, we'll be able to extract the data from the flash drive using the submarine's onboard systems. If not, *Michigan* will launch one of her UAVs with the flash drive aboard."

Brackman fell silent and the men around the table waited for additional questions from the president. After none were forthcoming, SecDef Jennings spoke, his voice subdued. "Mr. President. Request permission to engage the People's Republic of China."

As Jennings waited for the president's response, the only sound in the Situation Room was the faint whisper of cold air blowing from the ventilation ducts above. On the wall across from the president, the display flickered silently.

Finally, the president gave the order. "Engage the People's Republic of China with all conventional forces at our disposal."

GAMBIT ACCEPTED

15

USS *MICHIGAN*

Five hundred feet beneath the ocean's surface, Captain Murray Wilson felt the vibration through the submarine's deck as he leaned over the Navigation Table in Control, examining the ship's progress toward their new operating area. The main engines were straining, pushing the eighteen-thousand-ton submarine forward at ahead flank speed, through the Luzon Strait into the Philippine Sea. During their transit, Wilson had slowed every twelve hours to proceed to periscope depth to check the broadcast for new messages. No new orders had been received, expounding on their original, ambiguous *proceed to designated operating area.*

Wilson checked the clock in Control. It was midnight and Section 2 had just relieved the watch. The watchstanders were settling into their routine in the chilly Control Room, and the Fire Control Technician was wearing a green foul weather jacket to keep warm. A few years earlier, his face would have been illuminated by the green combat control display, the hue of his features matching the color of his jacket. Tonight however, a myriad of colors played off his face.

Although *Michigan* was a Trident submarine, it was a far different ship today than when it was launched over thirty years ago. When the START II treaty went into effect, reducing the allowable number of ballistic missile submarines from eighteen to fourteen, the Navy decided to reconfigure the four oldest Ohio class submarines as special warfare platforms, replacing the *Kamehameha* and *James K. Polk,* which were approaching the end of their service life. Even better, in addition to carrying Dry Deck Shelters with SEAL mini-subs inside, *Michigan* and the other three SSGNs could be configured with seven Tomahawk missiles in twenty-two of the submarine's twenty-four missile tubes. Only seventeen of the tubes held Tomahawk missiles on this deployment, however. The two Dry Deck Shelters covered four of the twenty-two tubes, with Unmanned Aerial Vehicles in another.

During the conversion from SSBN to SSGN, *Michigan* and her three sister ships received a slew of other modifications. The combat control consoles were now the most modern in the submarine fleet, as were *Michigan*'s new Sonar, Electronic Surveillance, and Radio suites. *Michigan*'s old legacy combat control system—green screens, as the crew called them—had been replaced with the advanced BYG-1 Combat Control System, the dual multi-color screens on each console reflecting off the operator's face.

Wilson turned his attention to the electronic navigation chart and Petty Officer Second Class Bill Coates, on watch as Quartermaster. The young Electronics Technician was busy analyzing the ship's two inertial navigators for error.

"How're we doing, Coates?"

The petty officer looked up. "Good, sir. Both inertial navigators are tracking together." Coates reviewed the ship's projected position as *Michigan* continued its northeast advance. "Will we be staying at ahead flank the entire way, sir?"

Wilson nodded. "That's the plan, except for excursions to periscope depth. How long until we reach our operating area?"

Coates mentally converted the distance to their destination into time based on the submarine's ahead flank speed.

"Ten hours, sir."

The lighting in Control shifted to Gray, catching Wilson's attention. The watch section was preparing to proceed to periscope depth, and the Officer of the Deck's eyes would need time to adjust to the darkness above. The Officer of the Deck, Lieutenant Kris Herndon—one of three female officers aboard—was standing on the Conn between the two periscopes. She called out an order to the Helm, and *Michigan* began to slow and swing to starboard, checking its sonar baffles for contacts behind them. A few minutes later, the lighting was extinguished, drowning Control in darkness aside from the glow of red, green, and blue indicators on the submarine's Ballast Control and Ship Control Panels. Another order from the Officer of the Deck, and *Michigan* returned to base course.

Lieutenant Herndon stopped next to Captain Wilson. "Sir, the ship is on course zero-two-zero, speed ten knots, depth two hundred feet. Sonar holds three contacts, designated Merchant, all far-range contacts. Request permission to proceed to periscope depth to copy the broadcast and obtain a navigation fix."

"Proceed to periscope depth."

The ascent to periscope depth was uneventful, and *Michigan* was soon tilted downward, returning to the ocean depths. After the lighting returned to Gray, then White, a Radioman entered Control, message clipboard in hand, stopping by Captain Wilson.

"New orders, sir."

Wilson flipped through the message, reading the pertinent details. *Michigan*'s Tomahawks were being held in reserve. It looked like her SEAL detachment would get a workout instead.

16

BEIJING

Twilight was creeping across the city beneath a blanket of dark gray clouds as Christine exited the CIA safe house, stepping onto a sparsely populated sidewalk. A cold wind whipped down the narrow street as she moved toward a blue sedan containing a driver and a single passenger in the back. A third man held the rear door of the car open, and Christine slid into the sedan. Although she had never seen the driver before, she instantly recognized the man seated next to her.

Peng Yaoting had grabbed her from behind in the courtyard three days ago, leading her to the rear entrance of the CIA safe house. Peng explained he'd been notified of her impending arrival, intervening just in time. Once safely inside the CIA town house, Christine had offered Peng the flash drive, but the data couldn't be extracted—it was a secure flash drive, which required a password. More sophisticated equipment would be required to extract the data. That, of course, was why she was on her way to the port city of Tianjin with the flash drive in her pants. Her assignment as the courier pigeon would kill two birds with one stone.

Peng nodded to the driver's eyes in the rearview mirror and the car eased into traffic. Peng said nothing during the short trip to the Beijing South Railway Station. Christine knew the basic plan: a high speed bullet train to Tianjin, where she'd be picked up at the station and taken to the port, where an awaiting SEAL team would take her to a submarine loitering off the coast. They hadn't explained how she would get from the port to the submarine, but the fact they had encased her flash drive in a waterproof pouch told Christine the transit from Beijing to the submarine wasn't as straightforward as they made it seem. Especially in light of the checkpoints that had been set up to capture her if she attempted to escape Beijing.

Every transit system was being monitored. Cars were being stopped along every road leading out of the city, and passengers were being examined at the airport and rail stations prior to boarding. Fortunately, there were no road checkpoints between the safe house and the rail station, but exactly how she was supposed to board the train without being detected was still unclear. Her disguise was not particularly effective.

Christine's hair had been dyed a lustrous black and makeup applied to add color to her skin. And although she wore a black scarf framing her face, one direct look into her blue eyes would give it all away. A pair of dark sunglasses offered superficial protection, and Peng had assured her a Caucasian woman wouldn't be an unusual sight at the rail station. Despite China's invasion of Taiwan, citizens and tourists had continued their daily business and sight-seeing, safe from the carnage offshore.

As the car turned left onto Kai Yang Lu Street, Christine examined the Beijing South Railway Station in the distance—an oval-shaped structure of steel and glass, larger than most international airports. It was the second largest railway station in Asia, covering the equivalent of twenty football fields. Peng had briefly described the five-story facility—three levels underground and two above—explaining it was the best exit point from Beijing due to the sheer number of patrons; over thirty thousand passengers boarded trains every hour from twenty-four platforms, with a waiting area capable of holding ten thousand. If there was ever a place she could get lost in a crowd, it was the Beijing South Railway Station.

Christine had been dressed not only to blend into the crowd, but prepared to make a run for it if things didn't go as planned. Instead of high heels, fashionable black sneakers were paired with black slacks and a tan sweater. She carried no purse—a matching black fanny pack strapped to her waist contained her makeup and a fake passport. Inside the waistband of her slacks was sewn the flash drive she'd been given at the Great Hall of the People.

It was only a four-kilometer ride to the rail station, and ten minutes after departing the safe house, Christine's sedan pulled to a stop. Peng turned to Christine. "We won't have many opportunities to talk clearly from here on, so before we begin, do you have any more questions?"

Christine shook her head. Without another word, Peng stepped from the sedan and rounded the rear of the car, opening her door.

———

Peng escorted Christine into the rail station, his arm interlocked with hers, passing through sliding glass doors that opened as they approached. Pausing momentarily near the entrance, Peng's eyes swept across the terminal. Directly ahead, above a bank of twelve ticket counters, an electronic status board listed in red letters the trains departing, along with the departure time and platform in green. The railway station curved away from them in both directions, with additional ticket counters spaced at twenty-yard intervals. Queuing in front of the ticket counters and hurrying along the concourse were thousands of people, all too busy to notice the arrival of two more people headed out of the city.

Christine was relieved she wasn't the only Caucasian woman in the station. At least one in thirty persons was white; young men and women with backpacks slung over their shoulders, typically traveling in pairs, with older folks congregating in large numbers—tour groups, apparently. It seemed it was mostly business as usual in the station, with fair-skinned passengers in line at ticket booths, walking through the concourse, or passing through ticket gates on their way to the train platforms. The only indication something was afoot was the blue-clad police officers at every gate entrance, scrutinizing each passenger as they swiped their ticket to gain access to the train platforms.

Peng began moving again, pulling Christine gently along with his arm. Rather than procure a ticket at one of the manned booths, Peng approached an automated ticket machine. A swipe of an ID card followed by a credit card produced two powder-blue tickets from a slot in the machine. After returning his wallet to his pants, Peng examined the lines at the nearest entrance gate. He guided Christine to the third line from the right, falling in behind an older Chinese couple.

Christine and Peng worked their way toward the gate, where passengers swiped their ticket past an electronic scanner. Each woman passing through was examined by a police officer, whose gaze alternated between the woman's face and a sheet of paper in his hand; a picture of Christine, no doubt. Peng hadn't explained how they would make it past the officer, and as they drew closer to the gate, Christine's apprehension began to mount—the police officers were making anyone wearing sunglasses remove them so they could get a clear look at their face.

The Chinese couple in front of Christine passed through the gate and Peng handed one ticket to Christine, swiping the other as he stepped through. Stopping close to the police officer, Peng spoke in a low voice, his words unintelligible.

The police officer nodded thoughtfully, then Peng turned to Christine. "This way, Cathy."

It took a moment for Christine to realize he was talking to her. Or rather Cathy Terrill, the name on her fake passport. Christine swiped her ticket past the scanner, which blinked green in response, then stepped through the gate. But as she exited, the police officer held his arm out, stopping her.

"Ticket please. And remove your glasses," he said in English.

Christine paused, paralyzed for a second, wondering if something had gone wrong. She had assumed Peng selected this gate because the officer had been bribed or otherwise persuaded to let her pass through. But now he was insisting she remove her glasses. Not only would the officer get a clear view of her face, but so would the surveillance camera at the gate. Christine glanced in Peng's direction for guidance, but the officer shifted his position, placing his body between them.

"Remove your glasses," he repeated as he stood firmly in her way. Christine hastily considering her options, which weren't many—comply or flee into the crowd. But fleeing into the crowd would attract attention, ruining the plan to slip out of the city undetected. She had no choice. Reaching up with one hand, she slowly removed her glasses, handing her ticket to the officer with the other.

Attempting to look disinterested, concealing the panic rising inside, Christine glanced at the paper in the officer's hand as he examined her ticket. There were four pictures on the sheet, one in each quadrant. They were all of her, each one with a different hair color. Blond, brunette, red, and the final one was black, the same hue as her current dye. The last image was like looking into a mirror.

The officer's eyes went from her ticket to the paper in his hand, studying it for a moment before raising his eyes to her face. He stared at her for a moment, then reached toward her.

"Thank you," he said as he returned her ticket. "Your train boards at platform twenty-one, which is down the escalator to the left." His gaze shifted to the next passenger as Christine slid her sunglasses back on.

The officer stepped aside and Christine joined Peng, letting out a slow breath. Peng slipped his arm through hers again as he whispered in her ear. "He had to make you take off your sunglasses. Otherwise it'd be obvious he was letting you pass without examination. But he placed himself between you and the surveillance camera while your glasses were off."

"You should have told me ahead of time. I damn near had a heart attack."

Peng patted her arm. "I'm afraid things might get hairier than that before we're through."

Christine followed Peng down the nearest escalator, arriving at their platform. They stood amongst a throng of people and it wasn't long before a sleek white bullet train arrived, its sloping nose squealing to a halt just past them. A few minutes later, after passengers debarked from the other side of the train, the doors facing Christine slid open. She followed Peng toward the nearest door, then turned left down the center aisle. The railcar sported two blue upholstered seats on each side, and Peng selected the first pair of open seats, letting Christine slide into the window seat while he settled into the other. Christine kept her face turned away, gazing out the window as the last of the train's previous occupants disappeared up the escalators to the concourse or down to the parking levels below.

After an announcement in Chinese, a second one followed in English, explaining the train was the Beijing–Tianjin Intercity Express; anyone not desiring to proceed to Tianjin should disembark. The doors closed a moment later and the train eased out of the railway station, accelerating toward the outskirts of Beijing.

17

BEIJING

Xiang Chenglei sat behind his desk in the Great Hall of the People, staring at his rival seated across from him. Huan Zhixin, chairman of the Central Military Commission—de facto leader of the People's Liberation Army and twenty years younger, wore a smug smile befitting his arrogance. He had deliberately withheld information concerning Christine O'Connor's whereabouts, revealing that fact only seconds earlier.

"You've known all along where she is?" Xiang asked.

"Yes and no," Huan answered. "We know she's been at a CIA safe house here in Beijing. However, our informant has refused to disclose its location. What we do know is that O'Connor has now left the safe house."

"Where is she headed?"

"Our informant doesn't know the final destination, nor the route she's taking—only that she's headed to the coast for a rendezvous with American special forces."

"Why have you not told me earlier she was at a safe house here in Beijing?" Xiang asked.

"I had higher priorities than running down your wayward American."

"Her escape from the Great Hall is an embarrassment."

"Yes, it is." Huan offered another smug smile.

There was a strained silence as Xiang contained his anger, focusing his thoughts on managing the delicate relationship with the head of the People's Liberation Army. Huan coveted Xiang's position as general secretary and paramount ruler of China, waiting impatiently for him to retire. In the meantime, it was not beneath Huan to undermine his credibility, even in subtle ways like this.

It was Huan who broke the silence. "You need not worry, Chenglei.

O'Connor will be apprehended. Now that she's headed to the coast, we will find her. There are only so many ways to make the transit."

Huan pushed himself to his feet. "If you'll excuse me, I have important matters to attend to. Lead elements of the American Navy will be within strike distance by tomorrow morning."

A few minutes later, Huan entered his office on the perimeter of the South Wing of the Great Hall. As chairman of the Central Military Commission, his main office was in the nearby Ministry of National Defense compound, but Huan had arranged for an additional office—with a view—in the Great Hall of the People.

He settled into the black leather chair behind his desk, contemplating the upcoming briefing by the four PLA branch heads. Everything was proceeding as planned. Not only was the PLA offensive progressing smoothly, but *Huan*'s scheme to use the PLA offensive as a springboard to supreme leader of China was working brilliantly.

The first element of that plan—the elimination of Prime Minister Bai Tao—had been executed flawlessly. Bai Tao's resistance to using military force was the main obstacle to the PLA offensive, and Huan had arranged for the removal of that obstacle. Bai's death also opened a coveted spot on the nine-member Politburo Standing Committee.

Huan fumed as he recalled the events of a decade before. His uncle Shen's vote would decide whether Xiang or his rival would become China's new ruler, and Shen had proposed a deal. In return for Shen's support, one of the three positions normally held by China's paramount ruler would go to Huan, a rising star in the Party. It was not without precedent. Two previous men— Deng Xiaoping and Hua Guofeng—had ruled China while holding only one of the three positions. Xiang had capitulated to Shen's request.

However, Xiang had outmaneuvered them both. It was a given that the chairman of the Central Military Commission would be a member of the Politburo, but in a stunning move, Xiang had blocked Huan's election. Without membership in the Politburo, there was no way Huan could be elected general secretary. Xiang had seen through their ultimate plan and had cut Huan off at the knees. But that would soon be rectified.

The PLA offensive was the perfect vehicle for Huan's ambition. Once the vaunted American Pacific Fleet was defeated, Huan's prestige would increase tenfold, and not even Xiang could block his election to the Politburo.

Huan smiled. Xiang was a fool, blind to the political implications of defeating the United States. Once Huan was elected to the Politburo, Xiang's days were numbered.

18

TIANJIN, CHINA

From the seat pocket in front of her, Christine pulled out a brochure containing information written in both Chinese and English. She and Peng were riding in a China Railways CRH3 electric-powered train, reaching a top speed of 350 kilometers per hour during the thirty-three-minute transit to central Tianjin, with select trains continuing on to the Tianjin port district of Tanggu. As the train picked up speed, it wasn't long before they were sweeping past factories and highways, the buildings and roads a blur.

Civilization soon gave way to the country as the train sped southeast toward the coast. Peng had purchased two second-class tickets, the lowest of three fares. Even so, smiling attendants in black and purple uniforms worked their way down the aisle, handing bottled water to passengers. Peng took both bottles without a word, offering one to Christine as the attendants stepped into the adjacent railroad car, passing through sliding glass doors. Christine took a sip, then slid the bottle into the seat pocket along with the brochure.

Eight minutes into their journey, they made the first of three stops along the way. The next twenty-two minutes passed uneventfully, the express train traversing almost the entire route on viaducts above the cities and countryside, the viaducts giving way to standard ground rail as they approached Tianjin. It was dark by the time the train slowed to a halt at the Tianjin Railroad Station. Peng put his hand on Christine's arm as most of passengers filed out of the railcar, explaining their destination was one stop farther, Tanggu.

The last of the exiting passengers stepped off the car, but the doors remained open. Peng's grip on Christine's arm tightened and she looked up, following Peng's eyes. In the adjacent car, two armed soldiers were examining the remaining passengers, each soldier periodically referring to a sheet of paper in their hands. Peng stood, pulling Christine with him down the aisle, stepping off the train just as the door slid shut behind them. Fifty feet in each direction, additional pairs of PLA soldiers had stopped several passengers, comparing their images to those on the sheet in their hand. Luckily, an escalator was directly across from their railcar exit and Peng led Christine onto the descending stairs.

Peng turned to Christine as the escalator moved downward. "They've started checking the trains to Tanggu. We'll have to get there another way."

As Christine navigated the busy Tianjin Railway Station with Peng at her side, she could sense Peng's tension mounting. Although there had been no PLA soldiers in the Beijing South Railway Station, they were posted sporadically throughout the Tianjin station. Peng kept his distance from the soldiers as he navigated the railway station, and he soon found what he was looking for, turning right and passing beneath a sign marking the entrance to the Binhai Mass Transit system, one of the few signs in both Chinese and English. After proceeding down another escalator, Christine realized they had switched from aboveground rail transportation to the subway.

Another stop at an automated ticket machine procured the necessary tickets to board the Line 9 train, and Christine followed Peng through the turnstiles to the loading platform. The subway was cramped, allowing Peng and Christine to meld into the throng of people. While they waited, Peng made a short phone call with his cell phone. The train arrived a few minutes later, and the mass of bodies moved almost as one into the white and red cars.

Peng grabbed one of the center poles in the subway car as the doors closed behind him, swinging around and stopping Christine in front of him, keeping her faced away from the platform. After a quick glance at the subway car's other occupants, Christine's grip on the pole tightened; there were far fewer Caucasians on the subway compared to the Intercity Express railway, the odds of her standing out much greater. That fact was not lost on Peng. With one hand high on the pole and another gripping an overhead strap hanging from the ceiling, he did his best to shield Christine's face from others inside the car. None of the other passengers paid any attention to Peng or Christine, however.

The subway train resumed its journey with a lurch, stopping every few minutes at additional stations. Staring over Peng's shoulder at the reflection in the window, Christine tried to determine whether PLA soldiers or police officers were stationed at the platforms at each stop. There were none she could see, and she sensed Peng relaxing as they worked their way down the Line 9 stops without any sign of passengers being scrutinized as they got off. At each stop, more passengers got off than on, the throng of people thinning until there were fewer than a dozen passengers remaining, most of them sitting on the hard plastic seats lining the sides of the subway car.

The train ground to a halt at the Donghai Road station, the twenty-fifth and last stop along Line 9, and the doors whisked open. Peng waited until the car emptied, then took Christine by the hand, following closely behind two couples engaged in conversation. There were no soldiers or police officers on the platform, only a few passengers awaiting the train's arrival. After a short ride up an escalator, Peng and Christine emerged into the open night air, the subway exit illuminated by harsh white lights.

The subway emptied into a parking lot abutting a two-lane road leading away from the station. The two couples in front of Christine continued toward one of the cars, while Peng and Christine turned right toward a passenger drop-off and pick-up area. From the corner of her eye as they made the turn, Christine noticed someone following about a hundred feet behind them. She squeezed Peng's hand.

"I know," Peng said. "He was on the platform waiting for the train."

Christine stared ahead as they walked, fighting the urge to turn and get a better look at the man following them. Her brief glimpse had captured few details—a Chinese man of medium height and build wearing a black leather jacket over blue jeans.

Peng quickened his pace, which Christine matched, and during a subsequent turn to the right, Christine noticed the man was the same distance behind them, matching their pace exactly. As they headed down the final stretch of sidewalk, a black sedan turned the far left corner of the parking lot, speeding toward the pick-up area.

Peng spoke firmly. "When I say, run to the car. Understand?"

Christine nodded, then glanced behind her again. The man was speaking into the sleeve of his jacket. When he spotted the approaching sedan, he began sprinting toward them, pulling a pistol from inside his jacket.

"Run!" Peng shouted as he spun around, pulling his pistol from inside his jacket.

Christine broke into a sprint as the black sedan squealed to a halt at the pick-up area. Two shots echoed in the darkness and Christine felt a sting in her right arm. Her upper body twisted to the left and she lost her balance, tripping and falling onto the pavement. She hit the sidewalk hard, rolling to a stop a few feet later. Peng was suddenly there, dragging her to her feet as a second black car turned the corner of the parking lot. Its blue-tinted head-lights switched to high beam as the car bore down on them. Christine re-sumed her sprint toward the waiting sedan, glancing briefly behind her. The man who had been following them was sprawled facedown on the sidewalk.

Peng reached the car first, opening the rear door. Christine dove inside and Peng jumped in after her, the tires squealing as the sedan sped away with the door still open. The door slammed shut as the sedan took a hard right, followed by an immediate left.

Christine buckled her seat belt as the car took another hard right, turn-ing onto a highway entrance ramp. Her body pressed against the car door as they sped up the curving ramp. The car's trajectory straightened and she sank into her seat as the sedan accelerated. Over the driver's shoulder, she noticed the speedometer passing two hundred kilometers per hour and climbing.

They were speeding along a three-lane expressway suspended above the water, a causeway connected to a shoreline glowing in the distance. Atop the concrete barriers on both sides of the expressway, lamp poles bathed the cause-way in yellow light, reflecting off the water's black surface. Behind them, a car's blue-tinted headlights were soon joined by an identical pair.

The headlights disappeared frequently as Christine's car weaved in and out of traffic, but it didn't take long to realize the blue lights were gaining on them. Peng spoke to the driver in Chinese, his words short and strained, then turned to Christine, his eyes dropping to her arm. It wasn't until then that she remembered the sting that had caused her to trip and fall. Follow-ing Peng's eyes, she noticed the right sleeve of her tan sweater was stained dark red.

There was a hole in the sweater and Peng ripped a tear into the sleeve to get a better look. Blood was oozing from a bullet hole in her arm. Peng glanced around the back of the sedan and surveyed her clothing, searching for some-thing he could use as a tourniquet. Unfortunately, there wasn't anything he could use or tear into a suitable bandage.

"We'll take care of it once we reach the transfer point." He continued talking in Chinese to no one in particular. With two cars in pursuit only seconds behind, Christine wondered how they would make a successful transfer, whatever that entailed.

"Where are we headed?" she asked.

Peng turned and pointed toward a bright group of lights on the approaching shoreline. "Kiev."

His answer confused her. Kiev was the capital of Ukraine. Yet he had pointed to the coast not far away. Straining her eyes, she noticed an object illuminated under the bright lights. Slowly, the silhouette of a ship formed.

An aircraft carrier!

An aircraft carrier was tied up along China's coast. She was about to ask Peng to explain when their car sped beneath a green traffic sign. Beneath the Chinese symbols, the English translation announced the exit for the Binhai Aircraft Carrier Theme Park, and the answer became clear.

The aircraft carrier looming in the distance was the *Kiev*. After the fall of the Soviet Union, China had purchased the *Kiev* and her sister ship *Minsk*, both carriers rusting alongside their piers. CIA analysts initially thought the *Kiev* and *Minsk* would be refurbished and enter service in the PLA Navy, but the two carriers were instead turned into tourist attractions. In the distance, Christine could see jet fighters on the deck of the carrier, static displays instead of functioning aircraft.

There was a loud pop and a bullet hole appeared in the back windshield, a dozen cracks spidering outward from the small hole. Two more holes appeared and a second later the windshield shattered into a thousand pieces, the glass ricocheting inside the back of the sedan. Peng pushed Christine's head down and yelled, "Stay down." He turned and aimed out the back window, firing off three quick rounds.

Christine clamped her left hand over the bullet hole in her right arm, listening to the terse conversation between Peng and the driver between shots. The left window shattered beside her. The cars behind were gaining on them. Christine looked up as they passed beneath a sign announcing the fare for the expressway. Peering over the driver's shoulder, she spotted an eight-lane toll plaza spanning the expressway. They were traveling at 220 kilometers per hour, barreling toward toll lanes barely three meters wide, separated by concrete barriers painted with yellow and black stripes.

They weren't slowing down. Christine dropped her head as Peng swung his arm over her, shooting out the side window now instead of the back. Her eyes met Peng's for a split second as he ducked down, dropped an empty magazine from his pistol, and inserted another. He chambered a round and sat back up as he yelled to the driver.

Christine jerked forward against her seat belt as the driver hit the brakes, followed a second later by a jarring veer to the left. There was a loud crunch accompanied by a metallic screech, and Peng ducked down again, holding his hand up and firing out the side window into the car that was crunched up against theirs. Christine saw the tollbooth flash past them as their car passed through, creating a shower of orange sparks as the side of their car scraped the concrete barrier. At the same time, an explosion rocked their sedan, illuminating the night sky a reddish orange hue.

Christine peered out the back window as a fireball billowed upward from the toll booth, and chunks of metal and concrete bounced down the expressway after them. The other car had impaled itself on one of the concrete barriers between the toll lanes. Christine breathed a sigh of relief, cut short as the second car emerged from beneath the fireball, rocketing through one of the toll lanes.

Peng pushed Christine's head back down and resumed firing through the back window as incoming bullets pinged off their car's metal frame and thudded into upholstery. Christine felt the car begin to slow and she looked up, wondering if they were approaching the exit to the Binhai Aircraft Carrier Theme Park. She noticed a hole through the headrest of the seat in front of her. Their driver was slumped over the steering wheel, blood oozing from the back of his head.

In less than a second, several things went through Christine's mind. The first was that they were still traveling over two hundred kilometers per hour. The second was the gradual drift of the car across the three-lane highway toward the right side of the road. The third was the realization that either she or Peng would have to jump into the front of the speeding sedan and take control of the car.

Christine turned to Peng as he continued firing out the back window. "The driver's been shot!"

Peng fired off another round at the car behind them, which was gaining steadily.

"What?" he yelled as he turned his head toward Christine.

But before she could reply, her face was splattered with warm blood. Peng's head jerked forward and blood started pouring out the left side of his head. It seemed as if time slowed down for the next few seconds; Peng's face went slack and his eyes turned vacant, then he slumped forward into her lap, blood pulsing from his head onto her slacks.

It was suddenly clear which one of them would have to jump into the front seat. But just when she thought the situation couldn't get worse, the driver slid off the steering wheel, pulling it clockwise as he fell toward the center of the vehicle. The car careened sharply to the right, directly toward the concrete barrier along the side of the road.

Her car would impact the barrier in only a few seconds, insufficient time for her to climb into the front seat, or even undo her seat belt and reach forward to grab the steering wheel. She barely had time to brace for impact.

Christine jolted forward as the car crashed into the concrete barrier. The sharp sound of cracking concrete and crumpling metal filled her ears, ending a second later; it turned peacefully quiet and it felt as if she were floating in air. The front of the sedan tilted downward, then plunged into the dark lagoon surrounding the aircraft carrier *Kiev*, moored a hundred yards on her left.

The car sank into the lagoon, tilted down at a thirty-degree angle. Cold black water began pouring into the car through the broken side and back windows. Christine took one last breath as her head sank beneath the water's surface.

Looking around through murky water with her hair suspended beside her face, she could barely see as she sank toward the bottom of the lagoon. But she didn't need to see; she could feel her way out of the sedan and swim to the surface. She fumbled for the seat belt release, finally locating it. But it wouldn't unlatch, no matter how hard she pressed it. Guessing it was the weight of her body due to the downward slant of the car, she pushed against the front seat with her legs, sliding her body back into the seat, easing the strain on her seat belt. She pressed again firmly, but the latch still wouldn't release.

Christine's desperation mounted. She couldn't hold her breath for much longer. She gave one final shove with her legs, pressing her body back against her seat, then pressed down on the seat belt release with all her strength. But it still didn't unlatch.

As she looked up toward the blue-tinted light shimmering on the water's surface, she became light-headed. The loss of blood and the sudden exertion, combined with the depleting oxygen in her lungs, had taken its toll. As her thoughts faded into darkness, she saw a bright flash of metal and felt strong hands slipping under her shoulders.

19

USS *NIMITZ*

Night was retreating across the Pacific as Captain Alex Harrow stood on the Bridge of his aircraft carrier, supervising preparations for flight operations. Pointed into the brisk thirty-knot wind, USS *Nimitz* surged west into the darkness, plowing through ten-foot waves. Fifty feet below, a myriad of colored lights illuminated the Flight Deck, as the last of the first four F/A-18 Hornet fighter jets, its engine exhausts glowing red, eased toward its catapult. Along the sides of the carrier, additional Hornets were being raised to the Flight Deck from the Hangar below. As the twenty aircraft in Wing ELEVEN's first cycle prepared for launch, Harrow knew that twenty miles to the north, *George Washington*'s air wing was doing the same.

Lieutenant Leland Gwenn pushed forward on the throttles, easing his single-seat F/A-18C toward the carrier's bow. In the darkness, he watched the Director's yellow flashlights guide him toward the next stage of preparation for launch—the Director lifted his hands over his head, then pointed toward the Shooter.

The Shooter, also wielding yellow flashlights, continued guiding Leland forward, finally raising his right arm, flexed at the elbow, dropping it suddenly. Leland responded by dropping the Hornet's Launch Bar, which rolled into the CAT Two shuttle hook as the aircraft lurched to a halt. The Launch Petty Officer disappeared under Leland's jet, verifying the Launch Bar was properly engaged, and a moment later the Shooter raised both hands in the air. Leland matched the Shooter's motion, raising both hands to within view inside the cockpit, giving the Shooter assurance Leland's hands were off all controls. The Shooter pointed his flashlight to a red-shirted Ordie—an Aviation Ordnanceman—who took his cue and stepped beneath the Hornet, arming each bomb and missile.

As Lieutenant Leland Gwenn—call sign Vandal—waited for the Ordie to complete his task, he thought about that fateful day, eleven years ago. He was only seventeen, having just pled guilty to managing a ring of teenage car thieves. Standing before Judge Alice Loweecey, he was more jubilant than remorseful; his lawyer had informed him a deal had been struck that would allow him to avoid jail time.

Judge Loweecey had studied the documents before her in silence before lifting her eyes to the heavily tattooed teenager standing before her. Pushing her wire-rimmed glasses high onto the bridge of her nose, she cleared her throat and announced the decision that changed Leland's life. It was either three years in jail or three years in the Navy.

Fortunately, the Navy was exactly what he needed, levying a heavy dose of discipline and responsibility onto his young shoulders. He matured rapidly, eventually regretting his youthful indiscretions. After receiving his high school GED and impressing his Navy superiors, he enrolled in the University of Maryland as a Midshipman, with guaranteed acceptance into the Navy's flight school in Pensacola following graduation. He received his commission as an officer in the United States Navy, and eighteen months later earned his wings, also earning the well-deserved call sign of Vandal.

A loud roar to Vandal's right caught his attention as his wingman—Lieutenant Liz Michalski—in the F/A-18C on the starboard bow catapult streaked forward, her engines glowing white-hot as CAT One fired. Michalski's jet disappeared below the carrier's bow, reappearing a second later as it climbed in altitude, the glowing twin-engine exhaust growing smaller as it ascended. She would wait in a holding pattern for Vandal and the rest of Air Wing ELEVEN's first cycle.

A signal from the Shooter told Vandal his weapons were armed and it was time to go to full power. Vandal pushed the throttles forward until they hit the détente, spooling his twin General Electric turbofan engines up to full Military Power. As he confirmed the engines were at one hundred percent RPM and fuel flow, he knew that beneath the Flight Deck, steam was being ported behind CAT Two's massive piston, putting the catapult in tension. He then exercised each of the Hornet's control surfaces, moving the control stick to all four corners as he alternately pressed both rudder pedals.

Black-and-white-shirted Troubleshooters verified the Hornet's control surfaces were functioning properly and there were no oil or fuel leaks. Both men gave a thumbs-up and the Shooter turned toward Vandal, relaying the results of the inspection.

Satisfied his Hornet was functioning properly, Vandal returned the thumbs-up and the Shooter lifted his arm skyward, then back down to a horizontal position, directing Vandal to kick in the afterburners. Vandal's Hornet was unusually heavy tonight, with twin fuel tanks—one on each wing—and ordnance attached to every other pylon; tonight's takeoff required extra thrust. Vandal pushed the throttles past the détente to engage the afterburners, then turned toward the Shooter and saluted, the glow from his cockpit instruments illuminating his hand as it went to his helmet.

The Shooter returned the salute, then bent down and touched the Flight Deck, giving the signal to the operator in the Catapult Control Station. Vandal pushed his head firmly against the headrest of his seat and took his hands off the controls, and a second later CAT Two fired with the usual spine-jarring jolt. He felt his stomach lifting into his chest as the Hornet dropped when it left the carrier's deck. Vandal took control of his Hornet, accelerating upward.

As the seat pressed into him during the ascent, Vandal scanned the instruments in his cockpit. Michalski was in a holding pattern at twelve thousand feet. With a nudge of his control stick to the right, Vandal adjusted the trajectory of his climb, angling toward his wingman. A few moments later, he pulled up next to Liz Michalski, call sign Phoenix, who was stationed behind an F/A-18E configured as a tanker, topping off her fuel tanks. All the fighters in Air Wing ELEVEN's first cycle were heavy, consuming over one thousand pounds of fuel during their launch and climb to twelve thousand feet, and would top off their tanks before heading west. Vandal settled in fifteen feet away on Phoenix's nine o'clock position, waiting his turn behind the tanker while USS *Nimitz* completed launching its first cycle.

20

NINGBO, CHINA

Inside the East Sea Fleet command center, with six rows of consoles stretching into the distance, the lights were dim, imparting a feeling of twilight throughout the facility. The blue glow from the consoles illuminated the faces of the men and women manning them, while multicolored symbols appeared on flat screen displays crowding the walls, the blinking icons superimposed on electronic maps of the Western Pacific. At the back of the command center, Fleet Admiral Tsou Deshi studied the displays, monitoring the progress of their assault on Taipei. The first phase of the naval battle had gone exactly as planned, eliminating the American submarines stationed along the Chinese coast. However, as America prepared to engage with their powerful aircraft carriers, the success of the next phase hinged on the performance of the PLA Air Force.

The People's Liberation Army Air Force was the third largest in the world, second only to the United States and Russia, fielding over 1,600 aircraft, with just over a thousand being fourth-generation jets. The PLA had overwhelmed the much smaller ROC Air Force and destroyed their land-based air defenses, gaining complete control of the skies. But now, as Admiral Tsou studied the three waves of blue symbols marching toward Chinese Taipei, he knew the true battle for air dominance was about to begin.

However, that battle would not be waged by PLA aircraft. Even though most were fourth-generation aircraft, they were still inferior to American fighter jets. That task fell to advanced surface-to-air missiles China had spent the last decade developing. It would be missile against aircraft.

Although the air battle was being directed by the Nanjing Military Air Command, Tsou monitored the progress of the engagement from the East Sea Fleet command center. This was their Achilles' heel—in the end, it would all come down to whether the United States could gain control of the ocean and skies and cut off the flow of food and ammunition.

Admiral Tsou watched as a wave of red symbols appeared along the Chinese coast, marching east toward the blue icons. He stood tensely at the rear of the command center as he waited.

21

SCARLET ONE • VIPER TWO

In the cabin of the northernmost E-2C Hawkeye, operating above the Pacific Ocean at 25,000 feet, Lieutenant Commander Julie Austin peered over the shoulders of the two Lieutenants in the Combat Information Center, examining the displays on their consoles. Affixed to the top of the Hawkeye—call sign Scarlet One—the aircraft's twenty-four-foot-diameter circular antenna, a sophisticated radar capable of tracking more than two thousand targets, rotated slowly, searching the skies for enemy aircraft and missiles.

The two Lieutenants—the Radar Officer and the Air Control Officer—were tracking two sets of opposing contacts. The first set consisted of the aircraft from *Nimitz* and *George Washington*, headed west, along with a stream of aircraft from the northeast. The U.S. Air Force's largest combat wing, based at Kadena Air Base on Okinawa, was getting in on the action. F-15C/D Eagles and F-15E Strike Eagles were heading toward Taiwan.

Austin was concerned about the second set of contacts. Over three hundred bogies were inbound from the Chinese coast and had split into a large V, one prong headed toward the Air Force fighters and the other prong speeding toward the carrier aircraft. To the south of Scarlet One, three more Hawkeyes divided up the inbound contacts, relaying the bogies to their fighters.

Austin studied the display, attempting to determine whether the bogies were inbound aircraft or missiles. Finally, the Hawkeye detected electromagnetic signatures that corresponded to the Chinese *Hongqi* surface-to-air missile. *Nimitz's* and *George Washington's* first cycle of aircraft, along with Kadena's 18th Wing, had their work cut out for them.

As the red symbols marched over the outline of Taiwan on the electronic display, they were joined by another wave of twenty missiles originating from the east coast of the island. China had apparently transported surface-to-air missile batteries across the Strait to Taiwan, increasing the range of their missiles by two hundred miles. Until this moment, Austin had been comfortable with their station above the Pacific Ocean, well out of range of missiles fired from the Chinese mainland.

Lieutenant Commander Austin scanned the new wave of missiles, which were leading the barrage from the mainland by sixty miles. The inbound fighters from *Nimitz* and *George Washington* had dropped down to ten thousand feet, matched in altitude by the main mass of missiles. But the new wave of missiles from Taiwan remained at fifteen thousand feet. Austin wondered if the missiles were a new variant, designed to drop in altitude at the last minute. Sure enough, as the missiles approached the fighters, the altitude on the Combat Information Console display began changing. But the missiles were climbing, not dropping. It took a moment for Austin to realize the missiles weren't headed toward their fighters. It took another second to realize where they were headed instead.

Austin slammed down on the ICS intercom button, activating the speaker in the cockpit. "Incoming missiles, bearing two-seven-three!"

Fifty miles ahead of Scarlet One, Vandal monitored the missiles being relayed from the Hawkeyes behind them. The eighteen Hornets and Super Hornets in *Nimitz*'s first cycle were divided into nine two-fighter packages, with each package assigned a different ground-support mission once they reached Taiwan. At this point in their approach to the island, the eighteen fighters were strung out side by side at half-mile intervals, with Vandal, designated Viper Two, on the far left, and his wingman, Phoenix, in Viper One on his right. Two EA-18G Growlers—one on each side of the fighter formation—accompanied the strike force toward their targets, jamming incoming missiles and aircraft radars.

The first wave of missiles curiously passed overhead, and a moment later, the trailing missiles disappeared from his display, no longer relayed from the Hawkeyes behind him. Vandal shifted to his organic sensors, and the missiles reappeared. Most of the missiles were represented by a red 6, which corresponded to the Chinese *Hongqi* surface-to-air missile. Interspersed within the mass of *Hongqi* missiles were sixteen bogies with an unknown designation. These bogies weren't radar-guided or his Radar Warning Receiver would have classified them based on their electromagnetic signature. They were most likely heat-seekers, which Vandal hoped to defeat with the Hornet's flares and evasive maneuvering.

As Vandal studied the incoming bogies, they broke into two groups of eighty missiles—one group headed toward *George Washington*'s aircraft and the other group headed Vandal's way. He did the math. Eighty missiles against twenty aircraft. Not good odds.

The missiles closed the remaining distance rapidly, and Vandal discerned that four missiles were targeting his aircraft, each missile thirty seconds behind the other. Four more missiles were targeting Phoenix. As the first wave of missiles approached, Vandal's APG-79 indicated the incoming *Hongqi* had failed to lock on to his Hornet. The nearby Growler's electronic jamming was working well. Vandal broke left as his wingman veered right. The other Hornets took evasive action as the missiles reached them. As the first wave of twenty missiles passed by, two pinpricks of bright light illuminated the black sky, one to his immediate left and another in the distance to his right. Two of the missiles had found their target.

The initial engagement was ominous. With two aircraft lost in the first wave and three more waves of missiles coming, they'd lose almost half of their first cycle even before they reached Taiwan. Unfortunately, Vandal soon realized the situation was far worse. The aircraft shot down to his left was one of the two Growlers accompanying them. After checking his radar display, Vandal confirmed the Growler on the right side of the formation had also been lost. The unidentified heat-seeker missiles had taken out both of their radar-jamming support aircraft.

Without the Growlers, the remaining eighteen jets were more vulnerable. Vandal was about to find out just how vulnerable; the second wave of twenty missiles was approaching. The next missile targeting Vandal was a *Hongqi* missile with a radar-seeking head, so Vandal dispensed chaff from the fuselage of his Hornet, then broke left. His jet veered out of the way as the missile continued straight ahead, attracted by the cloud of aluminum-coated glass fibers. Vandal hoped the missile's proximity fuse would detonate as it passed through the chaff, but no such luck. This missile was a new generation, because it turned around and headed back toward Vandal's jet.

As the missile closed rapidly on Vandal's Hornet, this time from behind, Vandal dispensed more chaff, then pushed his stick forward, rocketing down toward the ocean. Instead of passing through the chaff and continuing straight ahead, this time the missile turned downward, following Vandal toward the ocean's surface. As the missile quickly closed the distance, Vandal kicked on the afterburners. He had only a few seconds to decide on his next course of action. The chaff wasn't going to destroy the missile following him. So he had to destroy it another way.

As his Hornet screamed toward the water, Vandal decided to wait until the last possible moment, then pull out of the dive. The maneuver would be a challenge; he couldn't pull more than nine g's without losing consciousness, while the missile could pull far more. As a result, the missile would gain on his aircraft during the turn, unless it was distracted.

Warning signs flashed inside his cockpit as Vandal headed straight toward the ocean's surface at maximum speed. He eased off on the throttles and pulled back on the stick, pulling his Hornet out of the dive, simultaneously dispensing chaff. It was an eight-g turn, and he tightened every muscle in his body, trying to keep the blood from draining from his head and losing consciousness. The legs of his G suit filled with air, helping to keep blood in the upper half of his body. Vandal grunted through the turn, leveling his Hornet off at five hundred feet. Barely a second later, the missile passed through the chaff and continued straight down, detonating as it slammed into the ocean's surface.

Vandal's relief was short-lived. His APG-79 alarmed again. Another *Hongqi* missile was descending in altitude and had already locked on to him. Somehow the Chinese were guiding these missiles to their targets. Perhaps long-range command and control radars had been moved onto Taiwan. Vandal decided to stay close to the deck and try the last trick in reverse. By the time the missile passed through the chaff and figured things out, he'd be long gone.

Another ten seconds and the missile was dangerously close. Vandal kicked in the afterburners, increasing speed. He waited until the last possible moment, then dispensed chaff again and pulled back on his stick, turning his Hornet skyward. As planned, the *Hongqi* passed through the chaff and continued straight ahead. Vandal watched on his display as the missile turned around, searching for him, but Vandal was already five thousand feet above it.

Vandal continued higher, leveling off at ten thousand feet, attempting to get his bearings on the remaining missiles and *Nimitz*'s first cycle of aircraft. A blue-white flame streaked by on his right. Phoenix had twisted her Hornet around and kicked in her afterburners. One *Hongqi* missile had just missed her but another was in hot pursuit. As he contemplated whether there was a way to help her, an alarm activated again in his cockpit. Two more missiles were headed toward him.

Vandal steadied up in the direction of the first missile, dispensing another round of chaff as he broke right. The thin aluminum-coated decoys worked again, and the missile lost track of Vandal's Hornet as it passed through the chaff. But it wasn't long before the missile turned around. Even worse, the second *Hongqi* was in front, headed directly for him. Compounding the problem, he had only one burst of chaff left.

As he analyzed his predicament—one missile behind him and another in front—he realized the two missiles were racing directly toward each other. He did a quick mental calculation, guesstimating that if he slowed about a hundred knots, both missiles would arrive at his Hornet at the same time—in about ten seconds. He eased off the throttles.

Just before the two *Hongqi* missiles closed on Vandal's Hornet, he dispensed his last round of chaff, then kicked in his afterburners and pushed down on the stick, vacating the area as quickly as possible. The two *Hongqi* missiles, decoyed by the chaff, continued straight ahead, locking on to each other and detonating above Vandal as he raced toward the ocean's surface.

Vandal pulled up as the illumination above him faded to darkness, leveling his Hornet off at seven thousand feet. He let out a deep breath, checking his instrumentation. There were no additional missiles locked on to him.

He spoke into his headset. "Viper One, how are you doing?"

Michalski's voice came across the radio. "I've got a *Hongqi* on my six. I'm out of chaff and out of ideas. I can't shake it!" Vandal glanced at his display. Phoenix was five miles to the north at ten thousand feet, headed his way.

Vandal got an idea. He banked his F/A-18 hard left into a 360-degree turn, climbing in altitude toward Michalski. Vandal adjusted the diameter of the circle so that he came out of the turn headed perpendicular to his wingman's flight path. Michalski was one of the best pilots in the squadron, and Vandal wasn't surprised she'd been able to keep the *Hongqi* missile at bay even without chaff, juking her Hornet at the last possible second as the missile approached, taking advantage of the missile's excessive speed.

The surface-to-air *Hongqi* were very large missiles compared to the air-to-air missiles aircraft carried, packed with fuel for the long transit from the coast. Their large size made them less maneuverable, which thankfully gave Michalski and the other pilots a fighting chance. But what the *Hongqi* lacked in agility had been replaced with persistence. Its guidance and control processing was advanced indeed. It was only a matter of time before Michalski maneuvered too soon or too late, and the missile would remain locked on and home to detonation.

Michalski had kicked in her afterburners again after her latest maneuver, and her Hornet was streaking toward Vandal, the missile in hot pursuit. Vandal thumbed the trackball on his flight stick, switching to his six-barrel Vulcan 20mm cannon as he spoke into his headset.

"Viper One, do you trust me?"

"Hardly!" Phoenix replied. "With a call sign of Vandal?"

Michalski had a point, but there was no time to debate its merits. "I need you to fly straight," Vandal replied. "No juking until I say so, okay?"

"Okay," Michalski repeated as her Hornet screamed by a half-mile in front of Vandal.

Vandal focused. He had timed it as best as possible—the geometry was perfect. The *Hongqi* missile was a mile behind Phoenix and closing fast, and the missile would cut across Vandal's flight path in about five seconds. It was going to come down to hand-eye coordination, and he was better than most. Maybe all those days skipping high school, hanging out at Fat Eddy's Billiards playing video games, would pay off after all.

The odds of hitting a missile with a gun were low, but it was worth a shot. Unfortunately, the *Hongqi* would get dangerously close to Phoenix. If he missed the missile and told her too late to juke out of the way . . .

Vandal caught the red engine exhaust of the missile in his peripheral vision. He fired his Vulcan gun, watching the path of the red tracers race out ahead of him, judging whether they would intersect the path of the missile streaking across the night sky. He would not get another shot. At the last instant, he adjusted his angle down a fraction of a degree, and the *Hongqi* missile slammed into the stream of 20mm bullets, breaking into fragments in an orange-red puff. A second later, Vandal passed above the missile debris, then banked left and kicked in his afterburners.

"Splash one *Hongqi* missile," he said as he pulled up alongside Phoenix.

"Thanks Vandal. I thought I was a goner." The faint glow from Michalski's cockpit instrumentation illuminated her profile, and he could see her turn her head toward him. He couldn't see her face behind her visor, but he knew she was smiling.

Now that the immediate danger for him and his wingman had passed, Vandal turned his attention to the rest of *Nimitz*'s first cycle of aircraft. A glance down at his display returned startling information: Vandal and Phoenix were the only two aircraft remaining. Another review of his instrumentation told Vandal they could not continue their mission. They'd consumed too much fuel during their evasive maneuvers. They'd have to head back to *Nimitz*. Vandal was about to inform Phoenix when her voice broke across his headset.

"Incoming bogies, bearing two-seven-three."

Vandal checked his display as his APG-79 alarmed. Six incoming bogies. A few seconds later, the APG-79 identified them as *Hongqi*.

They were out of chaff and low on fuel. Their only option was to run and hide. "Down to the deck! Head back to *Nimitz*."

Vandal pushed his stick forward, pitching the nose of his Hornet down. Phoenix followed, and both Hornets raced toward the ocean's surface. Vandal banked left and Phoenix right, the two jets turning back toward *Nimitz*, leveling off at five hundred feet. Vandal checked his APG-79. The *Hongqi* were closing and dropping in altitude.

As the *Hongqi* continued to close, Vandal had two choices—wait until the last second and then climb, or veer to the left or right. Without chaff, neither option offered a reasonable chance of success.

He checked his fuel gauge again. With the evasive maneuvers they were about to make, they weren't going to have enough fuel to make it back to *Nimitz*. They were too heavy—they had too much ordnance. Ordnance that was a liability as they headed home. It was useless against incoming missiles, and it weighed them down as they maneuvered their Hornets.

"Viper One. Drop all ordnance. We need to get lighter."

Phoenix acknowledged, and seconds later the two Hornets dropped their payload of bombs into the Pacific Ocean.

Vandal wiggled his flight stick back and forth. His Hornet felt lighter, nimbler. And just in time. The six *Hongqi* had closed on them, and it was time to maneuver. But then he decided against the two previous options. Instead of pulling up or veering to the side, he decided to descend even lower.

"I'm dropping down as low as possible. Let's see if we can lose the missiles in the ocean clutter."

Pushing his stick forward, Vandal eased his Hornet toward the ocean, dropping down to an altitude of fifty feet, dangerously close to the top of the waves breaking on the ocean's surface. On a calm day, flying this low was dangerous enough. But the higher the sea state, the more unpredictable the wave height. The weather had steadily deteriorated through the night, and average wave height was now between thirty and forty feet. One fifty-foot wave and it'd all be over.

Phoenix matched his maneuver, pulling up alongside him on his nine o'clock position. But the *Hongqi* missiles also matched their maneuver, descending to fifty feet, continuing to close. It looked like Vandal's last-ditch effort had also failed, when one of the missiles trailing them disappeared from the display. Vandal's best guess was that it had been taken out by a random fifty-foot wave. That meant fifty feet was too low to be flying. He called into his headset.

"Viper One. A wave just took out one of our bogies. We're too low. Come up to seven-five feet."

As Phoenix joined him at seventy-five feet, Vandal realized he had run out of ideas, and time. In a few seconds, the leading *Hongqi* missiles would reach them. He was confident he and Phoenix could evade the first missile. But without chaff, he and Michalski had the skill and equipment to evade—at best—one missile at a time. Two missiles would be far too difficult.

Michalski's voice cut across his headset. "Viper Two. Got any more bright ideas?"

"I got nothing," Vandal replied.

"Then I think it's time we part ways," Michalski said. "I'll see you back at the farm."

"Roger that, Viper One."

Michalski's Hornet banked left and then Vandal banked right, both jets continuing to skim along the ocean's surface. Vandal checked his APG. Three missiles had peeled off toward Michalski, while two followed him. A few seconds later, Michalski's jet rocketed skyward, her afterburners burning blue-white, with three red pinpricks following beneath her. She wanted maneuvering room, something she didn't have near the ocean's surface. But Vandal didn't see any hope in that course of action; there was no way she could outmaneuver three missiles. Hell, there was no way he could outmaneuver *two* missiles.

As the two *Hongqi* trailing him closed the remaining distance, Vandal realized he needed to make a decision—head skyward like Michalski or come up with some other plan. If only he had another burst of chaff, he could try the same trick on these two missiles as the last two. As he grasped for a plan, he finally decided to try the same ploy as before, only this time without chaff. It'd be risky, with nothing to distract the two incoming missiles from his Hornet. But if he could maneuver his aircraft out of the way fast enough, resulting in the two missiles locking on each other, it just might work.

Vandal increased altitude to one thousand feet to give himself some maneuvering room, monitoring the first incoming *Hongqi* on the APG-79. Just before the *Hongqi* closed to within range of its proximity fuse, Vandal juked hard left and kicked in his afterburners. The first missile sped by without detonating. Vandal juked hard left again, completing a 180-degree turn. He was now heading directly toward the second missile. As expected, the first missile turned around, and was now following him in hot pursuit.

He ran the mental calculations again, slowing his Hornet slightly so both missiles would reach his Hornet simultaneously. Only this time, there would be no chaff to confuse them while he attempted to evade. He would have to wait even longer, until the missiles were very close, so neither missile detected his evasive maneuver until it was too late, hoping neither missile passed close enough to his Hornet to detonate—but hopefully close enough to destroy each other.

Both missiles had closed to within fifteen seconds when a bright orange fireball erupted at two o'clock high. He dropped his eyes to his instruments as Viper One disappeared from the display. A lump formed in his throat as he realized Liz Michalski was dead. But he had little time to reflect on the loss of his wingman. He had more pressing concerns.

As the two missiles closed the remaining distance, Vandal opted for a 3-D canopy roll at the last second. He pulled his control stick back hard and right, hopefully twisting out of the way as the missiles sped beneath him, hoping even more that his Hornet wasn't torn to shreds by debris from the two missiles as they exploded.

The plan was complicated and difficult to execute. Vandal timed it perfectly with respect to the trailing missile. His Hornet twisted out of the way of the *Hongqi*, and the missile was unable to change direction quickly enough, passing beneath Vandal's Hornet. However, the missile approaching from ahead arrived one second later than Vandal anticipated, and it noticed the target's sudden upward movement.

The missile turned sharply, slamming into the fuselage of Vandal's Hornet. The missile detonated, igniting the Hornet's two fuel tanks in secondary explosions. Shards of white-hot shrapnel tore through Vandal's body as the cockpit was engulfed in flames. Vandal, encased in the burning wreckage of his Hornet, plummeted toward the ocean's surface.

USS *NIMITZ* • USS *LAKE ERIE*

"Loss of Four-Alpha-One and Four-Alpha-Two."

The Strike Controller's report aboard *Nimitz* was professional and monotone, failing to match the panic rising inside Captain Alex Harrow. Standing in the aircraft carrier's Combat Direction Center, Harrow had monitored the carrier air wing's engagement with the Chinese missiles. The number of missiles was impressive, with China expending over four missiles for each aircraft. Even worse, the capability of those missiles was much better than expected. *Nimitz* and *George Washington* had lost their entire first cycle of twenty aircraft each.

Standing beside Harrow was the CAG, Captain Helen Corcoran, Commander of Carrier Air Wing ELEVEN. Her eyes were focused on the Video Wall, a collection of two eight-by-ten-foot displays mounted next to each other, with a half-dozen smaller monitors on each side. With her features illuminated by the blue glow of the CDC's equipment consoles, her face had paled as the Wing's losses mounted. The United States would prevail in this conflict—of that Harrow was sure. The price America would pay in the process was the only variable. Unfortunately, those losses were mounting at an unexpected rate.

A second wave of red symbols appeared on the screen, headed toward *Nimitz* and *George Washington*'s second cycle of aircraft. Unbelievably, the second wave of missiles was just as dense as the first. As Harrow evaluated their Wing's predicament, Captain Sue Laybourn, the Operations Officer or OPSO, approached the two Captains. "*George Washington* is recalling her strike package. Request your intentions."

Corcoran shifted her eyes toward Harrow. "I can't risk losing another twenty aircraft. Until we figure out how to effectively jam or decoy these missiles, I've got no choice."

Even though it wasn't his call—only the CAG or the Admiral in the Tactical Flag Communication Center aboard *Nimitz* could recall their fighters—Harrow nodded his agreement.

Corcoran turned to Captain Laybourn. "Recall the strike package."

Laybourn relayed the orders to the Strike Controllers via the Tactical Action Officer, and Harrow watched the electronic display on the Video Wall as the second and third cycles of Air Wing ELEVEN aircraft turned back toward the carrier. The first battle of the war would be chalked up as a Chinese victory; one third of *Nimitz*'s air wing had been destroyed while not an iota of damage had been inflicted upon Chinese forces. But just when Harrow thought it couldn't get worse, a wave of yellow symbols appeared on the display, originating from China's interior rather than the coast. A few seconds later, the yellow icons switched to red symbols with a sharp point, representing hostile surface-to-surface missiles. China was turning its attention from the inbound aircraft to the carriers that had launched them.

The OPSO stepped away to confer with the Tactical Action Officer, returning a moment later. "Multiple DF-21 missiles inbound. Request permission to set General Quarters."

"Set General Quarters," Harrow ordered.

Laybourn passed the order, and Harrow's stomach tightened as the *gong-gong-gong* of the ship's General Alarm reverberated in CDC, followed by the announcement, "General Quarters, General Quarters. All hands man your battle stations. Move up and forward on the starboard side, down and aft on port."

Ten DF-21 *Dong Feng* ballistic missiles were inbound toward the two carriers. In a few minutes, *Nimitz* and *George Washington* strike groups would engage missiles descending at 2.5 miles per second. The carriers were defenseless against this type of missile; not even their aircraft could shoot one down. That task fell to the strike group's Aegis class cruisers and destroyers, armed with SM-3 anti-ballistic missiles. With General Quarters called away, Harrow would normally have headed to the Bridge. However, there was little he could do against DF-21 missiles. It would be up to *Nimitz*'s escorts, and their efforts were more easily monitored from CDC. It was here that he would await *Nimitz*'s fate.

The DF-21 was a massive missile by anti-ship standards. Descending from an almost vertical trajectory, it was designed to impact the carrier's deck. Carrying a thirteen-hundred-pound warhead, a single *Dong Feng* missile would blast a forty-foot-wide crater in the Flight Deck, terminating the carrier's ability to conduct flight operations.

Harrow examined the left main monitor of the Video Wall, displaying the inbound missiles and the ships that would shoot them down. The fourteen Aegis class cruisers and destroyers were deployed in a semicircle to the west of *George Washington* and *Nimitz*.

As he examined the cruiser and destroyer icons, he heard Captain Laybourn beside him exclaim, "What the hell . . . ?"

Harrow looked down at Laybourn's console. It was cluttering with new missile contacts, appearing where the DF-21 missiles were, as if they were reproducing. Harrow figured these DF-21 missiles were a new variant, releasing smaller warheads, which would complicate the carrier's missile defense. The cruisers and destroyers in his strike group would have to start launching sooner, as there were a lot more targets now. But none of his escorts began firing. Harrow's eyes went to the video feeds, searching for evidence of missile launches. But there was nothing. The ships' vertical launchers were silent. Something was wrong.

Aboard USS *Lake Erie*, Captain Laybourn's counterpart watched in stunned silence as chaos erupted in the Combat Information Center. Ghost bogies had appeared on Lieutenant Commander Shveta Thakrar's console, and the trackers had begun flitting all over the place, switching between contacts. The *Lake Erie* was paralyzed, unable to determine which contacts were the real DF-21 missiles. The cruiser could no longer defend the carriers from the incoming missiles.

As the Tactical Action Officer, Thakrar was seated in the center of the "Front Table," or first row of consoles in the cruiser's Combat Information Center, with the ship's Captain on her left and the Combat Systems Coordinator on her right. Thakrar glanced up at one of the four fifty-inch flat panel screens on the bulkhead in front of her. The five incoming DF-21 missiles had morphed into over fifty bogies, and their Aegis Warfare System could not determine which contacts were the missiles and which were ghost contacts. As the Tactical Action Officer in charge of operations in CIC, it was Thakrar's responsibility to sort out this mess.

Thakrar turned in her seat and shouted over the cacophony of excited conversations. "Attention in CIC." She waited a few seconds for silence before continuing. "Status report."

The Systems Test Officer replied, "Every console in CIC is affected. The system is refusing to warm start. We've tried three times. It looks like the only option is a cold start."

Thakrar assessed the situation—it would take ten minutes for a cold start, and by then it'd be too late. The DF-21 missiles would have already hit the carriers.

"Not an option," she replied. "Any other ideas?"

There was strained silence for a moment, until the Combat Systems Coordinator next to her, Senior Chief Mario Caiti, spoke. "We could shift over to ACB-16. It's a developmental build, and they gave us the ability to warm start directly into it."

"ACB-16 isn't authorized for use," the Systems Test Officer interjected. "It's loaded aboard us strictly for testing."

Commander Thakrar evaluated Senior Chief Caiti's recommendation. There wasn't much time to debate how functional ACB-16 was, nor ponder how many rules they were about to break. She glanced to her left, at the *Lake Erie*'s Captain, Mary Cordeiro.

"Screw authorization," Cordeiro said. "Warm start into ACB-16."

The Systems Test Officer turned to his console, initiating a warm start of *Lake Erie*'s Aegis Warfare System into the test build. A minute later, the consoles in the Combat Information Center sprang to life. The operators focused on their screens, as did Lieutenant Commander Thakrar. To her relief, the system returned ten clean bogies, five headed toward *Nimitz* and five toward *George Washington*.

In *Nimitz*'s Combat Direction Center, Captain Harrow watched as SM-3s began streaking up from *Lake Erie*. But only *Lake Erie*. Her SM-3s headed toward the five missiles descending toward *Nimitz*, but *Lake Erie* had fired late, and had insufficient time to launch a second round if her SM-3 missiles missed. Harrow watched the display as four of the five missiles hit their target. But one DF-21 missile made it through. Now it was up to *Nimitz* to defend herself.

Captain Laybourn assigned the incoming DF-21 to the carrier's anti-air NATO Sea Sparrow Missile System and authorized *Weapons Free* for the Rolling Airframe missiles and CIWS Gatling gun. The DF-21 streaked down toward *Nimitz*. Sea Sparrow and Rolling Airframe missiles were launched in succession and both missed their target, leaving only the CIWS system. But Harrow knew the CIWS would be unable to engage a missile descending at such a high angle and speed.

The TAO announced, "Missile inbound. All hands brace for shock!"

Harrow counted down the seconds before impact, grabbing the nearest I beam to brace himself.

The DF-21 impacted *Nimitz*'s Flight Deck with a massive jolt. The explosion rumbled through the carrier, followed by tremors of secondary explosions. On the carrier's Damage Control Status Board, red symbols illuminated downward from the Flight Deck through the O-3, Hangar, and Main Decks, plus an additional three decks in a circular pattern radiating outward.

Harrow shifted his eyes to the video feeds canvassing the Flight Deck. Orange flames leapt skyward from a massive crater in the aft section of the Flight Deck, the fire licking the twisted metal edges of the gaping hole. He studied the red symbols on the status board, his eyes shifting uneasily toward midship, where the nearest ammunition magazine was located. If the fire caused the ammunition magazine to overheat, it'd be over. *Nimitz* would be turned into scrap metal.

Darkness enveloped CDC and the emergency battle lanterns flickered on in response. Harrow heard the forward emergency diesel rumble to life, telling him both reactors had SCRAMed, leaving *Nimitz* with minimal electrical power until one of the reactors could be brought back on-line. Even worse, the aircraft carrier was slowing; without an operable reactor she had no propulsion. As *Nimitz* drifted to a halt, Harrow's eyes shifted from the massive hole in its Flight Deck to the fires spreading on the Damage Control Status Board. The amount of damage they had sustained from a single missile was stunning.

Suddenly remembering *George Washington* had been targeted by five of the DF-21 missiles, Harrow turned his attention to his sister carrier. Operating twenty miles to the north, she was visible on video feeds streaming into *Nimitz*'s CDC, relayed from the one of the tanker Super Hornets circling above. Against the background of dawn's early light, five black plumes spiraled upward from the carrier, and incredibly, she was already listing heavily to starboard. She was taking on water. One of the DF-21s or the secondary explosions must have penetrated the carrier's hull beneath the waterline. The damage had to be catastrophic. Harrow's features hardened. It looked like *George Washington* was on its way to the bottom of the Pacific.

Harrow forced his thoughts back to *Nimitz*, and just as important, the two returning air wings. Both air wings would have to land on *Nimitz*. That was, *if Nimitz*'s crew was able to gain control of the fires and overcome the gaping hole in its Flight Deck. If *Nimitz* didn't return to flight operations, their aircraft would be forced to Bingo to Kadena or the Philippines, assuming they had enough fuel. If not, the pilots would be forced to eject and let their aircraft crash into the ocean, effectively neutralizing two of the Pacific Fleet's five carriers.

As Harrow dwelled on the disastrous scenario, three new symbols appeared on the left display of the Video Wall: red semicircles with the rounded end downward, representing submerged contacts. China's submarines were moving in for the kill. Without propulsion, *Nimitz* was a sitting duck.

THE SACRIFICE

23

CNS *CHANG CHENG*

Commander Zeng Yong rotated swiftly on the attack periscope of his Shang class nuclear-powered submarine, the CNS *Chang Cheng,* pausing for longer than he should have. It was a sight to behold: one of America's great aircraft carriers sinking. Zeng swung the periscope around, stopping to examine his target, the second carrier, marked by a single black plume on the horizon. Resuming his clockwise scan, he spotted two destroyers—one on each side of his submarine—forming a screen in front of his target. In a few minutes, Zeng and his crew would pass between the two warships and their helicopters equipped with dipping sonars and lightweight torpedoes. A few minutes more and their target would be within range of the *Chang Cheng's* heavyweight Yu-6 torpedoes.

The *Chang Cheng's* Periscope Attendant, standing between the submarine's two scopes, called out loudly, "Time!"

Zeng stepped back, pressing the *Lower Periscope* button on the bulkhead behind him. The scope had been up for thirty seconds, the time limit he had set for periscope exposure. Not only did Zeng need to worry about being detected by the sonar systems aboard the destroyers and their helicopters, he also had to ensure his ship wasn't detected by periscope search radars.

The attack scope descended to the bottom of the well and Zeng turned his attention to the fire control consoles just forward of the two periscopes, studying the red symbols on their screens. The two destroyers were holding steady on course and speed, giving no indication they had detected Zeng's submarine. It appeared the aircraft carrier was dead in the water, making his job that much easier.

Four days earlier, Zeng had left port along with two other Shang class submarines, and they had caught an American submarine monitoring the port of Zhoushan. Zeng's orders were clear. He had been surprised at how easy it was; the American submarine hadn't even fired back. Either the submarine's captain had been caught unprepared or the vaunted American Submarine Force was more propaganda than capability. Not a single United States submarine remained in the Western Pacific—every submarine on deployment had been sunk.

The Americans were arrogant, sending in their aircraft carriers without submarines to protect them. Is that how little they thought of their Chinese counterparts? The Shang class submarines were a marvel of engineering, built with the latest sound-quieting enhancements and new, sophisticated sensors, and his crew was well trained. Zeng's thoughts moved past the glorious moment when he would sink the American carrier, to his first engagement with a prepared American fast attack.

The Periscope Attendant called out, "Prepare!"

Zeng took station behind his attack periscope again, and a few seconds later, the Periscope Attendant followed up. "Next observation!" Zeng pressed the *Raise Periscope* button on the bulkhead, folding down the periscope handles as the scope emerged from its well. Placing his eye to the periscope, he swung it in the direction of the closest American destroyer, pausing to examine it for a second before continuing on to the second. Satisfied that neither destroyer had maneuvered toward them and no helicopters had repositioned along his path, Zeng stopped on the bearing to the American aircraft carrier. It was clearly visible now, no longer a gray speck beneath a spiraling black plume.

"Prepare for observation, Contact One!" Zeng called out.

The Fire Controlman announced, "Ready!"

"Bearing, mark!" Zeng pressed a red button on the right periscope handle, sending the bearing of the contact to fire control. "Range, one division, high power! Angle on the bow, starboard ninety!"

He stepped back and pressed the Lower Scope button as the Periscope Assistant announced, "Range, sixteen thousand, eight hundred yards!"

Zeng compared the visual range to the distance calculated by the submarine's automated fire control system. The range was an exact match, and the calculated speed of their target was indeed zero. Zeng smiled. With the American aircraft carrier dead in the water and a starboard ninety-degree angle on the bow, his torpedoes couldn't miss. The only question was how many torpedoes it would take.

One heavyweight torpedo would sink most combatants. An aircraft carrier would take several, depending on where along the carrier's keel the torpedoes exploded. Zeng decided to play it safe. The *Chang Cheng* had six torpedo tubes and they would therefore launch a salvo of six torpedoes. He wouldn't get a second chance. Once the torpedoes were detected, every anti-submarine sensor and weapon would be directed his way. He'd be forced deep, sprinting to safety before he could return to periscope depth, hopefully in time to savor the last minutes of the aircraft carrier sinking beneath the ocean waves.

Checking the fire control solution, Zeng calculated they would be within firing range in another two minutes. It was time to prepare their torpedoes. Standing between his submarine's two periscopes, Zeng gave the order.

"Prepare to fire, Contact One, all tubes!"

The men in Control responded immediately, powering up the Yu-6 heavyweight torpedoes loaded in their tubes and sending the target solution to the torpedoes' guidance and control computers. A minute passed and the submarine's Executive Officer announced, "Ready!"

"Open muzzle doors, all torpedo tubes!"

A minute later, Zeng received the report that all doors were open. Satisfied all preparations were complete, he approached the periscope for a final observation. Pressing the *Raise Periscope* button, he announced loudly, "Final Observation, Contact One!"

Zeng placed his eye to the scope again, swinging it in the direction of his target. At this range, he could almost see the texture of the black smoke spiraling upward. The target was still dead in the water. Zeng pressed the button on the periscope handle, sending a final bearing to fire control. Stepping back, he lowered the periscope. But just before giving the command to launch their six torpedoes, the Sonar Supervisor's voice blared across the speakers in Control.

"Incoming torpedo, bearing zero-nine-zero! An American MK 48!"

24

USS *TEXAS* • CNS *CHANG CHENG*

USS *TEXAS*

Standing in the Control Room of his Virginia class fast attack submarine, Commander Jim Latham peered over Petty Officer Colby Marshall's shoulder, watching the green inverted V on his console speed toward the red semicircle to the west. His crew was at Battle Stations, every console in Control manned, with supervisors crowding behind them. Commander Latham noted with satisfaction that there was little change in their target's position or course. In less than a minute, their torpedo would detect Master One.

Texas had been speeding west at ahead flank for the better part of four days, reactor power pegged at one hundred percent from the moment they received their orders. They'd had a head start on the rest of the Pacific Fleet; *Texas* was already outbound on the first leg of her six-month West Pac deployment, headed to relieve USS *Jacksonville* in the East China Sea. But as *Texas* surged westward, Latham had been informed they would not relieve the Los Angeles class submarine. *Jacksonville* had been sunk.

Texas, however, was no Los Angeles class submarine. She was the second of the new Virginia class, quieter at ahead full than a Los Angeles class submarine was tied to the pier. And *Texas* had a full Torpedo Room of the Navy's newest Heavyweight torpedo, the MK 48 Mod 7 CBASS, built with state-of-the art processors loaded with advanced search algorithms.

Commander Latham had timed it perfectly. The Chinese submarine hadn't detected the launch of their quiet MK 48 torpedo and he had let it close to almost point-blank range before activating the torpedo's sonar. The Chinese crew probably had no idea they had less than a minute to live. Data from the torpedo began streaming into the combat control system through the thin wire trailing behind their weapon. Their torpedo was increasing speed and the frequency of its sonar pings. It was homing on its target.

CNS *CHANG CHENG*

Zeng spun toward the sonar display between the two periscopes, observing the bright white trace burning in at 090 degrees. How had an American submarine approached to within firing range undetected? That was an important question, but the most pressing issue was evading the incoming torpedo. That effort began with speed, and his submarine was at periscope depth, lumbering along at five knots.

He shouted out his orders. "Helm, ahead flank! Hard left rudder! Launch torpedo decoy!"

Confusion reigned in Control as the *Chang Cheng* began evasive maneuvers. They were still in the middle of Firing Procedures, their torpedoes locked on to the disabled aircraft carrier. Zeng needed a torpedo to fire back at the American submarine. To do that, he would have to cancel his Firing Order. Zeng decided the carrier could wait; it would still be there after the American submarine was dealt with.

"Cancel Fire, Contact One! Reactive Fire, bearing zero-nine-zero, Tube One!"

The *Chang Cheng*'s Weapons Officer acknowledged the Captain's order, reassigning the torpedo in Tube One to the initial bearing of the incoming torpedo, back down the throat of the American submarine that had fired it. It would take less than thirty seconds; their torpedoes were already powered up and the torpedo outer doors were open, but Zeng was distracted by the frantic report from Sonar over the speakers in Control.

"Torpedo is homing! Ignoring torpedo decoy!"

Zeng's face went slack. They had detected the American torpedo only twenty seconds ago and it was already homing on his submarine, disregarding the decoy they had launched. The American submarine Captain had placed his weapon perfectly, giving Zeng insufficient time to react. As the pings of the incoming torpedo's sonar echoed through the *Chang Cheng*'s hull, Zeng realized the American Submarine Force was as capable as China feared.

USS *TEXAS*

The fast attack submarine shuddered and the sonar screens whited out as the shock wave from the explosion swept past USS *Texas*. Latham's Weapons Officer called out, reporting their torpedo had exploded.

"Loss of wire continuity. Final telemetry data correlates with Master One."

Less than a moment later, the Sonar Supervisor confirmed their torpedo had sunk its target. "Hull breakup noises, bearing two-seven-zero."

Latham glanced at the geographic plot on one of the combat control consoles. Where there was one Chinese submarine, there would soon be another. They had to stay focused and begin their search for the next one. However, *Texas* would not hunt alone. Two fast attack submarines from Guam were close on *Texas*'s heels, only an hour away. And not far behind them, twenty-four more fast attack submarines from Hawaii and the West Coast of the United States were surging west at ahead flank speed. China had caught the three deployed American submarines by surprise. The remaining twenty-seven fast attack submarines in the Pacific Fleet would not be caught unaware, and China would pay dearly for what it had done.

"Conn, Sonar. Hold a new contact, designated Sierra one-five, possible Shang class nuclear submarine, bearing two-five-zero."

Latham acknowledged Sonar's report. A second Chinese submarine, just south of the first one, was no doubt creeping toward *Nimitz*. He stood erect, making his announcement loudly so everyone in Control could hear. "Designate Sierra one-five as Master Two. Track Master Two." Turning to his Weapons Control Coordinator, Latham followed up. "Assign presets for Master Two to Tube Two."

Sonar called out again. "Conn, Sonar. Hold a new contact, designated Sierra one-six, also possible Shang class nuclear submarine, bearing two-eight-eight."

Latham frowned. They'd have to prosecute both submarines simultaneously, engaging first one, then the other. "Designate Sierra one-six as Master Three. Master Two is Primary contact of interest, Master Three is Secondary. Assign presets for Master Three to Tube Three."

Texas had its hands full, engaging two submarines at once. Unlike the

Chinese submarine they'd just sunk, these two crews knew an American submarine was in the area and would not be surprised. Still, *Texas* was the quieter submarine, carrying more sophisticated sensors and weapons. It looked like Commander Latham and his crew were going to have a busy day.

25

BOHAI SEA • USS *MICHIGAN*

The gentle vibration pulsing through Christine's body finally woke her up. Her eyes fluttered open but her vision remained shrouded in darkness. Breathing was an effort for some reason, and she felt something over her face. The upholstered seat of her sedan had somehow turned into hard metal, and she was cold, shivering beneath a thin, metallic blanket. There was a source of heat on her right side. She leaned toward it and her arm ignited in pain, clearing the fog from her mind.

Christine realized she had a full-face diver's mask on, and the pieces of the puzzle came together. She was underwater. Looking around closely, she made out the dim outline of the vehicle she was in—a James Bond–like mini-sub with two men in black scuba gear seated in front of her in the open-top submarine. Between the two men, she could see the faint illumination of green electronic displays. A third diver sat beside her on the right, his arm wrapped around her shoulder.

The man beside her noticed her movement and released his arm from around her. He reached down, retrieving a thin tube he bent with both hands. The tube began to glow a soft green and he held up one hand, displaying five fingers. Christine shook her head, not understanding. The man retracted one finger, then another, until there were none left, then returned to five fingers. Christine nodded her head this time, pretty sure he meant they would reach their destination in five minutes.

The man dropped the glow stick over the side and wrapped his arm around her again. Christine had no idea who he was, but she welcomed the warmth of his body, shifting her weight gently toward him, careful not to place too much pressure on her arm. She felt around inside the thin blanket. She was still in her clothes, but a bandage had thankfully been taped to her arm. The last thing they needed was a trail of blood in the water. With her luck to-night, sharks wouldn't be far behind.

Five minutes later, Christine felt the submersible slowing, and for the first time she noticed there was a second, identical mini-sub ten feet to her left with four divers in it. It drifted to a halt as Christine's vehicle continued toward a mammoth black shape materializing out of the darkness. They were headed toward a submarine, coming up from astern over the submarine's missile deck. At the forward end of the deck, just aft of the sail rising before her, were two nine-foot-diameter chambers, each with their door swung open ninety degrees.

Christine's submersible slowed to a hover behind the right chamber, sinking until it came to rest with a gentle bump on a set of rails extended from the chamber. Two divers appeared along each side of the submersible, quickly latching it to the rails as the two men in front of the mini-sub and the one beside her pushed themselves up and out of the vehicle. The man next to Christine extended his hand, guiding Christine out of her seat as she shed her blanket. With a powerful kick of his fins, he pulled Christine into the chamber.

Christine joined the three men from her submersible on the starboard side of the chamber, and once their vehicle was retracted inside, they were joined by the four divers who had tended to the mini-sub. The large chamber door shut with a gentle thud. Red lights flicked on, and an air pocket soon appeared at the top of the chamber, the water level gradually lowering. When the water level fell below her neck, Christine and the divers removed their facemasks.

The man next to Christine turned toward her, and she stared into the eyes of someone she hadn't seen in over twenty years. Jake Harrison flashed a brief smile before he spoke.

"Welcome aboard *Michigan*, Chris. It's been a long time."

Before Christine could respond, Harrison continued, "How's your arm? I did the best I could underwater."

Glancing down, Christine noticed what looked like two giant Band-Aids taped to her arm, one on each side. The bullet had passed clean through, entering the back of her triceps and exiting the front of her arm.

She looked up at Harrison, her teeth chattering between words. "You did great." She knew she should say more, but had difficulty finding the right words. She would need time to process her thoughts. And emotions.

The water finished draining from the chamber and Harrison stood. "Do you feel strong enough to make it on your own?"

Christine nodded. Although her arm ached, she felt fine otherwise, except for the deep chill throughout her body. Harrison shed his scuba gear and assisted with Christine's, then escorted her to the rear of the chamber, dropping down through two hatches. Christine followed, shivering uncontrollably, climbing carefully down a metal ladder inside what looked like a missile tube. Two levels down, she stepped onto a steel deck in a space outfitted with showerheads along the perimeter of the tube.

Harrison spun the hand wheel of a two-foot-diameter hatch in the side of the tube, and the hatch opened outward. He stepped through, thrusting his hand back inside to help. Christine took his hand and slid through feet-first. She emerged to be greeted by Harrison and three men wearing blue coveralls—a Commander and two enlisted petty officers based on the insignia on their collars—standing in a narrow passageway.

The Commander surveyed Christine with a critical eye, glancing at her arm as he wrapped a thick blue blanket around her. "I'm Commander Joe Aleo, Miss O'Connor, the Medical Officer aboard. I understand you've been shot in the arm. Do you have any other injuries?"

Christine shook her head, still shivering. "I think I'm fine otherwise."

"Let me get some quick vitals on you first, then we'll get you warmed up."

He guided Christine to a short equipment cabinet nearby, using it as a makeshift chair. Christine slid onto the top of the cabinet, her teeth chattering as one of the petty officers wrapped a blood pressure cuff around her left arm and the Commander pulled a small flashlight from the breast pocket of his coveralls. After a quick examination of her pupils, heart rate, blood pressure, and injured arm, Commander Aleo seemed satisfied.

Stepping back, he turned to Harrison, hovering nearby during Christine's evaluation. "We've got it from here. Thanks, Lieutenant."

"Sure thing, Doc. I'm going to warm up in the shower," Harrison replied, then turned to Christine. "See you around, ma'am." He stepped back through the hatch into the missile tube, pulling the door shut behind him.

Aleo turned to the two petty officers. "We need to warm Miss O'Connor up as well."

One of the petty officers replied, "Should we kick Lieutenant Harrison out of Tube One and send him to Tube Two with the other SEALs?"

Aleo thought for a moment. "No. We'll need more privacy to coordinate everything. Take her to one of the Missile Compartment heads." He returned his gaze to Christine, his eyes examining her from her chest to her feet. "I'll get some dry clothes for you, and do my best to find something that fits. What size shoes do you wear?"

"Size seven and a half, women's." Aleo gave her a blank stare for a second before Christine clarified. "That'd be a size six in men's."

Aleo smiled. "Thanks, Miss O'Connor. I'll see what I can do."

The two petty officers acknowledged Aleo's order, then led Christine to a staircase at the forward end of the compartment. After descending to the next level, they headed to the starboard side, then aft until they reached a bathroom, which consisted of a pair of shower stalls on one side and four sinks on the other, with a bank of three toilets against the far wall.

"Stay in the shower until you're warmed up," one of the petty officers said. "Just holler if you need anything. We'll be waiting outside."

The petty officer closed the door and Christine turned her attention to the three-by-three-foot showers. She selected the first stall, adjusting the water temperature to as hot as she could stand it, then stripped her wet clothes off, dropping them on the floor. Stepping into the shower, she pulled the curtain closed behind her. She let the hot water cascade over her head and down her shoulders, letting the warmth seep in, alternately letting the water flow over her chest and down her back.

The submarine began to tilt and Christine braced herself against the shower wall until the deck leveled out. She stood under the shower, her skin eventually changing from pasty white back to its normal color. The chill faded from her body, yet she was still shivering. She wondered why, then realized she wasn't shivering; she was trembling.

She had survived by the narrowest of margins. Along the way, Peng and their driver hadn't been so fortunate. Why did she get to live while others died? She was going to chalk it up to luck, but then she recalled a flash of metal and strong hands pulling her from the car at the bottom of the lagoon. No, it wasn't luck. One of the SEALs, probably Harrison, had cut her seat belt and pulled her from the wreck. Christine took a deep breath, forcing herself to breathe slower, trying to release the tension from her body. Her trembling gradually eased, then stopped.

Deciding the shower had done its job, she turned off the water and pulled back the curtain in search of a towel, and was startled to find another woman leaning against the bank of bathroom sinks, towel in hand. She was dressed similarly to the men she'd seen so far, wearing one-piece blue coveralls and white sneakers. Her blond hair was cropped short and she was remarkably tall, almost six feet.

She stepped forward, handing the towel to Christine. "Lieutenant Commander Kelly Haas, Miss O'Connor. Welcome aboard *Michigan*."

Christine took the towel and began drying herself as Kelly continued her introduction. "I'm the submarine's Supply Officer and one of three female officers aboard."

Christine recalled that the Navy had finally decided to integrate women into the Submarine Force, and in 2012 the first wave of female officers, in sets of three due to the officer stateroom sleeping accommodations, had begun reporting aboard Ohio class SSBNs and SSGNs.

As Christine finished drying herself, her eyes went to a stack of clothes on the sink next to the Lieutenant Commander. Kelly followed her gaze. "I was able to scrounge up two female coveralls that should fit. We call them poopie suits." She paused, eyeing Christine's naked body critically. "Although they'll be a tight fit in the chest area for you. I think they do that on purpose." Kelly offered a wry smile. "As for underwear, we don't have any in supply, so I had to borrow some. Doc said you were pretty close in size to Lieutenant JG Clark." Kelly placed her hand on the set of white bra, panties, and socks. "As long as wearing someone else's underwear doesn't squick you out." She offered another wry smile. "Hmmm, bra size is going to be a problem. Lieutenant Herndon may be able to help out. Just skip it for now."

"No worries," Christine said as she exchanged the towel for the clothing. "Anything dry right now will be wonderful."

"Great," Kelly replied. "Let's get you dressed and introduced to the ship's Captain. Or would you rather go straight to Medical?" Kelly eyed the bandage on Christine's arm.

"I feel fine. Just a flesh wound," Christine said, wondering if Kelly would get the *Monty Python* reference.

Kelly laughed. "All right. Captain first, then Medical. Then we'll get you settled in. You'll be berthing with the XO. He's got a spare bunk in his stateroom and a private bathroom he shares with the Captain. Overall, it's probably better than cramming you into our stateroom and forcing Clark and Herndon to hot-rack. Plus, all the dignitaries sleep in the XO's stateroom. We can't be treating you any different because you're a woman, right?"

"Right." Christine agreed in principle, although she honestly preferred to be crammed in with the women.

As Christine donned the dry clothing, she asked Kelly about her age. "You look a bit older than I'd expect a new submarine officer to be, fresh out of college."

"I'm thirty-three," Kelly replied, "on my third sea tour, although this is my first submarine. The first trio of female officers sent to a submarine typically includes a more senior Supply Officer who can provide guidance to the two junior officers. I've already been around the block a few times, just on top of the ocean's surface, not beneath."

Christine zipped up her coveralls, which fit remarkably well aside from being tight around her chest, then donned a pair of new white sneakers, which turned out to be a perfect fit. She tied her hair into a knot behind her head, then examined herself in the mirror. Under the harsh fluorescent lighting, with no makeup and wet, stringy hair dyed jet black, she looked like death warmed over. But at least she was alive. And she had delivered the flash drive to the submarine.

She bent down to her wet slacks on the floor, sliding the flash drive, still in its waterproof bag, from the slit in the seam, and deposited it into the right pocket of her coveralls.

She stood and turned toward Kelly, who opened the door to the bathroom.

"Follow me, ma'am."

Lieutenant Commander Kelly Haas led the way forward, describing the submarine compartments along the way, then up a staircase, which the crew called a ladder, two levels into Control. There were about ten men in the twenty-by-thirty-foot Control Room, crammed with equipment consoles and two periscopes, both lowered. Haas and Christine stopped near four men leaning over an electronic display table—a Captain, a Lieutenant Commander, and two Lieutenants. The four men didn't notice Christine's arrival in Control; they were engaged in a quiet conversation as they examined an electronic map of the coast and nearby islands, filled with dozens of red symbols.

The four men looked up as Lieutenant Commander Haas spoke. "Excuse me, Captain. Miss O'Connor is here to meet you."

The Captain turned to greet Christine. He was much older than the other three men, by at least ten years, his gray hair giving away his age. He extended his hand, accompanied with a warm smile on his face. "Welcome aboard *Michigan*, Miss O'Connor."

Christine rarely read people wrong, and she noticed a darkness in the Captain's eyes that belied his friendly demeanor. Glancing at his nametag on his blue coveralls, she realized why. A pit formed in her stomach and she felt the blood drain from her face. Moments earlier, she had laid eyes on a man she hadn't seen in over twenty years. Now, she stood before the last man she wanted to meet.

Captain Murray Wilson.

26

USS *NIMITZ*

Standing on Vulture's Row, on the port side of the aircraft carrier's Island superstructure, Captain Alex Harrow leaned over the railing in the brisk wind, surveying the damage to *Nimitz*'s Flight Deck. Black smoke from the fires raging belowdecks billowed upward from the forty-foot-wide crater, but the immediate danger had passed. Although the fires still burned, the carrier's ammunition magazines were no longer threatened. USS *Texas* had also arrived, already sinking two Chinese submarines and prosecuting a third. Unfortunately, while *Nimitz* had been given a reprieve, the two air wings circling above weren't as fortunate.

Carrier Air Wing ELEVEN Commander, Captain Helen Corcoran, joined Harrow on Vulture's Row, assessing the damaged Flight Deck in silence. The Iraq War veteran didn't need to say anything; her eyes said it all. In less than twenty minutes, her jets would begin falling from the sky, their fuel tanks empty. Likewise for *George Washington*'s air wing, circling in tandem with *Nimitz*'s above the lone remaining carrier. Corcoran had considered Bingoing all aircraft to Kadena Air Base on Okinawa, until the Air Force fighters recalled by 18th Wing had been shot down by another swarm of missiles. Their aircraft were safer inside *Nimitz*'s screen of destroyers and cruisers. However, if Harrow didn't return *Nimitz* to flight operations, figuring out how to land jets on three-fourths of a Flight Deck, what remained of two air wings would crash into the Pacific Ocean.

Restoring the nuclear reactors to operation was crucial. Control rods in both reactors had unlatched from the impact of the DF-21 missile, and both plants had been shut down by the reactors' core protection circuitry. Reactor Department personnel were frantically inspecting both reactor plants for damage, and Harrow had already given permission to conduct

Fast Recovery Start-Ups if no damage had been incurred. If there was any possibility of returning to flight operations, *Nimitz* needed both reactors on-line. He needed speed.

The only way Corcoran's jets could land was if *Nimitz* was racing into the wind, allowing the aircraft to land at a relatively slow speed. Not only had the missile blasted a crater in the Flight Deck, it also damaged the four arresting cables. The jets normally latched one of the arresting wires with their tailhooks as they landed, slowing the aircraft to a halt in two seconds. Without arresting cables, the aircraft would have to slow using nothing but their brakes. Even with the carrier at ahead flank, recovering aircraft without arresting cables and with a forty-foot hole in the Flight Deck would normally be an impossible feat.

Thank God for bad weather. Harrow looked up into the overcast skies, blustery winds blowing beneath a heavy blanket of steel-gray clouds. The winds were now howling from the south at sixty knots. If *Nimitz* could restore propulsion and head into those winds at maximum speed, they might have a chance. As Harrow wondered how much longer it would take to restart the reactors, the lights inside the Bridge flickered. The normal fluorescent lighting blinked on, and the yellow emergency lighting faded. Harrow left Vulture's Row, stepping inside the Bridge as a report came across the announcing circuit.

"Bridge, DC Central. Fast Recovery Start-Up of both reactors is complete. Ready to answer all Bells."

Harrow turned to the Conning Officer, Lieutenant Nathan Reynolds. "Bring her into the wind and increase speed to ahead flank."

Lieutenant Reynolds complied. "Helm, all ahead flank. Right full rudder, steady course one-eight-zero." As Harrow's wounded carrier turned into the wind, his eyes shifted between the Voyage Management System—displaying ship's speed—and the MORIAH wind velocity display. Captain Corcoran stopped beside him, no doubt doing the mental calculations, determining if the carrier's speed combined with the blustery headwind were enough to offset the speed of the aircraft as they landed.

As *Nimitz* steadied on course 180, the Air Boss, stationed in the Tower one deck above the Bridge, reported over the 23-MC, "Bridge, Tower. I need a Green Deck. Aircraft 612 is on emergency fuel and making its approach. 714 and 628 are also inbound."

Harrow looked aft through the Bridge windows, but couldn't see the approaching aircraft. Thick black smoke from the fire belowdecks roiled upward through the gaping hole in the Flight Deck, obscuring his vision. Landing would be even more perilous than he had envisioned. Land too early and the aircraft's landing gear would catch on the twisted metal edges of the crater, tearing the jet to pieces. Land too late and the aircraft would careen off the front of the carrier's bow. To complicate matters further, the pilots would be landing blind, their vision obscured by the thick black smoke trailing behind *Nimitz*.

To compensate for the lack of visibility, Corcoran had ordered automated landings, directing combat systems to recalculate the landing point to just forward of the crater in the Flight Deck. Unfortunately, that solved only one of the problems. The other was wind speed.

"It's not going to work," Corcoran said.

Harrow turned back to examine ship and wind speed, then ran the numbers, confirming Corcoran's assessment. The relative speed of the approaching aircraft was still too high; they wouldn't be able to stop before running out of runway. Harrow worked through the calculations again, determining how much faster *Nimitz* would have to travel.

They needed five more knots.

But the carrier was already at maximum speed, both reactors operating at one hundred percent power.

Harrow turned toward Corcoran, his eyes locking with hers. In a few minutes her jets would begin dropping from the sky, the pilots ejecting as their engines flamed out—two entire air wings lost, with the pilots splashing into waters infested with enemy submarines. With only *Texas* protecting them, *Nimitz* couldn't loiter while the strike group rescued their pilots. As distasteful as it was, the safety of his carrier and the six thousand men and women aboard were a higher priority. He would be forced to abandon the pilots. There was nothing he could do about it.

The hell there was.

Harrow picked up the handheld wireless. "DC Central, Bridge. This is the Captain. Put the RO on line."

A few seconds later, the Reactor Officer responded. "RO."

Harrow needed to eke out five more knots from the main engines. With both reactors already at full power, there was only one option.

"RO, Captain. Override reactor protection and increase shaft turns to one hundred ten percent power." There was silence on the line. Harrow knew what his Reactor Officer was thinking. He'd been ordered to break the most sacred rule in the nuclear power navy.

Violate reactor safety.

But Harrow had the authority and no alternative. He wasn't going to lose what was left of two air wings because of a measly five knots. It was likely there was enough of a safety margin to allow reactor operation at one hundred ten percent power for the time required to retrieve the two air wings. If the reactors required new cores when this was over, so be it.

The Reactor Officer finally acknowledged Harrow's order. "Override reactor protection and increase shaft turns to one hundred ten percent power, both reactors, RO, aye."

Harrow returned his attention to the Voyage Management System, and a moment later, the carrier's speed began inching upward. The Air Boss's voice came across the 23-MC again. "Bridge, Tower. One minute before the first recovery. I need a Green Deck and I need it now!"

The digital speed indicator ticked upward, increasing in one-tenth-knot increments as the first jet descended toward the carrier's Flight Deck. Harrow moved next to the Captain's chair. He had no choice. Reaching over to the communication console, he pressed the small green button, giving the Air Boss a Green Deck for flight operations.

Harrow joined Corcoran at the port Bridge windows, looking aft as his stomach turned queasy, waiting to learn if they had increased speed enough. The incoming pilot would be blind now, enveloped in the thick black smoke trailing behind the carrier. The seconds ticked away and there was still nothing.

The first jet emerged from the black plume, its wheels touching down just past the edge of the crater. The Hornet's ailerons flared upward and a puff of white smoke appeared by the jet's tires, the smoke trailing from the aircraft's landing gear as it sped toward the bow. Harrow leaned forward, urging his ship faster through the water, buying the extra few feet that would let the aircraft stop before it ran out of real estate. The jet screeched to a halt with its nose landing gear only four feet from the end of the Flight Deck.

Harrow let out a sigh of relief as the jet turned sharply to starboard, moving slowly out of the way as a second jet emerged from the black smoke, touching down with a screech and a puff of white smoke from its tires. As the first jet moved toward the forward starboard elevator, the second jet also ground to a halt four feet from the carrier's bow.

One by one, Captain Corcoran's air wing, followed by *George Washington*'s, landed safely aboard USS *Nimitz*.

27

USS *MICHIGAN*

In the submarine's Radio Room, just forward of Control, Christine stood between Captain Murray Wilson and the ship's Executive Officer, waiting while the submarine's leading Radioman, Chief Jeff Walkup, slid Christine's flash drive into a laptop computer. It was their last chance to retrieve the data from the small device she'd been handed in the Great Hall of the People. Although *Michigan*'s crew was normally prohibited from inserting flash drives into their computers for fear of viruses, they'd been given the go-ahead to use stand-alone computers. Unfortunately, none of the computers so far could access what appeared to be a simple flash drive.

The last few hours aboard *Michigan* had passed quickly. Following her introduction to Captain Wilson, the submarine's Medical Officer had followed up with an extensive evaluation, replacing the ad hoc Band-Aids applied by Lieutenant Harrison during her underwater journey with a white gauze bandage wrapped around her upper arm. There was little collateral damage aside from the small hole in her arm, which Commander Aleo had thoroughly disinfected, then stitched shut on both ends. Her arm now rested in a sling, which made traversing through the submarine's hatches difficult, with only one arm to keep her balance.

As Lieutenant Commander Kelly Haas explained, Christine had moved in with the Executive Officer. She'd been given his bunk, with the submarine's second-in-command moving to the spare upper rack. She hadn't had a chance to interface much with Lieutenant Commander Paul Greenwood though, as he had been busy assisting Wilson in Control during their tense transit through the Bohai Sea.

Chief Walkup removed the flash drive from his computer, turning to

Christine and the two officers beside her. "It's a secure flash drive, which requires an encryption key."

"Encryption key?" Wilson asked.

"A password," Walkup explained. "But good luck breaking it. Depending on the length of the password, you could be talking over a trillion possibilities. And if the password uses Chinese characters instead of English letters and numbers, you can add a lot more zeros to that number. If you want to break into this flash drive, we're going to need to get it to one of our three-letter agencies."

Chief Walkup handed the flash drive back to Wilson.

Wilson studied the flash drive in his palm before replying. "The Pentagon wants this data immediately, by whatever means required." Wilson handed the flash drive to his XO. "Prep for UAV launch."

A few minutes later, Christine stood next to the Executive Officer in the aft port corner of Control as *Michigan* prepared to ascend to periscope depth. As the Officer of the Deck made final preparations, Lieutenant Commander Greenwood filled Christine in on the details of *Michigan*'s UAVs. "We've got two types of Unmanned Aerial Vehicles aboard. The first is the Switchblade, which we launch out the bottom of the submarine from our Trash Disposal Unit. Unfortunately, our little shit-bird—pardon the French—doesn't have the required range. We've got to get the flash drive to Okinawa, which means we'll have to use one of our large UAVs. We have seven UAVs instead of Tomahawks stored in Missile Tube Ten."

Moments earlier, Greenwood had handed Christine's flash drive to an awaiting Missile Tech, who opened a hatch in the side of the missile tube and removed an access panel in the launch canister, inserting the drive into a compartment in the UAV. Greenwood explained the UAV would be ejected to the ocean's surface, where its container would pop open and deliver an electric charge to the UAV, launching it. The UAV was an electric fuel cell-powered X-wing airfoil with just enough range to reach the Air Force base on Okinawa.

Lieutenant Cordero, the submarine's Officer of the Deck, announced *Michigan* was proceeding to periscope depth, and all conversation in Control ceased. It was imperative they ensure there were no Chinese forces nearby that could detect their launch. As the submarine rose toward the surface, Christine leaned forward, compensating for the ten-degree up angle. The only sound in Control was the occasional depth report from the Diving Officer of the Watch.

The submarine's angle leveled off and Cordero began circling on the Conn, twisting the periscope in a continuous clockwise rotation, searching the horizon for nearby ships.

After determining there were no ships that were a collision hazard, Cordero announced, "No close contacts!"

Muted conversations resumed in Control, accompanied by the faint staccato chirp from the early warning antenna mounted on top of the periscope, searching the surrounding airwaves for enemy radars. Cordero followed up with several revolutions with the periscope optics at maximum elevation, scouring the sky for aircraft capable of detecting their periscope.

A moment later, Sonar reported no contacts, followed by the operator in Radio who monitored the submarine's Electromagnetic Surveillance Measures (ESM) equipment, who reported there were no contacts exceeding a signal strength of five, and none with threat parameters. Lieutenant Cordero, meanwhile, followed his quick assessment of the surface and air with a detailed survey of all quadrants in high power, finally reporting to the submarine's Captain that the ship held no air or surface contacts.

Satisfied it was safe to launch their UAV, Captain Wilson rose from his chair on the Conn and entered *Michigan*'s Battle Management Center, located aft of the Control Room, where the submarine's crew conducted Tomahawk mission planning and coordinated its SEAL operations.

Christine followed Wilson into the room, which was crammed with twenty-five tactical consoles, each with a keyboard and dual trackballs plus two color displays, one mounted over the other. Thirteen of the consoles were mounted on the port side of the ship with an aisle between them—seven consoles facing outboard and six inboard, while the other twelve consoles on the starboard side faced aft, arranged in four rows of three. Mounted on the aft bulkhead were two sixty-inch plasma screens, along with a third sixty-inch display on the forward bulkhead behind Christine.

Only one of the twenty-five consoles was manned this morning, and Captain Wilson stopped behind the petty officer manning the middle console on the port side. Wilson glanced at the display on the forward bulkhead, watching a video feed from a camera mounted on the back of the submarine's sail.

Next to Wilson stood the ship's Weapons Officer, Lieutenant Karl Stewart, who wore a sound-powered phone headset, a communication system that functioned using the energy of the speaker's voice, a critical circuit should the submarine lose electrical power. Stewart held the mouthpiece close to his lips, waiting for the order from Captain Wilson.

"Prepare to launch UAV."

Stewart acknowledged Wilson's order, then ordered Missile Control Center, one deck below, "Open Missile Tube Ten."

On the video screen in the Command Center, Christine watched the muzzle hatch atop Tube Ten lift slowly upward, coming to rest in its open position a few seconds later.

"Ready to launch UAV from Missile Tube Ten, MAC One," Stewart announced.

"Launch UAV," Wilson ordered.

Lieutenant Stewart relayed the Captain's order over the sound-powered phones and a few seconds later, a canister was ejected from Missile Tube Ten, disappearing as it streaked toward the ocean's surface.

Wilson's and Stewart's attention turned to the petty officer in front of them. A minute later, after manipulating a trackball and flipping through several screens on the lower display, the petty officer announced, "Positive control of UAV obtained, sending landing coordinates now."

A few seconds later the evolution was complete—*Michigan's* UAV was on its way to Okinawa.

28

WASHINGTON, D.C.

In the Situation Room beneath the West Wing of the White House, the conversation took a turn for the worse as the president aimed pointed questions at the next man in the military chain of command. The president was seated at the head of the conference table, flanked on his left by Secretary of Defense Nelson Jennings and Captain Steve Brackman, while on his right sat chief of staff Kevin Hardison and Secretary of State Lindsay Ross. The rest of the chairs around the table were empty. Jennings had planned to bring along the Joint Chiefs of Staff for today's meeting, but at the last minute decided to leave them in the Pentagon for a final review of Pacific Command's plan for full response, now that three additional carrier strike groups were almost within striking distance of Taiwan. Jennings was well briefed on the plan and could explain it to the president. But first, he had to explain what had happened to the first two strike groups.

"How the hell did they sink one of our carriers?" the president asked.

"We almost lost both carriers," Jennings clarified, not helping the situation. The president stared at Jennings, waiting for an answer. Jennings continued, "China was able to insert malware into our Aegis software build, then activate it via our own tactical data links. The malware disrupted the Aegis Warfare Systems aboard our cruisers and destroyers, and they couldn't shoot down most of the incoming missiles.

"The good news, however, is that *Lake Erie* was able to bring up her Aegis fire control system using a software build that was loaded on the cruiser for developmental testing. It's a new version, which didn't have the malware embedded in the Fleet release software."

"What are we doing about this malware and China's hijacking of our tactical data links?"

"General Krae at Cyber Warfare Command, along with everyone at N6, is working to identify and close the holes in our tactical data links. Concerning the malware in our Aegis software, now that we know what to look for, NAVSEA has already identified the malicious code and has developed a software patch to remove it.

"As far as the larger malware issue goes, we're combating a difficult problem. All China has to do is flip a programmer at one of our defense contractors, who inserts a segment of code that lies dormant during normal operations. If the code remains dormant during developmental and operational testing, there's really no way for us to find it.

"We're actually very lucky, Mr. President," Jennings continued. "If NAVSEA hadn't been able to identify the malware and confirm they can remove it, I'd be sitting here advising you to throw in the towel. Without the ability to shoot down China's DF-21 missile, we couldn't risk bringing our carriers within launch range of Taiwan. And without carrier strike group support, we can't land our Marine Expeditionary Forces. It would have been *game over*. China has prepared incredibly well for this campaign and we're still in it by sheer luck."

"It could have been far worse," Captain Brackman added. "Our war plans called for initial support with only two strike groups. If we had waited and engaged with the entire fleet, we could have lost every Pacific Fleet carrier. At first blush, it seems like losing a carrier was a serious blow, but in hindsight, we were fortunate. We forced China to reveal their hand, and now we can compensate when the entire fleet engages."

"Speaking of engaging," the president replied, turning to Secretary of State Ross, "how are we doing on the diplomatic front? I've talked with Russia's president and Japan's prime minister, and although they agree with our response, I haven't been able to convince them to assist us militarily. What are you seeing at your level?"

"We've had discussions with the Japanese," Ross answered, "but Article 9 of their constitution prohibits offensive military action. Since Japan hasn't been attacked, they can't aid our defense of Taiwan. Russia is unwilling to intervene, fearing a potential land battle against a standing army of over one million men, with another two million reserves who can be called up."

Ross added, "South Korea has North Korea breathing down its neck, and it can't afford to suffer significant losses in an engagement with China. Our other Pacific Rim allies have also refused to assist, afraid of provoking China into a retaliatory attack."

"What about a U.N. resolution, condemning China and authorizing military force to defend Taiwan?" Hardison asked.

"Member nations are extremely upset at China's use of force to unify the two Chinas, and a resolution condemning China's aggression should be approved within the next day or two. However, a resolution authorizing military force by the United Nations must come from the Security Council. Unfortunately, China is one of the five permanent members on the Security Council and will veto any resolution authorizing the United Nations to intervene militarily."

Ross examined the solemn faces of the men at the table, then returned her attention to the president. "I'm afraid that no one in the region is willing to engage China."

The president frowned. "So it looks like we're going it alone." He paused for a moment, then directed his next question at SecDef Jennings. "How are we going to compensate for the Aegis malware and new Chinese surface-to-air missiles? I don't want to lose another four carriers and their air wings."

Jennings replied, "First, we'll download the Aegis software patch to all our cruisers and destroyers in the Pacific. It's risky, since it hasn't gone through operational testing, but it's our only option."

"Why not use the new version *Lake Erie* used?" the president asked.

"It doesn't have full functionality," Jennings replied. "It was loaded to test new variants of our Standard SM-2 and SM-6 missiles, and thankfully it had SM-3 capability. But it's not fully integrated with the rest of the Aegis Warfare System yet."

The answer appeared acceptable to the president, so Jennings continued. "Second, we need to address the new Chinese surface-to-air missiles. They're a mix of new-generation radar-guided and heat-seeking missiles. We'll compensate for the radar-guided missiles by doubling the number of radar-jamming Growlers accompanying each cycle of fighters, and using the telemetry data we received during the first encounter, we're modifying the Growler's infrared-red jammers to be more effective against these new heat-seeking missiles. These changes should significantly increase the air wings' survival rate.

"One piece of good news," Jennings added, "is that Christine made it safely aboard USS *Michigan*. She suffered a minor injury—a gunshot wound to her arm—but will be fine. The even better news is that she delivered the flash drive she was given by the head of President Xiang's security detail, and it's been transported by one of *Michigan*'s UAVs to Okinawa. Unfortunately, we don't know what's on the flash drive, because the drive is encrypted. It's being transported to a cryptology center at the Office of Naval Intelligence, and they'll inform us once it's been decrypted."

"That *is* good news," the president affirmed. "I've been worried about Christine. Should we wait to find out what's on this flash drive before we engage China again?"

"We don't have that luxury," Jennings answered. "We have no idea how long it will take to decrypt the drive, and we can't wait. We have to land our MEFs before we lose the last beachhead on Taiwan. At the current rate of China's advance across the island, we can't delay."

The president sat back in his chair for a moment, evaluating the information discussed this evening. Finally, he sat up, a hard gaze focused on SecDef Jennings. "I realize things don't go as planned during war, gentlemen, and China has had a few surprises up their sleeve, giving them the advantage up to now. It's time we turn the table on our Chinese friends. When will the rest of Pacific Fleet be ready to engage?"

"The three additional strike groups will be within launch range by tomorrow night, Mr. President. *Nimitz* is conducting repairs and should also be able to participate." The president nodded as Jennings continued. "I have to warn you, sir, that we're placing the entire Pacific Fleet at risk. Everything hinges on this Aegis software patch—it's not fully tested. We'll be bringing all four carriers within range of their DF-21 missiles, and if the patched Aegis software build malfunctions, we could lose every carrier."

After a moment of quiet reflection, the president replied, "I understand. Continue with your plans."

29

USS *NIMITZ*

Four hundred miles east of Taiwan, USS *Nimitz* loitered in placid waters under a clear blue sky, a light breeze the only reminder of the passing storm. With the sun a few degrees above the horizon, the orange sunlight reflected off glassy waters as Captain Alex Harrow stood on the Flight Deck, a foot from the edge of the crater created by the DF-21 missile. The fires belowdecks had been extinguished and two-thirds of the forty-foot-wide hole had already been covered, thick metal plates welded into place and supported with I beams. Red sparks and molten slag spit into the air as the ship's welders continued repairs.

Harrow hadn't asked the Chief Engineer which bulkheads had been cut down to obtain the material; sealing the hole was the only thing that mattered. Now that the storm front had passed, Harrow could no longer use the strong winds to his advantage. *Nimitz* would launch its air wing soon, and when it returned, the aircraft would need the entire Flight Deck to land.

They didn't have much time to complete the repairs. The rest of the Pacific Fleet had arrived and the other three carriers were preparing to launch their air wings. To the south, Harrow could see USS *Lincoln*, a tiny speck on the horizon. Farther south were *Stennis* and *Vinson*, and arrayed in front of the four carriers were the strike groups' fifty-six cruisers, destroyers, and frigates.

Lagging behind, well out of range of Chinese ballistic missiles, were the Pacific Fleet's two Marine Expeditionary Forces, embarked aboard amphibious assault ships, transport docks, and landing ships—two divisions of Marines plus two Marine air wings, waiting for the Fleet to clear a safe path to Taiwan.

The DF-21 missiles still posed the most significant threat. Until the launch-

ers were taken out, the Fleet would have to rely on SM-3 missiles for defense. Fortunately, the DF-21 missile appeared to have one weakness. Although
the missile had a theoretical range of seventeen hundred miles, Navy intelligence had determined the missile could be effectively targeted out to only
seven hundred miles, which corresponded to the range at which *Nimitz* had
been attacked two days earlier. The four carriers would soon close to within
range of the DF-21, and Harrow hoped this time the outcome would be
much more favorable.

In a few minutes, Harrow would turn *Nimitz* west again and order ahead
flank speed, generating headwind to assist his aircraft during launch. Thankfully, both reactors could be brought up to full power. Radiation levels and
chemistry analysis of primary coolant had determined that neither reactor
had sustained damage during the few hours operating above one hundred
percent power.

As the first Hornet rose toward the Flight Deck from the Hangar Deck
below, Harrow felt a deepening uneasiness. China had prepared well for
America's initial response, and would undoubtedly be prepared for the onslaught of the entire Pacific Fleet. The United States Navy would not make
the same mistakes this time, underestimating not only the capability of
Chinese missiles, but the accompanying cyber warfare that made the missiles much more lethal. Their Aegis escorts had new software, their fighters
were loaded with additional chaff, and each wave of aircraft would be supported by the Wing's entire complement of EA-18G Growlers, the aircraft
refueled in-flight so they could support all three cycles. As Harrow turned
and headed toward the carrier's Island, he wondered if those adjustments
would be enough.

30

USS *MICHIGAN*

As the eighteen-thousand-ton submarine leveled off at periscope depth, the top of the sail four feet beneath the ocean's surface, Christine checked her watch. Standing in the aft port corner of Control, Christine waited for Captain Wilson to man Battle Stations; in less than twenty minutes, *Michigan* was supposed to begin launching her Tomahawk missiles. As Wilson peered through the submarine's periscope, Christine's thoughts drifted to the orders that had been streaming into the submarine over the radio broadcast. *Michigan* had been tasked with launching all of her Tomahawk missiles. That wasn't surprising considering the circumstances. What was surprising was that the missiles would be launched without a single target assigned.

The Tomahawk missiles loaded aboard *Michigan* were the new Block IV Tactical Tomahawk, or TACTOM variant, capable of loitering after launch, doing donuts in the air while awaiting targeting information. Although Tomahawk cruise missiles were extremely accurate, capable of flying through the window of a house, it took hours for launch orders to be generated, transmitted, and loaded aboard older variants, plus additional time spent during the missile's transit to its destination. During that time, enemy units or mobile launchers could reposition, resulting in the Tomahawk destroying a vacant building or deserted patch of dirt. The new TACTOM missiles overcame this deficit. They would already be launched and loitering nearby, reducing the time between identification and ordnance-on-target from hours to mere minutes.

Wilson stepped back, turning the scope over to Lieutenant Cordero as an announcement came over the Conn speakers. "Conn, ESM. Hold no threat radars."

Cordero acknowledged ESM's report as Wilson stepped toward the communications panel on the Conn. Wilson pulled the 1-MC microphone from its holster and issued the order his crew had been waiting for.

"Man Battle Stations Missile."

The Chief of the Watch, stationed at the Ballast Control Panel on the port side of Control, twisted a lever on his panel, and the loud *gong, gong, gong* of the submarine's General Emergency alarm reverberated throughout the ship. As the alarm faded, the Chief of the Watch picked up his 1-MC microphone, repeating the Captain's order. "Man Battle Stations Missile."

Men streamed into Control, taking their seats at dormant consoles, bringing them to life as they donned their sound-powered phone headsets. Sonar Technicians and Radiomen passed through Control on their way to the adjoining Sonar and Radio Rooms, while supervisors gathered behind their respective stations in Control.

Wilson stepped off the Conn, leaving the safety of the ship in the XO's and Lieutenant Cordero's capable hands, then headed down the ladder to Operations Compartment Second Level. After receipt of launch orders yesterday, Wilson had briefed Christine, explaining the process and where she could observe if desired. She followed Wilson down the ladder and a short distance aft, stepping into Missile Control Center.

Like the Navigation Center behind the Control Room, which had been converted into a Battle Management Center, Missile Control Center had also been transformed during the submarine's conversion to SSGN. The refrigerator-sized computers had been replaced with servers one-tenth their size, and a Tube Status Control Display was now mounted along the starboard bulkhead. The ballistic missile Launch Console on the aft bulkhead had been replaced with four consoles of the same type used in the Battle Management Center and in Control. The two workstations on the right were Mission Planning Consoles. The third workstation was the Launch Control Console, and the fourth workstation, on the far left, displayed a map of *Michigan*'s operating area, which was overlaid with one green and several red hatched areas.

Wilson stopped behind the Launch Control Console next to Lieutenant Karl Stewart, the submarine's Weapons Officer, who had been up all night supervising the Tomahawk mission planning teams. Stewart looked over one shoulder of the second class petty officer manning the console, while Wilson looked over the operator's other shoulder. Glancing at the fourth console,

Wilson verified that *Michigan* was within the green hatched area—the submarine's launch basket, where all of *Michigan*'s Tomahawk missiles were within target range.

Lieutenant Stewart reported to the Captain, "Five minutes to window. Request permission to launch Salvo One."

Wilson replied, "Permission granted. Launch Salvo One."

Following Wilson's order, there was no flurry of activity. Stewart simply turned back toward the Launch Control Console, his eyes focused on the time display as it counted down the remaining five minutes. At ten seconds before the scheduled launch, the launch button on the Launch Control Console display, which had been grayed out until this point, turned a vivid green. The Launch Operator announced, "In the window, Salvo One."

Lieutenant Stewart replied, "Very well, Launch Operator. Continue."

Finally, the digital clock on the Launch Operator's screen reached 00:00:00. The Launch Operator clicked the green button, and *Michigan*'s automatic Tomahawk Attack Weapon System took control.

"Opening Tube Seven," the Launch Supervisor reported as the green indicating light for Tube Seven turned yellow. Shortly thereafter, the indicating light turned red. "Hatch, Tube Seven, open and locked."

A few seconds later, the Launch Operator reported, "Missile One, Tube Seven, away."

The first of *Michigan*'s Tomahawk missiles had been ejected from the submarine, the missile's engines igniting once it was safely above the ocean's surface. In rapid succession, another missile followed every five seconds, with the Tomahawk Attack Weapon System automatically opening and closing the Missile Tube hatches as required. *Michigan*'s Tomahawks were streaking west; the Pacific Fleet's counteroffensive had begun.

31

WASHINGTON, D.C.

It was 7 P.M. when the president stepped into the Situation Room, taking his seat at the head of the rectangular conference table. Seated next to the president and across from SecDef Nelson Jennings, Captain Steve Brackman held the remote control in his hand, pointing it toward the ten-foot-wide monitor on the far wall. The president said nothing as the nine men and women seated at the conference table stared at the display in silence, watching their Pacific Fleet move west toward Taiwan.

As the president's senior military aide, Brackman had the honor of manipulating the display, zooming in and out upon request, and shifting to alternate displays as the battle unfolded. The monitor was zoomed out to a bird's-eye view of the Western Pacific, displaying the east coast of China, Taiwan, and the Japanese islands to the north. On the right side of the screen, four blue symbols, representing their carrier strike groups, moved across a red dashed line marking the effective range of China's DF-21 missile.

A few minutes after the president's arrival, an inverted U, shaded light blue, appeared next to each carrier strike group as they began launching their air wings. Brackman's grip on the remote tightened. If China employed the same tactics they had used against *Nimitz* and *George Washington*, it wouldn't be long before a barrage of missiles emerged from the Chinese coast and the occupied portions of Taiwan, speeding toward the carriers and their air wings.

Minutes ticked by like hours as the first cycle of each air wing assembled above their carriers, the eighty aircraft finally speeding west toward Taiwan. When they were halfway to the island, red symbols began appearing over China's coast and Taiwan, moving east. The launches continued for several minutes, the missiles breaking into two groups. The nomenclature next to the symbols told Brackman that China had launched eighty DF-21 missiles toward the four carriers and over three hundred anti-air missiles toward the incoming aircraft. Shoulders tensed and eyes tightened as the men and women in the Situation Room watched the red and blue symbols march toward each other.

The last three carrier strike groups had been loaded with every SM-3 missile in the Navy's arsenal. The Navy had downloaded the software patch for the Aegis fire control system onto their cruisers and destroyers, and everyone in the Situation Room was nervous about whether the Aegis Warfare System would remain functional. But what if China simply launched more DF-21 missiles than the Pacific Fleet had SM-3s to shoot them down with? Brackman ran the numbers. They had sufficient SM-3s to handle the first wave of eighty incoming DF-21s.

Turning his attention to the missiles speeding toward their aircraft, Brackman wondered if the modifications made to the air wings would also suffice. The three air wings aboard *Lincoln*, *Vinson*, and *Stennis* had been augmented with additional radar-jamming Growlers, stripped from the Atlantic Fleet's air wings. The density of China's anti-air missile attack against *Nimitz*'s and *George Washington*'s aircraft had been astounding, and additional Growlers were essential.

Meanwhile, what wasn't on the display were the locations of their twenty-seven fast attack submarines. Each submarine had a chunk of ocean assigned, and they could be anywhere inside their operating area, hunting down their adversaries. The performance of the fast attacks was critical, ensuring the four aircraft carriers were safe from submarine attack, as well as clearing a path to shore for the two Marine Expeditionary Forces.

The twenty-seven fast attacks were divided into three sets of nine. The first nine submarines were positioned in front of the carrier strike groups, pushing forward in narrow operating lanes as they searched for Chinese submarines. The other two formations of nine submarines were located on the flanks, angling toward the north and south entrances of the Taiwan Strait. Their mission was to break through the Chinese submarine blockade, clearing a path for the four carrier strike groups to sweep inside the Strait, cutting off the flow of supplies to the Chinese troops on Taiwan.

Brackman's attention returned to the DF-21 missiles speeding toward the carriers. Blue symbols began appearing next to each carrier strike group, angling toward the incoming DF-21 missiles. Their Aegis class destroyers and cruisers were launching a matching barrage of eighty SM-3 missiles. There was a collective sigh of relief in the Situation Room—their Aegis Warfare Systems were still functional.

Brackman zoomed in until the individual SM-3 missiles from the *Nimitz* Carrier Strike Group and the incoming DF-21 missiles were shown on the monitor. One by one, the SM-3 missiles intercepted their counterparts, performing admirably. Of the twenty DF-21s targeting *Nimitz*, only three made it through. Seconds later, another round of SM-3 missiles streaked toward the remaining DF-21s, and the last three missiles were destroyed.

Shifting the display to the other three carrier strike groups, Brackman observed similar results. The aircraft carriers had survived the initial attack. Brackman then examined the anti-air missiles racing toward the carrier air wings. Leaving the display on the unit level, he selected the first cycle of aircraft as they approached Taiwan.

The eighty jets were arranged in a linear formation, with each group of twenty aircraft escorted by four EA-18 Growlers, one at each end and the other two above and below the center of the formation. The Growler jamming worked well, as the majority of the missiles streaked past the aircraft. But a substantial number found their mark, indicated by the blinking—then disappearing—blue symbols. It was surreal, watching men and women die, their deaths represented by icons vanishing from the screen. As the red symbols streaked by and faded into oblivion, Brackman tallied up the losses: fifteen of the eighty aircraft had been shot down. But even though it was difficult to accept the loss of life, the men and women in the Situation Room realized they had weathered the storm of Chinese missiles.

Now it was time to strike back.

Satellites in orbit had been repositioned to identify the location of the *Hongqi* surface-to-air and *Dong Feng* DF-21 missile batteries, and while the president and his entourage had been watching the battle unfold in the Situation Room, men and women in Tomahawk Mission Planning Centers had been working furiously, sending targeting coordinates to *Michigan*'s and *Ohio*'s Tomahawks loitering in the Taiwan Strait, circling just above the ocean waves. Brackman figured half of them had already received their targeting information and were now heading toward the Chinese coast. But Tomahawks weren't the only weapons headed China's way. Additional ordnance was plummeting from high above.

As the Tomahawk missiles streaked along the ocean's surface toward the *Hongqi* missile batteries, one hundred B-1B bombers were releasing two-thousand-pound bombs with GPS-guided JDAM kits at their targets—the DF-21 ballistic missile launchers. Whether China had additional DF-21 missiles would quickly become a moot question. They would soon lack the batteries to launch them.

Brackman shifted the display and zoomed in until icons representing the Chinese missile launchers appeared. The *Hongqi* missile batteries were located sporadically in Taiwan and densely along China's east coast, with the DF-21 missile launchers farther inland. Brackman watched as the blue symbols representing Tomahawk missiles and GPS-guided bombs reached their targets, each red symbol blinking in response. Unfortunately, destruction of those batteries couldn't be confirmed immediately; the flashing icon simply indicated ordnance had arrived at the missile battery location. Whether the launchers had been destroyed would be determined via optical satellites. Unfortunately, that assessment would take several hours.

Now that the carriers and their air wings had weathered the initial onslaught, the men and women around the conference table settled in for the long haul. Tension eased from their bodies as they leaned back in their chairs. It was going to be a long night.

Brackman took a sip of his lukewarm coffee, placing the white Styrofoam cup onto the conference table where it joined another two dozen partially full and empty cups. The tension and silence of the first few hours had been replaced by the murmur of quiet conversations, loosened ties, and unbuttoned shirt collars as the men and women around the table monitored the battle's progress and awaited word of the underwater conflict. So far, the SOSUS arrays on the ocean floor and the towed arrays deployed from SURTASS ships had reported thirty-one underwater detonations: eleven in front of the carrier strike groups and ten each along the north and south entrances to the Taiwan Strait. Only three American submarines had been confirmed sunk. The other twenty-eight detonations were presumably the demise of a Chinese counterpart.

As the American submarines advanced, a path was being cleared for the Marine Expeditionary Forces. On the monitor in the Situation Room, the ocean between the carrier strike groups and Taiwan was divided into twelve squares—four columns wide by three rows deep. The first two rows had turned a solid green, 7th Fleet confirming that the eight operating areas had been cleansed of Chinese submarines. One of the nine American submarines in that sector had been sunk, and four of the remaining fast attacks had moved into the last row of operating areas while two loitered on each flank, ensuring no Chinese submarines slipped in behind the front line. Finally, the indication everyone awaited appeared on the monitor.

One of the squares in the third row turned green, and a minute later, a second one adjacent to it also illuminated a matching color. A safe path to Taiwan had been established. Within minutes, the two Marine Expeditionary Forces would begin surging toward beachheads on Taiwan's coast.

But that was only half of the battle. As long as China maintained their supply lines intact, time was on their side. To defeat the Chinese invasion of Taiwan, the Pacific Fleet had to cut off the flow of supplies across the Strait. Unfortunately, the Fleet couldn't do that with the carriers stationed east of Taiwan.

It was a simple numbers-and-distance problem. With the carriers stationed east of Taiwan in deep water, it would take time for the aircraft to make the trip inside the Strait, locate and destroy their target, and return to their carrier for refueling and rearming. If the Chinese had been supplying their troops on Taiwan with only a few large supply ships, this wouldn't have been a problem; their supply lifeline would have been severed within hours.

But China had built thousands of small supply ships, most only twenty feet long and powered by a single outboard motor, ferrying supplies across the Strait in a dizzying array of activity. As a result, the Pacific Fleet could not take out the supply ships fast enough. They needed to shorten the fighter turnaround time—they needed to get the carriers inside the Strait. The United States knew it, and so did China. They had blockaded the Strait with a dozen submarines on both the northern and southern entrances. The Pacific Fleet had its work cut out for it.

As Brackman wondered how their effort to break through the blockade was progressing, a small window appeared in the lower right corner of the monitor, displaying the image of a Navy Admiral. Brackman manipulated the remote control in his hand, and the Admiral appeared full screen. It was Admiral Vance Garbin, in charge of Pacific Command.

"Good evening, Mr. President." The Admiral's voice warbled over the long-distance encrypted video feed from his command center in Hawaii.

"Evening, Admiral. What have you got?"

"Satellite recon of Chinese missile battery sites confirm ninety-eight percent of the missile launchers have been destroyed. What remains can be easily handled by our carrier strike group cruisers and destroyers. Also, I have confirmation from 7th Fleet that our submarines have broken through both ends of the Chinese blockade of the Taiwan Strait. With your permission, Mr. President, I will order the Pacific Fleet into the Strait to cut off the Chinese invasion."

The president glanced at SecDef Jennings, who nodded his concurrence. Turning back toward the monitor, the commander-in-chief spoke firmly. "Order the carrier strike groups inside the Taiwan Strait."

32

BEIJING

In the South Wing of the Great Hall of the People, Admiral Tsou strode briskly down the corridor, his lone footsteps echoing off marble walls. At the end of the long corridor, urgently assembled in the conference room, Huan Zhixin and the eight members of the Politburo awaited his report. Although Admiral Tsou would normally have been flanked by two Captains—his aide on one side and his chief of staff on the other—he would deliver the news alone today. It was only fitting; the amphibious assault on Taipei had been his plan. His and his alone, convincing the Politburo it was the only path to success.

Tsou reached the end of the corridor, pausing momentarily with his hand on one of the two immense wooden conference room doors. He found it difficult to contain his emotions. For any man, especially one in his position, it would not be proper to display such a lack of control. Straightening his back, he pushed the door firmly. It swung noiselessly inward, revealing the impatient faces of President Xiang and the other seven Politburo members seated around the conference table, plus Huan Zhixin, seated along the perimeter.

Taking his place at the front of the conference room, Admiral Tsou faced the eight men in China's Politburo. Their faces were difficult to read. As was his, he supposed. After clearing his throat, he began.

"As you are aware, the American Pacific Fleet launched a counteroffensive with four carrier strike groups and twenty-seven fast attack submarines. The Americans were able to discern the malware in their Aegis software and implement a fix, and as a result, our *Dong Feng* missiles have been rendered ineffective. Their submarine force has proven extremely capable, clearing a path to Taipei for their Marine Expeditionary Forces, and has broken through our blockade of the Taiwan Strait. We've lost all submarines assigned to the blockade, with confirmed kills of only three American submarines.

"The United States has dealt equally well with our *Hongqi* missile batteries, destroying all but seven launchers. There is nothing left to deter the American carrier strike groups from entering the Taiwan Strait, cutting off supplies to our one hundred thousand troops on Taipei. Even now, satellite reconnaissance reports the four American strike groups are entering the Strait, two through the northern entrance and two from the south. Their air wings are now within striking distance of all resupply nodes."

Admiral Tsou paused, waiting for the Politburo to absorb the information and its implications. His eyes met President Xiang's for a moment, then passed over each man in the room. Finally, Tsou could no longer contain the emotion. A broad smile spread across his face, matched by wide grins displayed by Huan and the eight men around the table.

The smile faded from Admiral Tsou's face as he continued, his features returning to their normal, stoic state. "Everything is proceeding exactly as planned."

EN PASSANT

33

PANAMA CITY, PANAMA

Seated alone at a table for two on the patio of the Miraflores Café, Daniel
DeVor leaned back in his chair, a drink in his hand, admiring the crimson
sun as it set into the lush green canopy of the Arraiján rain forest. He wished
instead he could have watched the sun sink below the waters of the nearby
Pacific Ocean, hoping to observe a rare flash of emerald green as the last light
of day slipped beneath the horizon. According to legend, one who has seen
the Green Ray is able to *see closely into his own heart* and *read the thoughts of
others*. To Daniel, only the first part mattered. He didn't care what moti-
vated his Asian friend. Understanding why he had agreed to the man's plan
was where his thoughts dwelt tonight.

The decision had been a difficult one, and even now Daniel struggled with
his conscience. Three years ago, the family farm in West Virginia was about
to go under. The rising price of fuel, combined with four summer droughts,
had wiped out what little savings his father had squirreled away and no bank
was willing to extend additional credit. Fortunately, an opportunity arose
from an unlikely source. Chris Stevenson was a complete stranger the day
he pulled up a chair at this very café three years ago. But while Daniel knew
nothing about Stevenson, the thin Asian—with a fake American name, no
doubt—knew everything about Daniel's dire situation.

A pact had been proposed and after much consideration, Daniel had accepted. No one would be injured and his family would benefit. That's what
mattered, he told himself. His father's debt was paid and a comfortable an-
nuity established for Daniel's parents. In return, Daniel had agreed to complete a predetermined task.

Three years had passed without hearing from Stevenson and Daniel had
slowly convinced himself he would never be asked to complete the task. But

Stevenson had been waiting in his car by the curb when Daniel stepped from his house today. The conversation was short and Stevenson left behind the brown satchel currently at Daniel's feet, along with a clear warning of what would happen should Daniel fail to fulfill his end of the bargain.

Daniel finished his drink, placing the glass onto the thin cardboard coaster on the table. Pulling a ten dollar bill from his wallet, he placed it next to his glass, then stood, grabbing the brown satchel firmly. With one last glance at the Panama Canal stretching before him, he turned and headed toward the café's exit.

Ten minutes later, Daniel approached the security checkpoint to the Panama Canal's Miraflores Locks. With his heart racing, he emptied his pockets into a small container and placed it on the X-ray machine conveyor belt next to his satchel, then stepped through the metal detector. The technician monitored the display as the briefcase exited, sliding slowly toward Daniel. As he reached for his satchel, he froze when the technician spoke.

"Bag check."

The conveyor halted, Daniel's satchel only a few inches away from his outstretched hand. A second security guard stopped across from him, retrieving the satchel from the conveyor belt. With feigned disinterest, Daniel looked past the guard toward the lock entrance, only twenty feet away.

After taking the satchel to a side table, the guard opened the case. Daniel's heart hammered in his chest as the guard eyed the contents suspiciously, tilting the case as he examined the assorted items, finally pulling out an old iPod, one of two Chris Stevenson had given Daniel earlier that day. Both were filled with an explosive supposedly ten times more powerful than C-4.

The guard glanced at the iPod in his hand and the matching device in the satchel. "Why do you have two iPods?"

"They're older versions and don't have much memory. I need two to hold all my songs."

The guard studied the iPod in his hand. "Yeah, these are pretty old. Why don't you buy a new one?"

"Easier said than done, with what they pay us around here."

The guard grunted in commiseration. "Don't I know it. You should get a new iPod Touch. You can even watch movies on those things."

"Already on my list." Daniel smiled.

After a final examination, the guard started to return the iPod to the satchel when it slipped out of his hand. Daniel watched the iPod fall, almost in slow motion, toward the concrete floor. He lunged forward, his hands closing around the iPod just before it hit the ground.

"Sorry," the guard said sheepishly. He took the iPod from Daniel's hands and placed it back into the satchel. "Thank you," he said as he handed the bag back to Daniel, the guard's eyes already shifting to the next person in line.

Daniel took the satchel and exited the security checkpoint, his heartbeat slowly returning to normal.

Fifteen years ago, Daniel had been hired by the Panama Canal Authority to oversee maintenance of the canal's elaborate lock system. Ships entering the canal on either end were raised eighty-five feet as they passed through the locks, and lowered back to sea level after their transit. Each set of locks had gates, which, when closed, formed a chamber within which the water level could be adjusted. Each gate was over six feet thick, with some as tall as eighty-two feet, weighing over seven hundred tons.

Instead of heading to his office, Daniel crossed over one of the Miraflores Locks' massive gates, headed toward a center causeway separating the dual lock system. After stepping onto the causeway, Daniel descended a narrow staircase. The smell of damp, century-old concrete greeted him as he continued down the steps leading to one of two tunnels that ran the length of the locks. Daniel stopped where East Gate 3 was attached to the center causeway on a pair of two-foot-diameter pintle hinges. Destroy one of the hinges while there was a water level imbalance, and that half of the gate would shear away, disabling the lock for weeks, if not months.

Opening his satchel, Daniel retrieved one of the iPods and placed it against the metal access plate where grease was periodically pumped into the upper hinge. The magnet on the back of the iPod adhered to the metallic frame. After a few taps and swirls of the iPod's click wheel, the timer was set for ten minutes. Another tap and the timer began counting down. Daniel hurried to the adjacent tunnel, running parallel to this one, where he affixed the second iPod in a similar location for West Gate 3. Checking his watch, Daniel set the iPod timer to seven minutes, synchronizing both iPod countdowns.

Five minutes later, Daniel was in his office, standing at the window overlooking the Miraflores Locks, counting down the remaining two minutes. Container ships had just exited both of the upper locks, and their water level was twenty-seven feet higher than the locks below. Just as he checked his watch again, the floor of his office rumbled and windows rattled. He looked up to see half of East Gate 3 shear away from its upper hinge. The massive gate tilted back toward the lower lock, ripping away from its bottom hinge. Twenty-six million gallons of water in the upper lock, no longer held in place, surged into the lower lock, spilling over the lower gates into the Pacific Ocean. Seconds later, Daniel felt another rumble, and half of West Gate 3 also sheared away.

The Panama Canal was now impassable.

34

ISMAILIA, EGYPT

Caleb Malcom knelt in the darkness, his knees sinking into the soft sand at the base of the escarpment, sloping thirty feet up toward the clear night sky. His knees sank farther than they would normally have, for tonight he carried an extra sixty pounds slung across his left shoulder and in the black rucksack strapped to his back. The two men accompanying him, one on each side, also knelt low to the ground, their features illuminated by bright white security lights located just over the top of the embankment. Each of the two men, also clad in black, carried a matching rucksack and identical weapon slung across their shoulder.

There was no cloud cover tonight and the temperature had plummeted. Malcom's breath condensed into fine white mist as he exhaled, recovering from his sprint across the flat expanse of sand between the security fence and the base of the escarpment. The security patrol had passed by only three minutes ago, so they had seventeen minutes to accomplish their task and retreat through the hole they had cut in the fence. Their vehicle was just over the ridge, and they'd be long gone before the security forces arrived. Malcom glanced at each man beside him, ordering both men to begin their ascent in ten seconds.

After ten years in the military in one of the Army's elite units, Malcom had been hired by Bluestone Security, spending six years protecting supplies en route to forward bases. However, after America withdrew from Iraq, his employment had been terminated due to lack of contracts, and with no job came no money. After becoming accustomed to a $200,000 annual salary, it wasn't long before Malcom racked up serious debt and was willing to entertain more creative methods of employment.

Chris Stevenson had approached Malcom two weeks ago, offering a

lucrative deal. Malcom considered declining, but only for a moment. Someone would take the job, and it might as well be him. It would be easy to
accomplish the mission; he knew men who would assist, had access to the
required weapons, and knew contacts in the region who could perform reconnaissance. The decision was easy.

It was difficult tonight, however, climbing the steep embankment. Malcom's feet slipped in the loose sand, but less than a minute later, all three
men crested the top of the escarpment. Stretching into the distance in both
directions lay the 120-mile-long Suez Canal, and directly in front of Malcom transited the *Aegean Empress*, a 200,000-ton oil tanker passing from the
Red Sea into the Mediterranean. A half-mile in front of the *Empress* was another tanker, and behind, a third. He had timed it perfectly.

Malcom slipped the RPG-29 from his shoulder and shrugged off his rucksack, as did the two men beside him. It took only five seconds to load the
anti-tank round, another five to stand and hoist the launcher into position,
and another five to take aim on the *Aegean Empress*. After a quick glance at
the two men beside him, Malcom shouted his order. All three men fired simultaneously, their projectiles streaking through the darkness.

The anti-tank round sliced through the *Aegean Empress*'s hull just above
the waterline, igniting the ship's oil tanks in a jarring explosion. A fireball
billowed hundreds of feet skyward, illuminating the three men atop the escarpment in a burst of orange light. Two rumbles in the distance followed,
accompanied by similar pulses of light.

There was no time to be wasted. Security forces would be converging on
their location within minutes. Malcom slung the RPG over his shoulder
but then paused, staring dispassionately at the oil tankers burning brightly
in the darkness. He found it odd, but he felt no adrenaline rush from his
destructive endeavor. The thought of what awaited him in his bank account,
however, was quite exciting. Reaching down, he grabbed his rucksack and
slung it over his other shoulder as he began working his way down the steep
embankment.

35

USS *NIMITZ*

USS *Nimitz* surged south at ahead full, alternately launching and recovering aircraft on its patchwork Flight Deck. Twenty miles to the north, USS *Lincoln* followed behind as the two carrier strike groups entered the northern entrance of the Taiwan Strait. Arrayed to the west, cruisers and destroyers mirrored the carriers' movement, establishing a screen against Chinese missiles. Unseen in the waters ahead, twelve fast attack submarines straddled the width of the Strait, searching for Chinese submarines. Meanwhile, two hundred miles to the south, another twelve American submarines were headed north, leading the other two carrier strike groups through the Strait's southern entrance.

Nimitz was at General Quarters, and Captain Alex Harrow stood his watch on the Bridge, supervising his carrier's flight operations. Their aircraft had fared well thus far, losing only ten percent of their fighters. Anti-air missile defense and enemy fighter resistance was almost nonexistent as *Nimitz*'s F/A-18 jets struck supply nodes along the Chinese coast and beachheads on the west coast of Taiwan.

It would take another twenty-four hours to completely cut off the supplies flowing across the Strait. The number of ships ferrying equipment from China to Taiwan was impressive, but the four carrier strike groups had been whittling away at the small transports all morning.

Harrow looked out the Bridge windows, observing one Super Hornet descending from the Flight Deck to the Hangar on Elevator 1 while another ascended on Elevator 3, the fighter's normal allotment of self-defense missiles cut in half, increasing its payload of anti-ship missiles. There had been only sporadic Chinese fighter jet activity, and CAG Captain Helen Corcoran had decided to alter the mix of defensive and offensive weapons, increasing the wing's kill rate.

It was just too easy. Harrow's gut told him something was wrong, but there was nothing to confirm his fear. Everything was proceeding exactly as simulated in countless war games.

36

YǏN BISHOU
FUJIAN PROVINCE, CHINA

Just above the island of Taipei, a shimmering orange sun was climbing into a deep blue sky, bathing the cliffs rising from the Chinese mainland in gentle warmth. Deep inside the volcanic cliffs, harsh fluorescent lighting illuminated a cavern carved from the mountain's innards. Through the center of the mile-long cavern, with wharves lining each side of the man-made harbor, a channel flowed into the Taiwan Strait. Moored to the wharves were twenty-four Yuan class diesel submarines, their crews assembled topside, standing in formation. A hundred feet above the submarines at the inland end of the cavern, Admiral Tsou Deshi stood behind a narrow terrace, surveying *Yǐn Bishou* and the East Sea Fleet's flotilla of attack submarines with pride.

It had taken ten years to construct *Yǐn Bishou*, its creation concealed from America and their satellites in orbit. The United States was focused on *Sanya*, another underground base at Hainan Island. China had stationed their nuclear-powered submarines at *Sanya*, knowing it would focus America's attention there, and help keep *Yǐn Bishou* concealed.

America believed the only threat to their Navy was China's nuclear-powered submarines. If the Pacific Fleet had remained in deep water east of Taipei, that assessment would have been correct. But that wasn't the case today. The Pacific Fleet had been lured into the Strait. True, America had sunk many submarines and destroyed hundreds of missile batteries, but that was part of the plan.

In the next two hours, twenty-four new Yuan class submarines, just as advanced as their nuclear counterparts, would sortie to sea. Additionally, these submarine crews wielded a potent advantage. But before his crews sank the dagger into the American Navy, Admiral Tsou felt it fitting to offer a few words of encouragement.

Tsou spoke loudly, his voice carrying across the cavern. "Today, you will battle America, an enemy bent on the destruction of our country. They send their fleet to the shores of our homeland, attempting to subjugate us to their will. But their Pacific Fleet is overconfident. Today, America will feel the full might of China's Navy, and you will deliver a death blow, ending America's domination of the high seas." Tsou paused a moment before continuing. "I am proud of the men standing before me, ready to serve the people. This will be our finest hour."

Tsou turned to Admiral Guo Jian, commander of the East Sea Fleet, standing beside him. "Commence operations."

37

OFFICE OF NAVAL INTELLIGENCE, SUITLAND, MARYLAND

"This is taking forever."

Inside the four-story National Maritime Intelligence Center in eastern Maryland, Cindy Pon stood with a coffee mug in her hand, peering over Jay Wood's shoulder, examining his computer monitor. She had stayed late tonight, in case her analytical and language skills were required, but the decryption algorithms were still crunching away, the contents of the secure flash drive still unknown. Cindy took a sip of her coffee; it was 10 P.M. and she needed a caffeine jolt before the drive home.

Sitting at the workstation in front of her in the windowless, high-security enclave, Jay monitored the progress of the algorithm running on the computer, attempting to break the encrypted flash drive they had received from Okinawa two days ago.

"Have faith," Jay said without taking his eyes off the monitor. "It's just a matter of time."

Only twenty-seven years old, Jay Wood was ONI's best cryptologist. He had spent the last two days running various algorithms on the drive, evaluating how each algorithm performed before selecting the next. He had already determined which algorithm had been used to encrypt the flash drive, and was now attempting to determine the encryption key. Unfortunately, the key permutations were almost endless, and the process took time. The encryption key at the bottom of the monitor continued morphing—it had now increased to fifteen digits, each digit rapidly scrolling through the over-fifty-thousand characters of the Chinese language. Cindy had a hard time wrapping her mind around the number of permutations possible. A trillion had twelve zeros. The number of permutations in a Chinese encryption key with fifteen digits had seventy zeros. It definitely could take *forever*.

"I'm calling it a day," Cindy said. "If you happen to decrypt the drive before morning, give me a call. Also let Jina Hong know. She's got the night shift and will take a look at whatever you've got before I get in."

Jay nodded absentmindedly. He was focused on the monitor. Several of the encryption key digits had stopped changing, each displaying a different Chinese character. One by one, the other digits locked.

"Bingo!" Jay said. "Don't go anywhere, Cindy." He opened up a new windowpane on the monitor, displaying the icon of the flash drive they were attempting to access, then positioned the pane above the encryption key. He double-clicked on the icon, and several Chinese characters appeared on the screen.

"Your turn," he said.

Jay slid his chair out of the way as Cindy pulled one up, taking Jay's place at the workstation. She read the Chinese instructions on the monitor—they directed her to enter the encryption key. She had to type in the fifteen Chinese characters displayed below. The problem was she was using a computer keyboard with English letters and Arabic numbers.

Fortunately, this computer was loaded with the necessary software, allowing Cindy to type Chinese characters using pinyin—a method of writing Chinese using the English alphabet. She typed in the pinyin name for the first Chinese character, selecting the exact variation of the character from a pop-up menu. One by one, she entered the encryption key, then looked over at Jay.

Jay nodded. "Hit Enter."

Cindy reached over and hit the Enter key, and the icon on the screen opened, revealing a folder. She double-clicked on the folder and it opened to reveal eleven files with names in Chinese. The first four were titled after the PLA's four main branches: *Ground Forces*, *Navy*, *Air Force*, and *2nd Artillery Corps*, the last branch being in charge of China's nuclear and conventional ballistic missiles. The second set of files was named after China's seven military regions. An analyst at the Office of Naval Intelligence, she opened the *Navy* file first.

The file opened up into a PDF document. Cindy skimmed the Chinese characters, attempting to gain a basic understanding of the content. As she translated the Chinese to English in her mind, she realized she was reviewing a battle plan. She digested page after page, soon realizing the battle plan was divided into two phases. As she began to read Phase 2, she broke into a cold sweat. She slowed down, reading and then rereading the key elements of the plan.

'My God," she said, not realizing she was thinking out loud.

"What is it?" Jay asked.

She turned to Jay. "If China has developed the capabilities in this document, the Pacific Fleet is in big trouble." She reached for the phone and dialed the Director's home number, wondering if it was already too late.

38

USS *TEXAS*

Course 170, Speed 10, Depth 200.

In the crowded Control Room, Commander Jim Latham leaned next to the Quartermaster, reviewing the ship's log as USS *Texas* searched the surrounding waters. They'd been at Battle Stations for twenty-seven hours straight, beginning with the assault on the Chinese blockade of the northern entrance to the Taiwan Strait, with *Texas* near the center of the twelve fast attack submarine juggernaut. Chinese submarine resistance had been dense but inept. Only one American submarine had been lost while all twelve Chinese submarines opposing them had been sunk, and *Texas* and the other American fast attack submarines were now headed south, sanitizing the entire Strait.

Latham had shifted his crew to a port and starboard Battle Stations rotation at the sixteen-hour point. He could push his crew only so far before they began to lose their effectiveness. Luckily, there appeared to be few Chinese submarines remaining. They had encountered only two in their operating area after breaking through the blockade, and both of them were the oldest and noisiest submarines in the Chinese Navy, easily sunk.

After reviewing the ship's position in their operating area, Latham stepped away from the Navigation table, headed toward the Officer of the Deck's Tactical Workstation near the front of Control, examining the Combat and Sonar consoles along each side. It had taken him a while to get used to the design of the Virginia class submarine, with Sonar in Control instead of a separate room, the Sonar consoles lining the port side of the ship, the combat control consoles on starboard. And while Sonar had been added to Control, the periscopes had been removed. Virginia class submarines employed photonics masts, which didn't penetrate the pressure hull—there was no periscope to press your eye against or dance with for countless hours in endless circles. The Officer of the Deck instead sat at his workstation, raising and lowering one of their two photonics masts with a flick of a switch, rotating it with a joystick, like a kid's video game. The image was displayed on one of two monitors at his workstation.

Even more unsettling was the Virginia class ship control watch section. The four watchstanders on previous submarines—the Helm and the Outboard, who manipulated the submarine's rudder and control surfaces; the Diving Officer of the Watch, who supervised them; and the Chief of the Watch, who adjusted the submarine's buoyancy and controlled the masts and antennas—had been replaced by two watchstanders—the Pilot and Co-Pilot—who sat at the Ship Control Panel. The Pilot controlled the submarine's course and depth while the Co-Pilot adjusted the submarine's buoyancy and raised and lowered the masts and antennas.

As Latham stopped behind the Officer of the Deck, a report from Sonar came across the speakers in Control. Even though the Sonar Supervisor stood only a few feet away, he spoke into his wireless headset.

"Conn, Sonar. Hold a new contact on the towed array, designated Sierra five-seven, bearing two-zero-zero, classified submerged. Analyzing."

"Sonar, Conn. Aye," Latham replied as he turned to his left, examining the display on one of the Sonar consoles. A faint white trace had appeared to the south. Apparently, at least one Chinese submarine remained. Hopefully this would be another of the noisy Ming class, an easy kill. Latham decided to maintain course to keep the submarine's towed array, streaming a half-mile behind *Texas*, stable while Sonar analyzed the contact's frequency tonals.

A moment after the initial report, the Sonar Supervisor followed up. "Conn, Sonar. Sierra five-seven is classified Yuan class diesel submarine."

Latham's stomach tightened. Intel messages had reported the entire inventory of Yuan class submarines had been sunk. Those reports were obviously wrong, and *Texas* was now facing the most capable diesel submarine in the Chinese Navy.

Commander Latham stopped beside his Executive Officer, Lieutenant Commander John Milligan, to examine the contact solution on one of the BYG-1 Combat Control System consoles. The Yuan class submarines were quiet, which meant this contact would be much closer when detected than the previous two Chinese submarines. That meant there was a higher probability *Texas* would be counter-detected.

Milligan examined the three combat control consoles in front of him, then turned to Latham. "Ready to maneuver."

Latham decided to turn to the west, placing the contact on his submarine's beam. "Pilot, right full rudder, steady course two-seven-zero."

The Pilot acknowledged as he tilted his joystick to the right, and *Texas* began swinging to starboard. A moment later, *Texas* was steady on its new course. A few minutes later, after their towed array straightened out behind them, data streamed into their combat system again. As the Fire Control Party analyzed the contact's new bearing rate, another report from Sonar came across the Control speakers.

"Conn, Sonar. Now hold Sierra five-seven on the spherical array sonar."

Latham exchanged a concerned glance with his Executive Officer. The spherical array was less capable than their towed array, picking up contacts at closer ranges. In this morning's water conditions, Yuan class submarines would become detectable on the spherical array at eight thousand yards. Sierra five-seven was approaching too close for comfort.

Lieutenant Commander Milligan noted Sonar's report, ordering the three men manning the combat control consoles to override the automated algorithms.

"Set range to Sierra five-seven at eight thousand yards, speed four." Their target was a diesel submarine, most likely searching the water at slow speed. Milligan guessed four knots.

With a target range of eight thousand yards and a four-knot speed, the ship's combat control system slewed the contact's solution to a course heading almost directly toward them. Latham wondered if the Chinese submarine had already detected *Texas*, but there had been no indication thus far; no change in contact course or speed; and more important, no torpedo launch transients. Latham examined the combat control automated algorithm. It had converged on a similar solution to what the Executive Officer had forced, off by only six hundred yards in range, one knot in speed, and twenty degrees in course. Close enough for a firing solution.

The Executive Officer agreed. "Sir, I have a firing solution."

Latham announced, "Firing Point Procedures, Sierra five-seven, Tube One."

Thirty seconds later, Commander Latham began receiving the expected reports.

"Solution ready," the Executive Officer announced.

"Weapon ready," the Weapons Officer called out.

"Ship ready," the Officer of the Deck reported.

Texas was ready to engage.

Latham gave the order. "Shoot on generated bearings."

The firing signal was sent to the Torpedo Room, initiating the launch sequence for the torpedo in Tube One. Latham listened to the whirr of the submarine's torpedo ejection pump and the characteristic sound of the four-thousand-pound torpedo being ejected from the submarine's torpedo tube, accelerating from rest to thirty knots in less than a second.

Sonar monitored their torpedo, referring to it as *own ship's unit* so their reports wouldn't be confused with information about an incoming torpedo.

"Own ship's unit is in the water, running normally."

"Turning to preset gyro course."

"Fuel crossover achieved."

"Shifting to medium speed."

Their MK 48 Mod 7 torpedo had turned onto the ordered bearing and was speeding toward its target.

Less than a minute later, their MK 48 torpedo went active, filling the water with sonar pings, searching for its target. It took only three pings before the Chinese submarine was detected and verified, and Sonar picked up the characteristic torpedo response.

"Own ship's unit is increasing speed and ping interval."

The Weapons Officer followed up, confirming Sonar's observation as he read the telemetry data being sent back to the ship over the thin guidance wire trailing behind the torpedo.

"Own ship's unit is homing!"

Latham turned toward the combat control consoles, monitoring the performance of his weapon. Everything was proceeding well.

A powerful sonar ping echoed through the submarine. A report from the Sonar Supervisor followed. "Conn, Sonar. Sierra five-seven has gone active."

Before Latham could acknowledge, the Weapons Officer called out, "Own ship's unit has shut down!"

Latham responded coolly. "Firing Point Procedures, Sierra five-seven, Tube Two."

The Fire Control Party repeated their previous preparations, readying another one of their MK 48 torpedoes for launch. The required reports flowed from Latham's well-trained crew.

"Solution ready!"

"Weapon ready!"

"Ship ready!"

Latham quickly ordered, "Shoot on generated bearings!"

A second torpedo was ejected from *Texas*, and Latham waited expectantly for Sonar to announce the torpedo milestones as it pursued its target. Their first torpedo had malfunctioned. Torpedoes weren't one hundred percent reliable—there were too many single-point failures, from its electrical, fuel, and hydraulic systems, to the microprocessors in the torpedo's brain and the algorithms loaded onto them.

Their new MK 48 Mod 7 torpedoes had performed exceptionally well thus far, all eight of their previous shots finding their mark. Latham figured they were due for a bad apple. His crew responded swiftly, placing a second torpedo in the water before their target counter-fired. Latham listened closely as Sonar called out this torpedo's milestones.

"Second fired unit is in the water, running normally."

"Turning to preset gyro course."

"Fuel crossover achieved."

"Shifting to medium speed."

Latham turned his attention to the nearest combat control console, displaying an electronic map of their operating area, with an inverted green V representing their torpedo speeding toward the red icon representing their target. A moment later, the Weapons Officer called out the next torpedo milestone.

"Second fired unit has gone active."

A few seconds later, another powerful sonar pulse echoed through Control.

As the echo from the sonar pulse faded, the Weapons Officer called out, "Second fired unit has shut down!"

A pit formed in Latham's stomach. His mind churned as he initiated the process to send a third torpedo after their adversary.

"Firing Point Procedures, Sierra five-seven, Tube Three!"

The Fire Control Party responded quickly, preparing the MK 48 torpedo in Tube Three for firing. But Latham could see the worried looks on his crew's faces as they cast furtive glances at each other and in their Captain's direction. The odds of a malfunctioning MK 48 torpedo were very low; the probability of two consecutive failures infinitesimal. And both torpedoes had shut down immediately after their contact had gone active.

The idea that their adversary could shut down every torpedo was terrifying. It meant their submarine was defenseless and the outcome of this engagement unfavorable, to say the least. There was only one way to determine, without a doubt, whether their torpedo shutdowns had been unlucky coincidence—and that was to put a third weapon into the water.

But before Latham could give the order, he heard the Sonar Supervisor shout into his headset, "Torpedo launch transients, bearing one-nine-five. Correlates to Sierra five-seven!"

Latham turned toward the Sonar consoles as a bright white trace appeared on the spherical array broadband display.

The Sonar Supervisor followed up a few seconds later. "Torpedo in the water, bearing one-nine-five!"

Latham responded instantly. "Torpedo Evasion! Pilot, right full rudder, steady course two-eight-five. Launch countermeasure!"

The Pilot twisted his joystick to the right and rang up ahead flank on his display, sending the propulsion command to the Engine Room where the Throttleman began spinning open the ahead throttles. The fast attack submarine's powerful main engines sprang to life, churning the water behind them as the propeller accelerated *Texas* to maximum speed. As *Texas* began turning to starboard, one of the Fire Control Technicians clicked the Countermeasure Launch button on his display, ejecting a torpedo decoy into the water.

"Torpedo bears one-nine-five!"

Sonar called out the bearing to the incoming torpedo every ten seconds, and Latham carefully monitored its bearings. As the fast attack submarine initiated evasive maneuvers, the disciplined Fire Control Party completed the steps required to launch another MK 48 torpedo.

"Solution ready!"

"Weapon ready!"

"Ship ready!"

Latham gave the order to shoot, and the Fire Control Party's eyes were glued to the Weapon Coordinator's screen and their ears tuned for Sonar's report, awaiting word on the performance of their third torpedo. It achieved its initial milestones, turning toward its target. But shortly after it went active, another powerful sonar ping from Sierra five-seven echoed through Control, and the dreaded report from the Weapons Officer followed.

"Third fired unit has shut down!"

Commander Latham stood there a moment, absorbing the somber truth. *Texas* was defenseless, unable to sink their adversary. His job now was to extract *Texas* from this disastrous scenario, figure out what had gone wrong, and correct it before returning to battle.

"Torpedo bears one-nine-three!"

Latham observed the red lines appearing on the combat control display. Both bearings cut across the location of their decoy.

"Torpedo bears one-nine-one!"

The incoming torpedo was falling behind as it homed on their decoy. But before Latham could breathe a sigh of relief, another report from Sonar blasted across the speakers in Control.

"Torpedo launch transients, bearing one-eight-zero!"

Their adversary had also determined their first torpedo had been fooled by a decoy and had launched a second torpedo. The first decoy had worked. Hopefully a second would perform just as well. Latham called out, "Launch countermeasure!"

A moment later, a second decoy was ejected from the submarine's external launchers in the ship's hull, its position annotated on the geographic display as a white scalloped circle. Latham waited to determine whether the decoy would suck up the second torpedo chasing them.

"First torpedo is range-gating, bearing one-nine-zero! Second torpedo bears one-eight-zero."

The first torpedo was still homing on their decoy. However, the verdict was still out on the second torpedo.

"Second torpedo bears one-eight-zero!"

Latham looked up at the Ship Control Panel. *Texas* was at maximum speed now, but its propeller was making a tremendous amount of noise. He had traded stealth for speed, but he had no choice. He had to put enough distance between *Texas* and the torpedoes chasing them to prevent the torpedoes from detecting the submarine.

"Second torpedo bears one-eight-zero!"

Concern worked its way across Latham's face. The second torpedo remained on a constant bearing. That meant it had detected *Texas* and was adjusting its course to close on its target. He examined the geographic display again, confirming his assessment. Based on the bearing lines, the second torpedo had passed by their decoy and was headed straight for them.

"Second torpedo bears one-eight-zero. Range gating. Torpedo is homing!"

The torpedo had locked on to *Texas*. Latham's options were limited. He constructed the scenario's geometry in his mind. With *Texas* on a westerly course and the torpedo on a constant bearing of one-eight-zero, that meant the torpedo was on an intercept course, angling northwest. *Texas* had to turn to the northeast.

"Pilot, right hard rudder, steady course zero-six-zero!"

The crew held on to their equipment consoles as the Pilot tilted his joystick to hard right. Submarine maneuvers were normally benign, but a hard rudder at ahead flank would whipsaw the submarine around. Latham grabbed on to the Officer of the Deck's workstation as *Texas* banked to starboard. As *Texas* steadied on its new course, he returned his attention to the geographic display, attempting to discern whether his maneuver had had the intended effect. The rapid turn had put a knuckle in the water, which would temporarily blind the torpedo as it passed through.

"Second fired torpedo bears one-eight-five!"

Commander Latham held his breath, waiting for the next report from Sonar. It appeared the torpedo had maintained course. But sonar bearings occasionally wobbled. The next bearing to the torpedo would determine whether his maneuver had been successful.

"Second fired torpedo bears one-nine-zero!"

Latham let out a sigh of relief. The second torpedo was speeding behind them. But just when things appeared to be looking up, the Sonar Supervisor made another report.

"Conn, Sonar. Torpedo launch transients, bearing zero-eight-zero!"

Latham spun toward the sonar display. A second white trace had appeared—another torpedo in the water from a different submarine—this time fired from almost directly ahead. The sonar trace was burning in much brighter than the torpedo behind them. This torpedo had been fired from close range.

"Conn, Sonar! Third torpedo is homing, bearing zero-eight-zero!"

The torpedo's pings echoed through the submarine's hull, growing louder at each interval.

This torpedo was already homing, which meant it was within two thousand yards. *Texas* was barreling straight toward it and would close the distance in just over a minute. Latham quickly evaluated the few options that remained.

One minute to impact.

Launching a torpedo decoy wouldn't work, even if *Texas* turned out of the way. The larger fast attack submarine would remain in front of the decoy, attracting the incoming torpedo.

"Third torpedo bears zero-eight-zero!"

Silence gripped Control as Sonar reported the torpedo's bearing every ten seconds. Latham searched for a way out of their predicament, and they were running out of time.

Fifty seconds to impact.

There was one option left—an Emergency Blow, filling the water around the submarine with a massive burst of air. The air pockets would distort the torpedo's sonar pings, blinding the torpedo momentarily while *Texas* ascended. Hopefully, the torpedo would pass under the submarine.

Forty seconds to impact.

But if *Texas* blew, they'd be a sitting duck. They'd end up on the surface, vulnerable and noisy, unable to submerge while it waited for its Main Ballast Tanks to vent the air trapping the submarine on the surface.

Thirty seconds to impact.

But if they didn't Emergency Blow, the torpedo would blast a hole in the submarine's pressure hull.

Latham made his decision.

"Emergency Blow all Main Ballast Tanks! Full rise on the Stern and Bow Planes!"

The Co-Pilot reached up and tapped the Emergency Blow icon on his screen, opening the valves to the ship's high-pressure air banks. Thousands of cubic feet of high-pressure air spewed into the submarine's Main Ballast Tanks, pushing the water down and out through the flood grates in the bottom of the submarine.

Twenty seconds to impact.

Latham held on to the OOD's console as the ship pitched upward thirty degrees. As *Texas* ascended, the air finished pushing the water out of the ballast tanks, then spilled out through the grates in the ship's keel, and *Texas* left massive air pockets in its wake as it sped toward the ocean surface. The torpedo chasing them was temporarily blinded, but would it pass underneath them without regaining contact? The rumble of the air spewing from the flood grates began to ease.

Ten seconds to impact.

Latham counted down the final seconds in his mind, gripping the edge of the OOD's workstation as he reached zero.

But nothing happened.

Had the torpedo passed by, or had he calculated the time to impact incorrectly?

He waited a few more seconds, in case his mental calculations had been off. But then Sonar's report clarified what had just occurred.

"Third torpedo bears two-six-zero."

The torpedo had passed underneath *Texas* and was now on the other side, speeding away.

"Conn, Sonar. Torpedo is opening range."

Texas pitched forward, returning to an even keel. Latham checked the submarine's depth; they had reached the surface. Now that they had arrived there, it was time to leave. They were trapped on the surface by the air in the Main Ballast Tanks, and modern submarines traveled more slowly surfaced than submerged due to their hull design. Plus, their propeller cavitated on the surface, a beacon of sound for the Chinese submarines pursuing them. They needed to submerge again before they got another torpedo rammed down their throat. But before he gave the order to vent the Main Ballast Tanks, another report from Sonar echoed across Control.

"Conn, Sonar. Up Doppler on third torpedo! Torpedo is turning toward us!"

Latham cursed under his breath. Their adversary must still have wire guidance to their torpedo, inserting a torpedo steer back toward *Texas*. Still, the course of action was the same. He called out, "Vent all Main Ballast Tanks!"

The Co-Pilot tapped his display on the Ship Control Panel again, opening the vents to the submarine's Main Ballast Tanks. Latham knew that geysers of water spray were jetting into the air from the bow and stern of the submarine as the tanks vented, allowing water to flow back up through the flood grates in the keel. But would they submerge in time?

With the third torpedo racing back toward them, he needed to move *Texas* out of the torpedo's path before it acquired them again. He examined the sonar display on the Conn, selecting the optimal course.

"Pilot, hard left rudder, steady course three-five-zero."

Sonar's next report cut off the Pilot's acknowledgment.

"Third torpedo is homing, range two hundred yards!"

Twenty seconds.

Latham considered launching another torpedo decoy. But *Texas* was wallowing on the surface, unable to put much distance between the submarine and the decoy. The torpedo would lock on to the much larger, more realistic target.

Ten seconds.

It was hopeless. There was no way they could evade the incoming torpedo. Latham grappled with his grim conclusion.

USS *Texas* was going to the bottom.

However, there was one essential task they had to complete before then. Latham shouted out, countermanding his earlier order. "Co-Pilot, shut all Main Ballast Tank vents! Raise the Multifunction Mast!"

The Co-Pilot looked up in surprise but quickly complied, shutting the vents. Another tap and he raised the communication antenna. Latham didn't get an opportunity to explain, because *Texas* jolted as a deafening sound rumbled through Control. The Flooding alarm began wailing throughout the ship, followed by a report on the 4-MC emergency circuit.

"Flooding in Operations Compartment! Flooding in Operations Lower Level!"

Latham shouted into the open microphone. "Radio, this is the Captain. Patch me to CTF 74! Whatever lineup is fastest!"

As he waited for Radio to complete the lineup to his operational commander, Latham hoped he had bought enough time. He'd shut the vents, trapping the air inside the Main Ballast Tanks to add buoyancy to the submarine, counteracting the flooding. *Texas* was still going to the bottom, but it would take a few seconds longer, hopefully long enough for him to inform his superiors that China had discovered a way to dud his torpedoes.

The red light on the handset by the side of the OOD's workstation lit up, followed by Radio's report over the 27-MC. "Captain, Radio. Patch complete."

Latham grabbed the handset, then, over the roar of the inrushing water, which had filled the bottom of the Operations Compartment and was now spewing into Control, he yelled into the mouthpiece, hoping the Radioman on the other end understood him.

39

NINGBO, CHINA

Standing at the back of the East Sea Fleet command center, Admiral Tsou studied the pair of ten-by-fifteen-foot flat screens at the front of the room, surveying the status of China's war with the United States. The screen on the right displayed a map of the earth, overlaid with American military and GPS satellites in their orbits around the planet. The screen on the left displayed a map of the Taiwan Strait. Blue icons depicted U.S. surface ships, which had entered the two-hundred-mile-wide waterway, while red icons along China's coast marked the positions of forty *Hong Niao* surface-to-surface missile batteries, which had remained concealed thus far in the war.

The positions of China's and America's submarines were not marked, as their locations were unknown. But earlier today, China's submarines had surged to sea, and Tsou eagerly awaited the results of their engagements with their American counterparts.

Captain Cheng Bo, in charge of the East Sea Fleet Command Center, approached, stopping in front of Tsou. "I have good news, Admiral. The captain of *Jiaolong* has reported in. The Yuan sonar pulse is working as expected, shutting down the American torpedoes. *Jiaolong* sank a Virginia class submarine, and we have detected six additional underwater explosions. I expect the results of those engagements to be favorable as well."

Tsou did not respond, waiting for one additional report.

Cheng continued, "General Cao has also notified the command center. All Fourth Department cyber warfare units are ready, awaiting your command."

Admiral Tsou nodded this time, then replied, "Bring all missile batteries on-line and order the Fourth Department to commence operations."

Captain Cheng acknowledged, then headed toward the Command Center supervisor, seated at his workstation behind six rows of targeting consoles. After a short discussion, the supervisor typed orders into his computer. At the front of the command center, red flashing Chinese symbols appeared on the left screen, directing all console operators to order the *Hong Niao* batteries on-line and assign contacts to their launchers. Tsou watched as the red icons along China's coast switched to green.

Tsou's attention turned to the right screen, displaying the American military and GPS satellites in orbit. A moment later, the icons turned from green to red as the Fourth Department cyber warfare units initiated the first phase of their attack.

China's preparations over the years had come down to this moment.

40

FUJIAN PROVINCE, CHINA

Along the shore of the East China Sea, in a dark room deep inside sloping cliffs, Captain Zhou Pengfei stood tensely behind one of the eight consoles in the control room, his face illuminated by blue icons moving south through the Taiwan Strait. As Zhou studied the display, his thoughts drifted back a few days, to the unexpected visit by his country's president. That Xiang Chenglei had visited three times meant his missiles would play a crucial role in the battle. But none had been fired so far. However, he had received orders a few minutes ago. All forty batteries were to open fire precisely at noon. He checked the clock on the nearest console, its red numbers contrasting with the blue icons on the monitor below.

Two minutes to go.

Zhou stepped next to his Targeting Officer, reviewing the missile assignments. Their thirty-two missiles had been assigned to the lead American carrier strike group heading south. Five quad-launchers would target the carrier, with the remaining dozen missiles directed against the cruiser, destroyer, and frigate escorts. One missile was enough to cripple an escort, but an aircraft carrier was another matter. It would take several direct hits to seriously harm one, and a few torpedoes to finish it off. However, with the aircraft carrier's escorts destroyed and fires raging inside the carrier, it would make it easier for their submarines to move in for the kill.

One minute remaining.

Captain Zhou reached up, pressing a button beneath the display. Turning toward a second monitor, Zhou watched the portal at the front of the missile battery casement retract slowly upward, providing a flight path for the missiles. A wide, yellow shaft of light streamed into the dark launch chamber, reflecting off the missiles' white skin. Zhou glanced at the electronic clock above the display, counting down the seconds. When the clock reached noon, he gave the order to his men.

"Fire!"

41

USS *NIMITZ*

The General Alarm was sounding throughout the carrier as Captain Alex Harrow slid down the ladder to 3rd Deck. *Nimitz* was fifty miles into the Taiwan Strait when things took a turn for the worse. At five minutes before noon, the Navigator reported all satellites had gone down—GPS, tactical links, even their communications satellites were unresponsive—leaving only line-of-sight voice, which was cumbersome at best. Moments later, the first barrage of missiles appeared on the horizon, slamming into the carrier's escorts.

Harrow decided to swing by CDC before heading to the Bridge. He stepped into the noisy Combat Direction Center, locating the Operations Officer, Captain Sue Laybourn, huddled over the Tactical Action Officer's shoulder. Laybourn looked up as Harrow stopped next to her, updating the ship's Captain. "The first round of cruise missiles was targeted at our escorts. The *Lake Erie* and *Shiloh* have been hit, along with four destroyers and one frigate."

Captain Helen Corcoran exited Air Ops at the back of CDC, joining Harrow as the three Captains examined the Video Wall on the aft bulkhead, the left eight-by-ten-foot monitor displaying a video feed of their escorts to the west. Black smoke spiraled upward from seven ships; half of their escorts had been hit. As Harrow wondered how badly they were damaged, Captain Laybourn filled in the missing details.

"Our cruiser and destroyer Aegis Warfare Systems are completely off-line. They went down just before noon, when we lost our satellites. They're trying everything, but their systems won't respond. It seems China fooled us into thinking we had a solution to their malware in our Aegis Warfare System, saving their real assault for now."

"What does this mean for the strike group?" Harrow asked.

"Our escorts still have their close-in weapon systems," Laybourn replied. "But they're not very effective against these Chinese missiles. They're a new variant we haven't seen before. They travel at Mach speed and hug the ocean's surface. They also make last-second evasive maneuvers, making it difficult for our CIWS systems to lock on to, resulting in a seventy-five percent miss rate."

As Harrow digested the grim news, red icons began populating the right display on the Video Wall, annotating another wave of incoming missiles. Twenty-eight missiles were targeted at the seven undamaged escorts, four per ship. Harrow watched tensely as each ship was able to shoot down only one of the four incoming missiles. Harrow felt helpless as the twenty-one surviving missiles slammed into his seven remaining escorts.

Black-fringed orange fireballs billowed up from the stricken ships, and Harrow wondered how they could remain in operation. But his concern was overshadowed by another wave of red icons appearing on the display. It didn't take long to determine that twenty missiles were headed toward *Nimitz*. With the carrier's escorts unable to defend *Nimitz*, that task fell to Captain Laybourn. Harrow looked on as Laybourn ordered *Weapons Free* and put the ship's missile and CIWS systems in auto.

With both sets of missiles traveling near the speed of sound, it took only a few seconds for the scenario to play out. Five of the carrier's ESSM and Rolling Airframe missiles hit their targets, and the remaining fifteen Chinese missiles continued onward. The carrier's CIWS Gatling guns activated as the missiles approached, churning out 4,500 rounds per minute. But the missiles began evasive maneuvers as they approached the carrier, veering left and right at unpredictable intervals, and only two of the fifteen missiles were destroyed by the carrier's last-ditch self-defense system.

Seconds later, the thirteen remaining missiles slammed into *Nimitz*. Explosions rumbled through CDC, and thirteen sections of the Damage Control Status Board illuminated red. All thirteen missiles had impacted the starboard side of the carrier, below the Flight Deck. Two missiles penetrated the Hangar Deck, and secondary explosions rippled through the ship as ordnance staged for reloading aircraft detonated. *Nimitz* had well-trained Damage Control Parties, and Harrow knew they were responding quickly. But thirteen simultaneous fires, compounded with secondary explosions, would strain his crew.

Harrow glanced at the monitors, displaying black smoke rising from every surface ship in his carrier strike group. They could not continue their mission, launching sorties against targets in China and Taiwan. They'd be lucky to exit the Strait alive. His job now was to recover his aircraft and retreat to the far side of Taiwan, where they could regroup and lick their wounds.

Harrow picked up the microphone. "Bridge, Captain. Reverse course and exit the Strait at ahead flank." He turned to Captain Corcoran. "Recover the air wing. I don't know how much longer we'll be able to conduct flight ops." He followed up with an order to Captain Laybourn. "Direct all escorts via line-of-sight comms to reverse course and exit the Strait at maximum speed."

Corcoran and Laybourn acknowledged Harrow's orders as a bright flash lit up the Video Wall. USS *Lake Erie* had disintegrated in a massive explosion. The fires must have reached her magazine. A somber quiet descended upon CDC as Harrow and his crew reflected on the loss of the cruiser and the men and women aboard.

Harrow returned to the Bridge as *Nimitz* sped north, black smoke trailing behind the carrier. Only six of the thirteen surviving escorts had managed to keep up, black smoke likewise rising from their superstructures. As *Nimitz* continued north at ahead flank speed, a gut-wrenching sight greeted Harrow's eyes. The scattered remnants of the *Lincoln* Carrier Strike Group were adrift, eleven of the carrier's fourteen escorts ablaze, with three oil slicks on fire marking where the three missing warships had sunk beneath the ocean waves.

Thick, black smoke was pouring from every opening of USS *Lincoln*, and she was dead in the water. There were dozens of black puncture wounds in the side of the aircraft carrier where she had been struck by missiles, and the carrier's Island superstructure was completely destroyed, reduced to a mangled heap of blackened, twisted metal. *Lincoln* was also listing twenty degrees to starboard. She'd been torpedoed as well. *Lincoln* would not survive. Without propulsion, it was only a matter of time before she was finished off.

Harrow couldn't pull his eyes from the burning aircraft carrier. This wasn't supposed to happen. The United States Navy was the most powerful navy in the world. Yes, a few ships would be lost in an all-out confrontation with

China or Russia, but the United States would easily prevail. At least that's what the war games had proven. Disbelief washed over Harrow.

How had they been so wrong?

The aircraft carrier's Officer of the Deck, Lieutenant Commander Michael Beresford, stopped beside Harrow, staring at their sister ship. Harrow's thoughts turned to the status of their aircraft when Beresford spoke. "*Lincoln*'s air wing has been directed to land on *Nimitz*."

Harrow nodded. It looked like Captain Helen Corcoran had picked up yet a third air wing. It was going to be a crowded ship. Luckily, the fires on the Hangar Deck had been extinguished, and the elevators between the Hangar and Flight Deck were still operational.

Harrow's thoughts returned to *Lincoln*, listing even farther to starboard now. *Lincoln* had been torpedoed, so Chinese submarines were out there, and Harrow struggled to understand where they had come from. Both strike groups had been traveling at ahead full, so whatever submarine had torpedoed the *Lincoln* couldn't have snuck up from behind. It must have slipped through the fast attack screen in front. But Harrow had difficulty believing the Chinese submarines had defeated their American counterparts.

With his thoughts dwelling on the underwater threat, he glanced at the MH-60R anti-submarine warfare helicopters, hovering nearby with their sonars dipped beneath the ocean surface, searching for Chinese submarines. The carrier's fast pace was hindering the MH-60Rs, forcing them to reposition frequently to keep up.

The first indication that *Nimitz* was in jeopardy was when a torpedo suddenly dropped from one of the MH-60Rs hovering eight thousand yards off the starboard bow. Harrow's eyes followed the Lightweight torpedo into the ocean, his eyes drawn to a thin streak of light green water headed toward *Nimitz*. The information coalesced quickly in Harrow's mind. The MH-60R had detected a Chinese submarine and attacked it. But not before the submarine had launched a Heavyweight torpedo toward *Nimitz*.

Lieutenant Commander Beresford also noticed the light green streak of water. He assumed the Conn from the more junior Conning Officer as he bellowed out, "Lieutenant Commander Beresford has the Deck and the Conn! Left full rudder!" The Helm acknowledged and *Nimitz* began twisting to port. After assessing the torpedo's approach angle, Beresford followed up, "Steady course three-three-zero!"

Nimitz steadied up on its new course and Harrow watched as the torpedo traveled in a straight line; it hadn't detected the carrier and would pass behind them. He was about to breathe a sigh of relief when he remembered the Chinese Yu-6 torpedo, when fired in surface mode, was a wake homer. It would detect the carrier's white, frothy wake, then turn back and cross it again and again, weaving its way up the carrier's trail.

There was no point in launching torpedo decoys. As a wake homer, the Yu-6 was programmed to ignore acoustic decoys. As the light green trail crossed the carrier's wake, Harrow watched the torpedo turn toward *Nimitz*, beginning its snakelike approach, weaving back and forth across the carrier's wake, slowly gaining on them. Their only hope was to confuse the torpedo by maneuvering the aircraft carrier back across its own wake, forcing the torpedo to decide which way to continue. However, Harrow was no ship-driver; like all aircraft carrier commanding officers, he was a pilot. To evade the incoming torpedo, he would have to rely on the experience of his General Quarters' Officer of the Deck, Lieutenant Commander Beresford.

"Left full rudder!" Beresford called out. The Helm complied and the hundred-thousand-ton carrier tilted to starboard as the pair of twenty-by-thirty-foot rudders dug into the ocean. Beresford kept the rudder on as the carrier circled around. Beresford was conducting an Anderson turn, a complete circle. As the torpedo followed behind them, once *Nimitz* crossed its wake where they began their turn, the torpedo would be forced to choose which wake to follow. Hopefully, it would choose the wrong one.

Nimitz crossed its original wake a minute later, the torpedo not far behind. "Shift your rudder!" Beresford ordered, "Steady course north."

Beresford was steering the carrier off on a thirty-degree tangent to their original course, hoping the torpedo chose the wake heading to the left rather than the right. All eyes on the Bridge turned aft, watching the snaking torpedo reach the two intersecting wakes. Harrow momentarily lost the torpedo's light green trail as the torpedo traveled into the intersection of the wakes, his hope rising each second the torpedo failed to reappear. Finally, a light green trail emerged, snaking along the starboard wake.

The torpedo hadn't been fooled.

By now the torpedo was a thousand yards behind *Nimitz*. Harrow estimated they had less than a minute before it reached the carrier's stern, the last place he wanted to get hit by a torpedo. It would destroy the rudders and propellers, reducing the carrier to a drifting hunk of metal, awaiting the coup de grâce. As the torpedo steadily gained on *Nimitz*, Harrow glanced forward. One of *Lincoln*'s escorts, USS *Bunker Hill*, with black smoke billowing upward from fires raging inside the cruiser, was adrift just off the port bow, five hundred yards ahead.

"Head for *Bunker Hill*!" Harrow shouted to his Officer of the Deck.

Beresford looked ahead, quickly deciphering Harrow's plan. "Helm, come left to course three-five-zero."

The Helm complied, and *Nimitz* steadied up on its new course, headed toward *Bunker Hill*. The Helmsman turned to the ship's Officer of the Deck, looking for a new Helm order.

Beresford replied calmly, "Steady as she goes."

Lieutenant Commander Beresford had maneuvered the carrier perfectly. They would collide with the cruiser in a glancing blow just before the torpedo reached *Nimitz*. As *Nimitz* passed by *Bunker Hill*, the expanding wake would encapsulate the cruiser, and it was possible the torpedo would detonate on *Bunker Hill* instead of the carrier speeding away. Harrow had no idea if it would work. But it was a plan that offered hope.

Hell, it was his *only* plan.

Beresford took station next to the Helm, talking quietly to the nervous Helmsman as he maintained *Nimitz* on the ordered course, speeding toward the cruiser. Returning his attention to the torpedo chasing them, Harrow watched it slowly close on the carrier's stern. The torpedo was now centered in the carrier's wake, only two hundred yards behind. Harrow shifted his gaze from the torpedo chasing them to the cruiser they were about to ram. Counting down the seconds, Harrow braced himself for impact.

A screech of metal tore through the air as the starboard side of the carrier's bow collided with the cruiser. *Nimitz* listed slightly to port as the cruiser scraped down the starboard side of the carrier, sparks flying. *Nimitz* rolled back to even keel as *Bunker Hill* cleared the carrier's stern, and Harrow stared aft at the torpedo chasing them. *Bunker Hill* was now encapsulated within the carrier's wake, and the torpedo veered toward the cruiser, exploding a second later.

A two-hundred-foot-high plume of water jetted into the air, whipsawing *Bunker Hill* like a rubber toy, breaking the cruiser's keel, splitting the ship in half. The two halves of the cruiser started taking on water, the stern and bow tilting upward as *Nimitz* sped away with a new lease on life.

Nimitz's six escorts had fallen far behind by now, struggling to keep up with the speedy aircraft carrier. There wasn't much Harrow could do for his escorts. *Nimitz* would remain at maximum speed. Now that they had successfully evaded the torpedo, he could return to base course and initiate flight operations, retrieving the air wings circling above. Due to losses sustained to date, *Nimitz*'s and *George Washington*'s air wings were about half-strength, with *Lincoln*'s around eighty percent. It was going to be a crowded carrier. They were going to have to pack them in tight on the Hanger and Flight Decks.

Harrow was about to issue orders when the Tactical Action Officer's report blared across the Bridge speakers. "Torpedo in the water, bearing zero-four-zero relative!" Harrow looked up through the Bridge windows.

Forty degrees off the starboard bow, a light green trail had appeared in the water, streaking toward *Nimitz*. Before Beresford could order evasive maneuvers to the west, the TAO reported, "Torpedo in the water, bearing three-zero-zero relative!" Another light green streak appeared just off the port beam.

Two other Chinese submarines had joined the hunt for *Nimitz*, bracketing the carrier.

There was nowhere to turn. Reversing course wasn't an option, with the first submarine following behind. Turning to port or starboard wouldn't work either, with torpedoes closing from both sides. Harrow evaluated the options, eventually deciding to maintain course. Maybe, if *Nimitz* was able to increase speed, the carrier could thread the needle between the two torpedoes. But *Nimitz* was already at ahead flank. Harrow needed more speed, and the only option was increasing reactor power above the authorized limit. Harrow had done it successfully once. Perhaps he could do it again.

Harrow picked up the 23-MC, issuing orders to DC Central. "RO, Captain. Override reactor protection and increase shaft turns to one hundred twenty percent power."

The Reactor Officer acknowledged, and Harrow felt vibrations in the deck as the main engines began straining under the increased steam load. *Nimitz* surged forward as the carrier's four propellers churned the water, and Harrow watched his ship increase speed, first one knot and then another. Stepping close to the forward Bridge window, Harrow studied the trajectory of the incoming torpedoes. Both torpedoes were continuing in a straight line, and just when it looked like there was a chance the torpedoes would pass astern of the carrier, first one, then the other torpedo veered toward *Nimitz*. Both torpedoes had been wire-guided toward the carrier.

A few seconds later, the first torpedo hit *Nimitz*. An explosion on the starboard side of the ship rocked the carrier, and a geyser of water jetted a hundred feet above the ship, falling down upon the Island and Flight Deck like rain. A moment later, a second deafening explosion rocked *Nimitz*, this time on the port side.

The Flooding Alarm sounded, followed by emergency announcements, reporting flooding in both Engine Rooms. He could feel his ship begin to slow, and a glance at the ship's speed displayed on the Voyage Management System confirmed that *Nimitz* was coasting to a halt.

The aircraft carrier's fate was sealed.

Without propulsion, the ship no longer had its most important asset—speed. It would be a sitting duck, waiting to be finished off by however many torpedoes it took. And there would be no place for *Nimitz*'s and *Lincoln*'s air wings to land. There was a bitter taste in Harrow's mouth as he turned to his Officer of the Deck. "Order the air wings to land on one of the carriers to the south."

Lieutenant Commander Beresford stared at Harrow in silence. The blood had already drained from Beresford's face and it seemed to pale even further after Harrow's order. Beresford stuttered as the words tumbled from his mouth. He started over, and Harrow soon realized the reason for his OOD's ashen features.

"Sir, the *Stennis* and *Vinson* have been sunk. CDC reported the loss of both carriers a half-hour ago."

Harrow had been preoccupied, focused on saving his ship and hadn't taken the time to get an update on the other carriers. As he contemplated the fate of the six thousand men and women on each carrier, as well as the air wings that had nowhere to land, the TAO's voice boomed across the MC speakers again.

"Torpedoes in the water!"

Six more torpedo trails had appeared, three approaching from the port side of the ship and three from starboard. As the torpedoes raced toward *Nimitz*, Harrow realized there was nothing more he could do. He dwelt at first on the fate of his crew—the men and women who would not return home. But then his thoughts turned to the carriers they'd lost—*George Washington*, and now *Lincoln*, *Stennis*, and *Vinson*, with *Nimitz* soon joining their fate. Only now did Captain Alex Harrow appreciate the enormity of the Pacific Fleet's defeat.

NANJING, CHINA

THE PIT OF TEN THOUSAND CORPSES

A brisk morning breeze blew across the lower reaches of the Yangtze River, flowing up the eastern slope past Xiang Chenglei as he stood alone at the edge of a moat surrounding the Wall of Victims. To his left and right, rising from granite flagstones surrounding the memorial, bronze statues depicted the suffering: a man carrying dead and maimed relatives away; a dead mother sprawled on the ground, her baby suckling her breast; a family fleeing toward safety. In front of Xiang, one memory rose taller than the rest—a twenty-foot-high statue of a mother mourning, her face turned skyward as she held a dead child in her arms. Xiang dropped his eyes from the mother's face, and as he turned east toward the orange glow on the horizon, it was fitting his next thought was that of the rising sun.

Japan, the Empire of the Rising Sun, was guilty of atrocities difficult to comprehend. In December 1937, Nanjing—the capital of China at the time—fell to the Japanese Imperial Army. In the following six weeks, over 300,000 unarmed men, women, and children were slaughtered by Imperial soldiers; firing squads and beheadings were common. Mass graves were prevalent throughout the city, and beneath Xiang's feet lay the remains of ten thousand corpses. During the Second Sino-Japanese War, which raged from 1937 to 1945, the Japanese Imperial Army slaughtered 23 million ethnic Chinese.

Even more repulsive was that the atrocities weren't simply the result of out-of-control army units. Murder and rape of civilians was endorsed by the Japanese High Command, even sanctioned and encouraged by Japan's supreme leader. Emperor Hirohito's "Three Alls" edict, promulgated in 1942, directed the Japanese Imperial Army to "kill all, burn all, and loot all." After the war, the Japanese people and their emperor refused to acknowledge the magnitude of their cruelty, choosing to minimize what had occurred. Perhaps a sincere apology after the war would have assuaged, to some degree, the resentment harbored by the Chinese people; provide some measure of comfort to mitigate the hate.

Comfort and Hate. As a child, the word *comfort*—even the concept— was forbidden in Xiang's home. His mother loved him, he knew, but she would never comfort him. She wouldn't speak the word or even allow it to be uttered in her presence. It was not until Xiang became a young man that he learned the gut-wrenching reason for his mother's aversion to the word. Although Japanese atrocities during the war knew no bounds, many attractive Chinese women were spared; they had their uses. As the Japanese Army occupied eastern China, Comfort Houses stocked with women of every Asian ethnicity were established to satiate the physical desires of the Imperial solders. One of those young women was Xiang's mother.

Only fifteen years old, Lijuan was raped day and night for months. Serving up to thirty men each day, Xiang's mother came to truly understand the Japanese meaning of the word *comfort*. After a year of sexual slavery, she was discarded in a back alley in Nanjing, gaunt and listless, her body and mind broken. She was one of the lucky ones. Only twenty-five percent of comfort women survived, with the vast majority of those unable to bear children due to the injuries inflicted and venereal diseases contracted.

Japan had never formally apologized for the atrocities committed against the Chinese people, and some government leaders even asserted the Nanjing massacre had never occurred. Halfhearted attempts had been proffered by various government officials, but true *dogenza* had never been performed. That, however, would be rectified, and the emperor of Japan would soon bow before Xiang, his forehead touching the ground at the feet of China's supreme leader.

A movement at the edge of the memorial caught Xiang's attention. Striding across the gray granite slabs, Huan Zhixin approached, flanked by two members of the Cadre Department in their black suits.

Huan stopped next to him. "Everything is ready, General Secretary. Your helicopter awaits."

Xiang's eyes lingered on the bronze statue of the mother holding her dead child. After a long moment, he turned away, joining Huan as they moved toward the waiting aircraft.

The rhythmic beat of the Harbin Z-15's twin engines filled Xiang's ears as the helicopter sped northeast toward the coastal city of Yancheng. Xiang peered through the window as the outskirts of Yancheng appeared through a break in the clouds. A moment later, he caught his first glimpse of the Nanjing Army Group, comprised of the 1st, 13th, and 31st Armies, which would spearhead the assault on Japan. The 130,000 men were assembled in formation on the parade field below, bleeding over into the adjoining grassland. The mass of men in their green camouflage uniforms stretched to the horizon, the red pendants at the head of each unit fluttering in the breeze.

Xiang had traveled the 120 kilometers from Nanjing in silence, collecting his thoughts. The North Sea Fleet, held in reserve up to now, had been augmented with twenty-four Yuan class diesel submarines and what remained of the East and South Sea Fleets. Xiang knew Admiral Tsou had stood before his men yesterday, inspiring them to serve the people. This morning, it would be Xiang's turn to stand before the Army, explaining why he had been forced to make this decision. Explaining why many of them would not return home.

The helicopter landed gently on the black tarmac. An escort was waiting, headed by General Zhang Anguo, who would command the three army groups leading the assault. The stocky General with short-cropped, silver hair saluted as Xiang stepped out of the helicopter. Xiang returned his salute, then extended his hand.

Zhang's grip was firm and strong as he greeted his president. "The men are assembled for your review. Loudspeakers have been placed throughout the formation so every man can hear your words." Xiang nodded his appreciation, walking between Huan and General Zhang toward the platform. Like Xiang, Zhang and Huan were quiet, all three men lost in their own thoughts.

Xiang ascended the ceremonial podium and stopped behind a wooden lectern near the front, while Huan and General Zhang took their seats in a single row at the back. Xiang placed his hands along the lectern's edges, feeling the strength of the purple-brown zitan wood. He hesitated before he began, searching for the strength that had suddenly become elusive. The strength to send even more men to their death.

Japan was a more formidable opponent than Taiwan, but with the United States Pacific Fleet unable to assist, success was inevitable. The price China would pay, however, was unclear; how many of the men standing before him would die on Japan's shores was unknown. He told himself again his actions were justified, that the prosperity of the many required the sacrifice of the few. America had given him no choice.

With the destruction of the Pacific Fleet, the only threat to China's flank was the Japanese Navy. By themselves, Japan could be dealt with. Unfortunately, although the Pacific Fleet had been destroyed, America had two fleets, and its Atlantic Fleet would soon be on its way. Once China's true intent was revealed, Japan and America would undoubtedly join forces. That was something Xiang and Admiral Tsou would not allow. In the process, a long-standing wrong would be rectified.

Xiang lifted his gaze to the mass of men assembled across the country-side, then issued the traditional greeting his troops were expecting.

"Welcome, comrades." His voice boomed from the loudspeakers.

"Greetings, Leader!" The 130,000 men responded in unison, their voices reverberating across the field.

"Comrades, you are working hard!"

"To Serve the People!"

As the echo of the Nanjing Army Group's response faded, Xiang was filled with pride. The men standing before him were no less dedicated to their country than he, willing to sacrifice their lives. But as they prepared to land upon the shores of Japan, Xiang must ensure his men understood the reason for their assault. This was not about revenge. He would not let his men commit the same atrocities their parents and grandparents had endured.

As he began his speech, he told himself again that this was an honorable task. He—as well as the men standing before him—truly Served the People.

43

NINGBO, CHINA

Dawn was beginning to break across the east coast of China as a black sedan headed toward a four-story windowless building in the distance. Admiral Tsou sat in the back of the car along with his aide, neither man speaking. Even though it was morning, Tsou felt weary, having slept only four hours each night since the Chinese offensive began. It was here, eight days ago, that he had briefed his admirals on the plan, sending them to sea with the confidence they would defeat America's Pacific Fleet. They had accomplished the seemingly impossible task, paving the way for the next phase of the campaign.

Tsou's sedan pulled to a stop at the front of the East Sea Fleet headquarters. The two men stepped from the car and entered the building, proceeding to the underground Command Center. Tsou paused after entering the room, examining the dual ten-by-fifteen-foot displays at the front of the Command Center. The map on the left screen had shifted north, displaying China and the Japanese islands. Along China's coast, green icons crowded the eight major ports of the North Sea and East Sea Fleets, the icons annotating the location of China's three army groups that would lead the assault. Further inland, another mass of icons was blinking green, indicating the second wave of three additional army groups had begun their transit to the coast.

Along China's shore across from Japan, more green icons depicted the location of mobile missile launchers that had been moved into position to support the assault. At sea, Chinese surface ships loitered near the northern end of the Taiwan Strait, only five hundred miles from the southernmost Japanese main island, giving no indication they would soon be heading north at ahead flank speed. China's submarines, however, had already begun the transit, and were just now approaching Japanese surface ships at sea, preparing to attack.

The screen on the right displayed the order of battle of the first three army groups, their icons lined up neatly in columns. Over one hundred infantry, armor, artillery, and support units had loaded aboard their amphibious assault ships during the night, their icons toggling from red to green as they completed boarding their transports. Tsou's timing was perfect; the last of the icons turned green.

Admiral Tsou headed to the communications suite at the back of the Command Center, settling into a chair at the head of the conference table in the small, rectangular room. Seated around the table were several admirals, including Admiral Guo Jian, commander of the East Sea Fleet, on Tsou's left, and Admiral Shi Chen, in command of the North Sea Fleet, on Tsou's right. But the most important man was not present—General Zhang Angou's image appeared on the video screen at the front of the conference room, broadcast from the Nanjing Military District headquarters, where he would oversee the amphibious assault on Japan. The General stood stiffly at the other end of the transmission.

Tsou smiled inwardly. Even when Zhang was relaxed, he looked like he was standing at attention. It was always difficult to interpret the general's formal facade. Tsou knew that Zhang, like him, had never been enamored of his assignment. But both men had prepared diligently. Tsou would use China's Navy and Air Force to clear a safe path to Japan and transport Zhang's men and equipment ashore. Zhang would take over from there. It appeared that all army units were ready, but Tsou needed confirmation.

"Good morning, General," Tsou began. "I have indication that all army units are loaded aboard their transports. Is that correct?"

"Yes, Admiral. All three army groups have boarded their assault ships and we are ready to commence operations."

Tsou replied, "I will inform you once all Japanese surface ships have been eliminated and a safe corridor for the transit has been established by our submarines. Good luck, General."

General Zhang nodded, then his image disappeared from the screen.

It was quiet in the conference room as the admirals waited for Tsou to speak. The Fleet Admiral examined the solemn faces of the men seated at the table, then gave the order.

"Begin the assault on Japan."

44

TOKYO, JAPAN

Seated at his desk on the third floor of the Ministry of Defense headquarters, Major Suzuki Koki riffled through the papers in his in-box, searching for the monthly report on enlisted recruiting results. Finally locating it, he placed the manila folder in front of him, pausing to gaze out his window at the grove of camphor trees abutting the south side of the Ministry complex. Through a break in the trees, he could see his favorite coffee shop along the busy Yasukuni Dori Boulevard. He glanced at the empty coffee mug on his desk. Time for a refill.

Only three months ago, he was the Commanding Officer of an infantry company in 34th Regiment, and coffee would have been served upon his arrival at work and refilled at the nod of his head. But now that his tour had ended and he had been reassigned to the Ministry of Defense headquarters, Suzuki was *small fry*—a term he learned working at the American Embassy in Tokyo earlier in his career—barely senior enough to garner an office cube with a view. As he reached for his coffee cup—he'd have to refill it himself this morning—the wail of the city's emergency warning sirens carried through the building.

Suzuki searched his memory, but as far as he knew, no emergency drills were scheduled for today. As people around the office stood in their cubes, staring at each other with puzzled expressions, Suzuki swung toward his computer and pulled up the calendar containing Japan's emergency drill schedule. His memory was correct; there was nothing scheduled. He switched his monitor over to the classified computer system in case it was a real emergency. Messages from the Japanese Self-Defense Force communication center began filling his in-box.

Suzuki skimmed the contents of each message, disbelief spreading across his face. What was occurring was inconceivable—a direct assault on the Japanese mainland. During World War II, America had been forced to abandon its plans to conquer the Japanese islands; the casualty estimates were unacceptably high. President Truman decided instead to drop two atomic bombs on Japan, forcing a swift and relatively painless—at least from the American perspective—end to the war.

But the Japanese military was a shell of its former self. Politicians unwilling to believe war was a real possibility had gutted the Japanese Self-Defense Force over the years. Japan's leadership had abdicated its responsibility to defend their people, depending instead on the improbability of conflict and the might of the United States. As long as the American Pacific Fleet prowled the ocean, China could not threaten Japan. But America's Pacific Fleet had been destroyed.

Japan would have to defend itself without America's assistance, pitting its paltry military against the might of the People's Liberation Army. The Japanese Self-Defense Force Navy consisted of only eight guided missile destroyers, twenty-nine small destroyers, and sixteen submarines of various ages—and the Army could muster only eight combat divisions and six brigades, barely eighty thousand combat troops, spread across the four main islands.

With a few mouse clicks, Suzuki shifted from the classified messages to the tactical display fed from the Command Center in the reinforced bunkers below ground. The Chinese assault was massive and well coordinated: Japanese radar installations and missile batteries had dropped off-line, satellites were down. JSDF warships, both pierside and underway, were being bombarded with missiles skimming across the East China Sea from the Chinese mainland.

China and Japan were at war again.

Suzuki decided there was no further need to review the paperwork in his in-box. He, along with thousands of other augmentees, would leave their desk jobs in the city, reporting to infantry units to reinforce the front lines. There was no hesitation. Suzuki left his computer on as he headed for the stairway, grabbing his uniform hat hanging from the coatrack along the way.

MIDDLE GAME

45

ARLINGTON, VIRGINIA

Night was settling over the nation's capital as a trio of black Suburbans passed over the Arlington Memorial Bridge, crossing the Potomac River into Virginia. In the backseat of the middle SUV, Captain Steve Brackman sat next to the president as their vehicle took the first exit after the bridge, turning south on Jefferson Davis Highway before peeling off toward the Pentagon. In the distance, bright lights lit the Pentagon's River Entrance portico and the stepped terrace extending two hundred feet toward the Potomac River. While the river's waters flowed calmly east toward the Chesapeake Bay, Brackman knew the mood inside the Pentagon was nothing less than frantic.

Two days ago, bad news began streaming into the military's headquarters, growing progressively worse until leadership had been forced to accept the unthinkable. The United States Pacific Fleet had been defeated. But it hadn't simply lost the battle, returning home to fight another day; almost the entire Fleet had been sunk. The military high command was scrambling to understand how that had occurred and to identify their options. They'd been unable to tear themselves away from the Pentagon to brief the president, so the president decided to visit them instead.

The three Suburbans pulled to a stop in front of the Pentagon, and moments later the president and Brackman, accompanied by the usual entourage of Secret Service agents, were striding down Corridor 9 toward the National Military Command Center, relocated to the Pentagon's basement during the last phase of the building's fifteen-year renovation. Upon reaching the entrance, Brackman entered the cipher code, holding the door open for the president of the United States.

The scene inside Command Center was chaotic. The secretary of defense and the Joint Chiefs of Staff were standing around the main conference table, its surface strewn with papers, arguing among themselves, while three other flag officers gathered at end of the table, engaged in an animated discussion. The twenty-by-forty-foot monitor hanging from the far wall was a veritable cemetery map, marking the locations where the Pacific Fleet ships had been sunk, their blue icons blinking against the black background. The conversation in the Command Center ceased when the president entered the room, the admirals and generals turning in his direction.

The president headed toward the conference table, taking his seat without a word. SecDef Nelson Jennings and the nine flag officers followed the president's example, quietly settling into their chairs while Brackman took the twelfth and final spot at the other end of the table, directly across from the president. The president turned to Jennings, seated to his right, and spoke calmly.

"Bring me up to date."

Jennings looked uncomfortably across the table before beginning, his eyes scanning the Joint Chiefs of Staff. The chairman, General Mark Hodson, sat across from Jennings on the president's left, flanked by the four service chiefs—Army, Navy, Air Force, and Marine Corps. On the other side of the table, beside SecDef Jennings, sat the vice chairman and three additional flag officers Brackman recognized as Rear Admiral Michael Walker, head of Naval Special Warfare Command; Major General Carl Krae, head of Cyber Warfare Command; and Rear Admiral Tim Moss, Program Executive Officer (Submarines). Jennings turned toward the president, answering his question.

"As you're aware, Mr. President, the Pacific Fleet has been virtually destroyed and China now controls the entire island of Taiwan. Unfortunately, China has their sights set not only on Taiwan, but on Japan as well. They've landed three army groups—over one hundred thousand men—on Japan's four main islands, with another three army groups moving toward China's coast. To prevent us from assisting Japan, China has also attacked every American military facility in the region with DF-21 missiles, including all of our air bases. The largest combat wing in the Air Force, located at Kadena Air Base, is completely out of action. Every runway has been destroyed, as well as seventy-five percent of the wing's tactical aircraft. The situation is the same on every air base—the runways are too damaged to use.

"We can replace the aircraft, but without an air base in the region to operate from, China has taken Air Force tactical air support out of the mix. The only way we can provide persistent airpower is with our carriers, and they've addressed that issue as well. We've lost four more carriers, leaving no operational carrier in the Pacific.

"It appears China is neutralizing all threats along its coast, creating an almost impenetrable defense along the inner island chain. Without the Pacific Fleet to penetrate that barrier, China will have secured its flank."

"Secured its flank for what?" the president asked.

"Our best guess is this is a prelude to a push south, toward resources vital to their economy."

"So this is what it's all about."

Jennings nodded. "Yes, sir. Taiwan was just a feint, drawing the Pacific Fleet into the Strait where it could be destroyed."

The president replied curtly, "What do we have left? How can we help Japan?"

Jennings glanced at Admiral Grant Healey, Chief of Naval Operations. "Not much remains of the Pacific Fleet," Admiral Healey began. "Four Pacific carriers, plus the Atlantic carrier *Lincoln* and most of their surface escorts, have been sunk. Additionally, China has infected our MK 48 torpedoes with malware, which shuts down the torpedo whenever a Chinese submarine emits a sonar pulse at a specific frequency. As a result, we've lost every fast attack submarine in the Pacific. Only our SSGNs—*Michigan* and *Ohio*—have survived, along with the two MEFs aboard their amphibious ships. We've assigned every P-3 we have to an anti-submarine barrier between China and the amphibs to protect them, and so far China seems content to keep their submarines close to shore. But without the Pacific Fleet to ensure safe passage to Japan, our two MEFs are useless, stranded at sea. As far as our strategic forces go, our ballistic missile submarine fleet remains intact, and every SSBN has sortied to sea, ready to launch at a moment's notice."

There was silence as the president and his military advisors digested Admiral Healey's last statement. Brackman hoped everyone considered this a conventional war only—the United States would not resort to the use of nuclear weapons unless they were used against them first.

The president seemed to share Brackman's position, turning the conversation back to conventional forces. "What about reinforcements? Can we send the Atlantic Fleet into the Pacific?"

"We can, Mr. President," Healey answered. "But it will take much longer than normal. The Miraflores Locks in the Panama Canal have been destroyed and three oil tankers were sunk in the Suez Canal. This means Atlantic Fleet ships will have to travel around the bottom of Africa or South America. The nuclear-powered carriers can make it in three weeks, but they'll be slowed down by the conventional-powered ships. Taking into account the speed of our refueling tankers, we're talking a month before the Atlantic Fleet carrier strike groups reach Japan. By all accounts, that will be too late."

"Additionally," General Hodson added, "China has developed a way to jam every U.S. military satellite. GPS, recon, and communication satellites are down. The only comms we have with the Fleet right now is via the X37B Orbital Test Vehicle—a small drone version of the space shuttle, outfitted with sensor and communication packages. We have two X37s. One is already in orbit and we'll be sending the second one up as quickly as possible, which will give us limited message capability. Without our satellites, Pacific Command is paralyzed. What little we could glean of the situation has come from weather satellites, their optics refocused on the Western Pacific."

General Hodson sorted through the papers on the conference table, locating a stack of black-and-white photographs, which he spread across the table for the president to review. Of the fifty-six surface ships that entered the Strait, only a dozen remained afloat, each one on fire, black smoke angling upward as the winds blew westward. The four carriers that had entered the Taiwan Strait were missing; they were on the bottom of the Pacific Ocean.

"What about Air Force bombers," the president asked, "operating from Guam?"

General Mel Garrison, the Air Force chief of staff, replied, "Long-range bombers remain a viable asset. However, due to the long flight times, we're unable to maintain a persistent presence. For the scenario we're talking about, we need constant tactical air support. That means Air Force fighters operating from bases in the region, or carriers off the coast. We have neither."

A somber silence enveloped the Command Center as the General's words sank in. As Brackman surveyed the officers seated around the table, he sensed something he had never felt before. The United States military had always been confident, convinced they would prevail in any conflict. Tonight, there was desperation in their eyes as they attempted to come to terms with the

United States' defeat. Yet at the same time, he sensed a grim determination. A determination shared by their commander-in-chief. His expression hardened as he spoke.

"You're not giving me any solutions, gentlemen. I want options!" The president slammed his fist on the table, punctuating his statement.

There was a long silence before a general on SecDef Jennings's side of the table spoke. "Two can play this game, Mr. President."

The president turned toward Major General Carl Krae, head of Cyber Warfare Command, who followed up. "China knew they couldn't defeat us in a fair fight, so they cheated."

"How's that?" the president asked.

"Cyber warfare," General Krae replied. "They figured out how to jam our satellites and infect our weapon systems with malware. But two can play this game."

"Explain, General."

General Krae turned to the two-star Admiral seated beside him. The Admiral introduced himself first. "Rear Admiral Tim Moss, Mr. President. With the data on the flash drive Miss O'Connor obtained, we know how to revise our torpedo algorithms to make them immune to the Chinese sonar pulse. Even better, we can add an algorithm that will make our torpedoes home on the sonar pulse, virtually guaranteeing a hit."

"That's well and good, Admiral," the president replied, "but we don't have any fast attacks left in the Pacific. And with both canals unusable, no way to get the Atlantic Fleet submarines there in time. So how does that help us?"

A smile flickered across Admiral Moss's lips. The unexpected glimmer of confidence caught Brackman's attention, and he glanced first at the president, then back to Moss as the Admiral continued. "Our submarines don't have to head south, under Africa or South America, to reach the Pacific. They can travel over the top of the world, under the polar ice cap, cutting the transit time to Japan to twelve days. By the time they exit from beneath the ice cap, we'll have a fix for our torpedo software they can download and install into their torpedoes."

The president absorbed the Admiral's words, identifying its major flaw. "Our satellites are down, so how are our submarines going to download the new software?"

Moss turned to the two-star Admiral beside him. "Rear Admiral Michael Walker, head of Naval Special Warfare Command, will explain."

"We bring the satellites back up," Admiral Walker offered.

The president raised an eyebrow. "And how do we do that?"

"Like General Krae mentioned, two can play this game. It won't be easy, but pending your approval, we'll send a SEAL team from USS *Michigan* into China to inject a virus—developed by General Krae's team—into the PLA's command and control system. The virus will disrupt the jamming of our satellites and take down every Chinese satellite in the process, as well as knock every new-generation Chinese missile battery off-line. With our satellites up, we'll be able to download the new torpedo software to our submarines and bring our GPS-guided weapons back into play, all while we cripple Chinese command and control and their missile batteries."

"How do we get the virus to the *Michigan* with our satellites down?" the president asked.

"We can transmit the software via one of the X37s. The virus will be a relatively small program, which the X37 communication suite can transmit while it passes overhead. For the large torpedo software download, however, we'll need our normal communication satellites, which have a geostationary orbit and a larger data rate."

"The plan sounds doable, but what's the point? We can't help Japan defeat China with just submarines. We don't have any carrier strike groups left in the Pacific, and the Atlantic Fleet carriers will take too long to get there."

Admiral Healey, Chief of Naval Operations, answered. "There is one additional Pacific Fleet carrier, *Ronald Reagan*, in overhaul at Pearl Harbor. If we can get her underway, we'll land an augmented Atlantic Fleet carrier air wing aboard."

General Ely Williams, Commandant of the Marine Corps, joined in. "And then we can take advantage of the one flaw in China's battle plan. They struck our Pacific Fleet too early, before either MEF landed on Taiwan. Had they waited, both Marine Corps divisions would have been stranded on the island. However, both MEFs are at sea and available. Additionally, TWO MEF from the East Coast was deployed to the Mediterranean, and their ships made it through the Suez Canal before it was sabotaged. That gives us three MEFs in the Pacific, and if we can clear a path to Japan, we can land three divisions of Marines to assist, as well as bring three Marine air wings into play."

"There's one weakness in our plan," Admiral Healey added. "It's crucial that the three MEFs be protected from air attack while they off-load their Marines and equipment. China has destroyed or has control of every air base in the region, meaning our air support has to come from ships. *Reagan* will be augmented with two additional Super Hornet squadrons, but that gives them only seventy-two aircraft to defend against the entire PLA Air Force, which had over one thousand fourth-generation fighters at the beginning of the conflict. We don't know how many aircraft they've lost in the battle for Taiwan and Japan, but it's likely they can throw several hundred aircraft at the *Reagan* Task Force.

"In that case, they'll overwhelm the outer layer of our air defense, leaving it to *Reagan*'s surface ship escorts, consisting of only six cruisers and destroyers. If China takes out *Reagan*'s escorts, or they simply run out of anti-air missiles, we could lose not only *Reagan*, but every amphibious ship in the Navy, not to mention stranding or sinking three Marine divisions and their equipment."

As the president absorbed Admiral Healey's grim assessment, General Williams picked up the conversation. "We have a partial solution, Mr. President. Our Marine air wings normally include Harrier jets for ground support. However, we can replace two squadrons with Joint Strike Fighters. The Marine Corps has the Bravo version of the aircraft, which has a short takeoff and vertical landing capability and can deploy from our amphibious assault ships. We can configure the Joint Strike Fighters for tactical air support instead of ground support, augmenting *Reagan*'s air wing. The fly in the ointment with this plan is that the Joint Strike Fighter hasn't been authorized for combat yet—but with your approval, we can deploy them."

"The same goes for the Navy," Admiral Healey joined in. "We also have two squadrons of Joint Strike Fighters, which we can land aboard *Reagan* in place of two Super Hornet squadrons. That would give us almost a hundred fighters, of which half would be the new Joint Strike Fighter, which is far superior to anything in China's arsenal."

There was silence in the Situation Room before SecDef Jennings summed everything up. "There's a lot that has to go right with these plans, Mr. President, but we believe it's doable."

After a long moment, the president announced his decision. "Proceed with your plans, gentlemen. Send the Atlantic Fleet carrier strike groups into the

Pacific and the Atlantic submarines under the ice. Get *Reagan* underway, augmented by Joint Strike Fighters, and insert the SEAL team into China." The president paused, fixing each General and Admiral at the table in succession with a steely glare.

"This time, failure is not an option."

46

PEARL HARBOR, HAWAII

As nightfall retreated across the Pacific Ocean, the Pearl Harbor Naval Shipyard, normally placid at this time of day, was a frenzy of activity. Although the skies were clear, a cyclone of men and machines had converged on a large gray warship moored in Dry Dock One. Heavy cranes lifted ordnance across the wharf onto the ship, while smaller cranes swung pallets of supplies to sailors waiting topside. Along the wharf to the south, in a small building serving as the ship's temporary offices, Captain Charles "CJ" Berger stood at the window, oblivious to the cacophony of sounds around him. He stared at the naval message in his hand in stunned silence.

It was an impossible task. He'd been given seven days to get underway and another twenty-four hours to piece his aircraft carrier together enough to conduct flight operations. Four squadrons of Super Hornets, along with two squadrons of Joint Strike Fighters and a slew of Growlers and Hawkeyes, were scheduled to land aboard his carrier in eight days, where they would be packed inside the Hangar and on the Flight Deck, butts to nuts as if it were a crowded men's locker room. As Berger wondered how he would fit all of the aircraft aboard his carrier, he looked up toward the dry dock, and the collection of gray parts one might call a ship.

USS *Ronald Reagan* was in the middle of a yearlong overhaul, scheduled to replace USS *George Washington* as the Fleet's Japan-based carrier. However, now that *George Washington* had been sunk, it looked like that replacement would occur sooner than planned. Unfortunately, the shipyard had spent three months tearing Berger's ship apart and had just begun the painstaking reassembly with refurbished and replacement systems. There was a modicum of good news; this was a non-refueling overhaul, so both reactors and their engine rooms were still operational. Propulsion would not be a problem.

However, the Flight Deck was in tatters, all four catapults and the arresting wires completely disassembled. It would take a Herculean effort to undock the ship—two weeks minimum—and another month to reassemble the required systems and train his crew to safely conduct flight operations.

There was a knock on the door and Berger acknowledged. Captain Tim Powers, his Executive Officer, arrived with the Shipyard Commander, Captain Debra Driza, and a half-dozen civilians. His XO's face was flustered. Although they hadn't exchanged words after the XO handed the message to Berger this morning, he no doubt shared his Captain's opinion the task was impossible. However, the first words out of Captain Driza's mouth indicated the Shipyard Commander did not share those feelings.

"We'll have you underway in seven days as directed, CJ." The civilians shot uneasy glances in Driza's direction as the Captain continued. "Hull integrity will be restored and we'll flood down the dry dock in seven days. Will you be able to bring at least one reactor and engine room up by then?"

Berger was caught off guard by the Shipyard Commander's optimism. It took a second to digest her question, realizing the onus had been placed upon his crew. "Yes," he answered. "We'll be ready to get underway." Berger still grappled with the impossibility of the shipyard's task, but pushed past it. "What about supplies?"

"As you can see, we've already begun," Driza replied, "but we'll only have enough time to load one month of consumables and sixty percent of your ordnance."

Berger nodded, a frown on his face. "That'll have to do then. Will we be able to top off JP-5?"

"Yes, jet fuel won't be a problem."

"What about my catapults, arresting wires, and elevators?"

"We'll work around the clock until you undock, and we'll have shipyard Tiger Teams aboard to continue reassembling your critical flight systems along the way. You should have at least one arresting wire and elevator in operation by the time the air wing arrives. The Tiger Teams will continue working as you transit the Pacific, and your carrier should be fully operational by the time you reach Japan."

Berger nodded again, not yet sharing the Shipyard Commander's optimism. They needed a minor miracle. He turned to his Executive Officer. "Round up the department heads. We've got some work to do."

47

USS *MICHIGAN*

Inside the submarine's cramped sick bay, measuring only six feet wide by fifteen feet long, Christine O'Connor sat on the cold metal examining table, her legs dangling off the edge as the ship's Medical Officer, Commander Joe Aleo, prepared to inspect her right arm. Christine removed the sling from her shoulder, then unzipped her blue coveralls down to her waist, exposing her white T-shirt. After she pulled her right arm from the coveralls, Commander Aleo peered closely at the bullet's entrance and exit wounds.

As Aleo examined the wounds, Christine's thoughts drifted to the message they had received a few hours earlier. Two days ago, the United States Pacific Fleet had been virtually wiped out. *Michigan's* crew had been in the dark at first—the submarine message broadcast had gone down as the four carrier strike groups swung inside the Taiwan Strait. *Michigan*, along with her sister SSGN, *Ohio*, had been left behind on the east side of the island to protect the amphibious ships from any Chinese submarines that slipped past the fast attacks.

It had been maddening, cut off from communications, unable to determine what was going on, able to discern only that the situation had taken a turn for the worse when the amphibious ships suddenly reversed course, heading away from Taiwan at maximum speed. Unable to obtain further orders, Captain Wilson decided to accompany the Marine Expeditionary Forces east into deep water. As *Michigan* searched the skies for a radio signal, it was only a few hours ago that the submarine had received a lone transmission.

The content of the message spread through the crew like wildfire, and after the shock wore off, the Navy SEALS had gone to work, converging on the Battle Management Center. The Navy SEALS were nothing like what Christine had imagined. Instead of Rambo, they more closely resembled computer geeks. Thus far, they huddled around their laptop computers and consoles in the Battle Management Center, meticulously reviewing mission plans. In her limited interactions with the SEALs, they had been polite and respectful, not the aggressive, testosterone-laden demeanor she expected from the Navy's elite killers.

Commander Aleo released Christine's arm, pushing the sling to the side of the examining table. "You won't need this anymore. The wound has healed nicely and you should have full use of your arm in another week, after your triceps muscle finishes healing. Feel free to use your arm as much as you want, so long as you can tolerate the pain. Take one of the eight-hundred-milligram pills of ibuprofen if the pain gets too bad."

Aleo stepped to the side and Christine hopped off the examining table, flexing her arm again before shrugging back into the top of her coveralls, zipping up the front.

"Thanks, Doc." Christine had learned a lot during her short time aboard *Michigan*, and had picked up some of the unique vocabulary. Whether the submarine crew included a Corpsman or a Medical Diving Officer like Commander Aleo when SEALs were aboard, they were universally referred to as *Doc*.

"No problem, Miss O'Connor. Let me know if you need anything else." Aleo unlatched the door to his infirmary, holding it open for Christine.

Christine stepped out of Doc's office into the starboard side passageway of Missile Compartment Second Level, almost running into someone as she rounded the corner. A quick glance told Christine the Navy SEAL standing in front of her was no computer geek. Lieutenant Jake Harrison had just stepped out of the showers, wearing nothing but a pair of flip-flops and a white towel held loosely around his waist with one hand, a toiletry bag in the other. Damp brown hair clung to his forehead, and Christine couldn't keep herself from surveying his broad shoulders, her eyes involuntarily moving to his muscular chest, then down to his abdomen, where a long, flat expanse of muscles disappeared beneath the white towel. There was no way around it; Jake was still an attractive man.

But Harrison was no youngster. He was the same age as Christine, much older than his rank implied. He had enlisted twenty-four years ago, commissioned an officer after reaching the rank of Chief. If the quiet rumors were true, they had been an eventful twenty-four years. The Navy SEALs aboard

Michigan were tight-lipped about the missions they'd been on, but Christine had gleaned that Harrison had led numerous forays against insurgents in Iraq and Afghanistan.

Christine caught a smile from Harrison in her peripheral vision, and she realized she was still staring at the top of his white towel. She looked up toward his deep blue eyes, the temperature of her cheeks rising. She'd hoped he hadn't noticed her stare or her reddening face. He was undoubtedly used to those kinds of looks from women, even if that woman happened to be the president's national security advisor.

However, Harrison wasn't staring at her face, and Christine's blush turned even warmer when she realized Harrison had taken advantage of the few seconds while her eyes wandered. The blue coveralls she wore fit snugly to her curves, and Harrison wasn't the first man aboard to have his eyes drawn to her breasts, straining inside the confining jumpsuit.

Harrison's eyes met hers, and neither person said a word for a moment, until he broke into a wide grin. "Good afternoon, Chris," he said as he gripped the towel tighter around his waist. "Sorry for the lack of clothes. But I see you're also missing some attire."

Christine didn't understand his comment until she followed his eyes to her right arm. "Oh, my sling. Doc just took a look and said I don't need it anymore." She flexed her arm into a muscle pose, wincing as her triceps burned from the effort. She suddenly felt embarrassed, showing off like a teenage boy on the beach, a strange role reversal.

"That's good to hear," Harrison replied. "Then it won't be long before you'll be working out with us SEALs. I mean, not that you need to work out. You're still in great shape."

Before she could respond, Lieutenant Karl Stewart, *Michigan*'s Weapons Officer, turned the corner behind Christine. "Oh, there you are, Miss, O'Connor. The Captain asked me to remind you about the mission brief in the Battle Management Center at 1500." The Weps' eyes went to Harrison, standing naked aside from the towel wrapped around his waist. "You better get a move on, Jake. You're up in fifteen minutes."

"I'll be there," Harrison replied. "I just wanted to clean up before the brief." He nodded his respect to Christine as he stepped around her and continued on his way.

With Lieutenant Stewart standing beside her, Christine resisted the urge to turn and watch Harrison as he headed down the starboard side passage-way. The muscles rippling down his back would have been a pleasant sight.

Fifteen minutes later, Christine was seated at one of the twelve consoles on the starboard side of the submarine's Battle Management Center, along with Captain Wilson, his Executive Officer, and the submarine's four department heads—the Weps, Eng, Nav, and Suppo. Navy SEALs, led by Commander John McNeil—head of the four platoons of SEALs aboard, occupied the remaining five consoles, with another seven SEALs gathered at the back of the room. At the front of the Battle Management Center, Lieutenant Harrison stood beside one of the two sixty-inch plasma displays hanging from the bulkhead. This time, Harrison was fully clothed, wearing the standard Navy blue camouflage uniform, similar in design to what the Marines wore, as opposed to the solid blue coveralls worn by the submarine crew.

Commander McNeil kicked off the mission brief, beginning with a summary of the information provided in the message received by *Michigan* in the early morning hours. "As you're aware, our response to China's invasion of Taiwan did not go as planned. All five carriers have been sunk, along with most of our surface combatants and every submarine except for *Michigan* and *Ohio*."

McNeil paused momentarily, his thoughts no doubt matching those of every person in the room. The crew of every fast attack submarine in the Pacific Fleet—over three thousand men—were now entombed inside steel coffins resting on the ocean bottom. No one commented during McNeil's temporary pause, and he continued his brief.

"China defeated our Pacific Fleet because they were able to jam our military satellites, knock our Aegis Warfare Systems off-line, and dud our torpedoes. The mission we've been assigned will reverse that advantage. Lieutenant Harrison will brief the details." McNeil turned to Harrison.

"In a nutshell," Harrison began, "our job is to insert a virus into the Chinese command and control network, which will disrupt their jamming of our satellites as well as disable Chinese command and control and every new-generation Chinese missile launcher. To accomplish this, we must inject our virus into the central command and control node—the communications center in China's Great Hall of the People, located in Beijing."

Harrison pressed the remote control in his hand, and the monitor beside him energized, displaying a map of the Western Pacific. "We've got more planning to do, but here's what we've got so far." Harrison zoomed in toward China, stopping when the coastal waters to the west of Tianjin filled the screen. Several miles offshore, a green X blinked on the display.

"First, *Michigan* must reach this location in the Bohai Sea, which puts our SEAL Delivery Vehicles in range of the Chinese coast. From there, we'll launch two SDVs with six SEALs—four in one and two in the second, with the remaining space used to transport the weapons and equipment we need. I'll lead the mission, with the rest of the team comprised of Chief O'Hara, Garretson, Crane, and the girls."

Christine didn't understand who Harrison meant by *the girls*, but it seemed it was a reference to two large, muscular SEALs standing at the back of the group, who fist-bumped each other as Harrison continued. "We'll be met at the insertion point and escorted to a CIA safe house in Beijing, where we'll rest during the day before the hard part begins—entering the Great Hall of the People."

Harrison pressed the remote again, and the display shifted to a satellite view of the Great Hall of the People. "We haven't received any mission Intel, so we'll have to go with what's in our database. The communications center is located on the third floor of the South Wing. That means we'll enter along the south side of the building, breaking through an emergency exit door or through a window. Of course, the doors and windows will be alarmed, so we'll have to move fast once we're inside. Unfortunately, we don't have schematics of the building, so we'll have to sort out a path to the communications center once we're inside.

"Every member of the team will be trained on what type of computer terminal we need and how to upload the virus, since there's no telling how many of us will reach the communications center. I won't lie to you—although I expect at least one of us will reach our objective, it's unlikely any of us will make it back out. We'll have the element of surprise on the way in, but not on the way out."

Harrison paused for a moment, letting his bleak assessment sink in. After his eyes scanned the other five SEALs assigned to the mission, he turned first to Captain Wilson and then to Commander McNeil. "Subject to your questions, sir, this concludes my brief."

Silence settled over the Battle Management Center as Christine digested the assignment—practically a suicide mission. If they could gain access to the Great Hall of the People without being noticed, however, they might be able to slip in and out quietly, returning safely to USS *Michigan*. As she stared down at her hands, locked around her knee, she remembered a crucial detail about her escape from the Great Hall. She released her knee and turned her right hand over, examining her palm. The palm Yang Minsheng had entered into the security system, which gave her the ability to unlock the security doors throughout the building.

Christine raised her hand. "I can get you into the Great Hall of the People."

There was a surprised expression on Harrison's face as he asked, "And how would you do that?"

Christine explained how her palm print had been entered into the security system and how she had opened the security doors as she escaped from the Great Hall of the People. As long as her entry into the security system hadn't been discovered, gaining entrance into the building would be easy compared to forcing their way in. Additionally, she recalled the commands Yang had entered to pull up the schematics of the Great Hall on the security panel, which would allow them to determine the best route to the communications center. However, after explaining how she could help, Harrison brushed her off.

"Thanks for the offer, Miss O'Connor, but I'm afraid that's not an option. This mission is far too dangerous for a civilian, and frankly, your participation would be more of a hindrance than a help."

Christine could feel the heat rising in her cheeks, driven by a confluence of emotions. Her offer of assistance had been dismissed, and she wondered whether it was because Jake cared about her, or because he thought she was a helpless woman. As far as she was concerned, both of those reasons were unacceptable.

"I disagree with you on both points," Christine replied. "Whether this mission is too dangerous for me is my decision, not yours, and as far as being more of a hindrance than help, I doubt that. Whatever difficulties my presence creates will be far outweighed by gaining clandestine access to the Great Hall of the People. I recommend you reassess your position, *Lieutenant*." Christine's eyes bored into him.

Harrison was undeterred. "That's my professional assessment, Miss O'Connor, and you will *not* be a member of this mission unless I am over-ridden." Harrison glanced at Commander McNeil, seated next to Captain Wilson.

After a long moment, McNeil replied. "You have valid points, Miss O'Connor, and your offer of assistance is accepted." He looked toward Harrison. "Plan accordingly."

"Yes, sir," Harrison replied curtly, displeasure on his face as he wrapped up the mission brief. "Everyone is dismissed except O'Hara, Garretson, Martin, and Andrews. Crane, you're out. Your seat has been taken by Miss O'Connor." Harrison cast a scowl in Christine's direction. "Miss O'Connor, I'll brief you separately on what to expect during the mission."

Christine nodded, uncertain whether to be pleased or angry at Harrison's reaction. One thing was certain, however: a private conversation with him was long overdue.

An hour later, Christine was seated alone in the Executive Officer's stateroom, having asked the XO for an opportunity to speak with Lieutenant Harrison privately. She was seated in the XO's chair, one leg crossed over the other, facing the closed door. An extra chair had been dragged into the stateroom, positioned only a few feet away. Not that there was much choice. No matter where she put the chair in the small stateroom, in a few minutes she would be uncomfortably close to a man who had never been far from her thoughts.

Twenty-four years ago, Christine had left Fayetteville and Jake Harrison behind, headed to Penn State on a four-year gymnastics scholarship. Regardless of Harrison's opinion, it had been a difficult choice, leaving the man she loved behind. There would be time for marriage and children, just not then. But after graduating with a degree in Political Science, she'd been swept into a life of Washington politics. She'd get in touch with Jake soon, she kept telling herself, when the time was right. Only by the time she was ready, Jake had chosen another woman. Apparently, eleven years was too long to wait. Christine settled down instead with Dave Hendricks, their marriage ending after a turbulent ten years, his life ending three years later in the kitchen of her town house. But that was not entirely her fault.

There was a knock on the door.

Christine answered. "Come in."

The door opened, revealing Lieutenant Harrison standing in the entrance, his stiff posture accompanied by cold, dark blue eyes. He'd been summoned to the XO's stateroom not by Christine, but by the president's national security advisor, made clear when she instructed the Messenger of the Watch. She was still steamed about how Harrison had treated her during the mission brief, dismissing her ability to contribute.

There was an awkward silence as Harrison stood in the doorway at attention. Finally, he spoke first. "You requested my presence, ma'am." His tone was formal, his face expressionless.

Harrison's demeanor made Christine regret the words she relayed through the Messenger of the Watch. This wasn't how she wanted things to go.

"Please be seated, Jake." She used his first name and put a warm smile on her face.

"I prefer to stand, Miss O'Connor." He kept his eyes focused straight ahead, looking at Christine only when he spoke.

She fought back the desire to put a hard edge into her voice, ordering him to take a seat as directed. Instead, she decided to try again.

"Jake, I apologize for the wording of my request. I don't want to talk to Lieutenant Harrison, the Navy SEAL. I want to talk with Jake Harrison, the man I once dated." Christine said nothing more, waiting for his response.

After a moment, Harrison's eyes drifted toward Christine, and the stiffness in his shoulders softened. "Request permission to close the stateroom door."

"Please do."

Harrison stepped inside the stateroom and closed the door behind him, then grabbed the vacant chair and swung it around backward as he sat in one fluid motion. He folded his arms on the back of the chair and stared into Christine's eyes. He was only an arm's length away, his chair a few inches from Christine's legs.

"What would you like to talk about, Chris?" His demeanor had softened, but his eyes and voice were still hard.

"It's time we cleared the air, Jake."

Harrison nodded subtly. "Me first or you?"

"I'll start." Christine locked her fingers around her knee. "I don't want our personal past to affect our professional present, and I think there might be some of that going on here."

"What makes you say that?"

"You had to be ordered to include me on the mission, when my participation makes perfect sense."

"It does not make perfect sense, Chris. I explained my position during the brief, and it has nothing to do with the fact that we were once engaged."

"We were never engaged!"

Harrison pulled back a bit. "You said yes, and the ring went on your finger. That sounds like an engagement to me."

"I changed my mind and returned the ring the next morning."

"Still," Harrison insisted, "I believe my statement is more accurate than yours."

Christine pursed her lips together a second before replying. "All right, I concede your point. But that has nothing to do with today's discussion."

Harrison blurted, "It has *everything* to do with today's discussion!" He clamped his mouth shut a second too late; the words had already been spoken. He paused a moment before continuing, his eyes searching hers. When he finally spoke, the hard edge was gone from his voice.

"I loved you then, and I still love you today in some capacity. I don't want anything to happen to you, and if you accompany us, you won't make it back. We'll have the element of surprise on our side when we enter the Great Hall of the People, with or without your help. Making it back out is another issue altogether, and odds are none of us will. My professional opinion is that we don't need your assistance, so I see no point in needlessly sacrificing your life."

Christine let Harrison's words sink in, but she kept going back to the one phrase, trying to put it into context.

I still love you . . .

The words had an unexpected effect on her, and only then did she realize she had wanted to hear those words from the moment she laid eyes on him in the Dry Deck Shelter. She struggled to maintain her composure, her mind going in several different directions at the same time. Finally, she decided it was best she get off this track. Now was not the time to let long-buried emotions surface.

"Fair enough," Christine replied. "I respect your opinion, but I don't agree, so I'm going with you. Hopefully this will be the last of that discussion." She paused before continuing. "Now it's your turn. It sounded like there was something you wanted to get off your chest as well."

"All right," he said. "I'll get straight to the point." Only he didn't. He fell silent for a while, searching for the right words. He finally found them.

"I wasn't good enough for you, was I?"

Christine hesitated before replying. *How is it he still doesn't understand?* "You were more than good enough for me, Jake. It's the timing that wasn't good."

"The timing for what? Love? There's a right time and a wrong time to fall in love?"

"We were only eighteen."

"We were old enough."

"I wasn't ready. I had a gymnastics scholarship to college and I spent my afternoons and evenings in the gym. I didn't have time to be a wife or—God forbid—a mother at that age."

"I didn't ask you to become a mother, only a wife."

Christine waved away his words. They had rehashed this issue dozens of times. Neither could persuade the other, and it appeared things hadn't changed. "We've been over this before. I loved you and would have married you if you had waited for me."

"I waited long enough. It looked like you were more interested in being wed to Washington politics than to me. Did I embarrass you? Were you too afraid to introduce a simple corn-fed Midwestern boy to your sophisticated friends? An enlisted man to boot?"

"You could have been an officer—you could have gone to college with me and earned a commission instead of enlisting."

"I *am* an officer, if you haven't noticed. And the path I chose was far more difficult and honorable than simply being knighted an officer because I graduated from college. I *earned* my commission, working my way up the enlisted ranks, and I'm a far better man for it."

"That's not what I meant, Jake. I meant we could have gone to college together—you had the grades, just not the desire. We could've graduated and built a life together."

"And I could've ended up with a bullet in my head."

Jake's words sliced through Christine, leaving behind the image of her ex-husband's body on the kitchen floor of her town house, blood spreading across the stone tiles.

"That's so unfair, Jake." It was Christine's turn to pull back slightly, the memory of her struggle with her ex-husband flooding her body with emotion. "Dave drove a knife almost straight through my neck."

Harrison's eyes moved toward the thin scar on the left side of her neck, barely discernible now. "I'm sorry. It must have been difficult for you." He reached toward her, his fingers caressing the faint, inch-long vertical scar.

The warmth of Harrison's fingers, his gentle touch, sent shivers through Christine's body. She pulled away even farther. There was another awkward silence until he lowered his hand to his side.

"I'm sure you gave Dave a run for his money," Harrison added. "I've never met a woman as strong as you. Or as flexible." He broke into a wide grin.

Christine couldn't help but smile at the memories; the times they'd escaped to the loft in his father's barn, spending hours talking, and . . . She suddenly found herself leaning toward Harrison. She needed to change the subject.

"So, are you married?" She already knew the answer, but she and Harrison had never discussed it.

"Yes," Harrison answered. "It took me a while to find someone like—" He stopped, his eyes probing Christine's, until she mentally finished his sentence.

Like me.

She could feel the heat in her neck rising toward her face, and she searched for a way to divert her thoughts, to hide the feelings surging inside her while she struggled to discern their meaning. *Is it possible I've never gotten over him?*

"Do you have any kids?" she asked.

"I have one daughter. A ten-year-old. She's into gymnastics, like you." Christine smiled as Harrison continued. "Speaking of gymnastics, it looks like you haven't wandered far from the gym." He surveyed her body, his eyes moving slowly up her lean legs and narrow waist, his gaze undressing her along the way. Had any other man ogled her so blatantly, Christine would have slapped him. Instead, she struggled to keep from taking his hand, pressing it against her cheek. Her bed lay just a few feet away, and she fought the urge to lock the door and pull Harrison into her arms, dragging his hard body on top of hers.

There was a knock on the stateroom door, thankfully distracting Christine from her thoughts. "Enter," she said.

The door opened, revealing the XO. "Oh, I didn't realize you two were still talking."

"That's quite all right, sir," Harrison replied as he stood. "I've still got some mission planning to do, now that Miss O'Connor is accompanying us. I better get hot."

Speaking of getting hot, Christine thought as Harrison left the stateroom and Lieutenant Commander Greenwood entered. She hoped neither man noticed how warm her skin felt.

48

USS *RONALD REAGAN*

"Sir, casting off all lines."

"Very well." Captain CJ Berger acknowledged the Officer of the Deck's report as he reviewed the status of his aircraft carrier from Auxiliary Conn on the starboard side of the Island. Night had settled over Oahu, and the deck lights illuminated the large warship floating in Dry Dock One of the Pearl Harbor Naval Shipyard. Along the dry dock wharves and on each side of the ship, personnel were casting off the mooring lines, and inside the ship, the Sea and Anchor Detail was set, the crew ready to get *Reagan* underway. Whether the ship itself was ready was another question altogether.

The last seven days had been a nightmare. After receiving the order to get underway in a week, Berger had met with his department heads, concluding their pre-underway checklists were useless. The ship was still in pieces with many systems inoperable, preventing the completion of pre-underway checks on what was usually considered essential equipment. Berger decided instead to wing it, tossing the checklists into the recycle bin and ordering his department heads to rely on the crew's experience, especially on their seasoned Chief Petty Officers. Tell each division Chief to be ready to get underway in seven days and leave it at that.

One crisis after another had reared its ugly head, each one presenting a seemingly impossible problem to surmount. But his crew and shipyard personnel resolved each issue until only one remained. One that Captain Berger was staring at, midway down the aircraft carrier's starboard side. Both nuclear reactors were up and Electrical Division was in the process of disconnecting shore power. From the look of things, however, the long list of problems plaguing their underway preparations hadn't reached an end. The ship was due to get underway in two minutes and shore power was still connected.

The ship's Chief Engineer entered the Bridge wearing an unpleasant expression. Stopping next to Berger, Commander Andrew Fellows explained. "We're having a problem disconnecting shore power. The pierside relay has failed and the shore power cables are still energized. The shipyard estimates it will take four hours to replace the relay."

Based on the orders hand-delivered to Berger the previous day, getting *Reagan* underway on time was crucial. They had already been delayed twelve hours due to complications, consuming what leeway existed, and they couldn't afford another four-hour delay.

Berger asked his Chief Engineer, "Are all personnel clear of the shore power connections?"

"Yes, sir," Fellows replied.

Returning his gaze aft, Berger noted the dry dock caisson had been removed, providing egress into the channel where four tugs waited, their white masthead lights reflecting off the black water, ready to twist *Reagan* onto its outbound trajectory. Turning to his Officer of the Deck, Berger ordered, "Get the ship underway, Lieutenant."

Fellows blurted out, "Sir! Shore Power is still connected."

"Not for long," Berger replied, failing to keep a grin from creeping across his face. "We won't need shore power anytime soon. Besides, I've got two dozen shipyard Tiger Teams aboard, and I'm sure there are a few electricians who can repair the damage."

Commander Fellows nodded slowly as the Officer of the Deck complied with Berger's order. "Helm, all back, one-third."

Berger felt the subtle vibration in the deck as the aircraft carrier's four propellers began churning the water. Slowly, the hundred-thousand-ton carrier started moving aft, pulling the shore power cables taut as the ship eased out of Dry Dock One. As *Reagan* continued aft, the shore power cables ripped from the ship in a brilliant shower of yellow sparks.

A grin settled on Commander Fellows's face. "Sir, shore power has been disconnected."

Seconds later, the Officer of the Deck reported, "Shifting colors, Sir. The ship is underway."

"Very well, men," Berger replied.

Very well, indeed.

49

BEIJING

In the Great Hall of the People, the early morning sun slanted through tall colonnade windows as Xiang strode down a corridor along the eastern facade. Huan joined him on his right as they traversed the long hallway toward the conference room, where the other seven Politburo members awaited Xiang's arrival. The unscheduled meeting had been arranged barely an hour ago; it was necessary to evaluate the new American threats.

Although China's military offensive was proceeding as planned, a few wrinkles had appeared. The United States was creative in its response, and whether the new American initiatives posed a threat to China's plan was a question Xiang and the rest of the Politburo wanted answered.

Huan pushed the heavy conference doors inward, providing passage for China's president. The other seven members of the Politburo were already seated around the polished ebony conference table. Huan took his seat along the perimeter of the room as Xiang settled into his chair at the head of the table.

At the front of the conference room, Admiral Tsou stood at attention, awaiting acknowledgment from Xiang.

"At ease, Admiral."

Admiral Tsou relaxed somewhat, although most would still have described him as standing at attention.

"Before you begin this morning's brief, Admiral, I commend you on the success of your plan thus far. Your preparations were meticulous and the execution, flawless."

Admiral Tsou nodded in appreciation. "Thank you, Mr. President."

"However," Xiang added, "even the best-laid plans can go awry, and it has come to our attention that America has not conceded defeat. Can you expound on their response and how we plan to counter it?"

Admiral Tsou answered, "The United States is responding in ways both expected and unexpected. I'll begin with the expected. The first phase of our offensive—the invasion of Taipei—produced the desired result. America committed its Pacific Fleet and most of it was destroyed. America still has their Marine Expeditionary Forces, but without the Pacific Fleet to clear a safe passage for them ashore, the MEFs will remain at sea aboard their amphibious ships, unable to assist Japan.

"However, the United States is attempting to rectify that. Satellites have detected the Atlantic Fleet carrier strike groups heading south, presumably around the tip of South America or Africa into the Pacific. We also detected Atlantic Fleet submarines sortieing from their homeports, all headed north during their surface transit to their dive points. We suspect they are headed beneath the polar ice cap and will reach the Pacific in the next few days. We're not sure what their plan is once they reach the Pacific, since their torpedoes can also be disabled.

"Additionally," Admiral Tsou added, "satellite recon has determined that America was able to get their last Pacific Fleet aircraft carrier, *Ronald Reagan*, underway during the middle of a one-year overhaul, and an Atlantic Air Wing has departed the East Coast of the United States.

"However, my assessment is that the Atlantic Fleet carriers and the *Reagan* pose no threat to our plans. We will sink *Reagan* once it comes within range of our *Dong Feng* missiles, and the Atlantic Fleet carrier strike groups will arrive too late. We also have plans to address the Atlantic Fleet submarines making the under-ice transit. Without getting into the details, let me assure you that most of these submarines will never reach Pacific waters, and any that do will meet the same fate as their Pacific Fleet counterparts. We did not expect America to give up after their Pacific Fleet was destroyed, and we have prepared well for their response.

"Now for the unexpected. America is planning to insert a SEAL Team into Beijing from one of their guided missile submarines. We will eliminate this team once they arrive, hopefully after determining their objective. The United States has apparently identified a weakness in our plan, and it would be wise for us to understand and correct this deficiency." Admiral Tsou paused a moment before continuing. "Subject to your questions, this concludes my brief."

There was silence in the room as Xiang's eyes moved across the other seven men seated at the table. One by one, each man nodded their satisfaction. Xiang turned to Admiral Tsou. "Thank you, Admiral. Keep us informed."

50

SHEMYA ISLAND, ALASKA

On the westernmost tip of the United States, where the Alaskan archipel-ago curls north toward the frigid Russian peninsula of Kamchatka, a light snow was falling across an already-white landscape. On the shore of the small, four-by-six-mile island, inside a nondescript two-story building blending into the snowbanks, Tina Dill rubbed her cold hands together as she sat in front of her radar console, monitoring air traffic along the Pacific Northwest. She pulled her thick jacket close around her neck as she glanced at the air-conditioning vent in the ceiling, wondering if it was blowing hot air or cold. It seemed the temperature in the room had dropped ten degrees since she relieved the watch two hours ago.

Tina tried to remain focused, glancing at the other five operators at their consoles. They seemed similarly bored, despite America's predicament. The Pacific Fleet had been virtually wiped out, and now High Command—whoever that was—was worried China would send their Air Force east toward American bases on Guam and Hawaii, or even Alaska. Satellites in orbit would normally have detected China's bombers the moment they took off from their airfields, but China had managed to take the satellites down. However, Tina figured it didn't really matter.

Although the radar installation Tina worked at was a relic of the Cold War, it was up to the task. The COBRA DANE radar system, built in 1977, utilized a powerful phased-array radar, which was now incorporated into America's Ballistic Missile Defense System. Tina found it ironic the facility was built to safeguard the United States from the Soviet Union, given that her supervisor, seated at his desk behind her, was a Russian. Actually, Dimitrious Loupas was a U.S. citizen. After the collapse of the Soviet Union, Dimitri emigrated from Siberia to the United States with his family.

A blip on Tina's radar screen caught her attention. She sat up in her chair, selecting the sector in question, then zoomed in for a better look. A sortie of aircraft had taken off from Anqing Air Base in the Nanjing Military Region of China, headed out over the Pacific Ocean. A frown formed on her face; Anqing was the home of the PLA Air Force's 10th Bomber Division. Tina called for her supervisor over her shoulder.

"Dimitri. I've got multiple bogies departing China's airspace on course of zero-nine-zero. Probable *Xian* H-6 bombers." Tina began assigning CO-BRA DANE trackers to the aircraft.

Dimitri looked up from his computer, and a moment later was standing behind Tina, examining her display. "How many?" he asked.

Tina finished assigning the trackers. "One hundred and twenty." She looked up at Dimitri. "10th Bomber Division has only forty H-6s. They must have ferried 8th Bomber from Guangzhou and the 36th from Lanzhou to Anqing."

"That's every H-6 in their inventory," Dimitri replied.

As Tina and Dimitri studied the radar display, the aircraft began veering to the north.

"That's odd," Tina muttered. "Why would they head north?"

Dimitri peered over Tina's shoulder as the bombers steadied on a northeast course, paralleling the coast of Russia's Kamchatka Peninsula. "Yes, that is odd. I wonder where they're headed. They don't have the legs to reach the continental United States." The red icons continue their trek northeast, and Dimitri followed up. "Maybe they've implemented a refueling capability. Keep an eye on them, and if they go over the top, hand them off to NORAD."

"Will do." Tina's eyes narrowed as she studied the icons marching steadily northeast, wondering what the hell they were up to.

51

ARCTIC OCEAN

First Lieutenant Liang Aiguo examined the navigation display in the cockpit of his *Xian* H-6F bomber. His aircraft was flying over the Arctic ice cap, and there was still no indication of his target. Looking through his cockpit window, Liang could see additional *Xian* bombers strung out in a linear formation, the line of aircraft extending as far as he could see in both directions.

The voice of Liang's Navigator came across the speaker in his flight helmet. "We will reach the release point in five minutes."

Liang acknowledged the report, then returned his attention to the barren landscape. Five minutes ahead, there was nothing. Just ice and snow. He wondered what the purpose of his mission was. He studied his radar display again, then lifted his tinted visor and peered more closely through his cockpit window. All he could see was the flat white ice, interrupted by wandering ridges where the ice floes buckled.

"One minute to release point," the Navigator reported.

Liang lifted a switch on his panel, opening the bomb bay doors, then turned his attention to the ordnance they were about to drop on nothing. His aircraft carried twenty thousand pounds of free-falling bombs. Enough to blast a small city into the Stone Age. A green light illuminated on his panel, indicating the bomb bay doors were open and locked in place.

Liang activated the speaker in his flight helmet. "Bombardier, you have permission to drop."

The H-6's Bombardier acknowledged the order, and when their aircraft reached the release point, he began dropping their ordnance. To Liang's left and right, the entire line of H-6 bombers began releasing their payloads, the bombs falling to earth in a cascading rain of metal.

Liang shook his head. He had no idea why they were dropping their bombs here. But one thing was certain. They were going to blow the ice pack to bits.

52

USS *ANNAPOLIS*

Just below the Arctic ice cap, USS *Annapolis* surged south toward the Bering Strait and the Pacific Ocean, leading the twenty-four Atlantic Fleet submarines making the inter-fleet transit across the top of the world. Standing on the Conn of his Los Angeles class fast attack submarine, Commander Ramsey Hootman leaned against the railing, his eyes fixed on the display of his Sail High-Frequency under-ice sonar. His eyelids were getting heavier, but this was no time to leave Control for an hour or two down. *Annapolis* was approaching the most hazardous portion of her passage under the ice cap and there was no way he could tear himself away now. Had he managed the transit better, he might have been able to nab a few hours of sleep before reaching this point. But the ice pack seemed to be conspiring against him.

Two days earlier, *Annapolis* had slipped under the polar ice pack, proceeding at ahead flank through the deep water portion of the Arctic Ocean. The Commanding Officer's Eyes Only message had instructed him to abandon all caution; time was paramount. As *Annapolis* began the most dangerous leg of its underwater journey—transiting the Alaskan continental shelf toward the Bering Strait passage—Ramsey had maintained a high speed, slowing only to ahead full. But the high speed increased their peril.

The last portion of their voyage beneath the ice cap required transit in water depth less than six hundred feet. Although the bottom was mapped, not every feature was known and water depth could decrease rapidly. Additionally, although the thickness of the ice pack was normally uniform, there were also random ice keels jutting downward, blocking the submarine's path. Ramsey had already been forced to detour twice. That was difficult enough traveling alone, even more perilous with two submarines following closely behind.

Two Virginia class submarines, *New Hampshire* and the *Virginia* herself, were hot on *Annapolis*'s heels. Not far behind them were both of the Atlantic Fleet's SSGNs. Their loadout of 154 Tomahawk missiles each was sorely needed in the Pacific, now that *Ohio* and *Michigan* had launched theirs, and most of the surface ships were lying on the bottom of the Pacific Ocean.

As Ramsey pondered the Navy's decision to risk both of the Atlantic Fleet's SSGNs in the dangerous under-ice transit, his immediate concern was the two Virginia class submarines following closely behind *Annapolis*. The trio were transiting at an uncomfortably high speed, and if *Annapolis* had to slow down unexpectedly, he had to rely on the awareness of *Virginia*'s crew to prevent them from ramming into the back of *Annapolis*, and the same for *New Hampshire*'s crew behind *Virginia*, avoiding a disastrous underwater fender bender.

As if on cue, the Sonar Supervisor's voice came across the 27-MC. "Conn, Sonar. We're picking up some unusual broadband noise ahead."

Ramsey examined the spherical array display on the Conn. The background noise level directly ahead had increased significantly. The Sonar Supervisor followed up, concern in his voice. "Conn, Sonar. The intensity is increasing rapidly. If it continues at this pace, it'll interfere with our under-ice sonar. We won't be able to detect where the ice keels are."

As the Sonar Supervisor finished his report, Ramsey heard the unusual sound: a deep rumbling, audible through the submarine's hull. The watchstanders in Control exchanged questioning glances, and Ramsey's uneasiness grew as the volume increased. He walked over to the sonar shack, opened the door, and stuck his head inside the dark room, illuminated only by the glow from the sonar displays. The Sonar Supervisor was standing behind the three sonar operators on watch, pressing a set of headphones to one ear. The Chief looked up from the monitors as Ramsey spoke.

"Do you have any idea what it is?"

The Sonar Supervisor shook his head. "I've never heard anything like it. It isn't coming from a specific bearing. More like a wide swath, advancing toward us."

Ramsey returned to the Conn, viewing the broadband monitor with mounting concern. The increasing sound level was starting to blank out the forward sector of the spherical array sonar. Ramsey glanced at the monitor to the left. The same thing was happening to the under-ice sonar. In a few minutes *Annapolis* would be blind, unable to ping and detect a return from the ice above, or directly ahead. Ramsey turned toward the Officer of the Deck, stationed on the Conn between the two periscopes, staring at the under-ice sonar with the same concerned expression.

"Slow to ahead two-thirds," Ramsey ordered. "Inform *Virginia* and *New Hampshire* on underwater comms that we're slowing."

The Officer of the Deck complied, relaying the propulsion order to the Helm, and *Annapolis* began to slow as the rumbling continued to increase in intensity. The OOD attempted to contact the two fast attacks as directed, his voice going out on the underwater communication circuit—not much more than a speaker transmitting into the water. Ramsey hoped the two Virginia class submarines heard the report over the rising background noise.

Ramsey studied the sonar screens intently, searching for a clue to the unusual noise. It was broadband only, with no discrete frequencies, but as the sound grew louder, the rumbling was punctuated with loud bangs, which sounded like explosions. The noise was racing toward them, and in another minute, there would be so much noise in the water that their under-ice sonar would no longer be able to pick up its return. *Annapolis* was about to go blind, just like the two fast attacks behind her.

Three blind mice. Three blind mice.

The nursery rhyme rolled around inside Ramsey's head as he tried to understand what was happening. He was hearing explosions—he was certain of it—accompanied by the rumbling reverberations bouncing off the ocean bottom and the ice pack above. But then a new sound reached Ramsey's ears; sharp, ear-splitting cracks. Finally, it dawned on him.

"The ice pack is breaking apart!" Ramsey shouted to no one in particular. Someone was bombing the ice pack, blinding *Annapolis* and every Atlantic Fleet submarine making the under-ice transit. Even worse, as the ice pack broke apart, the jagged ice was shifting, twisting and repositioning, some fragments shifting up while others sheared downward, directly toward *Annapolis*. Although the submarine's steel hull was three inches thick, the ice keels would tear through the submarine's skin like papier-mâché.

Ramsey shouted so everyone in Control could hear him over the deafening noise. "This is the Captain. I have the Conn. Helm, back emergency!"

Annapolis began to slow as the propeller churned the water in reverse. Ramsey worried *Virginia* might ram into the stern, but he didn't have any choice. Until the situation stabilized and *Annapolis* could paint a picture of the underwater world with its under-ice sonar again, it was best not to move.

As Ramsey's submarine coasted to a halt, he called out, "Helm, all stop!"

The intensity of the noise peaked and then began to abate, but as the rumbling explosions swept past *Annapolis*, the sharp cracking sounds intensified. As his crew listened to the dreadful noise with upturned faces, *Annapolis* shuddered and began tilting to starboard, accompanied by a loud screech coming from the starboard side of the ship.

Ramsey held on to the Conn railing as the submarine listed fifteen degrees to starboard, the loud screech sounding like someone raking their fingernails down a chalkboard. An ice keel was shifting downward, impacting the submarine's hull, and Ramsey hoped the hull remained intact. Even though the water depth was less than Crush Depth, if the submarine went down under the ice pack, there'd be no way for the crew to escape.

The screeching sound ended and the submarine began to right itself. But as Ramsey breathed a sigh of relief, the Flooding Alarm activated, followed by a 4-MC emergency report.

"Flooding in the Engine Room. Flooding in Engine Room Upper Level."

There was little Ramsey could do. An Emergency Blow would send the submarine careening up toward the ice pack above, potentially impaling the submarine on another ice keel. If they couldn't stop the flooding and pump the seawater out of the bilges, they'd become a permanent fixture in the under-ice landscape. As Ramsey listened for the follow-up report from the Engine Room, the nursery rhyme began rolling around in his head again.

Three blind mice. Three blind mice.

USS *MICHIGAN*

Four hundred feet below the ocean's surface, as *Michigan* continued her west-ward transit toward China's coast, Christine O'Connor sat across from Cap-tain Murray Wilson at the small fold-down table in his stateroom, his dark brown eyes probing hers in silence. She had asked a straightforward yet dif-ficult question, one that had been hovering on the periphery of her mind from the moment she met Wilson in Control her first day aboard. It was obvious the answer was difficult as well; the submarine captain was search-ing for the right words.

For the last ten days, *Michigan* had been lurking east of Japan, guarding the amphibious ships from Chinese submarines while preparing for the SEAL mission. Twenty-four hours ago they had headed west at ahead two-thirds, stealthily approaching the Nansei island chain curling down from Japan's southwestern island of Kyushu. They would soon pass through the Tokara Strait, where they would likely encounter Chinese submarines protecting the supply lines to Japan from any American submarines that had survived the Pacific Fleet's demise.

Wilson had ordered the crew members not on watch into their bunks. He expected they would get little sleep from the time they entered the Strait until their mission was complete and *Michigan* was safe again in deep water. Christine had taken advantage of the temporary lull in the ship's activity to ask Wilson for a few moments of his time. As the second hand on the clock in Wilson's stateroom ticked toward the twelve o'clock position, Christine realized Wilson had been silent for over a minute.

Finally, Wilson answered. "No, I don't blame you for the predicament I was put in. It was the president's decision to sink the submarine my son was on, and he would have come to the same conclusion even without your rec-ommendation. It was the only option."

"Thank you for your understanding," Christine replied. "I keep telling myself the same thing. Yet it's hard not to feel responsible. For failing to stop the Mossad's launch order against Iran. For failing to devise a better response. For forcing you into an unimaginable position."

"No one forced me to do anything, Christine. Admiral Stanbury asked for my assistance, and I willingly gave it. We couldn't let *Kentucky* launch and annihilate an entire country. When you weigh the lives of seventy mil-lion versus one hundred and sixty, the scale tilts one way. Fortunately, things turned out better than they could have. But enough of that episode in our lives," he added. "What else would you like to know?"

Christine was happy to leave the *Kentucky* incident behind, moving to the next topic on her mind. "Why did you turn down flag rank, and end up in command of *Michigan* instead?"

Wilson leaned back in his chair. "I turned down promotion to Rear Admi-ral because I wanted to end my career at sea, not behind a desk. I told Stanbury what I wanted and he made the arrangements. There are only two submarines in the Pacific Fleet a captain can be assigned to—*Michigan* and *Ohio*, and *Michigan* was due for a change of command. A few strings were pulled, and I got the orders." Wilson smiled for the first time since their discussion began.

Their conversation was interrupted by the Officer of the Deck's voice, em-anating from the 27-MC speaker in Wilson's stateroom. "Captain, Officer of the Deck. Hold a submerged contact, designated Sierra four-five, bearing two-nine-three. Range and classification unknown."

As Wilson retrieved the microphone from its holster next to the speaker, Christine decided they were fortunate indeed to have Wilson in command, the most experienced submarine officer in the Fleet. Wilson spoke into the microphone. "Man Battle Stations Torpedo silently." The Officer of the Deck repeated back the Captain's order as Wilson stood, returning the microphone to its holster. "Let's head to Control."

Christine followed Wilson out of his stateroom and was almost bowled over by the Messenger of the Watch and LAN Technician of the Watch, sliding down the ladder from Control. One was on his way to the Chief's Quarters and officer staterooms, the other headed aft to rouse the crew from their bunks in the Missile Compartment. After the two men passed by, Wilson and Christine ascended the ladder into Control.

Michigan was still in its normal watch rotation, with only one-third of the crew on duty. The Officer of the Deck, Lieutenant Steve Cordero—the most experienced junior officer aboard—stood on the Conn between the two lowered periscopes, his eyes fixed on the sonar display. Wilson stepped onto the Conn, stopping next to Cordero, examining the display as he motioned Christine toward the fold-down chair on the starboard side of the Conn. Christine settled into the chair as she listened to the two men's conversation.

"Sir, the ship is on course two-nine-zero, ahead two-thirds, four hundred feet. Hold six surface contacts, all distant contacts. Sonar is still analyzing Sierra four-five."

Additional personnel began entering Control, energizing dormant consoles and donning sound-powered phone headsets as their displays flickered to life. The Executive Officer and Weapons Officer also arrived, followed by the submarine's Engineering Officer, Lieutenant Commander Kasey Faucher, who relieved Lieutenant Cordero as Officer of the Deck. Cordero manned the last dormant combat control console.

The XO hovered behind the three consoles keeping track of target position, while the Weps hunched over the Fire Control Technician at the Weapon Launch Console. The Weps cast furtive glances in the Captain's direction, and Christine wondered why, finally realizing the reason. If the submerged contact was a Chinese submarine, each torpedo aboard *Michigan* would become a dud as soon as the Chinese submarine transmitted a sonar pulse.

"Conn, Sonar. Sierra four-five is classified Yuan class diesel submarine."

Michigan was defenseless.

That fact was not lost on Wilson as he loudly announced, "This is the Captain. I have the Conn. Lieutenant Commander Faucher retains the Deck." He followed up immediately with, "Helm, ahead one-third," slowing the ship to its lowest bell, reducing the amount of noise put into the water by the submarine's propeller and main engines.

After peering over Lieutenant Cordero's shoulder, studying the combat control console display, Wilson issued another order. "Helm, right full rudder, steady course north."

The Helm twisted his yoke to the right and the submarine turned slowly to starboard, putting Sierra four-five on the port beam in an attempt to drive around it.

"Conn, Sonar. Hold a new contact, designated Sierra four-six, bearing zero-one-five, classified submerged. Analyzing."

It looked like *Michigan* had turned directly toward another Chinese submarine. Wilson ordered his submarine to reverse course. "Helm, continue right, steady course two-zero-zero." If they couldn't go around the first submarine on one side, they'd try the other.

Michigan eventually steadied up on its new course to the south. Wilson stood next to the Engineer on the Conn, studying the sonar display. He was waiting for their towed array sonar to finish snaking back and forth from the turn, straightening out so it could transmit reliable bearings. While they waited, Sonar followed up.

"Conn, Sonar. Sierra four-six is also classified Yuan class submarine."

Wilson acknowledged Sonar's report, and Christine's eyes shifted between Wilson and the XO, wondering if either submarine had detected *Michigan* yet. A torpedo in the water would be a clear indication, but could the crew figure it out some other way?

The XO spoke into his sound-powered phone mouthpiece, acknowledging a report from Sonar, and the three operators manning the submarine's combat control consoles began adjusting the parameters to the contact's solution.

A moment later, the XO announced, "Confirm target zig, Sierra four-five, due to upshift in frequency. Sierra four-five has turned toward own ship."

Wilson called out, "Helm, ahead two-thirds." *Michigan* was speeding back up, attempting to turn the corner around Sierra four-five. But then more bad news came across the 27-MC.

"Conn, Sonar. Hold a new submerged contact, Sierra four-seven, bearing one-eight-zero."

Wilson acknowledged, assessing the position of the third submarine—almost directly ahead—for only a second before issuing another order. "Helm, ahead standard. Left full rudder, steady course one-zero-zero."

With three submarines blocking *Michigan*'s path, there was no hope of slipping through, so Wilson had reversed course, heading out the way they had come in. It looked like they would have to fall back and attempt to penetrate the Chinese submarine barrier at some other point. As Christine wondered whether they would have better luck next time, a powerful sonar ping echoed through the hull.

"Conn, Sonar! Sierra four-five has gone active. Ping-steal range, six thousand yards." Seconds later, two more sonar pings reverberated inside control. "Conn, Sonar! Sierra four-six and four-seven have also gone active. Ping-steal range ten thousand yards each."

Wilson stepped off the Conn toward the combat control consoles on the starboard side of the ship. "Geographic display," he called out. The XO tapped Cordero on the shoulder and seconds later a geographic display appeared on the Lieutenant's console, displaying *Michigan* and the three Chinese submarines. They had *Michigan* bracketed, one behind with the other two on *Michigan*'s beam. As Wilson studied the display, a 27-MC report blared across the speakers.

"Torpedo launch transients, bearing two-eight-five! Correlates to Sierra four-five!"

Wilson responded immediately, "Helm, ahead flank! Launch countermeasure!"

The Helm rang up ahead flank on the Engine Order Telegraph, and Christine knew that back in the Engine Room, the Throttleman was spinning the ahead throttles open as rapidly as possible, pouring steam into the Main Engine turbines. One of the Fire Control Technicians seated at his combat control console pressed a button on his display, ejecting a torpedo decoy into the water. Christine felt tremors in the submarine's deck as the ship's propeller dug into the water, accelerating *Michigan* toward maximum speed.

"Torpedo in the water, bearing two-eight-five!"

Wilson stepped back onto the Conn, unfazed by Sonar's report, alternately studying the sonar and combat displays. The torpedo was chasing *Michigan* from behind, but with a Chinese submarine on each side of the ship, there was nowhere to turn. Unless the torpedo was distracted by *Michigan*'s decoy, it looked like the Trident submarine was headed to the bottom.

A bright white trace burned into the sonar display, but Christine found her eyes glued to the geographic display in front of Lieutenant Cordero. The torpedo chasing them was just now reaching their decoy. She watched intently as the torpedo passed by *Michigan*'s decoy, her heart sinking into her stomach. But then the torpedo turned around and headed back toward the decoy.

It worked. Christine watched as the torpedo swam in circles around the decoy, attempting to destroy the small countermeasure. But just when her spirits began to lift, another report echoed across the 27-MC.

"Torpedo in the water, bearing two-eight-three! Sierra four-five has shot a second torpedo!"

Christine looked up at Captain Wilson, still standing on the Conn, studying the Sonar display. A moment later he announced, "Launch second countermeasure." However, he issued no new orders to the Helm. With a Chinese submarine on either side, *Michigan* was constrained on course, so another torpedo decoy would have to do, along with the submarine's speed. *Michigan* was slow by American submarine standards, but she was nuclear-powered and could easily outrun the three diesel submarines chasing her. Outrunning their torpedoes was another matter.

Every ten seconds, Sonar called out the bearings to each torpedo, with red bearing lines annotated on several of the displays. A minute passed and the Navigator, supervising the various electronic plots, called out, "Second fired torpedo has been vectored around our decoy."

Wilson stepped off the Conn again and stopped by the geographic display, examining the bearing lines to the second torpedo. The torpedo had been steered forty-five degrees to the right, then back to base course chasing *Michigan*, passing to the right of the submarine's decoy. The Chinese torpedo was obviously wire-guided and the Chinese crew well trained. It would be a race to the finish, hinging on whether the torpedo ran out of fuel before it reached *Michigan*. The Trident submarine was already at ahead flank, so Christine figured they had a fighting chance. But as a glimmer of hope appeared, a series of reports echoed across Control.

"Torpedo in the water, bearing one-nine-zero! Correlates to Sierra four-seven!" A few seconds later, another report followed. "Torpedo in the water, bearing zero-one-zero! Correlates to Sierra four-six!"

Two more bright white traces appeared on the sonar monitor on the Conn, one on each side of the display. Every ten seconds, Sonar called out bearings to the three torpedoes chasing them, and not long after, solutions for the three torpedoes appeared on the geographic display on Lieutenant Cordero's console. The first torpedo was chasing them from behind, headed directly toward *Michigan*. However, the two on each side were fired at a lead angle, taking into account *Michigan*'s ahead flank speed, traveling to an intercept point ahead of the Trident submarine. *Michigan* was completely bracketed. They couldn't slow down and had nowhere to turn.

Christine sensed the restrained panic in the Control Room. The low murmur of orders and reports between watchstanders had ceased, the quiet in the Control Room pierced only by Sonar's announcements reporting the bearings to the three torpedoes. One by one, the watchstanders in Control looked toward Wilson, wondering if he would find a solution to their dilemma.

Wilson studied the geographic display on Cordero's console for a moment, his arms folded across his chest. The torpedo behind them had closed to within three thousand yards and would catch up to *Michigan* in four minutes. The torpedoes on each side of the submarine weren't far behind, only five minutes from impact. There was nowhere *Michigan* could go to evade the torpedoes, except up or down. The XO reached the same conclusion.

"Sir," Lieutenant Commander Greenwood called out, "recommend Emergency Blow."

"That won't work," Wilson replied. "We're too big and we won't change depth quickly enough. Even if we do, we'll be a sitting duck on the surface. However . . ." Wilson rubbed the side of his face as he stared at the geographic display, tapping Lieutenant Cordero on the shoulder a second later. "Overlay bottom contour."

Cordero complied, and after several push-button commands, depth contours appeared on the display. Each level of the ocean bottom was displayed in a different color, increasing in brightness from a dark blue to bright yellow, as the water depth decreased. Up ahead, to starboard, was a small patch of bright yellow.

Wilson turned toward the Quartermaster. "Report bottom type."

The Quartermaster replied, "Silt bottom, with intermittent rock formations."

Wilson suddenly ordered, "Helm, right full rudder, steady course one-seven-zero. Dive, make your depth seven-five-zero feet."

The Helm and Dive acknowledged, followed by another report from the Quartermaster. "Sir, charted water depth is eight hundred feet."

"Understood," Wilson replied. Stepping onto the Conn, *Michigan*'s Captain called out loudly, "Attention in Control. I intend to drive *Michigan* toward the bottom, searching for a rock outcropping along the way. If we detect one, we'll bottom the submarine on the opposite side, hoping the torpedoes chasing us lock on to the rock formation instead. Carry on." Turning toward the Quartermaster again, Wilson ordered, "Energize the Fathometer."

The Quartermaster complied, and seconds later the submarine's Fathometer began sending sonar pings down toward the ocean bottom, measuring the water depth beneath the submarine's keel. On the Fathometer display, Christine watched the depth steadily decrease as *Michigan* sped toward the ocean bottom. The Dive called out the submarine's depth change in one-hundred-foot increments, finally reporting, "On ordered depth. Seven-five-zero feet."

The Quartermaster followed up, "Eight fathoms beneath the keel."

The first torpedo was only two minutes behind them. *Michigan* would reach the shallow patch of ocean bottom in about the same time. Wilson's eyes shifted between the display on Cordero's console and the Fathometer readout as the three torpedoes sped toward them.

"Conn, Sonar." The Sonar Supervisor's report echoed across the quiet Control Room. "Torpedo bearing two-seven-zero has increased ping rate. Torpedo is homing!"

Wilson said nothing, his eyes fixed on the Fathometer. Suddenly, water depth began decreasing rapidly, reported by the Quartermaster. "Six fathoms beneath the keel . . . Five fathoms . . . Four fathoms . . ."

They were passing over a rock outcropping. But how high would it rise? Any higher than fifty feet and *Michigan* would slam into the rocks. With the submarine traveling at ahead flank, the rocky bottom would inflict significant, if not fatal, damage.

As the Quartermaster called out, "Zero depth beneath the keel," *Michigan* shuddered, knocking some of the personnel standing in Control off balance. Wilson grabbed on to the Conn railing, his eyes still fixed on the Fathometer. The Dive turned toward the Captain, looking for direction. *Michigan* was barreling along the ocean bottom at ahead flank speed, receiving who-knew-what kind of damage. Meanwhile, the torpedo behind them continued to close.

"Conn, Sonar. One minute to torpedo impact."

Sonar's report was barely audible above the racket as *Michigan* plowed along the ocean bottom, but the loud scraping sounds suddenly ceased.

Wilson immediately called out, "Helm, back emergency! Dive, bottom the submarine! Don't break the bow dome!"

Wilson had just ordered the Dive to perform something they had never trained on or even simulated. He would have to trust the Dive to figure out how to do it without wrecking the submarine, especially its bow-mounted sonar.

The Dive cast a worried glance at the Captain before turning back quickly toward the Ship Control Panel, simultaneously ordering the two planesmen in front of him, "Three down, Full Dive fairwater planes."

Christine felt tremors in *Michigan*'s deck as the ship's massive seven-bladed propeller began spinning in reverse. *Michigan* tilted downward three degrees as it slowed, and seconds later, a shudder traveled through the ship's hull as *Michigan* rammed into the ocean bottom again.

As the submarine's speed approached zero, Wilson called out, "Helm, all stop!" and the Helm twisted the Engine Order Telegraph to the ordered bell. The tremors beneath Christine's feet ceased, and *Michigan* came to rest at a ten-degree tilt to starboard. The racket of the submarine's grounding was replaced by a serene silence, penetrated only by the high-pitched pings of the torpedo behind them.

"Thirty seconds to torpedo impact." The Sonar Supervisor's report echoed across the quiet Control Room.

Christine examined the geographic display. The torpedo was approaching the protrusion in the ocean bottom *Michigan* had just passed over. If they were lucky, the torpedo would lock on to the rock outcropping instead of *Michigan*.

"Twenty seconds to impact."

A few seconds later, a deafening explosion filled Christine's ears, followed by hollow tings echoing through Control as chunks of rock bounced off *Michigan*'s steel hull. After another minute, the sound of high-speed propellers, accompanied by high-pitched sonar pings, streaked overhead from starboard to port, followed a few seconds later by identical sounds passing from port to starboard. The other two torpedoes had missed *Michigan*, hunkered down on the ocean bottom, indistinguishable from a large rock formation.

After the second torpedo passed overhead, Captain Wilson began issuing orders. "Rig for Reduced Electrical Power. Shut down the reactor."

The submarine's Engineer, on watch as Officer of the Deck, relayed the Captain's orders, and throughout the submarine, all nonessential equipment was secured, reducing the electrical demand to within the submarine battery's capacity. As the crew continued securing nonessential loads, Wilson tapped Lieutenant Cordero on the shoulder again.

"Relieve the Engineer as Officer of the Deck." Wilson turned to the Engineer. "Get the Turbine Generators and all nonessential loads secured as quickly as possible. The Chinese submarines are going to be overhead in a few minutes, sniffing around to ensure the first torpedo finished us off, and we need to look as much like a rock as possible. Also inspect the Engine Room to determine if we sustained any damage while driving along the bottom."

The Engineer acknowledged, and after he was relieved by Lieutenant Cordero, the submarine's senior department head proceeded aft. As the crew rigged the submarine for Reduced Electrical Power, the ventilation fans in Control drifted to a halt, and an uneasy silence settled over the Control Room. The nuclear-powered submarine's battery was small by diesel submarine standards, and wouldn't last long. Even if they successfully simulated a rock, they could not sit on the bottom forever.

Five minutes later, the Engineer's voice emanated from the speaker on the Conn. "Captain, Engineer. Both Turbine Generators are secured and the reactor plant is shut down. All nonessential machinery is secured. There is no noticeable damage in the Engineering spaces, although it looks like we sucked quite a bit of silt into the main condensers before we were able to secure the Main Seawater Pumps. Once we start the reactor back up again, we won't be able to sit on the bottom for long or we'll foul the main condensers."

Wilson acknowledged the Engineer's report, then queried Sonar over the 27-MC. "Report status of sonar systems."

The Sonar Supervisor replied, "We've lost the towed array, but the spherical array appears fully operational."

"Sonar, Conn, Aye." As Wilson examined the sonar monitor at the front of the Conn, a faint white trace materialized from the random static.

A moment later, the Executive Officer turned toward Wilson, one hand on his sound-powered phone earmuffs and his other holding the mouthpiece. "Sir, Sonar reports a new contact, Sierra four-eight, classified Yuan class submarine. Most likely one of the three previous contacts." Before Wilson could respond, a powerful sonar ping echoed through Control.

Conversation in Control ceased again as Captain Wilson and his men listened tensely with upturned faces, as if they could see the Chinese submarine lurking above them. Lieutenant Cordero joined Wilson in front of the sonar display. As the white trace and random static reflected off their pale faces, two additional faint white traces appeared on the monitor. Seconds later, two more pings echoed through Control, one slightly louder than the other.

Wilson turned to the Chief of the Watch, seated at the Ballast Control Panel on the port side of Control. "Chief of the Watch, pass over the X1J, secure all MC comms. Sound-powered comms only."

The Chief of the Watch acknowledged and passed the order over his sound-powered phones. A moment later, the ship's Engineer returned to Control. Wilson asked quietly, "How long will the battery last?"

"At the current discharge rate, six hours."

Wilson rubbed the side of his face again, eventually turning toward his Executive Officer. "XO." He motioned for Lieutenant Commander Greenwood to join him on the Conn.

As the XO stepped onto the Conn, Wilson relayed the Engineer's information. "Eng estimates the battery will last six hours. We might have to remain on the bottom much longer than that before we convince our friends we're dead, so we need to get the discharge rate down to a trickle. I'm taking everything off-line, including all tactical systems. Any objections?"

The XO shook his head slowly. "They're not doing us much good right now anyway."

Wilson issued new orders to Lieutenant Cordero, and one by one, the console displays in Control faded to black until every watchstander sat in front of a dormant console. The overhead lights in the Control Room suddenly extinguished, and a second later, yellow emergency battle lanterns flickered on, casting an eerie yellow pall across the men and equipment in Control.

Christine leaned toward Captain Wilson, catching his attention. "What do we do now?"

Wilson's dark eyes probed hers for a moment before answering.

"We wait."

54

WASHINGTON, D.C.

It was just after midnight when Captain Steve Brackman and the president descended the single flight of stairs into the basement of the West Wing, stepping into the crowded Situation Room. The entire military hierarchy was present—the Joint Chiefs of Staff, along with SecDef Jennings and various Cabinet members. In the few hours he'd been away, Brackman hoped the Japanese Self-Defense Force had stabilized its positions. But the look on the faces of the men in the room, accompanied by a glance at the eight-by-ten-foot monitor in the Situation Room, told Brackman the situation had deteriorated faster than expected.

In the eight days since the assault began, China had gained complete control of three of the four main Japanese islands; only portions of Honshu remained in Japanese hands. As expected, defense of Tokyo—the largest city on the island and the location of the Emperor's palace—was fierce. However, the PLA Army had pushed past both sides of the city and reached Tokyo Bay, completely encircling Japan's capital. Although the fate of the Japanese forces cut off in Tokyo was a concern, the status of Honshu's eastern shoreline was the more important issue.

The only way to defeat China was to land the three Marine Expeditionary Forces. Hopefully, with the Marines' superior air and ground firepower, along with the augmented air wing aboard *Reagan*, they could hold out until additional Marine Corps and Army troops arrived. Although the MEFs were equipped and trained for contested amphibious assault, the casualties suffered storming a defended beach could be enormous. Thankfully, most of the eastern shore of Honshu was still controlled by the Japanese Self-Defense Force. But at the rate the JSDF was retreating, there would soon be no viable beachheads in friendly hands.

The stress was getting to everyone. Brackman could sense the frustration smoldering inside the president, and discussions amongst the Joint Chiefs of Staff were on the verge of flaring into confrontations and accusations. How could the United States have been caught so flat-footed; how had malware been inserted into their weapon systems; and how were their satellites and tactical data links so easily jammed? Even worse, threatening to ignite the situation with its implications, not a single Atlantic Fleet submarine had emerged from under the Arctic ice cap. The lead submarines were now six hours overdue.

Brackman took his seat at the conference table as the president settled into his chair and asked for an update. Admiral Grant Healey, Chief of Naval Operations, answered. "*Ronald Reagan* continues toward Japan and has linked up with the three MEFs. We'd normally keep the MEFs well behind until the situation stabilizes, but we don't have time. We project we'll lose the last beach-head in three days, so we have to start moving toward shore. Of course, we'll have to call everything off without the Atlantic Fleet submarines. Without fast attacks to clear a safe path to Japan, *Reagan* won't be able to get close enough to sustain flight operations, and you can forget about landing the three MEFs. The Chinese submarines will sink the amphibs as they approach the coast."

The president nodded tightly as Healey fell silent. "What's the status of the Atlantic Fleet submarines?" the president asked. "Were they sunk when the Chinese bombed the ice pack?"

Healey hesitated a moment before answering. "I don't know, sir."

The president silently digested Healey's answer. Brackman had felt the uneasiness in the room deepen as each hour passed without word from any of their submarines. Each element of their plan had to succeed: the Atlantic Fleet submarines had to complete their under-ice transit, *Reagan* had to reach striking distance of Japan, and most important of all, the SEAL team had to succeed.

As the president stared at Admiral Healey in silence, Brackman was distracted by the appearance of a blue icon on the monitor hanging against the far wall; a lone symbol appearing in the Bering Strait between Alaska and Russia. The other eyes at the conference table followed Brackman's to the monitor, the mood lifting instantaneously as another icon appeared five miles to the east, and a few seconds later, another icon to the west. The lead Atlantic Fleet submarines had completed their under-ice transit and had entered the Pacific Ocean.

CASTLE

55

USS *ANNAPOLIS*

"No close contacts!"

As USS *Annapolis* reached periscope depth, the Officer of the Deck's announcement was the first piece of routine news Commander Ramsey Hootman had heard in a while. Just over a day ago, the ice pack above *Annapolis* had broken apart, sending jagged ice keels downward, crashing into the submarine's steel hull. But they were lucky; although the Engine Room hull had been deformed, the three-inch-thick steel hadn't been punctured. However, the seawater cooling system pipes had cracked in multiple places, spraying frigid water throughout the Engine Room, and Ramsey's crew had shut the Emergency Flood Isolation Valves. Six hours later, the seawater piping had been repaired and propulsion restored, and *Annapolis* had surged south again.

They were now in the Marginal Ice Zone just north of St. Lawrence Island in the Bering Strait, and as *Annapolis* cruised at periscope depth, the lack of announcements troubled Ramsey. The Quartermaster should have reported a GPS satellite fix by now, and there was no report from Radio either.

The Navigator stepped onto the Conn. "Sir, we've reported our successful under-ice transit and our position. There must be some sort of makeshift communication system overhead, because we received an acknowledgment, but nothing else. All satellites are still down. Unable to obtain a GPS fix or download the submarine broadcast."

"Understand," Ramsey replied.

This was not good news. The first order of business after completing an under-ice transit was to determine the ship's position. *Annapolis* had navigated across the top of the world using her two inertial navigators, and they had become unstable as they approached the North Pole. As a result, their estimated position could be off by several miles. They couldn't approach close to shore, clearing the way for the Marine Expeditionary Forces, without knowing exactly where they were. Even more important, they needed to download new software for their torpedoes. Both of those efforts required satellites.

Ramsey stepped off the Conn, stopping at the Navigation Table, joined by the Nav. Ramsey searched for a way to verify their position. The GPS satellites were still inoperable, and the old LORAN and Omega systems had been retired years earlier. As he studied the navigation chart, an idea took hold. They were just north of St. Lawrence Island, where the water shallowed rapidly—they could do a bottom contour fix. By comparing the water depth measured by the submarine's Fathometer to charted depth, they could verify their position, at least to within a hundred yards. Not good enough for launching ballistic missiles, but good enough for submarine warfare.

Ramsey explained the plan to the Nav, then turned to his Officer of the Deck. "Bring her down to five hundred feet, ahead standard, course two-zero-zero." The Officer of the Deck complied, and a moment later *Annapolis* tilted downward, increasing depth and speed.

56

USS *RONALD REAGAN*

Beneath gunmetal-gray clouds, a driving rain pelted USS *Reagan* as the aircraft carrier surged through dark green seas at ahead flank speed. As daylight faded, Captain CJ Berger surveyed the wet Flight Deck through the port Bridge windows, noting the slow, but steady progress of the shipyard's Tiger Teams, reassembling the aircraft carrier's arresting cables. It was a race against time.

The Atlantic Fleet air wing had been circling above for hours, taking turns refueling from a dozen tankers accompanying the aircraft. Whoever decided to augment the air wing with Air Force KC-10 refueling tankers was a wise man or woman. The speed at which the Tiger Teams reassembled *Reagan*'s flight systems was impressive considering the complexity of their task, but they still lagged behind predictions.

As difficult as it was to prepare *Reagan* to get underway, reassembling enough of her systems to conduct flight operations had been even more challenging. All four catapults were still inoperable, and the Tiger Teams had focused first on restoring the systems required for landing. Two of the ship's four elevators were back in operation, so ferrying aircraft to the Hangar Deck below wouldn't be a problem. Slowing the aircraft as they landed, their tailhooks catching an arresting wire, was the last remaining issue.

They had only ten minutes left to complete the repairs. The modified LANT air wing, consisting of four Super Hornet and two F-35C Lightning II squadrons, twelve Growlers, and four Hawkeyes, had sucked the refueling tankers dry and were approaching Bingo Fuel. Sending out another round of refueling tankers was not an option; the pilots could remain aloft for only so long. They would either have to begin landing now or head back to Hawaii for rest, followed by another attempt the following day. Landing the aircraft today wasn't essential, but Berger was more concerned with the pace at which his flight systems were being returned to service. The longer the arresting wires took, the longer it would be before the Tiger Teams turned their attention to the catapults.

Berger's thoughts were interrupted by the Air Boss's voice, coming across the 23-MC speaker from the O-9 Deck, directly above the Bridge. "Captain, Air Boss. Two Wire has been repaired. Request Green Deck."

Captain Berger reached over to the console beside his chair, pressing the small green button as he slipped the microphone from its clip with his other hand. "Air Boss, you've got Green Deck."

A moment later, the first aircraft materialized through the steady downpour, barely distinguishable against the backdrop of dark gray skies. Berger glanced at the Number Two arresting cable, stretched across the Flight Deck, hoping the arresting engines worked properly.

Berger's attention shifted between the wobbling jet, buffeted by strong winds as it approached, to the Landing Signals Officer, standing on the Flight Deck in the rain. The LSO held a radio handset close to his mouth with one hand, advising the approaching pilot on engine power and glide path. In his other hand, he held the *pickle switch* controlling the Optical Landing System, containing red *wave-off* and green *cut* lights, which directed the pilot to either abort the landing or make additional adjustments during his approach. Berger watched as the green *cut* lights flashed periodically during the jet's descent, sending last-second guidance to the pilot.

The Super Hornet angled down toward the deck, its tailhook extended. With only one operable arresting wire, the odds of a successful landing were reduced. Land a split second too late and the jet's tailhook would miss the cable. The pilot would have to *bolter*, pushing his engines to full throttle to regain sufficient speed for flight before he ran out of carrier deck.

Berger followed the Super Hornet in, its wings wobbling one last time before the jet touched down. The aircraft's tailhook snagged the arresting wire and the jet screeched to a halt. Forty-five seconds later, the fighter was headed to the forward starboard elevator as a second Super Hornet touched down. One by one, as darkness settled over the Pacific Ocean, the modified Atlantic Fleet air wing landed safely aboard the Pacific Fleet's last carrier.

57

USS *MICHIGAN*

Eight hundred feet beneath the surface, USS *Michigan* rested on the ocean bottom, listing ten degrees to starboard. Seated on the Conn, bathed in yellow emergency lighting, Christine rubbed the arms of her thick green jacket. With the ventilation fans and heaters secured, the temperature inside the submarine had plummeted, dropping until it matched the temperature of the ocean bottom. Moisture from the air condensed on the submarine's steel hull, trickling down the curved bulkheads, and the crew's breath condensed into white mist when they spoke.

Standing on the Conn next to Captain Wilson, Lieutenant Commander Faucher had just arrived after completing another review of battery voltage and discharge rate, ensuring there was enough power remaining to complete a reactor start-up. They were pushing the battery to its limit, and Christine could see the concern on Faucher's face, wondering if Wilson had pushed it too far. However, it didn't seem like they had any choice. Sonar pings still echoed periodically through *Michigan*'s hull. At least one Chinese submarine was still out there, unconvinced the American submarine had been sunk.

"We need to commence a reactor start-up now," Faucher repeated. "If we wait any longer, we won't have enough power."

Wilson shook his head. "We can't afford to start up yet. Our feedwater and seawater pumps are too loud. We have to wait until the Chinese submarines depart." A powerful sonar ping echoed through the submarine's steel hull, adding emphasis to Wilson's statement.

Faucher replied, his voice straining as he attempted to contain his frustration. "Then what is your plan, sir? How do we complete a reactor start-up without enough energy in the battery?"

Wilson hesitated a moment before answering. "We'll do a Fast Recovery Start-Up instead of a normal start-up. That will buy us an hour."

Captain Wilson's words seemed to hit the Engineer like a physical blow. Faucher straightened his posture and cast a glance in Christine's direction, aware she was sitting close enough to hear the conversation. He turned back to Captain Wilson, lowering his voice in a failed attempt to conceal his words. "That's not allowed, sir. We've been shut down for too long. If we conduct a Fast Recovery Start-Up from such a low temperature, we risk fracturing the reactor vessel. We're talking about a complete core meltdown if that happens."

Wilson's eyes locked onto his Engineer's face. "I understand, Eng. That's a chance I'm willing to take. It's my call. Enter it in the logs."

An uneasy silence hung in the air between the two men, interrupted by the submarine's Weapons Officer arriving in Control with a second class petty officer whom Christine recognized as Sam Walsh, a Machinist Mate assigned to Torpedo Division. The Submarine Force had eliminated the Torpedoman rating, and Machinist Mates now manned the Torpedo Room. Wilson turned toward the new arrivals.

"Sir," the Weps began, "Petty Officer Walsh may have a solution to our torpedo problem."

Wilson's eyes brightened as they shifted to the Machinist Mate. "What solution is that?"

Petty Officer Walsh explained. "The message we received said the algorithm that shuts down the torpedo is located on the primary Signal Processing card. I spent three years at our torpedo maintenance facility in Yorktown, and I know how to take apart the torpedo and remove the affected circuit card."

Wilson replied. "Will the torpedo function properly without this card?"

"It should, sir," Walsh replied. "There are two SP cards in each torpedo. They're not completely identical, but each has the ability to take over for the other if one card fails. If we remove the primary SP card, the secondary card will assume the first has failed and take over. The message we received implied the algorithm was loaded only on the primary SP card, so the torpedo should function normally after we remove it, ignoring the Chinese sonar pulse. I don't know that for sure, but I figure it's worth a shot."

"How long will it take to remove the card?" Wilson asked.

"With enough help and the proper tools, about two hours per torpedo. But I can do two torpedoes at once, one on the starboard side of the Torpedo Room and the other on the port side, without slowing me down too much."

Wilson nodded thoughtfully. "Great idea, Walsh." He turned to the Weps. "Get Walsh whatever help he needs. We've got another hour before we commence reactor start-up, and another hour before we'll be coming off the bottom. We may need a functioning torpedo or two about the time Walsh is finished."

"Aye, sir." The Weps and Walsh stepped off the Conn, the two men already conversing as they headed down the ladder from Control.

An hour later, Christine was in the Torpedo Room along with the Weapons Officer, watching Walsh and five other petty officers gathered in the center aisle of the Torpedo Room. The six petty officers were disassembling two of the submarine's MK 48 Mod 7 torpedoes, one on the inboard starboard stow and the other on the inboard port stow. Christine watched from the aft end of the crowded compartment, filled with eleven of the submarine's thirteen green MK 48 warshot torpedoes. The other two were still loaded in Tubes Three and Four, ready for launch.

Both torpedoes Walsh was working on had been separated into two pieces. On each torpedo, Walsh had removed the joint band connecting the Guidance and Control section to the torpedo's warhead, fuel tank, and engine. Thick black cables had been disconnected and were dangling from the torpedo innards, and Walsh and another petty officer were sliding a heavy, one-foot-long metal Guidance Control Box from the front half of the torpedo. The GCB was the torpedo's brain, containing the two SP cards as well as a slew of other critical microprocessors.

The GCB was extracted from the Guidance and Control section and placed onto a rubber mat between the two halves of the torpedo. Walsh removed the hex screws from the front plate of the GCB and stared into the torpedo's electronic brain. In the dim yellow emergency lighting, it was difficult to see inside, so the other petty officer grabbed a nearby flashlight, aiming the white beam into the GCB.

Walsh wrapped an electrostatic guard around his wrist, with the other end of the cord attached to the submarine's metal hull. He reached carefully inside the GCB, working his hand back and forth, extracting a four-by-eight-inch circuit card. He examined it closely, as if he could visually detect the faulty algorithm loaded onto one of the several dozen chips embedded in the green circuit board.

He placed the card on the rubber mat, then replaced the GCB's cover and tightened the fasteners. The Weapons Officer checked his watch for the hundredth time; it had taken just over an hour to get to this point. Walsh slid the GCB back into the Guidance and Control section, securing it in place with additional screws. Then he instructed the other petty officers to begin the process of rejoining the two halves of the torpedo. After observing their efforts for a moment, Walsh turned his attention to the torpedo on the port stow.

A powerful sonar ping echoed through *Michigan*'s hull, a stark reminder of the enemy awaiting them, and Christine decided to return to the Control Room. Wilson was still standing on the Conn, his arms folded across his chest, conversing with the Engineer and Navigator. As Christine approached the three men, the Navigator asked, "Why don't we stay on the bottom after the reactor start-up is complete, then wait until the Chinese submarines depart."

The Engineer shook his head. "*Michigan* isn't designed to sit on the ocean bottom. Our main seawater intakes are near the bottom of the hull, and we sucked in a significant amount of silt during the short time it took to shut down the reactor. If we stay on the bottom more than a few minutes after start-up, we'll foul the main condensers and lose all propulsion and electrical power."

Their conversation was interrupted by the high-pitched chirp of the 2-JV sound-powered phone system. Wilson picked up the 2-JV handset, flipping on the speaker so his two department heads could hear the report from the Engineering Officer of the Watch in the Engine Room. "Conn, Maneuvering. The battery has begun reversing. Three cells have changed polarity."

Three of the battery's 126 cells had been drained and were now attempting to recharge themselves, adding an additional demand on the remaining cells. As more and more cells reversed, the situation would rapidly deteriorate until the battery was completely drained, leaving no power for the reactor startup.

"Maneuvering, Conn," Wilson replied. "This is the Captain. Understand cell reversal has begun." Wilson placed the handset back into its cradle, looking back at the Engineer. "Looks like we can't wait any longer. Commence Fast Recovery Start-Up."

The Engineer acknowledged the Captain's order. As he left Control, Wilson approached the front of the Conn. His silver hair appeared almost blond in the yellow lighting from the emergency battle lanterns. He addressed all twenty-three watchstanders in the crowded Control Room, his breath condensing into fog as he spoke.

"Attention in Control. The battery has begun cell reversal, so we're commencing a reactor start-up. As we bring up the seawater, condensate, and feedwater pumps, we'll become more detectable, and we'll be helpless until we get an electrical turbine and propulsion restored. However," Wilson continued, "Petty Officer Walsh believes he can fix our torpedoes, making them impervious to the Chinese sonar pulse. He's working on two now, and they should be ready by the time we complete reactor start-up."

The crew sat up at their consoles as Wilson spoke, but when he finished, there was little for them to do. Their consoles were still dead, staring back at them with dark displays. Christine pulled back the left sleeve of her thick green jacket, checking the time. The reactor start-up would be complete in about an hour. She settled into the Captain's seat on the starboard side of the Conn, preparing to wait as the minutes ticked by.

Christine shivered inside her foul-weather jacket, observing Lieutenant Kris Herndon, the Officer of the Deck, standing between the two lowered periscopes, supervising the dormant Control Room. *Michigan* still tilted to starboard at a ten-degree list, but no one seemed to notice aside from the Night Baker, who entered Control carrying a tray of coffee mugs held at a slight angle. Petty Officer Sam Meade had somehow managed to brew hot coffee without any electrical power. Steam rose from the ceramic mugs as Meade made his round, exchanging twelve empty cups for full ones. He delivered the last three to the Conn before retreating down the ladder toward Crew's Mess.

Christine wrapped her cold hands around the hot mug as she took a sip of black coffee, savoring the heat more than the flavor. Wilson flipped on the 2-JV speaker, listening to the communications between Engine Room watchstanders and Maneuvering, where the Engineering Officer of the Watch directed reactor plant operations. They had commenced withdrawing control rods from the reactor core, adding a significant drain on the battery as the Control Rod Drive Mechanisms lifted the rods inside the uranium fuel cells. Additional battery cells began reversing, and Christine glanced at Wilson each time to assess his reaction. His face was placid, exhibiting no reaction to the news. Suddenly, an announcement came across the 2-JV.

"The reactor is critical."

Christine glanced at Wilson again, wondering if something had gone wrong, but there was still no response from the submarine's Captain. Lieutenant Herndon noticed the concerned look on her face, and spoke softly. "That's normal," she said. "It means the neutron fission rate in the core is self-sustaining, exactly where we want it. Neither too few fissions, eventually shutting down, nor too many, escalating out of control. Just like Goldilocks." Herndon smiled, and Christine almost laughed at the unexpected simile.

A few minutes later, another report emanated from the speaker. *"The reactor is in the power range. Commencing reactor plant heat-up."*

The minutes ticked away as the reactor plant increased temperature until another report came across the 2JV. *"Opening Main Steam One and Two."*

While the Engineering watch section worked quickly to bring up the electrical turbine generators, the emergency battle lanterns in Control continued to fade. Sonar was still down, and the combat control, navigation, and ship control consoles remained deenergized. The only indication of electronic life aboard *Michigan* was the Ballast Control Panel, the red and blue indicating lights casting an eerie glow on the Chief of the Watch's face. Another loud sonar ping penetrated *Michigan*'s hull, followed by a report over the 2-JV speaker.

"The port and starboard turbine generators are ready for electrical loading."

Upon hearing this report, the watchstanders in Control straightened in their seats, turning back toward their dark consoles, and one of the Fire Control Technicians cracked his knuckles in anticipation. A moment later, the bright white fluorescent lighting overhead flickered on and the emergency battle lanterns extinguished.

There was a chirp from the 2-JV circuit, and Lieutenant Herndon picked up the handset. "Conn. Officer of the Deck."

"Conn, Maneuvering. The electric plant is in a normal full power lineup. Main Engine warm-up in progress."

Herndon acknowledged, then turned toward Wilson, who ordered, "Secure the rig for reduced electrical." Herndon passed the order, and moments later, the Control Room sputtered to life, start-up screens appearing on the combat control consoles. The Ship Control Panel illuminated, as well as a plethora of displays and indicators on the Conn, and the ventilation fans began blowing welcome warm air from the vents.

The XO turned to the Captain. "Sonar reports cold start-up in progress. Six minutes remaining."

Wilson acknowledged, ordering Sonar to resume making reports over the 27-MC.

The combat control consoles completed their start-up before Sonar's, and the Weapons Officer peered over the Fire Control Technician's shoulder at the Weapon Launch Console, monitoring the status of their torpedoes. Weapons appeared in two of the submarine's four torpedo tubes. Tubes One and Two remained empty.

Wilson called out to the Weps, "Report status of Tubes One through Four."

The Weps turned toward the Captain. "Tubes Three and Four are loaded, flooded down, outer doors open. Weapons powered up. Still reassembling the torpedoes for Tubes One and Two. Estimate twenty minutes before we're ready to load."

Lieutenant Stewart's response was followed by a report over the 27-MC. "Conn, Sonar. Start-up complete. Hold a new contact, designated Sierra four-nine, bearing two-eight-zero. Analyzing."

Sonar bearings appeared on three of the combat control consoles, and the two Fire Control Technicians and Lieutenant Cordero began manipulating the trackballs by their keyboards, their hands moving faster than Christine's eyes could follow. The men flipped through various multicolored graphical displays, adjusting the contact's course, speed, and range. Behind them, the submarine's Executive Officer reviewed the three different solutions, eventually tapping one of the Fire Control Technicians on the shoulder.

"Promote to Master."

The Fire Control Technician complied as the Executive Officer read off the contact's estimated solution. "Sierra four-nine bears two-eight-five, range six thousand yards, course zero-one-zero, speed four." The XO turned toward Wilson. "But's that's a rough solution. We'll have a better estimate once we can maneuver and drive bearing rate."

"We'll come off the bottom once the main engines are ready," Wilson replied.

As the XO acknowledged, the overhead lighting in Control flickered, followed by another announcement from the 2-JV speaker.

"Loss of vacuum, starboard main condenser."

The report from the Engine Room was followed by the chirp of the 2-JV. Wilson retrieved the handset, and Christine listened to the conversation over the speaker.

"Conn. This is the Captain."

"Captain, Engineer. The starboard main condenser is fouling and we've shifted to a half-power lineup on the port turbine generator. We need to come off the bottom so we can restore vacuum and bring up the starboard side of the Engine Room."

"Understand," Wilson replied. He replaced the handset, turning to Lieutenant Herndon. "Hover at seven-six-zero feet."

Herndon gave the order. "Dive, engage Hovering. Set depth at seven-six-zero feet."

The Dive relayed Herndon's order to the Chief of the Watch seated beside him, manning the Ballast Control Panel. The Chief dialed in 760 feet and energized the submarine's Hovering system. Blue circles illuminated on the Ballast Control Panel, indicating valves in the hull were opening. The Chief of the Watch called out periodically as the submarine's hovering pumps pushed water from *Michigan*'s variable ballast tanks, increasing the submarine's buoyancy.

"Ten thousand pounds out."

The Chief of the Watch reported every ten thousand pounds out, and at the forty-thousand mark, *Michigan* began tilting to port, righting itself from its starboard list as it lifted off the ocean floor. A sonar ping echoed through Control just as *Michigan* began drifting upward, a stark reminder that at least one Chinese submarine was still searching for them. Christine shivered involuntarily from the combined cold and nervousness. She didn't know how sophisticated the Chinese sonar systems were and whether they could detect a submarine hovering forty feet off the ocean floor, or whether *Michigan* would still look like a rock on the ocean bottom.

"On ordered depth, seven-six-zero feet," the Dive announced.

Wilson removed the 2-JV handset from its holder. "Maneuvering, this is the Captain. We're forty feet off the bottom. Recover the starboard side of the Engine Room."

The Engineering Officer of the Watch repeated back the Captain's order, and as Wilson slipped the handset into its holder, another sonar ping echoed through Control. Sonar followed up a few seconds later, the Sonar Supervisor's voice emanating from the speaker. "Active pings bearing two-nine-zero. Correlates to Sierra four-nine. Classified Yuan class submarine."

The Executive Officer monitored the three men at their combat control consoles as they continued adjusting the contact's course, speed, and range. The contact solution was updated, followed by an announcement from the XO. "Hold Sierra four-nine on a course of zero-three-zero, speed three, range five thousand yards."

Before Wilson could acknowledge, the Sonar Supervisor's voice echoed from the 27-MC speakers again. "Upshift in frequency, Sierra four-nine. Contact has zigged toward."

Hands began moving again at the three combat control consoles as the operators updated their solution.

The Executive Officer called out, "Confirm target zig. Contact has maneuvered to a new course of one-one-zero." The XO stopped behind Lieutenant Cordero, directing him to shift to the geographic display. After a quick glance at the target solution, the XO looked up at the Captain. The Yuan class submarine had turned directly toward them.

Wilson picked up the 7-MC microphone. "Maneuvering, Captain. How much longer before the starboard side of the Engine Room is recovered?"

"Captain, Engineer. Estimate five minutes."

Another ping echoed through the Control Room, this one stronger than the previous ones. Wilson replaced the handset, his eyes scanning the combat control displays. Christine could feel the tension in the air, but the conversations in Control remained subdued. Lieutenant Cordero and the two Fire Control Technicians continued their target motion analysis, adjusting parameters, refining the target's new course, speed, and range.

After a moment, Wilson called out, "Designate Sierra four-nine as Master One. Firing Point Procedures, Master One, Tube Three. However," Wilson added, "we will not shoot unless fired upon. We will continue hovering near the bottom and hope we look enough like a rock outcropping that Master One won't expend a torpedo to find out."

As Wilson fell silent, the watchstanders began preparing to fire the torpedo in Tube Three. The Executive Officer stopped briefly behind each of the combat control consoles, examining the target solution on each one, finally tapping the middle Fire Control Technician. The Technician pressed a button on his console and the XO called out, "Solution Ready."

The Fire Control Technician at the Weapon Launch Console sent the course, speed, and range of their target to their MK 48 torpedo in Tube Three, along with applicable search presets, and a few seconds later, the Weapons Officer announced, "Weapon Ready."

Lieutenant Herndon followed up, reporting, "Ship Ready with the exception of full propulsion. Ready to answer bells on the port main engine only."

Michigan was cocked and ready, a single button push away from firing its torpedo.

Another sonar ping echoed through the Control Room, increased again in intensity. A report from Sonar followed shortly thereafter. "Sonar ping received at plus ten D-E. Corresponds to a depth of four hundred feet."

There was bright white trace on *Michigan*'s port beam, growing stronger by the minute. The XO cast frequent glances in Wilson's direction, waiting for the order to shoot. Christine knew what the XO was thinking. If they shot first, maybe they could surprise their target.

But that was risky. At this range, the Chinese submarine would detect *Michigan*'s torpedo launch. Walsh's modified torpedoes weren't ready yet, and the Chinese submarine might have enough time to dud their unmodified torpedo, then return fire. Wilson's alternatives were to either shoot first and almost guarantee their own destruction, or sit tight and play the odds their target would pass by without firing. Neither option seemed to offer a high probability of survival.

Another sonar ping penetrated *Michigan*'s hull, but this one was followed by two more pings in rapid succession. There was no visible reaction from Wilson, even though *Michigan* had apparently been detected and the Chinese submarine was refining its firing solution. A moment later, Wilson glanced at the clock above the Quartermaster's stand. It had been exactly five minutes since the Engineer's last update on the Engine Room start-up.

As if in response to Wilson's glance, the Engineer's voice emanated from the Conn speaker. "Conn, Maneuvering. Ready to answer all bells." But before Wilson could respond to the Engineer's report, the Sonar Supervision's voice blared across the 27-MC.

"Torpedo launch transients from Master One, bearing two-nine-zero!"

Wilson shouted out, "Helm, ahead flank! Launch countermeasure!"

The Helm twisted the Engine Order Telegraph fully clockwise, and Christine felt the submarine's engines spring to life, sending tremors through the deck. A few seconds later, a Fire Control Technician manning one of the combat control consoles called out, "Countermeasure away!" The torpedo decoy was launched none too soon, because Sonar followed up with a second announcement.

"Torpedo in the water, bearing two-nine-zero!"

The XO turned in Wilson's direction, awaiting the order to counter-fire. However, Wilson simply stood there, evaluating the sonar display on the Conn. After a moment of silence, interrupted only by Sonar's updated bearing to the torpedo over the 27-MC, the Executive Officer spoke. "Sir, recommend counter-fire."

"No," Wilson replied. "It'll be a wasted shot unless we can get close enough so they don't have time to dud the torpedo."

Wilson stepped off the Conn, stopping next to the Navigation table, examining the display. A bright white dot representing *Michigan* marched away from a scalloped circle annotating their torpedo decoy. A half-dozen red lines were drawn out from the submarine's track, recording the torpedo bearings called out by Sonar every ten seconds. Wilson attempted to determine whether the torpedo was headed toward *Michigan* or their decoy. It was difficult to assess because *Michigan* was still close to their countermeasure.

"Torpedo range, one thousand yards. Impact in one minute."

Christine's stomach tightened, realizing their fate would be determined by the effectiveness of their decoy. She felt helpless, sitting on the Conn as they counted down what might be the last minute of their lives. After the next announcement, her stomach settled low and cold in her gut.

"Torpedo is range-gating! Torpedo's homing!"

The torpedo had increased the rate of its sonar pings to more accurately determine the range to its target, so a refined intercept course could be calculated. The important question was whether the torpedo was about to intercept *Michigan* or their decoy behind them.

"Thirty seconds to impact!"

Michigan was approaching ahead flank and was a decent distance away from their decoy now.

"Fifteen seconds to impact!"

The torpedo's high-pitched pings could now be heard through *Michigan*'s hull. Conversation in Control ceased, the silence interrupted only by the periodic sonar echoes, which increased in intensity as the torpedo closed the remaining distance. Throughout Control, the crew braced themselves for the impending explosion as they counted down the remaining seconds.

Michigan shuddered as an explosion roared through the Control Room. Christine tensed, as did everyone in Control, listening for an emergency report. The seconds on the clock by the Quartermaster's stand ticked upward in slow motion as the crew waited.

After an agonizing fifteen seconds, Wilson ordered, "Helm, all stop, right full rudder." *Michigan* hadn't been hit. The torpedo had been distracted by their decoy, eventually locking on to the same rock outcropping as the previous Chinese torpedo.

Christine felt the tremors in the deck fade as the main engines fell silent. As the torpedo explosion echoed through the water, she wondered why Wilson had ordered all stop.

Wilson called out, "Attention in Control. I've secured the main engines so we can blend back into the ocean noise, masked by the echoes of the torpedo explosion. If Sierra four-eight continues down our trail, we'll have a nice surprise for him. We're not going to be where he expects us to be." Wilson looked at the Weapons Officer. "Speaking of surprises, how long until Tubes One and Two are loaded?"

The Weps answered, "Ten more minutes before both torpedoes are buttoned up, then we'll begin loading. However," Lieutenant Stewart added, "we won't know if the torpedoes are operable until we power them up and attempt to assign presets."

"I understand," Wilson replied. "We don't have ten minutes anyway. I intend to prosecute Master One with the unmodified torpedo in Tube Three once we regain contact." Wilson turned to the watchstanders in Control. "Check Fire, Tube Three. Resume tracking Master One."

Christine wondered what Wilson was up to. How were they going to employ an unmodified torpedo without it being dudded?

The geographic display on Lieutenant Cordero's console showed *Michigan* curling to the right, back toward the Chinese submarine, which was maintaining a straight course. Christine realized Wilson was attempting to circle around behind the Chinese submarine, their approach masked by the torpedo explosion still reverberating through the water. *Michigan* was temporarily invisible, and Captain Wilson was using that to their advantage.

The Helm called out, "Request orders to the Helm. Rudder remains right full, no ordered course."

Stopping behind the geographic display, Wilson evaluated the solution for Master One. *Michigan* had traveled almost in a complete circle, its speed bleeding off to five knots and still decreasing, with the submarine still hugging the ocean bottom at 760 feet, blending into the occasional rock outcroppings. The Chinese submarine was directly behind them again, steady on a course of one-one-zero at ten knots, depth four hundred feet.

Wilson finally answered the Helm's request for orders. "Steady course one-one-zero."

As *Michigan* lined up on the identical course of its adversary, the Chinese submarine remained steady on course, attempting to regain track of the American submarine as the echoes from the torpedo explosion faded. Just as *Michigan* completed it full circle, Christine heard the loud churn of a propeller through *Michigan's* hull as the Chinese submarine traveled overhead at four hundred feet, apparently unaware of the American submarine lurking below.

As the Chinese submarine passed above, a determined look settled on Wilson's face. He called out, "Helm, ahead two-thirds. Dive, make your depth four hundred feet. Use five up."

The Helm rang up ahead two-thirds on the Engine Order Telegraph as the Dive ordered full rise on the fairwater planes and a five-degree up-bubble on the submarine. The Outboard watchstander, seated on the Helm's left, tilted the stern planes until the submarine was pitched upward to the ordered angle.

The main engines returned to life, increasing *Michigan*'s speed to ten knots, matching its target. At the same time, *Michigan* drifted up toward four hundred feet. Christine glanced at the geographic display. They were only a thousand yards behind Master One, directly in its sonar baffles. Assuming the Chinese submarine wasn't employing a towed array, *Michigan* would remain completely undetected.

"On ordered depth, four hundred feet," the Dive announced.

Wilson stepped back onto the Conn as he called out, "Firing Point Procedures, Master One, Tube Three. Set tactics to Low speed/Low speed, passive search only. Extend enable point to intercept range."

The Weps acknowledged Wilson's order and relayed it to the Fire Control Technician at the Weapon Launch Console, who modified the presets of the torpedo in Tube Three. The Executive Officer stopped briefly behind each of the combat control consoles, examining the target solution on each one, finally tapping Lieutenant Cordero. Cordero pressed a button on his console and the XO called out, "Solution Ready."

Immediately following the XO, the Weapons Officer announced, "Weapon Ready."

Lieutenant Herndon followed up, reporting, "Ship Ready."

Wilson replied, "Shoot on generated bearings!"

Christine heard the whirr of the torpedo ejection pump as the four-thousand-pound torpedo was ejected from Tube Three. The Sonar Supervisor announced the torpedo milestones.

"Own ship's unit is in the water, running normally.

"Fuel crossover achieved.

"Steady on preset gyro course, Low speed."

Wilson's eyes shifted to the Weapon Launch Console, depicting their torpedo as a green inverted V heading toward a red semicircle representing Master One, which remained steady on course and speed—giving no indication it had detected the incoming torpedo. Thirty seconds after launch, *Michigan*'s torpedo had closed to within five hundred yards of its target. Wilson called out, "Wire guide Tube Three. Shift search speed to High-One and Enable the weapon."

The Weapon Launch Console operator sent the new commands to their torpedo over the thin copper wire trailing behind it. The Fire Control Technician reported, "Unit Tube Three accepted commands."

Sonar confirmed the torpedo was responding properly, announcing, "Own ship's unit has shifted to High-One and has gone active."

A few seconds later, the Weapons Officer called out, "Unit Tube Three is homing! Telemetry range, four hundred yards."

Their torpedo was sending data back to *Michigan* over its guidance wire, and the *Michigan*'s crew could adjust the target solution if the contact evaded. However, no adjustments would be necessary. The torpedo had begun homing and would adjust course on its own.

The Weps followed up. "Unit Tube Three still homing! Two hundred yards to contact."

Christine watched as the torpedo's track on the Weapon Launch Console merged with Master One.

A few seconds later, an explosion rumbled through Control.

Michigan shuddered as a shock wave passed by, followed by Sonar's report. "Explosion in the water, bearing one-one-zero!" Cheers erupted in Control, quickly dying down as Sonar followed up. "Conn, Sonar. Breaking-up noises, bearing one-one-zero."

Michigan had survived, and now they had to clear the area quickly. If there were other Chinese submarines nearby, they would converge on the explosion.

Wilson ordered, "Helm, ahead standard. Right full rudder, steady course two-eight-zero."

Michigan began reversing course to the west, away from the explosion reverberating through the ocean depths. Christine took in a deep breath, realizing only now how shallow her breathing had been. However, as the tension eased from her muscles, a powerful sonar ping echoed through Control.

Seconds later, the Sonar Supervisor's announcement struck fear back into her heart. "Torpedo launch transients, bearing three-one-zero!"

58

USS *MICHIGAN*

"Hold a new contact, designated Sierra five-zero, bearing three-one-zero! Yuan class submarine." Sonar's follow-up report echoed from the 27-MC speaker on the Conn.

Another Chinese submarine had materialized from the murky waters. This time, however, *Michigan* wasn't hugging the ocean bottom, masked by the reverberations of a torpedo explosion.

Before Wilson could engage the second Chinese submarine, he had to deal with the incoming torpedo. "Helm, ahead flank! Steady course two-two-zero. Launch countermeasure!"

The Helm acknowledged Wilson's order and rang up ahead flank, maintaining his rudder at right full. *Michigan*'s powerful main engines surged to life and a Fire Control Technician launched one of *Michigan*'s decoys into the water. Christine felt the engines vibrate through the deck again as *Michigan* swung rapidly toward its torpedo evasion course. However, as *Michigan* approached its new course of 220, there was another report from the Sonar Supervisor.

"Torpedo in the water, bearing two-three-zero! Hold a new submerged contact, bearing two-three-two, classified Yuan diesel submarine."

Christine was beginning to hate the sound of the Sonar Supervisor's voice. She followed Wilson's eyes to the sonar display on the Conn, where a second bright white trace had appeared next to an accompanying faint white line. *Michigan* was now heading directly toward another Chinese submarine and its torpedo. These two diesel submarines were probably the other two of the trio of Chinese submarines that had chased *Michigan* into the ocean bottom a day earlier.

"Launch countermeasure! Helm . . ." Wilson hesitated.

There was no good course to maneuver to. The Chinese submarines had *Michigan* bracketed. If Wilson put one torpedo on the beam in an attempt to drive out of its path, the other torpedo would end up directly ahead or behind, a recipe for disaster. Yet they had to turn somewhere, and fast. They were barreling directly toward the second torpedo.

Wilson finally completed his order. ". . . shift your rudder, steady course one-five-zero."

The Helm shifted the rudder to left thirty degrees, reversing *Michigan*'s turn to starboard. Wilson had decided to place the second torpedo on the beam, but that meant the first torpedo was chasing right up *Michigan*'s tail. At least they were headed away from it, buying precious time while Wilson developed a plan to save everyone's bacon.

Wilson calmly stepped off the Conn, stopping behind Lieutenant Cordero again. "Geographic display with geoplot overlay," Wilson commanded. Cordero pulled up the requested display as Wilson was joined by the XO. "We're going to maneuver between the two torpedoes," Wilson said. "To do that, I need to know their courses." Both men turned toward Lieutenant Cordero, who spoke calmly into the mouthpiece of his sound-powered phones.

"Sonar, PRI MATE. Report Sonar Search Plan range, Yuan class submarine."

Christine couldn't hear Sonar's response over Cordero's headset, but a few seconds later, Cordero began manipulating one of the trackballs, adjusting the range parameters of the torpedo solutions, overriding the automated algorithms. His hand fell still and he looked up at Captain Wilson, awaiting further direction.

"Use High Speed for a Yu-6 torpedo," Wilson ordered.

Cordero returned his attention to his display as he adjusted the speed of both incoming torpedoes, forcing them to fifty knots. Wilson examined the results of Cordero's analysis, then turned to the Ship Control Panel.

"Helm, left full rudder, steady course zero-nine-zero."

The Helm acknowledged and a second later *Michigan* was turning to port again. As the submarine steadied on course 090, Wilson returned to the Conn and addressed his crew. "Attention in Control. Both torpedoes were fired on a line-of-sight bearing vice corrected intercept. That means our best evasion course is to the east. If our countermeasures fail to decoy the torpedoes, we'll have to hope they don't detect us as they pass by. Carry on."

The Executive Officer ordered Lieutenant Cordero to enter the torpedo solutions into Combat Control, and the geographic display updated with projections of both torpedoes. Their paths formed a giant X, crossing two thousand yards behind *Michigan*.

It was quiet in Control, the silence interrupted only by the periodic torpedo bearings. Christine could see the strain on the crew's faces as they attempted to discern whether their countermeasures would decoy the torpedoes—and if not, whether the torpedoes would pass behind them without detecting their submarine speeding away.

Another 27-MC announcement. "First torpedo bears three-zero-zero. Second torpedo bears two-four-zero."

Two new bearing lines appeared on the geographic display. Both torpedoes were drawing aft, continuing their crisscross pattern. Christine watched the two torpedoes approach the decoys *Michigan* had left in its wake, waiting for a sign the countermeasures had worked.

"First torpedo bears two-nine-five. Second torpedo bears two-four-five. Both torpedoes approaching countermeasures."

Christine's eyes went to the geographic display again. Both torpedoes were within a hundred yards of *Michigan*'s decoys.

"First torpedo bears two-nine-zero. Second torpedo bears two-five-zero. Both torpedoes have passed our countermeasures."

The geographic display updated, verifying the Sonar Supervisor's report. Both bearings marched onward, giving no indication the torpedoes had been fooled by the decoys.

And so it had come down to this. *Michigan* would thread the needle between both torpedoes, hoping each would pass by without detecting them. Christine studied the geographic display, watching the red inverted Vs gradually gain on the white dot in the center. The two torpedoes continued their crossing pattern, drawing closer together as they converged on *Michigan*.

"First torpedo bears two-eight-zero. Second torpedo bears two-six-zero."

The Executive Officer joined Wilson on the Conn. Lieutenant Commander Greenwood was the Fire Control Coordinator, responsible for generating a firing solution for their targets. But he had no firing solutions; *Michigan* was evading at ahead flank and they had lost both Chinese submarines due to the turbulent flow of water across the submarine's sonar dome. Besides, it seemed pointless to Christine to launch another torpedo now. At least not until one of the two torpedoes Petty Officer Walsh was reassembling was ready.

Seemingly in response to Christine's thoughts, the Weapons Officer announced, "Reassembly of both torpedoes is complete. Loading Tubes One and Two."

Wilson acknowledged the Weps' report, his eyes never leaving the geographic display.

"Both torpedoes bear two-seven-zero."

The two torpedoes were now at their closest point of approach, and Christine heard the faint, high-pitched chirp of the torpedo sonars. She gripped the Conn railing tightly, hoping there was enough distance between *Michigan* and the torpedoes behind them.

"First torpedo bears two-six-five. Second torpedo bears two-seven-five."

Christine could feel the collective sigh in the Control Room. Both torpedoes were continuing on their original courses, which meant they hadn't detected their target. But now, instead of a narrow stern aspect, the torpedoes would pass by *Michigan* on its beam, getting a much clearer look at the 560-foot-long submarine. Although the torpedoes were now gradually opening, the danger hadn't passed.

"First torpedo bears two-six-zero. Second torpedo bears two-eight-zero."

Christine listened intently as the torpedo bearings marched up *Michigan*'s port and starboard side, until both torpedoes were abreast *Michigan* and opening. Christine assumed the torpedoes could look only in front of them, and apparently her assessment was correct, as the tension in the Control Room faded. The men at their consoles and the Supervisors began conversing and passing reports between them again.

They had survived. *Michigan* could now speed away and return later, attempting to slip through the Chinese submarine blockade at some other location. But instead of heading away, Wilson did the opposite.

"Helm, all stop. Left full rudder, steady course two-seven-zero."

Christine's jaw almost dropped. *Michigan* was turning around, pointing toward the two Chinese submarines behind them. Wilson explained.

"Attention in Control. We're going to turn and fight. We have a timeline to meet with respect to inserting our SEAL team, and we can't keep running away every time we're detected. We'll have surprise on our side—the last thing the Chinese expect is for us to turn and fight with a Torpedo Room full of defective torpedoes. Our opponents believe they are invincible, and we're going to use that belief against them. I've ordered all stop, reducing our noise signature so the Chinese submarines will lose contact on us. We'll wait until they're close and shoot two torpedoes in their face, and hopefully the Chinese sonar pulse won't shut down our modified torpedoes. Carry on."

Captain Wilson was placing a lot of faith in Petty Officer Walsh. Turning to fight would be either a brilliant tactical move or suicide, depending on whether Walsh had successfully modified the two torpedoes.

Michigan completed its turn to the west, gradually drifting to a stop while Lieutenant Herndon and Wilson stood on the Conn, scanning the sonar display for evidence of the Chinese submarines pursuing them. After a few moments, two faint white lines appeared on the display, accompanied by a 27-MC report from Sonar.

"Conn, Sonar. Regained Sierra five-zero and five-one, bearing three-zero-zero and two-four-zero respectively."

"Very well, Sonar." Wilson acknowledged Sonar's report, then announced loudly so everyone in Control could hear. "Designate Sierra five-one as Master One and Sierra five-zero as Master Two. Track Master One and Two."

Wilson glanced at his Executive Officer, who was already engrossed in the task of determining the course, speed, and range of the two Chinese submarines.

The Executive Officer finally called out, "I have a firing solution for both contacts."

Christine's eyes shifted from the sonar monitor on the Conn to Captain Wilson, expecting him to order Firing Point Procedures. But he just stood there. As Christine wondered what he was waiting for, her thoughts were interrupted by the Weapons Officer's report.

"Tubes One and Two are loaded. Powering up both weapons."

Wilson remained silent, and for the first time, Christine sensed the tension in his posture. Petty Officer Walsh hadn't been sure the torpedoes would function with the primary Signal Processing card removed, yet Wilson's plan hinged on two functional torpedoes.

"Both weapons have powered up, communicating with combat control," the Weps announced.

Wilson ordered, "Firing Point Procedures. Salvo from Tubes One and Two.

Assign Tube One to Master One, Tube Two to Master Two. Tube One first-fired. Set Short Range tactics and change Search Speed to High-One, both units."

The Executive Officer bounced between the three combat control consoles, eventually tapping Lieutenant Cordero and one of the petty officers on the shoulder as he announced, "Solutions ready."

Lieutenant Herndon reported, "Ship ready."

The Weapons Officer followed up. "Both tubes flooded down. Opening outer doors, Tubes One and Two. Sending presets to both units." Lieutenant Stewart returned his attention to the Weapon Launch Console as Wilson and the rest of the personnel in Control waited quietly. For what, Christine wasn't sure, but Wilson's eyes were fixed on his Weapons Officer.

As the crew waited for Weps' next report, the Sonar Supervisor's voice carried across Control. "Downshift in propeller blade rate, both contacts. Master One and Two are slowing."

There was no reaction from Wilson as he acknowledged Sonar. Lieutenant Herndon moved close to Wilson, speaking quietly. "Sir, we are at all stop. I recommend we put speed on the ship. If either submarine fires, we'll need speed to evade."

"No," Wilson replied. "I don't want them to realize we're pointed at them. What we lose in speed we'll gain in surprise."

Herndon nodded as the Weapons Officer called out, alarm in his voice. "Sir, weapons *not* ready! Neither torpedo is accepting presets."

Wilson snatched the 27-MC microphone from its holster, punching the button for the Torpedo Room. "Torpedo Room, Captain. Put Walsh on."

A moment later, the Torpedoman answered. "Petty Officer Walsh."

"Neither torpedo is accepting presets. Is there something we need to do?"

"No, sir," Walsh replied. "There's nothing we *can* do. It could be both torpedoes are running additional start-up diagnostics now that their primary SP cards are missing. Or maybe I should have left them in and short-circuited them, but I didn't know how to do that. I recommend we give them a little more time."

A powerful sonar ping echoed through the Control Room. Wilson's eyes went to the sonar display, showing a bright white blip on the bearing of Master One. "Time is a luxury we don't have, Walsh."

"Give them a few more seconds, Captain."

A second sonar ping penetrated *Michigan*'s hull, this one coming from the bearing corresponding to Master Two.

The XO turned toward Wilson as the Captain slid the 27-MC microphone back into its holster. "Both contacts have closed to three thousand yards and have slowed to ten knots."

Wilson acknowledged the XO, then called out, "Weps, report weapon status."

"Sir, both torpedoes are still refusing to accept presets."

An uneasy silence settled over Control as Wilson stepped off the Conn to examine the geographic display at Cordero's console. The two Chinese submarines were closing on *Michigan*, one from thirty degrees off the bow to starboard and the other from thirty degrees to port. It wouldn't be long before one or both submarines calculated a firing solution and sent a torpedo down *Michigan*'s throat.

Christine wondered what the two submarines were waiting for when she heard Captain Wilson mutter under his breath, "That's it, you overconfident bastards. Get nice and close, so your torpedoes won't miss this time."

It seemed this was part of Wilson's plan, remaining dead in the water, drawing their adversaries in close. For what purpose, Christine didn't know. But she figured she'd find out soon enough.

"Conn, Sonar. Master One and Two are opening torpedo tube outer doors."

The Executive Officer followed up, "Sir, both contacts have closed to within two thousand yards."

Wilson returned to the Conn, his eyes shifting between the sonar monitor and the geographic display. He seemed on the verge of issuing new orders when the Weapons Officer called out, "Both torpedoes have accepted presets! Weapons ready, Tubes One and Two!"

Wilson responded, "Match Sonar bearings and shoot! Helm, ahead flank!"

The two Fire Control Technicians at the combat control consoles updated the firing solution for each contact, and the Fire Control Technician manning the Weapon Launch Console pressed the launch button at the bottom of his display.

There was a high-pitched whirr as *Michigan*'s starboard torpedo ejection pump jettisoned the four-thousand-pound torpedo from Tube One, followed by the Weapons Officer's announcement, "First fired unit running, wire good, merging on bearing to Master One!" Seconds later, the unique whirr filtered through Control again as *Michigan*'s second torpedo was ejected from Tube Two. "Second fired unit running, wire good, merging on bearing to Master Two."

Meanwhile, the Helm had rung up ahead flank and *Michigan* was now surging directly toward the two Chinese submarines, splitting the distance between them.

Sonar's reports echoed through Control as they monitored their torpedo milestones.

"First fired—fuel crossover achieved."

"Turning to preset gyro course."

"Shifting to High-One speed."

Sonar repeated the announcements for their second fired unit. It appeared both torpedoes were functioning as expected. Whether they were now immune to the Chinese sonar pulse was another question, which would be answered soon. Another powerful sonar ping echoed through Control, this one at a slightly higher frequency.

The Weapons Officer hunched over the Weapon Launch Console, examining the data being transmitted back over the wire from each of *Michigan*'s torpedoes. Christine was relieved when Lieutenant Stewart called out, "Both units functioning normally!"

Wilson responded, "Pre-enable and shift both units to Slow speed."

Christine wondered what Wilson was up to as the Weps repeated back the order, then sent the commands to each torpedo over their guidance wire. *Michigan*'s two torpedoes turned off their sonars and coasted down, giving the impression they had been dudded by the Chinese sonar pulse.

Although an important element of Wilson's plan appeared on track, there was another aspect of his plan that worried Christine—they were barreling directly toward the two Chinese submarines, which would no doubt fire back.

Sure enough, Sonar reported, "Torpedo in the water, bearing two-four-zero!" Seconds later, the Sonar Supervisor followed up, "Second torpedo in the water, bearing three-zero-zero!"

The two Chinese submarines had counter-fired, and Christine wondered which direction Wilson would turn the ship to evade the torpedoes. But Wilson did nothing, leaving *Michigan* on a course of 270, headed between both torpedoes. He didn't even launch a torpedo decoy, but that was under-standable, given the decoy would be ejected behind them and do nothing to distract the torpedoes racing toward *Michigan*.

Wilson seemed oblivious to the danger speeding toward them. Instead, he focused on the geographic display, watching *Michigan*'s two torpedoes continue toward their contacts. The MK 48 torpedoes had reduced their speed, but instead of coasting to a halt, were continuing toward their targets at Slow speed, and were now only five hundred yards away. Apparently that was what Wilson was waiting for.

"Enable and shift Search Speed to High-Two, both units!"

The commands were relayed to *Michigan*'s torpedoes, and a moment later, Sonar confirmed the orders had been accepted. "Sonar, Conn. Both units have gone active, shifting to High-Two." Seconds later, the Weps called out, "First fired unit has acquired!" followed almost immediately by, "Second fired unit has acquired! Both units are homing!"

With both torpedoes at maximum speed, they closed the remaining distance in only fifteen seconds, the arrival of the first torpedo at its target announced by a deafening explosion rumbling through Control.

The Weapons Officer called out, "Loss of wire continuity, first-fired unit." A second explosion erupted as the first one died down. "Loss of wire conti-nuity, second-fired unit."

An announcement from Sonar followed, confirming *Michigan*'s two torpedoes had hit their mark. "Breaking-up noises from Master One and Master Two."

Unlike earlier, when they had sunk the first Chinese submarine, there was no cheering in Control. Two torpedoes were still bearing down on *Michigan*, both less than four hundred yards away. Wilson remained on the Conn, monitoring the sonar display, paying no attention to the red inverted Vs an-gling toward them.

Christine braced for the torpedo explosions as the red inverted Vs merged with *Michigan*'s white dot. But instead of jolting explosions, a loud metallic clank echoed from the port side of the ship, followed by an identical clank on the starboard side.

Sonar announced, "Both torpedoes have impacted the hull. Neither det-onated."

Questioning eyes turned toward Wilson, who let out a slow breath. "That's what I was banking on. These were Yu-6 torpedoes, with a minimum arming distance of one thousand yards. We were able to close both torpedoes before they armed."

Wilson had calculated everything perfectly, and they had sunk three Chinese submarines blocking their path toward the coast. Turning his attention to the SEAL team insertion, he ordered, "Helm, ahead standard. Right ten degrees rudder, steady course two-nine-zero."

The Helm acknowledged and rung up ahead standard as he twisted the rudder to right ten degrees. *Michigan* slowed, melting back into the ocean.

59

USS *MICHIGAN*

"Be *very* careful with this."

In the Radio Room just forward of Control, Christine watched Chief Jeff Walkup hand a USB flash drive to Lieutenant Harrison, standing beside her. The Chief held out the flash drive with two hands, cradling it like a vial of nitroglycerin as he added, "This is the electronic equivalent of the bubonic plague."

Harrison took the flash drive, placing it into a black, waterproof pouch he sealed as the Chief explained how to inject the virus into the Chinese communication center.

"Any USB port will do. The flash drive should load onto the desktop, regardless of the operating system used by the computer. Open the drive and inside you'll see a single icon. Double-click on the icon and the virus will take care of the rest."

Christine digested the Chief's instructions as her thoughts dwelt on the preceding forty-two hours. After sinking the three Chinese submarines, *Michigan* had headed quietly toward the Chinese coast, searching the surrounding waters for signs of other Chinese submarines. They had avoided detection as they closed on the SEAL team launch point, proceeding to periscope depth an hour earlier at exactly 4 A.M., as instructed.

A satellite of some type had been repositioned, allowing communications with *Michigan* for one hour, twice each day. During its last pass above the Western Pacific, it had downloaded the lethal computer virus to *Michigan*.

Harrison turned to Christine as he slid the pouch into the left breast pocket of his camouflage uniform. "Are you ready to suit up?"

"Into what?" Christine asked.

"You don't think you're going on a mission dressed like that, do you?"

Harrison's eyes darted to her blue coveralls for a second. "You'll need something more appropriate."

An hour later, the *Michigan* was back at three hundred feet, heading steadily toward the Chinese coast. Christine was seated in the Executive Officer's stateroom as Harrison arrived with a stack of equipment in his arms. After closing the door behind him with his elbow, he placed the gear on the XO's desk.

"This is your wet suit." Harrison held up a one-piece black wet suit with a zipper up the front and a hood. "We'll be traveling in water that's fifty-eight degrees Fahrenheit this time of year, and hypothermia will set in unless you're protected." He placed the wet suit back onto the desk, picking up a pair of rubber shoes in his right hand and a harness in his left. "Rubber booties and a double tank harness. We'll be underwater for a while, so you'll need two air tanks. Rubber boots, but no fins for you. I'll get you to the surface without them." Harrison returned the gear to the desk and he picked up the final piece of equipment. "A full-face mask, which supplies air you can breathe through your mouth or nose."

Harrison piled the equipment into a neat stack. "You wear nothing under your wet suit except underwear. Let me know if you need help getting dressed." Harrison flashed a mischievous grin. "I'll be waiting outside your stateroom."

Christine offered a condescending smile and matching tone of voice. "I'm sure I'll manage."

Five minutes later, after wriggling into her wet suit, Christine had donned the gear Harrison had deposited on the XO's desk. She opened the door to find Harrison leaning against the bulkhead, his muscular arms folded across his chest. He turned and eyed her from head to toe, reaching out to adjust the harness straps over her shoulders.

"Not bad for a novice." Harrison smiled warmly this time. "Wait in your stateroom while I suit up. I'll be back in a few minutes."

Harrison headed aft while Christine returned to her stateroom, closing the door behind her, settling into the XO's chair. As she waited in silence, outfitted in Navy SEAL gear, she reflected on the upcoming mission. Harrison believed their odds of making it out of the Great Hall were slim to none. Until this moment, she had refused to dwell on the possibility that she might not survive. But now, less than an hour from launch, a cold shiver slid over her body. Although her outward demeanor remained calm, inside she was beginning to panic.

Christine drew in a deep breath, exhaling slowly, trying to calm her nerves. She told herself that, one way or another, she would survive and return to *Michigan*. They would *all* survive.

Another knock and the door opened, revealing Lieutenant Harrison decked out in a matching wet suit and associated gear. He said nothing and Christine stood without a word. He turned and she followed him down the passageway, through the watertight hatch into Missile Compartment Second Level. The four SEALs who would accompany them were standing outside Missile Tube One, dressed like Harrison. They eyed Christine without greeting her. Their faces were grim.

Also wearing dour expressions were Captain Wilson and Commander John McNeil. Harrison and Christine stopped beside the six men, and it was Commander McNeil who spoke first.

"Does everything fit correctly?"

It seemed an odd question for some reason, like he was inquiring whether a new pair of shoes felt comfortable. She wondered if there was a more direct question he wanted to ask.

Are you ready to die?

Commander McNeil stared at her, and Christine realized she hadn't answered. "Everything fits fine, Commander."

McNeil nodded, then turned toward the four SEALs beside him, motioning to the first man. "Accompanying you is Chief Dan O'Hara, the senior enlisted man on the mission." O'Hara was the oldest of the four SEALs, the sides of his short red hair speckled with gray. O'Hara extended his hand. "Glad to have you with us, Miss O'Connor."

O'Hara's light blue eyes conveyed the sincerity of his words. As she shook his hand, McNeil continued the introductions. "Also on the team is Drew Garretson—Communicator; Tracey Martin—a Breacher, an explosives expert; and Kelly Andrews—Rappeler." Christine recognized Tracey and Kelly as *the girls* Harrison had mentioned during the mission brief, apparently due to their feminine first names. Both SEALs, however, were over six feet tall and two hundred pounds of solid muscle.

Christine shook each man's strong hand, ending with, "It's a pleasure to meet you."

McNeil added, "You'll be riding with Lieutenant Harrison in one SDV, with the other four SEALs in the other. Do you have any questions?"

Christine shook her head slowly.

"Let's get going then." Upon McNeil's order, Harrison approached an open hatch, about waist high, in the side of Missile Tube One, while the four other SEALs headed toward Missile Tube Two.

As Christine followed Harrison toward the hatch, Wilson reached out and touched her shoulder. She stopped, turning toward him as he spoke. "Be careful, Christine."

She eyed the submarine Captain, searching for the right response. She had no idea what to expect in the coming hours, or whether Harrison was right—that she would be more hindrance than help.

Christine nodded, then stepped through the hatch into the missile tube. Behind her, the hatch swung shut with a faint clank, and she watched the handle spin as the hatch lugs were engaged, sealing her and Harrison inside.

The seven-foot-diameter missile tube was brightly illuminated by fluorescent lights mounted overhead. Harrison and Christine stood on a metal grate in the second level of the missile tube, containing a steel ladder leading up two levels to another hatch. Harrison adeptly climbed the ladder and Christine followed carefully. She paused at the top of the ladder, peering into the relative darkness, bathed in diffuse red light. A hand thrust downward, and after she grabbed Harrison's hand, he pulled her up into the Dry Deck Shelter.

The Dry Deck Shelter was a conglomeration of three separate chambers—a spherical hyperbaric chamber at the forward end to treat injured divers; a spherical transfer trunk in the middle, which she and Harrison were currently in; and a long, cylindrical Hangar section containing the SEAL Delivery Vehicle—a black mini-sub resembling a fat torpedo—twenty-two feet long by six feet in diameter. The Hangar was divided into two sections by a

Plexiglas shield dropping halfway down from the top of the Hangar, with the SDV on one side and controls for operating the Hangar on the other side.

Harrison stepped into the Hangar and Christine followed, to find the Hangar already populated with five Navy divers; one on the forward side of the Plexiglas shield to operate the Hangar controls, and the other four divers in scuba gear on the other side of the shield. Harrison sealed the hatch behind him, then ducked under the Plexiglas shield.

Christine followed, stopping at the forward end of the SDV, which was loaded nose first into the Dry Deck Shelter. The SDV had two seating areas, one in front of the other, each capable of carrying two persons. Two large, black duffel bags occupied the rear compartment.

Harrison lifted a pair of scuba tanks from a rack in the DDS bulkhead, dropping them into Christine's harness behind her. After connecting her air hose to the tanks, he donned two tanks of his own, then helped Christine into the front seat of the SDV. Harrison put on his fins and climbed in beside her, then manipulated the controls in front of him. The SDV displays energized, illuminating the cockpit in a soothing green glow. A contour of the Chinese coast appeared on the navigation display. They were ten miles from shore.

Harrison put his facemask on, motioning for Christine to do the same. Then he popped his head out the top of the mini-sub, rendering a thumbs-up to the diver on the other side of the Plexiglas shield.

A few seconds later, dark water surged into the DDS, gushing up from vents beneath them, pooling at the bottom of the Hangar and rising rapidly. The DDS was soon completely flooded down, except for a pocket of air on the other side of the Plexiglas shield, where the Navy diver operated the Dry Deck Shelter. Christine heard a faint rumbling grind as the circular hatch at the end of the DDS opened. Through the murky water, illuminated by the green glow from the SDV console, she watched the two divers on each side of the SDV glide toward the chamber opening with a kick of their fins.

The divers pulled rails out from the Hangar onto the submarine's Missile Deck, and the SDV began moving backward. As they emerged from the chamber, Christine spotted the other four SEALs in a second SDV being hauled out of the other shelter, guided aft along rails by divers floating beside them.

The SDV exited the Dry Deck Shelter and Christine felt a subtle thud as the backward motion of the submersible ceased. Harrison manipulated the SDV controls and a gentle vibration began coursing through her body. The SDV's propeller had begun spinning, and the submersible lifted off its rails. It rose slowly, then began moving forward, passing above the Dry Deck Shelter and then along the starboard side of *Michigan*'s sail. After passing the sail, Christine spotted the other SDV on the port side of the submarine, and the two SDVs cruised over the submarine's bow fifteen feet apart. Turning around, Christine watched the black silhouette of USS *Michigan* fade into the murky water.

60

BOHAI SEA

Christine lost all sense of time as she cruised toward the Chinese coast. The underwater world was cloaked in darkness, illuminated only by the SDV console. Despite her insulated wet suit, a chill had set in and her muscles were tense from the cold. Christine sat quietly in the SDV as she tried to pass the time and chill away.

The vibrations pulsing through the SDV suddenly ceased and the mini-sub began slowing. Harrison looked up from the SDV console, peering ahead, and Christine followed his gaze. Barely discernible in the darkness, barnacle-encrusted wood pilings drifted toward them. Harrison deftly maneuvered the SDV, angling alongside the pilings, letting them pass slowly down the starboard side of the vehicle. A rusted metal ladder appeared between two of the wooden pilings, and Harrison shifted the propeller into reverse, then cut the engine after the SDV slowed to a halt. After a few taps of the controls, the SDV drifted downward, coming to rest on the sandy ocean bottom. A few seconds later, the other SDV settled on the ocean floor beside them, only a few feet away. Another tap and the SDV console went dark.

Yellow lights wavered on the water's surface, faintly illuminating the eerie underwater world. Christine watched as Harrison and the four other SEALs deftly extracted themselves from their SDVs. Harrison helped her out of the SDV, depositing her onto the side of the mini-sub where she hung on with one arm draped inside the cockpit. Then he grabbed the two black duffel bags from the back of their SDV, slung both bags over his shoulder, and sidled up against Christine as one of the other SEALs ascended toward the surface.

A minute later, the SEAL returned, offering a thumbs-up. He grabbed one of the duffel bags, rejoined the other three SEALs, and all four surged toward the surface. A moment later, Harrison gripped Christine's arm firmly and propelled them both upward with a powerful kick.

They slowed as they approached the surface, angling toward the rusted metal ladder. Christine grabbed on to the ladder while Harrison removed his fins, motioning for her to follow him up. After climbing a few of the rusted metal rungs, Christine's head emerged from the dark water. She pushed her facemask onto her forehead, taking a deep breath of the cool night air.

Harrison reached the top of the ladder and disappeared. Christine continued climbing, and after a few more rungs, reached the top of a wharf, framing what looked like an abandoned quay. The first four SEALs were arranged in a semicircular perimeter about twenty feet in diameter, each man on one knee wielding a Heckler & Koch MP7 submachine gun—a compact assault rifle barely more than a foot long with an extendable stock, an optical sight, and a suppressor screwed onto the barrel.

The wharf extended for several hundred yards in each direction, and a few hundred feet to the left was an abandoned two-story building. A sign above the dark entrance, inscribed in English, identified the building as the Xingang Port Passenger Terminal, which had been abandoned after the new terminal had been built a few miles away. They were in Tianjin, Beijing's neighboring port city.

Christine pulled herself onto the wharf, moving awkwardly toward Harrison; her muscles were stiff from the cold underwater journey. Harrison opened his duffel bag and retrieved a flashlight that he pointed inland, energizing it briefly three times. As Christine stopped next to Harrison, a pair of headlights appeared in the distance, and a white van soon approached the deserted wharf, stopping next to the five SEALs and Christine. A side door slid open, revealing one of the men from the CIA safe house.

Harrison picked up the duffel bag and guided Christine into the van, and they were joined by the four other SEALs as they collapsed their perimeter. The van sped away and Christine and the five SEALs settled into seats lining both sides of the van, while the Chinese man remained standing, gripping handholds suspended from the top of the van. He eyed Christine and the five men briefly before speaking.

"I am Tian Aiguo. Welcome to China."

In the back of the van, the SEALs shed their scuba gear, stripping the wet suits from their bodies, and put on the trousers and shirts that Tian pulled from a sack at his feet. Harrison helped Christine remove her gear and glanced at her wet suit.

"Tian has clothes for you, if you don't mind stripping down in the van. We won't look."

The underwater journey had sucked the heat from Christine's body, and the prospect of warm, dry clothing instead of a cold, damp wet suit outweighed her modesty. "I'll change."

Tian handed her a white towel, along with a loose-fitting white shirt and baggy khaki pants with a drawstring at the waist. Christine pulled her arms from her wet suit, wrapping the towel around her chest as she pulled the rest of the suit away from her body, steadying herself with a grip on Harrison's shoulder as the van jostled along the highway. True to Harrison's word, the six men averted their eyes as she changed into dry clothing.

"All clear," she announced, then tossed the towel back to Tian as he turned toward her.

Christine returned to her seat next to Harrison. Even though she'd changed into dry clothing, she was trembling from the cold. She could sense Harrison wanted to wrap his arm around her and pull her close, warming her with the heat of his body. But instead, he sat stiffly as the van bounced along. Minutes turned into hours as the van traveled through the night, and Christine found herself drifting into sleep occasionally, awaking each time to find herself leaning against Harrison's shoulder. He gave no indication that he noticed, and neither he nor the other four SEALs appeared tired. They sat staring ahead, occasionally murmuring something to each other in the darkness that she couldn't quite make out over the rumble of the van.

The outskirts of a large city became visible as dawn crept across the countryside, tall skyscrapers rising in the distance. They were traveling along a six-lane highway, three lanes in each direction, heading north into Beijing. The immense steel and glass oval structure of the Beijing South Railway Station appeared in the distance, and it seemed like it was a lifetime ago that she had boarded the white bullet train out of the city with Peng.

The van exited the highway onto Kai Yang Lu Street, and four kilometers later, the vehicle stopped in front of the same CIA safe house she'd left two weeks ago. Tian opened the side door from inside the van and stepped onto the sidewalk, then after a quick glance in each direction, waved them out. Chief O'Hara led the way, followed by the other three enlisted SEALs, then Christine and Harrison.

Fatigue set in as she stepped into the safe house. The underwater transit, followed by the uncomfortable journey in the back of the van had taken its toll, and her body was in desperate need of sleep. The plan, according to Harrison, was to sleep most of the day, then after a final mission review, head out after dark. From that point on, there would be no opportunity for sleep until the mission objective had been accomplished and the team had returned to *Michigan*, lurking just off the coast. *If* everything went according to plan.

61

BEIJING

Huan Zhixin strode briskly through the corridors of the Great Hall of the People, making the transit from his office on the perimeter of the South Wing to its center, where President Xiang and the other Politburo members had their offices. The floor transitioned from terrazzo to marble, and he passed between fluted columns on each side of the hallway, marking the beginning of the Politburo's official spaces.

Huan's plan to gain membership to the elite ruling Politburo was proceeding flawlessly. The American Pacific Fleet had been destroyed and although Admiral Tsou was the plan's mastermind, Huan, as head of the People's Liberation Army, would receive much credit. When it came time to fill Bai Tao's vacant seat, no other candidate could defeat him. However, the United States was up to something. It was important Xiang be briefed, so if things did not turn out well, Huan could somehow twist the situation around and make Xiang responsible.

Huan reached the president's office, ignoring the two Cadre Department bodyguards stationed outside as he knocked. He heard Xiang's voice through the door and entered, settling into a chair across from the president's desk.

Xiang ignored Huan's presence, continuing to review a document in a folder on his desk. Xiang's failure to acknowledge him was deliberate, he thought, treating him like a second-class Party member. Huan began to fume at the blatant disrespect. As he waited, he savored his pending election to the Politburo. Then, with his uncle Shen's support, it would be only a matter of time before he obtained the necessary votes to supplant Xiang as China's supreme leader. Xiang would pay for his insolence.

Finally, Xiang signed the document and looked up. "You have news?"

Huan got straight to the issue. "The American SEAL Team has reached Beijing."

"Where are they now?" Xiang asked.

"They're at the CIA safe house."

"Why are they here?"

"We don't know yet. However, our informant has been directed to determine the objective of their mission. Then we will send in our special forces and eliminate them."

"I thought you didn't know the location of the safe house."

"We do now," Huan answered, then explained. "We thought O'Connor's escape from the Great Hall was inconsequential, and not worthy of compromising our penetration of the CIA here in Beijing. We were not aware until later that a secure flash drive was missing, and that she might have it. The SEAL Team, however, poses a clear threat, and we have obtained the location of the safe house by paying our informant a very large sum."

Huan waited for additional questions, and Xiang asked the most important one. "When will the SEAL Team be eliminated?"

"Today," Huan answered, "after we determine the objective of their mission. Or nightfall, whichever comes first."

62

BEIJING

A light rain was falling from dark overcast skies, pattering softly against a grimy, four-pane window in a small second-story bedroom, furnished with a twin bed next to a rickety wooden end table. Christine's eyes fluttered open in the semidarkness as she stretched under the soft brown blanket. It was either dusk or dawn, based on the gray light filtering through the window. She poked her left hand out from beneath the covers, and brought her watch close to her face. After scrutinizing her watch in the dim light for a moment, she concluded it was 7 P.M.

She had slept most of the day. After arriving at the safe house, Tian had cooked breakfast for Christine and the SEALs, peppering them with questions about their mission. The SEALs were tight-lipped—they hadn't even told Tian their names—and Harrison had cut her off with a sharp, disapproving glance when she had begun to answer one of Tian's questions. Christine caught the hint—as did Tian, who apologized for prying. After cleaning up after breakfast, Tian took Christine and the SEALs' measurements for clothing that would allow them to travel from Guang Chang Boulevard to the Great Hall of the People without attracting attention.

Christine pushed the blanket aside, swinging her feet onto the cold wooden floor as she sat up on the side of the bed. Glancing at the end table, she eyed a travel kit Tian had dropped off. She grabbed it as she stood, then headed down the hall to the bathroom. After freshening up and returning the travel kit to her nightstand, she descended the stairs to the main floor.

Harrison and the other four SEALs were already downstairs. The Lieutenant and Chief O'Hara were standing in the living room while the other three SEALs—Garretson, Martin, and Andrews—huddled around a laptop computer on the small dining room table, the dark brown curtains by the dining room window drawn closed. The scarred wooden table their laptop rested upon was illuminated by a yellow, incandescent lamp hanging from the ceiling.

All five SEALs were dressed in civilian clothes—black trousers with the legs covering the top of their combat boots, each man wearing a different dark-colored polo shirt. Harrison and O'Hara were trying on black, loose-fitting windbreakers. Both SEALs had their MP7s attached to slings draped around their necks and under one shoulder. After zipping up their jackets, each man turned to examine the other.

"They'll do," O'Hara said as he unzipped and shrugged his jacket off, tossing it onto three other jackets lying across the back of the couch. Leaning next to the couch were three black backpacks Tian had also apparently procured, lying next to the SEAL duffel bags—now empty. Harrison left his jacket on and she could see a slight bulge in his right pocket, most likely the sealed pouch containing the flash drive loaded with the virus.

Lieutenant Harrison looked up as Christine reached the bottom of the stairs. "Good evening, Miss O'Connor. It's about time you woke up. I was about to knock on your door."

O'Hara turned toward her as did the other three SEALs, who looked up from the computer, and Christine suddenly realized she was wearing a thin white T-shirt with no bra. It was chilly in the room and the men noticed her body's reaction, their eyes moving from her face to her breasts, the outline of her nipples clearly visible through her T-shirt.

Christine crossed her arms across her chest as the front door opened. Tian appeared in the doorway, carrying a shopping bag in each hand. He kicked the door closed with his left heel as he entered the foyer and moved into the dining room, depositing the bags onto the table as Garretson closed the laptop lid.

Tian pulled the contents from the first bag, stacking them neatly on the table. "I've purchased suitable clothes for you, Miss O'Connor, along with an assortment of makeup products. I wasn't sure if you wanted any and I didn't want to wake you, so I took the liberty of picking up a few things."

Christine joined Tian at the table, noting a black pair of slacks, long-sleeve dark blue satin shirt, and a short black coat. Tian upended the second bag, dumping a shoe box and an assortment of makeup products onto the table. Christine opened the box and examined a pair of flat-soled shoes with a critical eye before deciding they'd be suitable for running if the situation demanded it. She slipped one on, verifying it fit.

Christine returned the shoe to its box, and after reviewing the products on the table, decided she'd skip the makeup.

"Thanks, Tian." Christine placed the clothes and makeup back into their bags and Tian disappeared into the kitchen, returning a moment later with a platter bearing a bottle of baijiu—a clear liquor sometimes referred to as Chinese vodka—and seven shot glasses, which he placed on the dining room table.

The three SEALs at the table perked up, and one of the *girls*, Tracey Martin, broke into a wide grin. "Now we're talking."

Harrison checked his watch. "We'll be leaving soon. No drinks."

"Oh, come on, Lieutenant," Martin pleaded. "One drink won't hurt anything. We've got a few hours to work it off."

Chief O'Hara interjected. "Shut your trap, Martin. You know better. No drinks."

The smile disappeared from Martin's face as the other *girl*, Petty Officer Kelly Andrews, smacked Martin across the back of the head. "What answer did you expect?"

Martin rubbed his head. "It can't hurt to ask." His eyes shifted from Andrews to the bottle of baijiu, then back to the computer. "Let's get back to business, then." He looked up at Lieutenant Harrison. "We're ready to run through it one more time, sir." He glanced at Tian, still standing next to the table.

Tian frowned, then returned to the kitchen as Garretson opened the top of the laptop, pulling up a satellite image of the Great Hall of the People. Harrison and O'Hara joined the three SEALs around the table as Christine scooped up her new clothes in one arm, the shoe box in the other.

Ten minutes later, Christine returned downstairs wearing her new clothes. They fit perfectly. Harrison and the other four SEALs were still gathered around the laptop, their eyes focused on the screen. Harrison looked up as Christine descended the stairs, but said nothing.

Tian exited the kitchen, appraising his selection of clothing. "You look fantastic, Miss O'Connor. I take it everything is suitable?"

"Yes, Tian. Thank you."

"If you'll excuse me," Tian added, "I have a few errands to run. I'll be back in an hour." Tian grabbed his jacket from the foyer coatrack, exiting the town house without another word.

As the front door closed, Harrison left the other four SEALs and headed toward Christine. O'Hara picked up the platter of baijiu and shot glasses from the table, entering the kitchen as Harrison guided Christine over to the living room where he dropped into a brown, dingy sofa. Christine settled in beside him.

"So," Harrison began. "How do you feel?"

"Good," Christine answered. "Although I'm still tired." She could tell Harrison wanted to talk about something important. He was just breaking the ice.

"That's typical," Harrison replied. "Long transits in cold water sap the strength from you. Even more so for someone not used to it. You'll bounce back soon enough, though." There was an awkward silence as Christine waited for Harrison to work toward what he really wanted to discuss. Finally, he continued. "This is a dangerous mission, Chris. I have no idea what we're going to run into once we enter the Great Hall, and I don't want to put you in harm's way. So I'm leaving you outside. Once you unlock the door to the Great Hall, I want you to return to the car and wait with Tian."

Christine shook her head. "That's not a good idea, Jake. There's no telling how many security doors you'll need to pass through once you get inside."

Harrison shrugged. "We'll manage."

Christine knew she had a point, so she pressed it. "We've already discussed this. I'm coming with you. The whole way, not just to the front door."

Harrison's eyes searched hers for a moment, then he nodded reluctantly. "Okay, Chris. You always were headstrong, and I see that hasn't changed. But I had to try." He stood, offering Christine his hand, pulling her to her feet.

As Christine stood, the dining room curtains billowed inward, small holes appearing in the fabric as high-pitched zings pierced the quiet town house. Christine froze, watching bullets puncture the bodies of the three SEALs gathered around the dining room table. She watched in stunned silence as the middle of the three SEALs slumped onto the table, his head coming to rest on the laptop, and the other two SEALs fell backward in their chairs onto the floor. She had no idea how long she stood there, but it must have been only a second before she felt Harrison's body slamming into her, knocking her onto the wooden floor.

Shards of glass from the dining room window and chunks of plaster ricocheted throughout the town house as Harrison protected her with his body. Turning her head to the side as bullets streamed into the town house, she spotted Chief O'Hara burst from the kitchen in a crouch, sliding next to the dining room table. One glance at the SEAL slumped over the table told O'Hara what he needed to know—blood trickled from a bullet hole in the center of Garretson's forehead onto the laptop, flowing over the sides of the computer and collecting in a red pool spreading slowly across the table's surface.

O'Hara extracted the laptop from under Garretson's head, then flung it across the floor toward Harrison and Christine. The other two SEALs were still alive, crawling toward the living room, leaving slick red trails behind them. Harrison rolled off Christine, joining O'Hara as each man grabbed an injured SEAL by the collar of his shirt, dragging them into the living room as bullets continued pelting the town house through the dining room window.

"Get the computer!" Harrison shouted to Christine as he grabbed one of the black backpacks and O'Hara grabbed a second. "Stay low to the ground!"

Christine crawled over to the computer, which had come to rest only a few feet away, as Harrison shouted again. "The back of the town house!"

Crawling on her hands and knees, Christine followed Harrison and O'Hara, pushing the computer down a narrow hallway as plaster fragments from the town house walls rained down on her. They reached the back of the town house, where a narrow door led to the alley from which Christine had entered the safe house with Peng two weeks ago. Harrison and O'Hara propped the two injured SEALs against the washer and dryer in the laundry room, then Harrison stood and drew his MP7 from the sling inside his jacket and approached the back door. He twisted the knob slowly, opening the door an inch. As he peered through the slit into the back alley, wood splinters began ricocheting past Harrison's head as the doorframe was peppered with bullets.

Harrison slammed the door shut, then retreated to the laundry room.

"Four men to the left." He squatted to help O'Hara tend to the two wounded SEALs as Christine leaned against the far wall. Harrison checked Andrews's pulse, but Christine could tell he was already dead. Leaning against the dryer, Andrews had a gaping hole in the side of his neck and the blood had stopped flowing; his eyes were frozen open and glazed. Martin was wounded in the chest and was having difficulty breathing. O'Hara ripped open Martin's shirt to examine the wounds. Christine could see red air bubbles forming as blood flowed from two bullet wounds, one on each side of his chest. Harrison and O'Hara exchanged grim looks.

"I know," Martin said. "Both lungs punctured." He grimaced as he spoke, then held his hand out. "Backpack."

Harrison opened one of the backpacks for Martin. "What do you have in mind?"

"The alley," Martin answered. "It's only a few feet wide. Blow a hole in the wall on the other side, and you can enter the adjacent building while the alley is clouded with debris." Martin rummaged through the backpack as Christine digested his plan—blow a hole into the building across the alley, then dash across as four men filled the alley with lead.

Piece of cake. But Christine couldn't think of a better idea.

"We're not leaving you behind," Harrison replied.

"Yes you are. I'll be dead in a few minutes, and you know it." Martin paused as he was wracked by a coughing spasm, spraying the floor with red specks. "If there's any chance of escape, you'll have to travel light and fast. That means without me."

Harrison and O'Hara exchanged glances again, and O'Hara nodded slowly. Harrison turned back to Martin as the injured SEAL pulled four thin blocks of C4 explosive from the backpack, each block wrapped in an olive-drab Mylar film. Martin peeled off the protective paper covering the adhesive on the back of three of the blocks, pressing all four blocks together as he explained.

"Assuming the wall across the alley is one foot thick, you'll need five pounds of untamped C4 placed against the base of the wall to blow a hole large enough for you to pass through."

Martin reached into the backpack again, retrieving a spool of detonating cord and a Gerber tool—a military version of the Swiss Army Knife—and cut off a four-foot length of det cord. He tied one end of the cord into a triple knot, then cut off the Mylar wrapper from one of the blocks of C4. Martin carefully sliced a wedge from the white, claylike plastic explosive, placed the knot of det cord into the divot, then molded the wedge of C4 over the knot so the det cord was firmly embedded in the five-pound block of explosive.

Another reach into the backpack retrieved a handheld initiator and a detonator clamp. Martin unscrewed the bottom of the small, cylindrical initiator, pulling out the detonator—a thin metal tube three inches long, connected to the initiator by shock tube, even thinner, hollow plastic tubing only three millimeters in diameter containing an explosive charge. Martin pulled out ten feet of shock tube, then slid the detonator into one opening of the clamp and the det cord into the adjacent opening. Martin squeezed the clamp shut, ensuring the det cord and detonator were held firmly in place. All in all, it had taken Martin just over a minute to assemble their *Get Out of Jail Free* card.

"This should do it." Martin wheezed the words out.

Harrison took the explosive assembly from Martin while O'Hara pulled the MP7 from Martin's sling, handing it to him grip first.

Martin nodded as he wrapped his fingers around the weapon, but then he placed the MP7 on the floor. "I have a better idea. Leave one of the backpacks with me." His breathing was already turning shallow and the color had drained from his face, leaving it a pasty white, dotted with perspiration.

After another glance between Harrison and O'Hara, Harrison began transferring items from one backpack to another, handing Martin a half-full backpack. Martin emptied the backpack onto the floor, creating a pile of additional blocks of C-4, det cord, and initiators. The injured SEAL began pressing eight more blocks of the plastic explosive together.

The steady stream of bullets piercing the front of the town house stopped, leaving behind an eerie silence. "Get going," Martin said.

Harrison took the laptop from Christine and placed it in his backpack, then stood and slung the backpack over his shoulder. He and O'Hara pulled their MP7s, taking up stations on either side of the door. Harrison turned to Christine. "Up against the wall, between the door and O'Hara." Christine complied, pressing her back against the wall. Harrison added, "I'll go first, then you, then Chief. Understand?"

Christine nodded, then Harrison pulled the safety clip from the initiator. He cracked the door open and tossed the block of C4 into the alley against the far wall. The doorframe splintered from another round of bullets, and Harrison stepped away from the door, flicking up a lever at the top of the initiator with his thumb.

An explosion rocked the alley, shattering the door as it blew back into the town house, the pieces flying down the hallway. Debris was still ricocheting inside the town house when Harrison jumped through the doorway, and Christine felt O'Hara's strong hand on her shoulder, pushing her forward. Christine stepped into the doorway, then bolted into the alley.

The alley was clouded with debris and the men guarding it must have been stunned, because there was no sound of gunfire as Christine followed Harrison into a dark opening across the alley. Harrison pulled to a stop a few feet into the adjacent building and Christine almost ran into him. A second later, O'Hara was at her side, the two SEALs assessing the situation.

They were in an old warehouse filled with stacks of crates about thirty feet high, illuminated by a string of lights along the perimeter of the building. The stacks of towering crates formed passageways down the length of the building, and Harrison took off in a sprint into the nearest aisle. Christine and O'Hara followed as Harrison turned right at the first intersection, then left after two more, resuming their original direction.

Christine and O'Hara caught up to Harrison at the other end of the building, where he had stopped in front of a locked door. Harrison fired twice into the lock mechanism, then kicked the door open. After a cautious glance outside in either direction, he disappeared through the doorway.

Christine followed, emerging into a deserted street, faintly lit by street lamps spaced every fifty feet. It was raining and a cold drizzle drifted down from an overcast sky, blocking out the moon and stars. Harrison sprinted toward a door in the building opposite them, firing into the lock mechanism as he approached, knocking the door open with his shoulder. But then he sprinted back toward the center of the street. Christine headed toward him, wondering what he was planning as they pulled to a halt beside a circular, three-foot-diameter manhole cover in the road.

After letting his MP7 fall to his side on its sling, Harrison lifted the heavy cover with both hands, sliding it aside, revealing a rusted metal ladder that disappeared into the darkness. Harrison descended, followed by Christine as the sound of voices and footsteps raced toward them from inside the warehouse. O'Hara dropped down into the hole after Christine, pausing at the top of the ladder, his chest still above street level. He took aim on the nearest two street lamps, one in each direction, squeezing off two quick rounds, dropping their section of the street into near darkness. He then pulled the manhole cover back into place. A low metallic grinding sound reverberated in Christine's ears until the plate dropped into its recessed location with a metallic clank, enveloping the two SEALs and Christine in pitch black.

Harrison's voice reached out to her in the darkness. "Sit tight."

Christine froze where she was, gripping the metal ladder.

A few seconds after Harrison's order, Christine heard a commotion above them; men shouting, accompanied by the sound of heavy boots. As she waited in the darkness, clutching the rusted metal ladder rungs, the ground trembled, followed by the rumbling sound of a distant explosion. Martin had detonated his C-4.

There was a burst of commotion from the men above them, but the sounds soon faded, eventually ceasing altogether. There was no sign of movement from the two SEALs, until the darkness surrounding Christine was dispelled by a beam of red light. Glancing down, she spotted a flashlight in Harrison's hand, which he shined around them, then down. They were in a concrete access shaft about five feet in diameter, descending another twenty feet into a tunnel. The light reflected off the tunnel floor, and Christine heard the sound of running water. She wondered if they were about to wade through a sewer pipe, but there was no offensive smell, only the ferrous tang of rusted metal.

"Let's go," Harrison whispered as he began descending the ladder.

Christine followed, glancing up occasionally at O'Hara and the manhole cover above him, which thankfully remained in place. As she worked her way down the ladder, she took the opportunity to catch her breath—she was winded from the sprint through the warehouse. Harrison and O'Hara, however, weren't even breathing hard, a testament to their conditioning. Christine made a mental note—if she survived this ordeal, she'd hit the treadmill more often. You never know when you'll have to flee for your life.

Shortly after resuming their descent, Christine reached the end of the ladder. Harrison was already standing on the tunnel floor, his boots immersed in a six-inch-deep stream of water. Christine stepped off the ladder into the cold water, rushing past the top of her ankles, and was joined by O'Hara a second later.

Harrison shined his flashlight down the tunnel, first one way, then the other. They were in a ten-foot-diameter concrete tunnel, containing nothing but a relatively clean stream of water flowing along the bottom.

"Looks like we're in a storm drain," Harrison commented quietly as he turned to O'Hara. "Which way?"

O'Hara glanced down at their feet. "I'd follow the water."

Harrison nodded his agreement, then began jogging down the tunnel, his flashlight beam cutting through the darkness ahead. Christine fell in behind Harrison, with O'Hara behind her.

Christine followed Harrison through the underwater maze, frequently reaching intersections where a decision was required. Each time they chose to follow the stream of water, which gained in volume at each intersection until it was now up to her knees, slowing down their pace. As they sloshed through the dark water, Harrison pulled to a stop, turning off his flashlight. In the distance, a faint white light penetrated the darkness.

"Stay here, Chris," Harrison ordered.

Harrison and O'Hara moved cautiously forward. She could barely hear them as they waded through the water toward the faint disc of light ahead. The two men disappeared, and it wasn't until then that she realized how cold she was again. She rubbed both arms with her hands, hoping to increase her circulation, but it made her shiver instead. Her hands were ice cold, sucking what heat remained in her arms through the thin satin shirt.

Christine had no idea how long she waited for the SEALs to return, finally spotting a red beam of light in the distance. Her eyes followed the swaying beam as it approached until Harrison materialized out of the darkness only a few feet away, the flashlight in his hand.

"We've reached the exit to the storm drain," he said. "It's safe."

He turned and Christine followed him a few hundred feet, pausing at the end of the storm drain, the stream of water continuing into a canal. Although it was still dark outside, the rain had ceased and the clouds had departed, leaving behind an array of stars shining down from a clear night sky. On Christine's right, the storm drain opening was illuminated by a street lamp atop a steep embankment crowned with a guardrail, and she heard an occasional car passing by.

Christine suddenly realized Harrison was no longer wearing his backpack or black jacket, and there was no sign of Chief O'Hara.

Harrison seemed to read her mind. "He's gone to figure out where we are."

The Lieutenant retreated twenty feet inside the storm drain, toward a four-foot-wide concrete ledge about waist high jutting from the side of the tunnel, where the backpack was sitting. He slid onto the ledge, his feet hanging over, then rummaged through the backpack until he pulled out what looked like a ruggedized BlackBerry. Christine joined him on the ledge as Harrison punched a number into the PDA, bringing it to his ear. After a moment, he frowned, tossing the PDA back into the backpack.

"Nothing," he said. "Satellite communications are still down."

Chief O'Hara appeared at the entrance to the storm drain. The older SEAL shrugged Harrison's jacket off, revealing his MP7 hanging from its sling around his shoulder. He tossed the jacket to Harrison.

"We're on the west side of a canal beneath Jiaosha Road," O'Hara said.

"Thanks, Chief, but it doesn't look like that info will help. Comms are down. I can't get ahold of anyone to let them know where we are. Looks like we'll have to make it back to the coast on our own."

"We're not heading to the coast," O'Hara replied. His voice was determined, and as the street lamp illuminated the silhouette of his face, Christine could see his jaw muscles working. "We lost Drew and the girls, and I'm not about to turn tail and call it a day without payback."

Harrison nodded almost imperceptibly. "What do you recommend?"

"We continue the mission. If we don't insert the virus, the *Reagan* Task Force is toast."

"You don't think the objective has been compromised?" Harrison asked.

"I don't," O'Hara answered. "Only the six of us knew our destination." He looked away for a moment before turning back. "I should have seen it coming. Tian was prying for information. Once he realized he was outta luck, he let his friends move in."

Like O'Hara, Christine figured she should have seen it coming. Her trip from the safe house to the coast two weeks ago hadn't gone as planned. Only now did she see the obvious signs. Chinese officials somehow knew she was headed to Tanggu, and they were checking the trains and watching the subway exits. Tian was the man who had held the car door open for her as she left the safe house, and although he hadn't known the details, he was aware of the basic plan to smuggle Christine to the coast. Her resolve crystalized. If she made it out alive, she'd see to it that Tian was tracked down and killed. What she would do between then and now, however, was up to Harrison.

Harrison considered the Chief's words at length, finally nodding his agreement. "We're behind schedule, but there's still time. As long as we get the virus loaded by 0700, there'll be time for our submarines to download the new torpedo software. We're low on ammo though. The extra magazines were in the third backpack. Transportation is going to be a problem too. I can't get ahold of anyone, and I don't like the prospect of stealing a car and driving into the city. Public transportation is out—we'll stick out like sore thumbs."

"Transportation won't be a problem," O'Hara replied.

Harrison raised an eyebrow. "How's that?"

O'Hara gestured toward Harrison's jacket, lying on the ledge beside the Lieutenant. "Check the left pocket." Harrison shot O'Hara a questioning look as he reached into his coat pocket, retrieving an iPhone. O'Hara added, "There's going to be one pissed-off dude when he wakes up from his five-knuckle nap."

Harrison cracked a wry smile as he turned on the iPhone. "Great job, Chief."

Christine watched as Harrison launched the Apple App store, her curiosity growing as he searched for and then downloaded a free app. Harrison noticed Christine's keen interest as he launched the application. "Don't ask," he said, the smile spreading across his face.

The application launched and the screen turned black except for a password entry, which Harrison typed in. The app accepted the password and a numeric keypad appeared on the screen. He punched in an eleven-digit number, then placed the phone against his ear.

After a moment, he spoke. "Harrison, Jake Edward." There was a short pause, then he followed with an eight digit alphanumeric code before continuing. "The team was ambushed in the safe house. Three down. O'Hara and Christine O'Connor also remain. Mission objective is still confidential and remains a go. Require transportation." There was another pause, then

Harrison spoke again. "I need a large, loose-fitting jacket and four MP7 forty-round magazines." Harrison nodded thoughtfully, then added, "We're in a culvert emptying into the west side of a canal beneath Jiaosha Road." There was silence again before Harrison ended the call with, "Understand. Standing by."

He pulled the phone from his ear—the screen had already gone blank—placing it on the ledge next to him.

"How long?" O'Hara asked.

Harrison shrugged. "Not sure. They'll call back once arrangements have been made."

"I'll take the first watch," O'Hara said. He looked at Christine as she sat on the ledge, his eyes surveying her from top to bottom. "You're soaked. We're going to need to warm you up."

The Chief's comment reminded Christine how cold she was. She was chilled to the bone and was shivering uncontrollably.

"You happen to be in luck," Harrison added. "You're in the company of highly trained SEALs, experts in thermal rewarming."

O'Hara grinned as he turned and headed toward the storm drain entrance, taking the first watch as Harrison slid next to Christine. He draped his jacket over her shoulders, then put his arm around her, pulling her close against his warm body. She rested her cheek against his muscular chest, instinctively wrapping her arm around his waist. Even though it'd been twenty-four years since he'd held her in his arms, it seemed natural. His fingers brushed a lock of hair away from her face, tucking it behind her ear, and that simple gesture brought back strong memories of chilly winter nights in the back of his Ford Escort, fogging up the windows, Jake holding her close afterward in his strong arms.

"You should get some sleep," he said softly. "This might be your last chance for a while."

Christine murmured her agreement as she closed her eyes. She could feel the fatigue seeping in. The sound of the water gurgling past her into the canal, combined with the heat radiating from Harrison's body, helped ease the tension from her muscles, and sleep began to wash over her like a warm sea. She had almost dozed off when the iPhone next to Harrison vibrated. Her eyes opened as Harrison picked up the phone. He typed his password again, then placed the phone against his ear.

After a short wait, Harrison replied with a single word. "Understand."

Christine closed her eyes again as Harrison placed the iPhone back on the ledge.

"Morning," was all he said.

63

BEIJING

It was still dark when Christine woke, her arm still around Harrison's waist, her cheek pressed against his chest. She pulled him closer as the cobwebs slowly cleared.

"Miss O'Connor," she heard him say, only his voice was different somehow.

She wrapped her arm tighter around his waist and snuggled deeper under his arm.

"Miss O'Connor," he said again in a strange voice.

She opened her eyes and looked up, confused when she saw the face of Chief O'Hara in the dim light. His arm was draped around her shoulders and she had her arm tight around his waist. Christine sat bolt upright, coming to her senses.

O'Hara seemed unfazed by her reaction. "It's almost time, Miss O'Connor," he said. "Transportation will be here soon."

Christine examined her surroundings—she was sitting where she had snuggled next to Harrison. The two SEALs must have switched places during the night for Harrison's turn on watch. She searched the storm drain, spotting the Lieutenant sitting near the opening where the water gushed into the culvert, staring into the distance. She glanced at her watch but couldn't determine what time it was in the faint light coming from the street lamp atop the embankment.

She turned to O'Hara. "What time is it?"

"Five A.M."

O'Hara stood, slinging the backpack over his shoulder with one hand while extending the other to Christine, helping her to her feet. She followed him to the storm drain opening where they sat next to Harrison without a word.

A few minutes later, a car stopped on the road atop the embankment. She could only see the top of a white sedan, its red hazard lights blinking in the darkness. An elderly Chinese man, with creased face and silver hair, appeared next to the guardrail, hands in his pockets.

Christine followed the two SEALs as they emerged from the storm drain and headed up the embankment. She stepped over the guardrail as Harrison and O'Hara stopped beside the man. There was a quick exchange of words and the three men headed toward the car.

"In back with Chief, "Harrison said as he opened the front passenger door. Christine followed Harrison's instructions and slid into the rear seat behind the driver. The four doors closed with solid thuds, and the elderly man turned to Christine.

"I am Yuan Gui," he said. He reached down toward Harrison's feet and pulled up a small canvas bag, retrieving three bottles of water he passed to Christine and the two SEALs. Christine eyed the bottled water in her hand suspiciously. After everything they'd been through, she wondered whether she could trust Yuan. However, Harrison and O'Hara broke the bottle cap seals and quenched their thirst, and Christine did the same as Yuan reached into the canvas bag again, retrieving a pistol.

"I have no extra magazines for your MP7s. However, I have two SIG P226s, with four magazines each. Will they do?"

Harrison and O'Hara exchanged glances, with O'Hara shaking his head. "We'll go with our MP7s," Harrison answered.

"Then how about this for the lady?" Yuan reached into the bag again, pulling out a small semiautomatic pistol with a silencer screwed into the end of the barrel. "A Glock 26."

"No thanks," Harrison answered, but Christine leaned forward quickly, taking the small subcompact pistol from Yuan's hand. "That'll be just fine," she said.

Harrison turned toward her. "Put the gun back."

Christine ignored him as she verified the safety was on, then dropped the magazine into her hand—ten rounds—then pulled back the slide valve, verifying the chamber was empty. She reinserted the magazine, then released the slide, chambering a round, then slid the subcompact pistol into the waistband of her pants. She looked up, and Harrison was staring at her with the same stern eyes he'd had when he tried to talk her out of joining them on their mission. She stared back at him with a dispassionate glare.

"Put the gun back," he said again. "Having you *help* will do more harm than good."

Harrison's overprotectiveness, combined with his dismissal of her ability to *help*, aside from gaining entry to the Great Hall, was a source of lingering irritation.

"My ex-husband taught me to shoot," she said. "At twenty-five feet, I can put a bullet through a man's head or heart, whichever is more appropriate." She glared coldly at Harrison.

O'Hara grinned, but she could see anger smoldering in Harrison's eyes. She wasn't giving the gun back, but she needed to diffuse the situation. "I promise not to use it unless you tell me first," she offered.

Harrison and Christine stared each other down, until Harrison finally acceded. "Have it your way," he said, "but let's get one thing straight. You will do *exactly* what I say from here on out or you'll be staying in the car with Yuan. Is that clear?"

"Crystal," Christine said dryly.

There was a momentary silence, broken as Yuan reached into the bag again, retrieving one final item—a black windbreaker, which he handed to O'Hara.

"So, where to?" Yuan asked as O'Hara took the jacket.

"The Great Hall of the People," Harrison answered.

Yuan raised an eyebrow, studying first Harrison, then O'Hara. Convinced Harrison wasn't joking, he engaged the clutch and shifted into first gear. The manual transmission grinded momentarily as the sedan pulled away from the guardrail into a U-turn, steadying up on the two-lane road leading back into Beijing.

64

USS *RONALD REAGAN*

Six hundred miles east of Japan, USS *Reagan* surged west at ahead full. Standing on the Bridge, Captain CJ Berger peered through the windows at the Flight Deck fifty feet below. The first four Super Hornets were in tension in their catapults, their engine exhausts glowing red in the darkness, waiting for the order to launch. Along both sides of the ship, the four elevators were loaded and rising upward, bringing additional Super Hornets topside from the Hangar Deck below. Not far behind *Reagan*, the three MEFs aboard their amphibious assault ships trailed, banking on the ability of the Atlantic Fleet submarines in front of them to clear a safe path ashore. Berger would have preferred to wait until the submarines had downloaded new torpedo software, but time was running out.

As anticipated, Japanese resistance had deteriorated, leaving only one beachhead in JSDF hands, and *Reagan* and the MEFs could wait no longer. Unfortunately, satellites and tactical data links were still down and Chinese command and control and their missile batteries were still fully operational, able to engage the carrier and its air wing as they approached Japan. In a few minutes, Berger would commence flight operations, launching *Reagan*'s air wing just outside range of China's DF-21 missiles. However, the aircraft had insufficient fuel to complete a round-trip to their current location; *Reagan* would have to close to within range of the DF-21 missiles to retrieve the aircraft after their missions were complete. With its small escort of only six surface combatants—all heavily damaged—the *Reagan* Task Force was ill equipped to defend against even a modest attack of DF-21 missiles. Chinese command and control and their missile batteries had better be disabled within the next two hours, or *Reagan* would end up on the bottom of the Pacific, just like its five sister carriers.

In front of *Reagan*, the Submarine Force had established a protective cone of submarines, proceeding in front of the carrier strike group and wrapping back along the sides of the trailing amphibs. However, they were currently nothing more than a sophisticated underwater alarm system. Although they could communicate with *Reagan* via line-of-sight comms and report enemy submarines, there was nothing more they could do. Their torpedoes were still infected with malware and would dud as soon as they received the first Chinese sonar pulse.

Reagan's Air Wing Commander, Captain Emil Jones, stopped beside Berger, his eyes following CJ's to the Flight Deck below. The two men stared through the Bridge windows in silence for a moment, until their thoughts were interrupted by the Air Boss's voice over the 23-MC. "Request Green Deck."

Berger pulled the mic from its holster as he pressed the green button. "Tower, Bridge. You have Green Deck."

Orders were relayed to the Flight Deck, and seconds later, the first Super Hornet, locked into CAT One, screamed toward the carrier's bow, the aircraft's white-hot engine exhaust fading in the darkness as it rose into the sky. The succeeding three aircraft were hurtled from the carrier's deck as the catapults shot forward, and additional Super Hornets moved toward the catapults, continuing the steady flow of aircraft launched into the darkness.

65

BEIJING

Night was still clinging to the city as a white sedan pulled to a stop along the side of Guang Chang Boulevard in the center of Beijing. Three doors opened and two men and a woman stepped from the car onto the sidewalk, the woman intertwining her arms through those of the two men, one on each side of her as they began strolling north. There were no other pedestrians within view as the sedan pulled away, and a moment later, the three individuals disappeared into the ringlet of cypress and pines surrounding the Great Hall of the People.

Christine paused for a moment to get her bearings, taking a deep breath of the cool night air. Her pulse was racing and she commanded herself to relax. But her heart kept pounding in her ears as O'Hara dropped the backpack from his shoulders, retrieving Christine's Glock, which she had handed over so it could be concealed in the backpack as they strolled along Guang Chang Boulevard.

O'Hara handed Christine the pistol, which she slipped back into the waistband of her pants, then focused on the reason she had accompanied the SEAL team—to discreetly gain access to the Great Hall. That meant finding the alcove she had entered when she escaped from the Great Hall two weeks ago. To Christine's left, the gray marble columns of the Great Hall's central entrance were illuminated by bright white landscape lighting. That meant the alcove was a few hundred feet to her right. Christine turned and led the two SEALs north.

Christine halted at the edge of the trees. The alcove was directly ahead, across twenty feet of paved road. The camera mounted above the door was operational this time, its red LED illuminated. Gaining access to the Great

Hall would be easy if Christine's palm print remained in the system. Gaining access undetected was another matter. Fortunately, six feet above the camera, a decorative balcony with black wrought iron railing extended over the exit, protecting the camera and the plasma display from the weather.

O'Hara dropped the backpack from his shoulders again, retrieving a black rappelling harness. After shedding his windbreaker and MP7, Harrison donned the harness, from which dangled a metal carabiner attached to a gear loop on the waist strap. Reaching into the backpack again, he pulled out a coil of thin nylon rope, a Mini Maglite with red lens, and a Gerber multitool. Harrison draped the rope over his shoulder and slid the Gerber and flashlight into loops sewn into his waist strap, securing each in place with a Velcro tab.

Reaching into the backpack one final time, Harrison retrieved the final device he needed, a metal shunt, which he attached to the carabiner on the front of his waist strap.

"All set," Harrison said, looking at Christine. "Wait here until I signal for you."

Christine's stomach knotted. Guards traversed the perimeter of the building, and she had no idea how long it'd be before the next pass. Once Harrison climbed the balcony and began disabling the camera, he couldn't duck back into the foliage if guards approached.

Without another word, Harrison and O'Hara dashed across the paved road, stopping against one of the ten-foot-tall walls forming the C-shaped alcove. O'Hara interlocked his fingers, forming a foothold for Harrison, which he used to scale the alcove wall. From there he was able to pull himself onto the balcony and over the railing as O'Hara sprinted across the paved road again, joining Christine along the tree line.

"You look left," he whispered, "and I'll watch right."

Christine acknowledged and peered left as directed. As she stared into the shadowy distance, she listened carefully to her surroundings. The chirping crickets she'd heard during her escape were still vocal, and there was the occasional car passing by on Guang Chang Boulevard. Thankfully, there was no indication—sight or sound—of approaching guards.

Harrison tied the end of his nylon rope to the wrought iron railing and gave it a firm tug to verify the railing was sturdy enough to handle his weight. Convinced it was, he slipped the nylon rope into the shunt attached to his harness, then tossed the free end of the rope over the railing. He climbed over the railing and stood facing outward, with his heels between the bars, then tilted forward as he fed the rope through the shunt with his right hand. A moment later his body was horizontal, dangling just beneath the balcony. A small kick sent Harrison slowly spinning, turning 180 degrees until he faced the building. He lowered himself slowly until he was just above the camera. After locking the shunt in place, Harrison retrieved the Maglite and the Gerber multi-tool, and began disassembling the camera.

Christine glanced back at Harrison periodically. It seemed like he was taking forever, but there was finally a double flash of the red Maglite in their direction, and Harrison dropped down into the alcove a second later.

"Let's go," O'Hara said after a final glance in both directions, grabbing the backpack beside him. Christine followed O'Hara across the concrete path, joining Harrison inside the alcove. Above them, two cut wires dangled from the top of the camera, and the red LED light was dark.

Harrison shed his rappelling harness, which he handed to O'Hara in exchange for his MP7. O'Hara returned the harness to his backpack, which he slung over his shoulder. Harrison turned to Christine. "Your turn."

Christine stepped in front of the plasma screen beside the door, flexing her hand involuntarily. She reached toward the screen, hesitating with her hand an inch away from the monitor, unable to shake the uneasy feeling something was about to go wrong.

"Only one way to find out," Harrison said.

Christine placed her palm firmly against the cold glass. The screen activated immediately, a vertical red line scanning her palm from left to right. The red line reached the edge of the screen and the monitor went dark. She waited for the door to unlock, her hand still pressed against the glass, but nothing happened. Seconds ticked away and there was still no reaction from either the plasma monitor or door.

There was a sinking feeling in Christine's gut and she was about to pull her hand away from the display when the door unlocked with a metallic *click*. She breathed a sigh of relief as O'Hara pulled the door open and Harrison peered around the doorframe. After looking in both directions, he waved them in, and Christine followed Harrison and O'Hara into the Great Hall of the People.

66

BEIJING

The door into the Great Hall of the People opened to a corridor that ran several hundred feet in both directions. The two SEALs took station on either side of the door, each monitoring a different direction while Christine stopped in front of the plasma display on the inside. She paused for a moment, closing her eyes to recall the characters Yang had tapped to pull up the building schematics. After convincing herself she knew the correct ones, she opened her eyes, then pressed the top right tab. A new screen appeared and she touched the middle right tab, her effort producing yet a third screen. A final tap returned the desired result; the schematics of the Great Hall of the People appeared on the display, each room labeled in Chinese.

After examining the schematics, Christine concluded she was looking at the main floor. Beside her, Harrison reached into his back pants pocket, pulling out a small green notebook. Flipping to the first page, he held it open next to the display. At the top of the page were two Chinese characters.

"We're looking for this room, on the third floor of the South wing."

Christine studied the characters, then returned her attention to the display, tapping the up arrow once to display the second floor. After surveying the schematics briefly to determine the best route upward, she tapped the display again and the third floor appeared. She shifted the schematics to the South wing with a swipe of her fingers. A moment later, she spotted the two Chinese characters atop a room in the center of the wing. The communication center was in the Politburo section, inside a ring of security checkpoints.

Figures.

"The communications center is here," Christine pointed to the room as Harrison peered over her shoulder. "We're in the northeast section of the Great Hall on the main level. We've got two problems. The first is that the central section of the Great Hall contains several large auditoriums we'll need to avoid and there are only a few corridors that cut across that wing. Best bet is the third floor, since there are a few extra corridors that pass over some of the smaller halls. The second problem," Christine pointed to several red symbols, "are the security checkpoints at the entrances to the South Wing, guarding the Politburo section of the building." Christine paused, waiting for Harrison's response.

"What about the sub-floors?" he asked. "Can we get to the South Wing below ground, then go up?"

Christine pulled up the first subfloor, then the second. After a quick examination, she shook her head. "The subfloors exist only in the North and South Wings, not in the Central section. Looks like the third floor is the best bet."

"I agree," Harrison replied. "What's the best stairwell to take?"

Christine selected the main floor again, noting a staircase in the farthest northeast corner of the building. "How about this one?"

Harrison nodded. "Looks good." He turned to O'Hara, who was alternately watching both ends of the corridor. "That way, Chief." Harrison pointed past O'Hara, down the long corridor.

O'Hara turned without a word and headed down the hallway at a slow jog. Christine followed, with Harrison a few yards behind. As O'Hara approached the first intersection, he stopped and shrugged his backpack from his shoulder, extracting a device with a small display and a thin, flexible snakelike cord. O'Hara pressed a button on the top of the display, turning it on, then with his back against the wall, fed the tip of the snakelike cord around the corner.

A camera on the end of the cord fed an image to the display in O'Hara's hand. The adjacent corridor was empty. It was still early, only 6 A.M. Without another word, O'Hara retrieved the backpack and crossed the hallway. After stopping at two additional intersections, examining each one in the same manner, O'Hara turned right, and after a few hundred feet, reached a staircase. O'Hara was about to begin the ascent when he froze. Christine heard footsteps echoing from the stairwell opening.

Harrison grabbed Christine's arm, pulling her away from the staircase as O'Hara slowly backed up as well. By the sound of the approaching footsteps, the individual would reach their level any second. O'Hara halted his retreat and raised his MP7 to the firing position.

A second later a man wearing a charcoal suit and red tie emerged from the stairwell, stepping onto the main floor of the Great Hall. O'Hara fired immediately and the man crumpled to the floor, blood flowing from a hole in the center of his forehead. The MP7, with the attached suppressor, barely made a whisper. Harrison checked the hallway for unlocked doors, locating one a few feet behind them. Finding the room vacant, Harrison helped O'Hara drag the dead man into the empty office, wiping up the trail of blood with the man's jacket.

After closing the office door, O'Hara returned to the lead, proceeding cautiously up the stairwell. Christine and the two SEALs soon emerged onto the third floor. It was thankfully unoccupied. From the length of the corridor, Christine could tell it extended across the central section of the Great Hall. O'Hara returned to a jog, with Christine and Harrison following him down the empty hallway.

The corridor turned to the right after a few hundred feet, and O'Hara pulled to a stop, extending the camera probe around the corner as he had done earlier. This time, O'Hara made a quick hand signal. Without a word, Harrison moved next to O'Hara, examining the display as Christine looked past Harrison's shoulder.

Around the corner and thirty feet down the hallway was a security checkpoint. The corridor was blocked by a metal detector and a baggage X-ray machine, manned by two armed guards. One man was standing on their side of the detector, chatting with the second guard, who was on the other side of the checkpoint, seated behind the X-ray machine. The first guard was standing in the open and would be easy to take out. However, the second guard was partially protected by the X-ray machine.

Harrison tapped his chest and then touched the display, pointing to the guard partially hidden behind the X-ray machine, then pointed across the corridor. O'Hara nodded; Harrison would *go long*, stepping out to the middle of the hallway to take out the guard behind the X-ray machine, while O'Hara wheeled around the corner simultaneously, taking out the other man.

O'Hara placed the camera on the floor by his feet, gripping his MP7 while Harrison moved in front of him. Harrison held his left hand up with four fingers extended, retracting one finger, then another, counting down. There were only two fingers remaining when a shout echoed down the corridor behind them.

Christine and the two SEALs turned toward the noise. Two armed security guards had turned the corner thirty feet behind them. Both men were dressed identically to the men at the security checkpoint, and were reaching for their pistols. It was just their luck. They had reached the security checkpoint at the end of a shift, and the two replacement guards had caught Christine and the SEALs by surprise.

O'Hara responded immediately, turning and firing four times, hitting both men twice in the center of the chest just as they drew their pistols from their holsters. Both men crumpled to the floor.

One of the security guards around the corner called out, the challenge unmistakable in the tone of his voice. Although O'Hara's MP7 had barely made a sound, the security guard had heard the shout from the other guard.

Harrison picked up the camera and poked the probe around the corner again, his eyes fixed on the display. One of the guards was walking down the hallway toward them and was less than fifteen feet away now. His pistol was drawn and ready, and the second guard had shifted his position, his body completely blocked by the metal detector.

"New plan," Harrison whispered to O'Hara. "You take out the lead while I go long, then we both advance until one of us gets a clear shot on the second."

O'Hara nodded, then turned to Christine. "Stay here until we call for you."

Christine was about to respond but never got the chance. O'Hara's eyes widened as he looked past her, then he shoved her against the wall with his left arm. Before she could figure out what was going on, a gunshot echoed down the corridor and O'Hara's head jolted backward. The SEAL dropped to his knees, then collapsed onto the ground, blood flowing from the right side of his forehead. Christine turned and looked down the corridor.

One of the two guards was still alive, lying prone on his stomach with his pistol in his hand, pointed toward them. From the corner of Christine's eye, she saw Harrison's hand swing up and he fired a single round, which hit the top of the guard's head in a red puff. The guard's face dropped to the floor, blood spreading across the terrazzo. Christine's eyes went back to O'Hara. Blood was pooling beneath his head and his eyes were frozen open.

Things quickly went from bad to worse. The guard advancing from the security checkpoint turned the corner, and it took only a second for him to assess the situation. As Harrison turned back around, the guard fired at point-blank range. Harrison seemed unaffected though, ducking and twisting around, firing up toward the man twice with his MP7. The guard's face went slack and the gun fell from his hand as he collapsed onto the floor.

A second later, a loud wailing alarm filled Christine's ears, and she could hear shouting from around the corner. She looked toward Harrison, only then seeing the pain in his eyes. His left shoulder slumped downward, arm dangling by his side, and a red stain was spreading over the shoulder of his shirt and down his sleeve.

Harrison glanced at O'Hara, then turned to Christine. "Follow me." He sprinted back down the corridor. Following closely behind, Christine could see the bullet hole in Harrison's shirt, behind his left shoulder. He turned left at the first intersection, and as Christine followed him down the maze of corridors, she realized he was working his way toward the perimeter of the building. A moment later, they reached the end of the hallway.

The wailing alarm suddenly ceased, and behind them, Christine heard men shouting. Harrison checked the last door on the left. It was unlocked and he stepped inside, closing and locking the door after Christine joined him inside what appeared to be someone's office. An oak desk was decorated with the usual assortment of paraphernalia—photos, in-box, pen-holder, and computer display, with a matching oak bookcase against one wall. Based on the quality of the furniture, it clearly wasn't a Politburo-level office, but the owner of the small office was high enough in the pecking order to warrant an office with a view; dark green curtains framed a closed, two-paned window.

Harrison stopped by the window and twisted the latch, swinging the two panes inward. Poking his head out the window, he looked to his left a moment before turning back toward Christine. His face was pale and beads of sweat were collecting on his brow, and he winced each time he drew in a breath.

"We're going to part ways here, Chris." His clipped his words short as he spoke, and Christine could hear the pain bleeding through his voice. Reaching into his jacket pocket, he retrieved the flash drive. He grabbed Christine's right hand, placing it into her palm. "They know we're here, and it's unlikely we'll make it past the security checkpoints. But there's a small ledge that runs the perimeter of the building. You can work your way past the security checkpoints and into the Politburo section of the building, then make your way to the communications center. I'll do my best to keep them occupied in the meantime."

Christine closed her fingers around the flash drive, absorbing Harrison's request. The success of the mission had literally been placed in her hand. She was at a loss for words as she slipped the drive into her pants pocket.

"The ledge is wider than a balance beam," Harrison added, "so I know you can do it. Work your way left until you get to the South Wing, then break into an empty office."

Christine was standing close to him and could smell the pungent scent of fresh blood. She glanced at his left shoulder, which was bleeding heavily. If it didn't abate, he wouldn't last long. "Let me take a look."

"I'll be fine," he said curtly.

She was about to argue when he suddenly stepped toward her, pulling her against his body with his good arm. As she looked up, his lips met hers, crushing against them as he pulled her even closer, his MP7 pressing into the small of her back.

The kiss was short but passionate. He stepped back, his eyes holding hers for a moment before he spoke. "Good luck, Chris. It's up to you now."

It was another few seconds before she broke from his gaze, then leaned out to examine the ledge. It was barely six inches wide, disappearing into the darkness after a few feet in each direction. Forty feet below her, perimeter lights illuminated the grounds surrounding the Great Hall. The ledge was two inches wider than the balance beams she had spent almost twenty years training on. She could easily work her way along the outside of the building. However, there was no padded mat four feet below. If she slipped off the ledge, she wouldn't survive the forty-foot drop.

It was the only viable option. Christine's pulse raced as she steadied herself with a hand on each side of the window, then lifted her right foot over the sill and onto the ledge. After a deep, shaky breath, she glanced one final time in Harrison's direction, then stepped out into the cool night air.

BEIJING

Christine leaned against the exterior wall of the Great Hall of the People, her toes hanging over the edge of the six-inch-wide ledge. Shuffling along one step at a time, she worked her way toward the South Wing. Another twenty feet and she would reach the first office in the Politburo section of the building. Thus far, the ledge had proved sturdy and her travel unremarkable. However, as she took another step, voices reached out to her in the darkness.

To Christine's left and below, there was the faint sound of men talking. Four men were approaching, each man wielding a flashlight, the white beams of light scouring the grounds outside the Great Hall. Christine froze, pressing her back against the building, hoping their attention remained focused on the ground below and not the ledge she was perched on. The men's voices became more distinct as they approached, and to her dismay, the men stopped almost directly below her as another four men approached from her right.

The eight men gathered beneath her, their conversations drifting into the air, their flashlight beams pointing toward the ground or into the ringlet of trees farther out. Christine prayed the men would move on, her anxiety increasing with each additional second they remained below. Finally, Christine sensed their conversation drawing to a close and she was about to let out a sigh of relief when the ledge under her right foot suddenly gave way, crumbling under the weight of her body.

She shifted her weight quickly onto her left foot, retaining her balance as several chunks of stone rained down toward the men beneath her, bouncing off the ground near the building in an impossibly loud crescendo of falling debris.

Flashlight beams shot toward the Great Hall, scouring the ground beneath her. A moment later, one of the shafts of light began working its way up the building's facade, examining the windows on the first floor, then the second. As the beam of light reached the third floor, Christine began to panic. To her right, she watched the light examine one window, then the next, moving methodically toward her, cutting from one window to the next.

Christine searched frantically for a solution. Glancing to her left, she spotted a window only six feet away. Perhaps, if she moved fast enough, she could hide inside the edge of the windowsill, where the ledge deepened to about a foot and a half. The flashlight beam shifted to the window on Christine's right. She had to move now.

She shuffled left in three large steps, ducking into the recessed window ledge as the flashlight cut across the building, pausing to examine the window where Christine stood. She plastered herself against the cold stone, hoping her body was concealed in the darkness. The light illuminated the window for what seemed like an eternity, then moved on, continuing its trek across the building's facade. As the beam of light reached the next window, a pair of pigeons took flight. A few seconds later, the light dropped to the ground and the two groups of men continued in opposite directions, continuing their search along the building's perimeter, their bright shafts of light fading into the distance.

Christine let out a deep breath—her pulse was racing and her body was trembling. She waited a few seconds, letting her heartbeat slow down as she collected her thoughts. It was only going to get tougher, she told herself. Her resolve solidified and she began moving again, working her way left toward the South Wing without further incident until a step with her left foot found nothing but air. After pulling her foot back onto the ledge, she looked down. The ledge ended.

Perfect.

She contemplated breaking into one of the offices she had passed, but that would put her on the wrong side of the security checkpoints. She needed to break into an office in the South Wing, not the Central Wing. And she needed to do it soon. The approaching day was an orange glow on the horizon—it wouldn't be long before she'd be easily seen on the ledge outside the building, and she was running out of time. The virus had to be inserted into the Chinese command and control network by 7 A.M. or the *Reagan* Task Force would be forced to abandon their mission to land the Marine Expeditionary Forces on Japan.

Christine's eyes went back to the ledge, noticing it began again after a four-foot gap, marking the transition between the Central and South wings. The only way to continue was to jump the four-foot gap.

Under normal circumstances the jump would be a piece of cake—she had spent eighteen years training and had become an Elite gymnast. Unfortunately, she would have to jump from an awkward stance, and when she landed, her left shoulder and hip would hit the building. She'd almost certainly lose her balance and fall off the ledge. She didn't have any choice though. Searching through her repertoire of beam jumps, she decided a half-turn leap might work—she would twist her body ninety degrees while in the air and land facing the wall, which solved the issue of her shoulder and hip hitting the building. But if her leap was off and she didn't land squarely on the ledge . . .

She'd come too far to turn back now: four dead SEALs, with Harrison injured and unlikely to make it back out alive. A four-foot jump was a risk she had to take. Turning to her left, she bent her knees carefully, lowering her body into a crouch, doing her best to maintain her balance. After a deep breath, she sprang toward the ledge four feet away.

At the apex of her leap, Christine twisted toward the building, her feet searching for the ledge as she fell. It seemed like she fell downward much longer than the one second it should have taken, but just when she was convinced she had missed the ledge, both feet landed on hard stone. Unfortunately, her jump was slightly off and only the balls of her feet hit the ledge. She was unable to flex her ankles quickly enough to maintain her balance, and she began tilting backward. She clawed at the building but there was nothing to grab on to. There was no way to stop it—she was falling off the ledge.

As her body tilted backward, she tried the only maneuver that gave her a chance. Instead of waiting until she completely lost her balance, she cut to the chase—she jumped off the ledge.

It was only a small jump backward, but it allowed her to fall from the building while her hands were still within reach of the ledge. As she fell, she swung her arms forward, hands outstretched, searching for the narrow ledge. Her palms hit the cold stone and her grip held as her body swung toward the building and smacked against the hard granite wall. The impact almost knocked the breath out of her, but her grip held.

Hanging from the stone ledge, Christine realized the six-inch ledge wasn't wide enough to pull herself onto it. She looked to her right, noticing another window a few feet away. Beneath the window, the ledge widened to a foot and a half again, giving her enough room to pull herself back onto the ledge. But to work her way to the window, she'd have to let go with one hand, supporting her weight with the other as she shuttled down the ledge. She tested the grip of her left hand—the ledge was still damp from the evening's rain, but her grip seemed firm.

After another deep breath, Christine shifted her weight onto her left hand as she slid her right down the ledge. Her left hand held and her body swung back to the right, shifting weight back onto both hands. She repeated the process until she was directly below the four-by-four-foot window. The curtains were drawn, a sliver of yellow light leaking though a vertical seam where they met. Christine pulled herself onto her elbows, then swung her right foot up onto the ledge. Here's where it got tricky. With a final heave, she lifted her body up and twisted inward, rolling onto the ledge, her back coming to rest against the window.

Climbing to her feet, she placed her eye against the window where the sliver of light leaked through. Inside was a well-appointed office. On the far wall, a built-in bookcase filled with leather-bound books overlooked a red upholstered sofa and two matching chairs arranged in a semicircle. The center of the dark wood floor was covered with a thick, pale blue rug with a five-foot-diameter ruby-red star embroidered in its center. She heard the murmuring of people talking, and as she shifted her eye first to the left, then right, she spotted two men in the room. The chairman of China's Central Military Commission, Huan Zhixin, was facing her, seated at a desk. Standing in front of the desk, with his back to Christine, was another man.

The two men were engaged in a heated conversation. Based on Huan's facial expression and animated gestures, he was upset about something. The discussion ended when Huan slammed his fist on his desk. He picked up a red folder, shoving it toward the man across from him, then stood abruptly and headed toward a door in the back of his office. The other man turned as Huan passed by, a malevolent glare in his eyes as they bored a hole in Huan's back, offering Christine a clear look at his face.

Tian, from the CIA safe house.

Her suspicions were confirmed. Tian had betrayed the United States, first during her transit to the coast two weeks earlier, then last night. She fingered the Glock, still stuck into the waistband of her pants. She needed to break into one of the offices in the South Wing of the Great Hall. This one was as good as any, and if she could slip into the office unnoticed, she could pay Tian back for his treachery.

The door to the office closed as Huan left, and Tian turned back around, placing the folder on Huan's desk. His back was to Christine as he opened the folder and studied the first page of the document inside. Christine pushed gently against the middle of the window and the two sides swung inward an inch. The window was unlocked.

Christine kept her eye on Tian as she pushed the window open a few more inches, wide enough to slide her hand through. She reached in, carefully pushing the right-side curtain out of the way, listening closely to ensure the movement created no sound. Christine froze as Tian reached down toward the desk, but he simply flipped the first page of the document over. Christine exhaled slowly, then pushed the other side of the curtain back, providing enough clearance to open the window wide enough for her to slip through. She glanced down through the glass panes—there was nothing beneath the windowsill inside the office, just a four-foot drop onto the wood floor.

Christine slowly pushed the two sides of the window open, then pulled the Glock from the waistband of her pants, disengaging the safety with her thumb. Kneeling down and supporting her weight with her left hand, she slid her left leg through the window, resting her thigh on the windowsill as she pulled the other leg through into a sitting position on the windowsill, her legs dangling over. She looked up at Tian, still studying the document. With a firm push off the windowsill, Christine landed on the wooden floor with a soft thud.

Tian turned around as Christine raised the Glock to a firing position. There was a shocked expression on his face as he slowly raised his hands. "What are you doing here?"

She should have pulled the trigger immediately and continued on. But there was one question she wanted to ask. She moved closer to Tian, keeping the Glock pointed at his chest. "Why did you betray us?"

Tian's surprised expression faded, his eyes turning cold, calculating. "I did not betray you. My colleagues were the traitors and they deserved their fate. As far as your SEAL friends go, they are enemy combatants and they paid the price." Tian's eyes went to the pistol in Christine's hand, then back to her face. "You didn't answer my question. Why are you here?"

Christine ignored his question again, suddenly curious why Huan was upset with him, considering the aid Tian had given. "Why was Huan angry with you?"

Tian frowned as he dropped his hands, folding his arms across his chest. "Because I failed to determine the objective of your mission. I called in our special forces too early."

Early enough.

Her curiosity satisfied, Christine decided it was time to move on. She'd already spent more time here than she should have. It was time for Tian to meet his fate.

Tian sensed her decision. "Kill me and your friend will also die."

Christine hesitated. "What do you mean?"

"One of your SEAL friends is in custody and is being interrogated. You can ensure his safety if you surrender and reveal the objective of your mission."

Had Harrison been captured? Or was Tian lying, buying time?

Christine searched Tian's eyes again and examined his expression, trying to determine if he was telling the truth. His face was an impassive mask, offering no clue. But after mulling his proposition, Christine decided it didn't matter.

"No deal," Christine replied.

It looked like Tian was about to plead his case again when there was a sound of a door opening behind Christine. Tian's eyes flicked over her left shoulder.

Huan had returned to his office. Christine squeezed the trigger, putting a bullet into the center of Tian's chest, then turned toward the door. But Huan had already closed the distance, blocking her right arm as she swung the Glock toward him. A second later, the air was knocked from her lungs as Huan punched her in the stomach. Christine doubled over as one of Huan's hands clamped firmly around her right wrist, and she could sense his other hand going for the pistol.

She felt Huan's grip on the Glock, twisting it from her hand. In desperation, Christine tried the only move she could think of. She lunged forward and tackled Huan, clamping her left arm behind his knees as she buried her shoulder into his waist. As Huan fell backward, he instinctively reached out with his right hand in an attempt to brace his fall, temporarily abandoning his attempt to wrest the Glock from her hand. But his left hand was still firmly clamped around her right wrist.

Huan landed on his back and Christine fell on top of him. She clambered to a sitting position with her legs straddling his waist and tried to aim the gun toward his head. But Huan had his arm extended, and she couldn't bend her wrist far enough. As she tried to determine what her next move should be, Huan's right hand swung up, his fist connecting solidly with the left side of her jaw.

Huan's punch almost knocked her off him, but she was able to maintain her balance as pain coursed through the side of her face. Huan's right hand reached toward the pistol.

Two can play this game.

One of the fundamental principles Christine learned during her self-defense course was to hit the perpetrator where it hurt. She pulled her left hand back and slammed her fist down into Huan's nose with all the force she could muster. Huan cried out in pain as blood spurted from his nostrils. His grip on her wrist loosened, and with a twist of her arm, she wrenched her hand free from his grasp.

She bent her arm toward Huan, hoping to get a clear shot at him, but Huan blocked her again with his left arm, then chopped across and down on her wrist with his right. The impact knocked the Glock from her hand and it slid across the smooth wooden floor, coming to rest under the sofa.

Without the gun, the encounter would turn into a physical battle she was sure to lose. Her only hope was to retrieve the Glock.

She pushed down on Huan's chest with both hands, springing to her feet, then dove toward the sofa. But Huan grabbed her left ankle as she leapt, and she fell onto her stomach, her outstretched hands at the edge of the sofa, only a foot away from the Glock. A second later, the distance to the pistol began to grow as she slid backward across the floor. Huan had scrambled to his feet and was pulling her away from the sofa by her ankle.

Christine twisted onto her back, kicking at his hands with her other foot, but her shoes were flat-soled and had little effect. After Huan dragged her to the center of his office, he released her leg and stomped down on her stomach. Christine doubled over from the pain, turning onto her right side, away from Huan. He circled around so he faced her, wiping the blood from his face with his sleeve.

"What are you doing here?"

Christine looked up at the man towering over her. "I thought I'd stop by for tea."

Huan kicked her in the stomach.

The kick caught her at the bottom of her rib cage, and she felt the bones crack. The pain was intense, magnified with each inward breath. Trying to protect herself from another kick, she curled into a ball, covering her face with her forearms, pulling her knees up to her elbows. Huan's kick had sapped the strength from her, and she needed a moment to recover.

"Tell me why you're here," he said, "and I will let you live."

Tilting her head up slightly, she peered between her forearms at Huan. As the pain coursed through her body, she realized there was a silver lining to her beating. As long as Huan interrogated her by himself, there was a chance she could escape. Once security guards arrived, it would all be over. She had to keep him engaged. As she looked up at him, she noticed the anger glowering in his eyes. She needed to keep him angry.

"Go screw yourself."

Huan kicked her again, but this time his foot glanced off her shins. Realizing his kick had little effect, he reached down, grabbing Christine by her hair and left arm, pulling her to her feet. White-hot pain shot through her ribs as she stood erect. Christine dropped her arms, protecting her ribs as best as possible. As soon as she dropped her arms, Huan pummeled her with another punch to her face.

Pain sliced through Christine's mouth as she reeled backward, tripping over Tian's body, her back smacking against Huan's desk as she landed on the floor. Blood trickled down her chin from a split lip as she tried to pull herself to her feet, her arms reaching out on top of Huan's desk. But before she could stand, Huan closed the distance, clamping his right hand around her neck. She tried to pry his hand away, but Huan grabbed her right wrist, pinning it on top of the desk. She continued prying with her left hand, but Huan was too strong.

Huan tightened his grip, pushing her head back against his desk at such a sharp angle it felt like her neck would snap any second. Pain shot through her chest as she arched back, trying to ease the angle. The tangy taste of blood seeped into her mouth between clenched teeth as Huan spoke again.

"I'll ask you one more time. Why did you come here?"

His hand squeezed her neck so tightly she doubted she could speak—she could barely breathe. Her plan to distract Huan from calling security had bought some time, but her situation hadn't improved. It was time for Plan B.

Whatever that was.

Out of the corner of her left eye, she noticed a lamp on top of Huan's desk. An emerald-colored glass lampshade, supported by a round column of one-inch-thick green marble, attached to an ornately carved metal base. It looked nice and heavy. And it was just within reach.

Plan B.

But she needed to distract him while she grabbed the lamp. Huan was standing over her, his feet straddling her thighs. Christine pulled her right knee up against her chest, ignoring the pain shooting through her ribs, then kicked up as hard as she could. Huan winced, but his grip around her neck held firm. He glanced down as Christine prepared for another kick, and that was all the distraction she needed. She stopped trying to pry Huan's hand from her neck and reached for the lamp. Her palm hit the marble and she closed her fingers around the smooth stone.

Huan noticed her movement, but it was too late. Christine's arm was already swinging upward. The base of the lamp hit Huan squarely on the side of the head, impacting his skull with a solid thud. Huan's hand around her neck went limp, and he collapsed onto the floor next to Tian, blood oozing from a four-inch gash in his scalp.

Christine dropped the lamp, then pulled herself to her feet, assessing the situation. Huan was either dead or unconscious—that was the good news. The bad news was that she couldn't stand straight without pain shooting through her chest. Pushing the pain from her mind as much as possible, she bent down, dragging Huan, then Tian behind the desk.

After pulling Tian on top of Huan, Christine stopped by the sofa, kneeling down to retrieve the Glock. With the pistol back in her hand, she paused at the door to Huan's office, glancing back to assess her work. Both men were hidden behind the desk, and by the time someone discovered the bodies, Christine would have uploaded the virus. The communications center was only a short distance away.

Turning the knob, she slowly pulled the door open, peeking out into the hallway. No one was there. Opening the door wider, she stepped into the corridor and turned right.

Christine hurried down the hallway, pausing briefly at two intersections to peer around the corner. Thankfully, the hallways were empty. Turning left at the second intersection, she stepped into a long corridor lined with doors along the right side. The entrance to the communications center was easy to identify. It was the only one with a security panel.

Stopping beside the door, Christine shifted the gun to her left hand, then placed her right on the center of the display. The bright red line appeared again, scanning her palm. A few seconds later, the door unlocked with an audible click. After returning the Glock to her right hand, Christine pushed against the door.

The door opened, revealing a dimly lit room containing computer consoles lining the far wall. There were four terminals, each one containing a keyboard and two displays, one above the other. Two of the consoles were occupied—one on the far left and the other on the far right, each by a man seated with his back to Christine. During her transit down the corridors, she had thought ahead, planning to coerce whatever information was required from whoever was in the communications center, tying them up or locking them in a closet afterward. She stepped into the room and shut the door behind her as both men turned in her direction. Their eyes widened when they spotted the pistol in her hand.

"Freeze! Do as I say and I won't harm you!" Christine hoped they understood English.

Apparently not.

The man on her left lunged forward, his outstretched hand reaching toward a red button protected beneath a hinged, plastic cover.

Christine aimed the pistol at his shoulder. She didn't want to kill him—one or both of the men might be instrumental in figuring out how to upload the virus. But there was little time to aim carefully before she squeezed the trigger.

The Glock recoiled in her hand with a whisper. Christine's aim was off and the bullet hit the man in the side of his neck. An unbelievably large gush of blood began spurting from the bullet hole. Christine stared in horror as the man clamped his hands around his neck, but blood continued to pulse from between his fingers. It was only a few seconds before the man slumped onto his console. Blood continued to ooze from the man's neck, coating his console and running onto the white tile floor in thin rivulets.

There was a flash of movement to Christine's right. The second man had bolted from his chair, headed to a side exit door only six feet away. Christine fired quickly, aiming for the center of the man's back. This time her aim was perfect and the bullet hit him right between the shoulder blades. The man collapsed against the door, then fell onto his stomach, his face turned to the side. His eyes were open and moving, but he was otherwise immobile. So much for the humane approach; her plan hadn't worked out too well.

After a final glance at the man by the door, Christine slid the pistol into her waistband and retrieved the flash drive from her pocket. Her eyes scanned the communications center, spotting two USB ports on the vertical portion of the first man's console. Christine stopped by his chair, pausing to examine him. The blood had stopped flowing from his neck; he was clearly dead. Christine shoved him onto the floor and took his seat, doing her best to avoid the blood coating the workstation. She inserted the flash drive into one of the ports, turning her attention to the two displays. On the bottom screen, various icons were loaded on what appeared to be a desktop, and Christine waited impatiently for the computer to recognize the flash drive.

A few seconds later, a new icon appeared. The name of the icon was written beneath it in Chinese characters she couldn't read, but she was certain it was her drive. Noticing a flat metal touchpad on the right side of the keyboard, she slid her finger across it and the arrow on the screen moved. After positioning the cursor over the icon, Christine tapped the pad twice and the icon opened into a window containing a single file. She repositioned the cursor and tapped twice again.

A horizontal status bar appeared on the display, with the color of the bar changing from left to right, turning from gray to bright blue. Beneath the bar, a digital timer appeared, starting at two minutes, counting down the time remaining until the process was complete. Christine watched the timer tick down, and when the time reached zero, the status bar turned green.

The status bar disappeared a few seconds later, leaving the desktop blank except for its icons. Christine waited for something to happen. She had no idea what to expect, and couldn't tell if the virus had accomplished its intended effect. She waited a minute, listening for approaching personnel as she examined the various displays in the communications center.

Nothing.

There was no indication that a lethal cyber virus had been injected into the Chinese command and control system. Deciding that waiting any longer would do no good, she pulled the flash drive from the USB port, sliding it into her pocket as she stood, turning her thoughts to escape from the Great Hall of the People for the first time.

The SEALs were supposed to get her out of the Great Hall, but she was on her own now. She needed a plan. She was inside the Politburo security perimeter, and successfully shooting her way out was iffy at best. She could head back out the way she came in, shuffling along the ledge outside the building, but it was daylight by now and she would be clearly visible, even to a casual observer. She needed a better exit plan, and the communications center wasn't the place to sort through the possibilities.

And then there was Harrison. Where was he? Had Tian told her the truth and Harrison had been captured, or was he hiding in an office somewhere, leaning against the wall as he bled to death?

Either way, she had to take care of herself now. She turned and headed toward the exit, stopping at the door. After listening for sounds, she cracked the door open and peered into the hallway. There was no one present. She stepped into the corridor, then turned around toward the plasma display beside the security door and pulled up the schematics of the Great Hall of the People. As she searched for an escape route from the building, an idea began to take hold.

ENDGAME

68

NINGBO, CHINA

Inside the East Sea Fleet's Command Center, Admiral Tsou stood at the back of the facility, his eyes skimming across six rows of consoles before coming to rest on the main screens at the front of the Command Center. The PLA was on the verge of capturing the last beachhead on Japan's main island, and only an injection of American airpower could stave off the advancing PLA forces. America's last aircraft carrier in the Pacific had launched its air wing, and China's new *Hongqi* surface-to-air missile batteries had locked on to the first wave, the aircraft almost within range. China was about to deliver the fatal blow.

Scattered across Japan in PLA-controlled territory, red icons marked the location of over one hundred mobile missile batteries, while three waves of blue symbols over the Pacific Ocean speeding west represented *Ronald Reagan*'s air wing. The aircraft were accompanied by twice the usual number of radar-jamming EA-18G Growlers for protection. But China's *Hongqi* missiles, far surpassing the capability of the Russian S-400 they had copied, would overwhelm them. In less than a minute, the lead missile batteries would begin firing, and America would be forced to accept defeat as the last remnant of their airpower in the Pacific was destroyed.

Tsou glanced at the timer on the main display as it counted down toward zero, when the first of their missiles would begin launching.

Only ten seconds remaining.

The consoles on the left side of the Command Center suddenly flickered off. In a cascade of darkening displays flowing left to right, console after console dropped off-line, their displays going black. The disciplined communications between console operators and their supervisors deteriorated into chaos as supervisors rushed to assist the nearest operators, directing them to reboot their consoles. One by one, the console screens turned blue, with white characters scrolling across the displays. After a few seconds, each screen went dark again. Operators frantically rebooted their consoles again, obtaining the same result; the displays went dark at the same point in the start-up process each time. Tsou looked toward the front of the Command Center. The main screens were frozen, no longer being updated. The entire Command Center was paralyzed.

Captain Cheng Bo, in charge of the Command Center, approached a moment later.

"A hard fault has occurred, Admiral. We must do a cold start of the entire system."

"How long will that take?"

"Ten minutes, sir. But it might not fix the problem. We have no idea what's wrong."

"Are we the only command center affected?"

The Captain shifted uncomfortably on his feet before continuing. "No, sir. All command centers are down, including weapon systems in the field linked to our tactical networks."

Captain Cheng's report was alarming. Their most potent missile batteries were linked to their tactical networks. That meant the *Hongqi* batteries, *Dong Feng* anti-carrier missiles, and *Hong Niao* surface-to-surface missiles were inoperable.

Admiral Tsou checked his watch. If the batteries could be brought up again, ten minutes was acceptable. When their missile batteries returned to service, *Reagan*'s aircraft, and then *Reagan* itself, would be destroyed.

69

USS *ANNAPOLIS* • CNS *JIAOLONG*

USS *ANNAPOLIS*

"Conn, Sonar. Hold a new contact, designated Sierra two-four, bearing two-six-zero. Classified submerged."

Standing on the Conn with his crew still at Battle Stations, Commander Ramsey Hootman acknowledged Sonar's report over the open mike. Ramsey glanced at the geographic display on the combat control console as a red half-circle appeared on the screen. It was almost certainly another one of the Yuan class submarines forming an underwater barrier two hundred miles east of the Japanese islands. And it was most likely the submarine that, earlier this morning, had almost sunk *Annapolis*.

He had pushed it too far, and they had barely escaped with their lives. *Annapolis* was stationed near the center of the Atlantic Fleet submarines, awaiting the arrival of both *Ronald Reagan* and their new torpedo software. In the meantime, their task was to probe the waters ahead, mapping out the defensive screen of Chinese submarines. The only wrinkle was—don't get killed in the process. With no functioning torpedoes to defend themselves with, that was easier said than done.

Annapolis had been counter-detected by a Yuan class submarine, and it had been a harrowing three hours, attempting to shake the Yuan that had caught a sniff of them. Ramsey had been tempted to kick it in the ass, going to ahead flank and vacating the area quickly. But that would have announced his presence to every Chinese submarine in the area. Not knowing if others were nearby that could have taken a shot at him while he fled, he decided to take his chances with the submarine that had detected him. It had been a cat-and-mouse game, with *Annapolis* constantly maneuvering, preventing the

Chinese submarine from obtaining a firing solution until *Annapolis* had sufficiently opened range and broken contact.

"Conn, Sonar. Sierra two-four is a Yuan class diesel submarine." Ramsey acknowledged Sonar. The cat was back, searching for its mouse.

Annapolis was at periscope depth now, its Type 18 periscope with its radio transmitter sticking above the water, along with the submarine's main communication antenna, scanning the skies in search of a signal and the torpedo software they desperately needed. But there was nothing. The submarine broadcast and all tactical data links were still down.

Ramsey retreated to the HDW fusion plot, aft of the periscopes. It was blank, lacking oceanographic, tactical, and even the basic navigation data it usually displayed. Thirty miles to the east, the *Reagan* Task Force was rapidly advancing. But without a submarine screen, the task force would have to turn around. The few surface ships and their anti-submarine helicopters would be insufficient to protect the task force. *Reagan* needed submarines, and the submarines needed the new torpedo software. That China had so thoroughly crippled the United States's military communications, robbing Ramsey of the software necessary to engage the enemy, was infuriating. He slammed his fist down on the HDW.

Seemingly in response to Ramsey's admonition, the HDW came alive. Red and blue icons began cluttering the display, and the submarine's GPS position appeared on the electronic chart. The Radioman's excited voice carried across Control.

"Radio, Conn. Communication satellites are back up. In sync with the broadcast. Download in progress!"

Ramsey stepped into Radio as the list of broadcast messages emerged from the printer. At the top of the list was the torpedo software download. It was a massive file by broadcast standards, and he'd been wise to raise the High Data Rate antenna. Once the download was complete, the file would be transferred to the BYG-1 Combat Control System via the submarine's SWFTS fiber optic tactical network, and from there to torpedoes loaded in their tubes, connected to Combat Control through a thick black cable attached to the torpedo tube breech door.

A few minutes later, with Ramsey back on the Conn, the Weapons Control Coordinator, Lieutenant Don Miller, announced, "Torpedo software update received and validated by combat control. Request permission to update weapons in tubes One through Four."

"Update all weapons," Ramsey ordered.

Lieutenant Miller acknowledged, and as he tended to the submarine's torpedoes, Ramsey prepared his submarine for combat. "All stations, Conn, proceeding deep. Dive, make your depth two hundred feet."

As *Annapolis* tilted downward, the Officer of the Deck lowered the scope into its well. Turning to the Chief of the Watch, Ramsey ordered, "Lower all masts." The broadcast was complete and the submarine's antenna no longer needed. Ramsey had skimmed through the several dozen messages, but none changed his immediate orders.

Sink all enemy combatants.

The one message Ramsey had scrutinized, however, detailed the changes to their torpedo software—and he had been pleasantly surprised. Not only had the malware been eliminated, making their torpedoes impervious to the Chinese sonar pulse, but the torpedoes were being reprogrammed to home on the pulse. The unique sonar frequency China had used to dud the American torpedoes would be used as a beacon.

The Weapons Control Coordinator called out, "Torpedoes in tubes One through Four have accepted the new software. Tubes One through Four are ready in all respects."

Annapolis was finally ready to engage.

CNS *JIAOLONG*

Commander Zhao Wei stood between the Search and Attack periscopes, surveying the men in Control with pride. His crew had performed well, sinking three American submarines so far, two of them the vaunted Virginia class. True, it wasn't a fair fight. But it served the Americans right. They had no business interfering in the conflict between communist and nationalist Chinese.

This morning, Zhao and his crew had almost sunk a fourth submarine. The Atlantic Fleet fast attacks had arrived and had taken up stations along China's defensive perimeter east of the Japanese islands, probing to determine the density and composition of the submarines opposing them. The

Americans were skilled; Zhao's sonarmen were able to detect only sporadic tonals, nothing they could lock on to. However, earlier today, a Los Angeles class submarine had ventured too close and Zhao's sonarmen had been able to place a tracker onto one of its frequencies. They had been close to a firing solution on three occasions, but the American submarine had deftly maneuvered each time, just before the XO had gained enough confidence. Finally, the 688 had slipped away, its tonal disappearing from their sonar screens.

However, they now knew what frequency to look for, and Zhao had pushed his submarine to the forward edge of his operating area, searching for his American foe. The next time they detected it, the American submarine would not get away.

USS *ANNAPOLIS*

Ramsey peered over the shoulder of Lieutenant Armando Hogarth, examining the solution to Sierra two-four. *Annapolis* had gone deep to five hundred feet and turned to the north, and they were waiting for the towed array to stabilize after the turn. Unfortunately, they didn't have much time to refine their target solution once it did.

The Japanese Self-Defense Force perimeter around the last remaining beachhead was collapsing, and *Reagan* and the Marine Expeditionary Forces were headed toward Japan at ahead standard. Ramsey figured he could get one leg in with Sierra two-four on his beam, and then he would have to push forward aggressively to stay ahead of the advancing surface ships. Such a high speed of advance was problematic, as it hampered *Annapolis*'s ability to search the surrounding waters and increased her detectability. But Ramsey had no choice. He'd been put between a rock and a hard place with the last-minute download of the new torpedo software.

The Officer of the Deck, Lieutenant Mike Land, approached, unable to conceal his concern. "Sir, we received an update to our Common Operational Picture while at PD. The *Reagan* Task Force is only ten miles behind us now."

"I understand," Ramsey replied. He checked the clock on the combat control console. The array should be stable by now. He called out to the overhead microphone.

"Sonar, Conn. Report time to array stabilization."

CNS *JIAOLONG*

"Control, Sonar. Detect nuclear reactor coolant pump frequency, bearing zero-eight-zero. Correlates to Los Angeles class submarine."

Commander Zhao smiled. They had found their adversary. He turned to the Helm. "Left standard rudder, steady course zero-eight-zero. Ahead full."

Jiaolong was a diesel submarine, normally maneuvering at slow speed to conserve the battery. Perhaps he could surprise his American foes and close to within firing range before they figured things out.

As Zhao and his crew prepared to send yet another American submarine to the bottom of the Pacific, he wished for a greater challenge. This Los Angeles class submarine, compared to the two Virginia class he'd already sunk, was a relic. A Seawolf—one of the three Cold War behemoths built when money was no obstacle, with eight torpedo tubes and even faster than the new Virginia class—now that would be a challenge. But for now, sinking an old 688 would have to suffice.

USS *ANNAPOLIS*

"Fire Control Coordinator, PRI MATE. Possible target zig, Sierra two-four. Upshift in frequency."

Ramsey listened to the report Lieutenant Hogarth made over the sound-powered phones. Hogarth had shifted to the Time Frequency display on his combat control console, analyzing changes in the contact's frequencies over time. Sierra two-four had either turned toward them or increased speed. Or both. Lieutenant Commander Ted Winsor, *Annapolis*'s Executive Officer, in charge of the Fire Control Party, would have to sort through the possible new course and speed combinations.

The two Fire Control Technicians and Lieutenant Hogarth were already adjusting their solutions, utilizing frequency and bearing information. Lieutenant Hogarth passed his assessment to the XO, who examined all three combat control consoles.

Winsor spoke into his mouthpiece. "Confirm target zig. Sierra two-four has turned toward and increased speed. Set range . . . ten thousand yards."

Ramsey stepped off the Conn, examining the new solution over Hogarth's shoulder. His solution had the contact on a course of zero-eight-zero, speed fifteen. It was headed directly toward them. Ramsey glanced at the other two combat control consoles. Their contact solutions varied by as much as thirty degrees in course and five knots in speed. The XO didn't have a firing solution. Even worse, with *Reagan* advancing toward them on one side, and now Sierra two-four headed toward them on the other, *Annapolis* was being squeezed from both sides.

Ramsey evaluated his predicament. He needed to sink Sierra two-four quickly. There wasn't enough time to prosecute the Chinese submarine the way he had been trained. After sorting through the options, he decided to throw everything he'd been taught about prosecuting enemy submarines out the window. "Helm, left fifteen degrees rudder, steady course two-six zero. Ahead full."

The XO, leaning over the shoulder of one of the Fire Control Technicians, stood erect, a surprised expression on his face. Winsor walked over to Ramsey.

"What are you doing, sir? You're heading straight toward the contact, taking our towed array out of the picture. And at this speed, with the flow noise over the bow, we might lose him on the spherical array."

"We don't have a choice, XO. *Reagan* and the amphibs are moving ahead. We have to push forward and clear a path."

"What's your plan?"

"This is probably the same guy we slipped away from earlier today, and he's being more aggressive. Let's give him what he wants." Ramsey called into the overhead mike. "Sonar, Conn. Line up to transmit mid frequency active, short pulse, forward sector, ten-thousand-yard range scale."

Sonar repeated back the order, then a moment later reported, "Conn, Sonar. Ready to transmit MF active, short pulse."

Ramsey ordered, "Sonar, Conn. Transmit MF active for ten seconds."

CNS *JIAOLONG*

"Target maneuver confirmed. Contact One has turned toward and significantly increased speed."

Zhao Wei listened intently to the report from his Executive Officer. A turn toward a contact was not unusual—submarines maneuvered frequently to sort out their target's course, speed, and range, occasionally pointing their target when held solely on the towed array. But a significant increase in speed made no sense. However, before he could contemplate the situation further, the Sonar Supervisor's report carried across the speakers in the Control Room.

"Control, Sonar. Contact One has gone active. Ten-second duration."

Zhao was perplexed by the new tactics of his American adversary. It was almost as if this American had grown tired of the cat-and-mouse game, and was taunting him. Daring him to shoot his torpedo and sink his submarine. It seemed the American believed his superior tactical skills and the speed of his nuclear-powered submarine could somehow save him and his crew.

Commander Zhao smiled. The American submarine would not get away this time.

He took his position on the Conn. "Prepare to Fire, Contact One, Tube One. Open muzzle doors, all torpedo tubes."

USS *ANNAPOLIS*

"Range to contact, six thousand yards," the XO announced. The two submarines were headed directly toward each other and closing rapidly. He tapped Lieutenant Hogarth on the shoulder. "Promote to Master." Turning to the submarine's Captain, he said, "I have a firing solution."

Ramsey reviewed the contact solution on the geographic display on the top panel of Hogarth's console. It was a risky plan, giving away *Annapolis*'s position with a non-covert pulse. But he had to increase the submarine's speed to stay ahead of *Reagan*, and would have been counter-detected anyway. Better to control when and where that detection occurred. The geometry was exactly what he wanted.

"Firing Point Procedures, Sierra two-four, Tube One," Ramsey announced.

The final preparations to shoot their torpedo, with its new software, began.

The XO verified the best of the three solutions was promoted to Master, then called out, "Solution ready!"

The Office of the Deck calculated the best torpedo evasion course and verified the submarine was ready to launch its torpedo decoys. "Ship ready!"

Finally, the Weapons Control Coordinator delivered the most crucial, and yet unverified report. "Weapon ready!"

Their MK 48 torpedo had accepted its target and search presets. But whether the torpedo was *truly* ready, its revised algorithms now impervious to the Chinese sonar ping, was still unknown. The two submarines were barreling toward each other, and Ramsey had little time to ponder the issue.

"Shoot on generated bearings!" He turned to the Helm. "Ahead flank!"

CNS *JIAOLONG*

"Torpedo launch transients, Contact One!"

The Sonar Supervisor's report blared across the speakers in Control, but Commander Zhao Wei listened calmly, waiting patiently for his crew to complete firing preparations. They were processing the orders smoothly and efficiently; there was no sense of urgency. The crew shared their Captain's confidence. Their opponent was impotent, and his torpedo would be dealt with once they had launched theirs in return. The outcome was not in doubt.

The XO turned to Commander Zhao. "All launch preparations are complete. Tube One is ready to fire."

Zhao nodded. "Fire Tube One."

USS *ANNAPOLIS*

"Torpedo launch transients, bearing two-six-zero!"

After launching their MK 48 torpedo, Ramsey had maintained *Annapolis* headed straight toward the Yuan, waiting until his adversary fired his torpedo. As a result, the incoming torpedo would be fired on a line-of-bearing solution, giving *Annapolis* the maximum possibility to evade. Maneuvering this close to a torpedo launch was risky, but the Chinese had probably never seen a 688 maneuver at high speed up close, and had no idea what she was capable of.

The Sonar Supervisor's report was what Ramsey had been waiting for. "Helm, hard right rudder, steady course three-five-zero. Launch countermeasure!"

Throwing the rudder over hard on a 688 while at ahead flank was a dangerous evolution if the crew wasn't properly trained. As the submarine heeled over during the turn, the rudder turned into a quasi-stern plane, which would send the submarine plummeting down toward Crush Depth unless the Helm and Outboard quickly compensated with the stern and bow planes.

The Helm twisted the yoke hard right. The rudder dug in and *Annapolis* snap-rolled to starboard, heeling over forty-five degrees as the bow swung around. Everyone and everything not strapped down or hanging on to something went sliding across the Control Room. Fortunately, most watchstanders were strapped into their chairs and the supervisors behind them grabbed on to nearby consoles, and Ramsey held on to the Search Periscope. The Helm and Outboard were well trained, maintaining the submarine on depth during the rapid turn, and the deck evened out as *Annapolis* steadied up on her new course.

Ramsey checked the fusion plot behind him, verifying their torpedo decoy had been launched. Now the questions were—would the Yu-6 torpedo suck up on their countermeasure, and would the Chinese submarine be around long enough to wire-guide it toward the evading *Annapolis*?

CNS *JIAOLONG*

"Target maneuver. Contact One has turned away."

Commander Zhao listened to the report from his Executive Officer, watching the contact solution update on the plasma display above the bank of fire control consoles. This old Los Angeles class submarine was surprisingly nimble. However, it would not get away—it could not outrun their Yu-6 torpedo once it was wire-guided onto the submarine's new course.

While the XO determined what that new course was, Zhao turned to a more pressing matter. The American torpedo was still inbound. He called to Sonar. "Transmit the MK 48 termination pulse."

The Sonar Supervisor acknowledged, and a few seconds later, a single pulse echoed into the ocean. However, instead of the usual report from Sonar— *MK 48 torpedo has shut down*, Sonar reported, "Control, Sonar. MK 48 torpedo remains inbound. Termination pulse had no effect."

Zhao quickly ordered, "Send MK 48 termination pulse again." As Sonar acknowledged, he turned to the plasma screen above the combat control consoles again, studying the geographic display with renewed interest. The MK 48 torpedo was dangerously close and Zhao had kept his submarine at ahead full, headed directly toward their adversary and their torpedo. He had waited to dud the torpedo, not wanting to interrupt his torpedo launch preparations. The Sonar Supervisor's excited report came across the Control Room speakers.

"Captain, Sonar. Second termination pulse sent. MK 48 torpedo has not shut down!"

Zhao called out, "Helm ahead flank! Right hard rudder! Launch decoy!" But he knew it was already too late. The MK 48 torpedo was less than two thousand yards away, and the decoy would not distract the American torpedo from the larger submarine beside it.

As Zhao's submarine began to swing to starboard, Sonar reported, "MK 48 torpedo is increasing frequency and speed! Torpedo is homing!"

USS *ANNAPOLIS*

"Target acquired!" the Weapons Officer announced, reviewing the telemetry data being sent back to *Annapolis* over the torpedo wire.

The position of the Chinese submarine on the combat system updated, but there was little change. Their solution had been almost perfect. Ramsey watched on the display as the green inverted V closed on the red U, the two symbols merging a few seconds later.

An explosion rumbled through the Control Room, announcing their torpedo software had indeed been corrected and their adversary vanquished.

"Loss of wire continuity, Tube One," the Weapon Control Coordinator announced.

Ramsey turned his attention to the Chinese torpedo, examining Lieutenant Hogarth's geographic display. The Yu-6 torpedo was circling their decoy, and there was no submarine to wire-guide it toward *Annapolis*. Ramsey turned back toward the Ship Control Panel.

"Helm, ahead standard. Left ten-degree rudder, steady course two-seven-zero."

Annapolis slowed, blending back into the ocean environment and reducing the flow noise across her sensors.

"Conn, Sonar. Hold a new contact, designated Sierra two-five, bearing two-nine-three, classified submerged."

Ramsey acknowledged Sonar. The Atlantic Fleet submarines now had functioning torpedoes. And they had plenty of targets to use them on.

The Unites States Submarine Force was back in business.

70

BOSO PENINSULA, JAPAN

On the eastern shore of the Chiba Prefecture, only three kilometers from the Pacific Ocean, Major Suzuki Koki picked his way through the rubble of the Iioka Railway Station, offering encouraging words to the remaining men in his company. Less than half of his men were alive and half of those injured, including him. His limp was getting worse, but he tried to ignore the throbbing in his left leg from the shrapnel buried in his thigh. He tried to hide the pain and set an example for his weary men.

His men were firing through jagged holes blown in the railway station wall, attempting to repel the latest PLA onslaught. After completing his round, his senses numbed by the staccato firing of rifles and the rumbling explosions of incoming artillery rounds, Suzuki leaned back against the cool cinder block wall, taking care not to put weight on his left leg as he slid slowly to the ground. Placing his pistol on the floor next to him, he winced as he pulled his left knee up with both hands to examine the deep gash in his thigh, protected from the dust and rubble by a wrapping of blood-stained gauze. Lifting the edge of the bandage up, he confirmed the bleeding had stopped. After the never-ending flood of bad news over the last eleven days, this was good news indeed.

Eleven days ago, seated at his desk in the Ministry of Defense Headquarters in Tokyo, he had watched China's surprise attack unfold on his computer monitor. Once the shock wore off, he had raced to the outskirts of Tokyo to join his unit. Japan was ill prepared for a land invasion, convinced their sea power would thwart any attempt. But China had prepared well and struck fast, devastating Japanese naval forces. With the American Pacific Fleet destroyed, there was nothing to deter the flow of Chinese soldiers and equipment onto the Japanese home islands.

The fighting had been fierce around the dozen Chinese beachheads on the western shore of Japan's main island, but the PLA gained a foothold and once they broke out from their beachheads, Suzuki's company, like the rest of the Japanese Ground Self-Defense Force, had been in full retreat mode. Until now, that is. Suzuki and the rest of 1st Division had been ordered to hold their position along the Sobu Rail Line at all cost; retreat or surrender was not an option. An explanation hadn't been provided, but given their proximity to the eastern shore, Suzuki figured the sixty kilometers of Kujukuri's straight, reef-less shore was the only viable beachhead remaining for America's Marine Expeditionary Forces.

Major Suzuki was in command of the entire 34th Infantry Regiment now. The Colonel—hell, every officer senior to him—had been killed or injured, those surviving too incapacitated to issue commands. By good fortune, Suzuki's regiment had linked up with a medical unit, and even now one of the Medics was making his way through the rubble, checking on the injured men assigned to the front line.

As the Medic made his way toward Suzuki, an explosion rocked the railway station. Twenty feet away, stone and men were blown backward as a gaping hole appeared in the railway station wall. As Suzuki gazed at the hole, he realized something had changed. This wasn't the result of an artillery shell. He rolled to his side, peering through a ragged one-foot-wide hole in the cinder block wall. Emerging from the tree line, a dozen turrets appeared, and he heard the faint clanking of metal treads.

The Chinese had ferried tanks onto the island.

The situation was hopeless. They needed shoulder-fired anti-tank missiles, weapons Suzuki's company didn't possess. Against advancing tanks, they'd be forced to wait until the tanks crashed through the railway station walls, then his men would toss grenades into the tank tracks, disabling them to prevent their advance toward the beach behind them. Unfortunately, there would be little left of Suzuki's company afterward. Protected behind each tank, a platoon of Chinese infantry was advancing toward the railway station. Once the railway station walls were breached, what was left of Suzuki's company would be overwhelmed.

However, his orders were clear.

This was their final stand.

There was a puff of white smoke from one of the tank turrets, and this time a section of the railway station to Suzuki's right vaporized in a shower of debris, ricocheting in every direction. Suzuki shouted to his men, but he couldn't hear himself—there was a loud ringing in his ears from the two explosions. No one responded as the dust drifted through the terminal, partially obscuring his vision. He pulled himself to his feet, ignoring the pain shooting through his thigh. If his men couldn't hear him, he would lead by example. He climbed over the rubble toward the nearest injured man, grabbing him under his shoulders, dragging him away from the gaping hole in the wall. His men recovered from their daze, scrambling toward the injured, pulling them to temporary safety behind intact sections of the railway station.

Once the injured men had been pulled to safety, Suzuki peered through the nearest hole in the wall. The tanks, which had closed half the distance from the tree line to the terminal, had turned their attention to adjacent buildings along the Sobu Rail Line, occupied by other 1st Division units. One of the tanks swiveled its turret back toward the Iioka Railway Station, and Suzuki swore he was staring right down the turret barrel. He fought the instinct to cover his head with his arms—there was no way to protect himself from a direct hit.

As Suzuki stared at the tank, waiting for it to fire, the turret exploded in a fireball of orange flame and black smoke, and the tank ground to a halt. The two adjacent tanks also erupted in fireballs roiling upward, one of the turrets blown completely off the tank base. A few seconds later, Harrier jets streaked overhead, headed inland as bombs fell toward PLA formations farther back. The horizon erupted in a mass of red-tinged fireballs, black smoke spiraling upward.

For the first time in eleven days, Major Suzuki Koki smiled.

The Americans had arrived.

71

BEIJING

It was a small, windowless office in the South Wing of the Great Hall. A single desk—decorated with framed photos, assorted knickknacks, and a computer monitor—occupied most of the floor space. Against one wall, a plain wooden bookshelf was crammed with notebook binders, pamphlets, and loose papers that threatened to spill onto the floor at any moment. The office door was solid—no window—offering privacy to the room's only occupant, who stood behind the desk searching through its drawers.

Earlier this morning, when Christine stepped from the communications center, the corridors in the distance had begun filling with civilians arriving for work. Although the East and Central wings of the Great Hall were locked down due to the SEAL team intrusion, the South Wing was open for business as usual.

She thought that was odd until she recalled the Pentagon on 9/11. After American Airlines Flight 77 crashed into the Defense headquarters, only a portion of the Pentagon was evacuated, and the secretary of defense met with the Joint Chiefs of Staff in the National Military Command Center in one part of the Pentagon, while fires raged in another. Political and military organizations had difficulty abandoning their communication hubs and would remain as long as they believed they were safe.

When she had reviewed the schematics of the Great Hall of the People this morning, searching for a way out, Christine had stumbled onto an idea. But first, she decided to duck out of the way, choosing an unlocked office belonging to someone low on the food chain. The room was small and the furnishings inexpensive. But it served Christine's purpose, offering a reprieve from discovery while she collected her thoughts and formulated her plan. Wandering around the empty Great Hall in the early morning hours was one thing. A Caucasian woman traversing crowded corridors during the day was another matter.

On second thought, crowded corridors might work to her advantage. In a few hours, it would be lunchtime and there would be many workers traveling the hallways, and hopefully a few Caucasians. Her review of the Great Hall's schematics told here there were representatives from several Western countries with offices in the South Wing. She might blend in long enough for her plan to work.

However, there were three items she needed, and as she riffled through the desk drawers, she finally spotted the first—a roll of tape. She required two more items. One was a badge. The personnel arriving for work wore badges, and she'd stick out like a sore thumb without one. The other item she needed was something she could hide her pistol in while traversing the halls. She had luckily selected a woman's office to hide out in, and she would almost assuredly arrive with a purse.

There was a knock on the door, accompanied by a loud, demanding request. Christine's heart leapt to her throat—it was most likely security guards searching the South Wing, room by room. With one and probably two dead SEALs in the Great Hall, they'd be searching for another man wielding an MP7, not a woman sitting behind a desk in her office. But that was true only as long as Huan was dead or unconscious. She cursed herself for not putting a bullet into his head. If he recovered, they'd know exactly who to search for and she wouldn't stand a chance.

The door was locked and Christine stood frozen behind the desk, hoping whoever was outside would move on. But then she heard the metal jingling of keys, and the round doorknob twitched. Another jingle and twitch. Whoever was outside had master keys and would eventually find the right one. If they discovered her in the office after she ignored their request to open the door, they'd be suspicious and examine her closely.

Her only hope was to open the door.

Christine walked toward the door, searching her memory for a Mandarin phrase that would suffice in this situation. Halfway to the door, she selected one, calling out, "It's nice to meet you!"

She winced after the words left her mouth, but it was all she could come up with on short notice, and she hoped the door muffled enough of her voice that her response was unintelligible. The keys stopped jingling and the doorknob fell still.

Christine forced a smile onto her face, then twisted the doorknob, disengaging the lock, and pulled the door open. There were three men in the hallway. The man in the middle, wearing a white shirt and blue tie, held a ring of keys in one hand. The other two men were uniformed security guards, their pistols drawn. Their eyes widened, no doubt surprised by the appearance of a Caucasian woman. If that wasn't enough, Christine realized her inability to carry on a conversation with them in Chinese would be even more suspicious. Her only hope was to brush them off quickly. She strung together two phrases that might work.

"Good morning. How can I help?"

Christine had been prepared to utter the second expression during the planned meeting with her counterpart two weeks ago. Unfortunately, the few remaining phrases she knew were insufficient to carry on a conversation with the three men in front of her. She probably wouldn't be able to work in "Thank you" and "It was a pleasure meeting you."

The guard on the right replied to Christine's greeting.

She had no idea what he had said.

Christine decided to cut the conversation short. That meant she had to answer the man's question with something that made sense. Unfortunately, she didn't understand his question. She guessed they were inquiring about the intruders in the Great Hall, wondering if she'd noticed anything suspicious. She decided to keep her answer simple.

"No," she replied in Mandarin, then turned and headed to her desk, hoping her answer was sufficient and that the men would move on. However, as Christine settled into her chair, the guard moved into the doorway and asked a second question, the tone more demanding.

This question was probably more pointed and Christine had no idea how to answer it. As she stared at the man in silence, she sensed him growing impatient. She had to answer, but how? Glancing at a thick manila folder on top of the desk, she latched on to an idea.

Twisting her face into an aggravated expression, she picked up the folder, waving it excitedly at the man as she replied in English. "Does it look like I have time for this? I've got to finish translating this for the general secretary by noon! Do you want to explain to him why I'm not finished?"

Christine prayed the man understood English. It appeared he did, or at least enough to understand her response. Fear flickered in his eyes for a second, then he bowed his head slightly. After uttering something else in Chinese, the tone of his voice subdued, he stepped back and closed the door. Christine waited tensely for a few seconds, then her shoulders slumped in relief.

After a long moment, she stood, focusing on the next two items required to accomplish her goal. Their owner would hopefully arrive anytime now.

She had to be ready.

It was only a few minutes later, with Christine seated behind the door with the Glock in her right hand, when the doorknob turned. Christine stood as the door opened, and it began to swing shut after a Chinese woman stepped into the office, headed toward the desk. After the door shut, Christine reached over with her left hand and pressed the lock in the center of the doorknob. The woman stopped at the side of the desk, noting the absence of her chair. She dropped her purse onto the top of the desk as she turned with a perplexed look on her face, searching the office for the wayward chair. The woman spotted three things almost simultaneously—the chair by the door, a pistol pointed at her, and Christine with her index finger over her lips.

The woman's jaw dropped but thankfully no sound came out. The finger over Christine's mouth and the Glock pointed in her direction had communicated the desired response and consequence if directions weren't followed.

"Do you understand English?" Christine asked.

The woman nodded, swallowing hard.

"Stay quiet and do as I say, and you won't get hurt. Understand?"

The woman nodded again.

Christine shoved the chair toward the woman. "Take a seat."

A few minutes was all it took before the woman was taped to her chair, her chair taped to a leg of the desk, and her mouth taped shut. Before taping the woman's mouth shut, no coercion was required to extract the required information. The woman confirmed the peak time for traffic in the Great Hall was during lunch. Christine didn't relish the idea of waiting the next four hours in the small office where she would be cornered if discovered, but the wait was worth the risk.

Christine stepped back to examine her work. It was possible the woman could wriggle her way out of the tape after she left, but Christine figured it didn't matter. She would need only a few minutes. In the meantime, the woman wouldn't need her badge. Christine transferred the badge from the woman's blouse to hers, then searched through the woman's purse on top of the desk, retrieving a compact mirror, which she opened in her left hand.

Huan's two punches to her face had done some damage, but thankfully the swelling had subsided. His first punch had caught her squarely on the left side of her face, but there was only a faint blue bruise along her jawline. The second fist to her face had done more damage, splitting open her upper lip. After entering the woman's office this morning, she had wiped her face clean with a tissue from the box on the woman's desk. She must have done a decent job, because the guard she encountered a few minutes ago didn't seem to notice. As she examined her face in the small mirror, tilting her head from side to side, she was pleased. The split lip had sealed, forming a thin scab. She ran her fingers through her hair, making herself as presentable as possible, then returned the mirror to the purse.

Christine glanced at her watch. It would be a few more hours before lunchtime, when the corridors would be sufficiently crowded for her journey. As long as the security guards didn't sweep by the office again in the meantime, her plan might work. A slim chance, but a chance nonetheless.

72

WASHINGTON, D.C.

In the Situation Room beneath the West Wing of the White House, Captain Steve Brackman took his seat at the conference table, waiting for the briefing to begin. Gathered around the table, with the president at the head, were Secretary of Defense Nelson Jennings and the chairman of the Joint Chiefs of Staff on one side, Captain Brackman and senior members of the president's Cabinet lining the other. At the front of the conference room, the image of Admiral Vance Garbin, head of Pacific Command, flickered on the large monitor.

"The SEAL team mission was a resounding success, sir," the Admiral began. "All PLA communication nodes and command and control centers are off-line, as well as their newest missile systems. Also, our Atlantic Fleet SSGNs launched over three hundred Tomahawk missiles, destroying the older Chinese missile systems that weren't networked. Between our Tomahawks, another round of B-1 bomber attacks, and the computer virus, Chinese air defense is practically nonexistent. Our aircraft have complete control of the skies over Japan.

"After our satellites came up, our submarines downloaded the new torpedo software, which has been extremely effective. The fast attacks sanitized the approach lanes for our MEFs, sinking over twenty Chinese submarines. Our fast attacks have penetrated the Nansei Island chain, and will soon be attacking Chinese ships ferrying men and supplies onto the Japanese islands."

"How are the MEF landings going?" the president asked.

"The beachhead has been secured and the MEFs are off-loading men and equipment. The three Marine air wings are providing support as ground forces move inland. Once we've gained control of an airstrip or the Marines finish building one, we'll begin moving Air Force fighter squadrons and Army troops in to assist. Unless something unforeseen occurs, Mr. President, this war is all but over."

The president nodded, a grim look of satisfaction on his face. "What about the SEAL team that injected the virus?"

"I'm afraid that's the only piece of bad news," the Admiral answered. "The virus was inserted five hours ago, but no one has exited the Great Hall of the People. We have to conclude the team members have been either killed or captured."

There was silence in the conference room as the president absorbed the Admiral's assessment. The mission had been an enormous success, but the men—and woman—had likely paid with their lives.

"Thank you, Admiral," the president replied. "Keep us informed if anything changes."

"Yes, Mr. President."

The view screen flickered off, and the president directed his attention to the men and women seated at the conference table. They were silent, awash in relief from the success of their counterpunch against China, but keenly aware of the probable death of the president's national security advisor. Finally, the chairman of the Joint Chiefs of Staff, General Hodson, expressed his condolences.

"Mr. President, I'm sorry to hear about Miss O' Connor."

The president remained silent for a moment, then leaned forward in his chair and placed his elbows on the table, his forearms crossed in front of him. "How well do you know Christine?"

The chairman answered, "Not very well, I admit. Our interactions were limited to the various briefings we attended together."

"Let me provide some background," the president began. "There are two important things you should know. The first is that she's a tenacious woman, willing to put up with a lot in an effort to achieve her goal. Hell, she puts up with me. And Hardison!" Hardison nodded glumly as the president continued. "She agreed to work in an administration of the opposite party, butting heads every day with the likes of me, Hardison, and SecDef, with the hope she could make sense out of our hare-brained national defense policies.

"The second thing you need to know is that Christine has a vindictive streak. You don't want to cross her or the United States. Do you remember the *Kentucky* incident?" The General nodded. "And you remember what happened to Israel's Intelligence Minister afterward?"

General Hodson replied, "He was assassinated by his own Mossad."

"Not the Mossad," the president replied. He kept his eyes locked on Hodson until what really happened dawned on him.

The General's eyes widened. "Christine killed him?"

"She insisted on the assignment," the President answered. "And she did a stellar job.

"My point, gentlemen," the president added, "is that I wouldn't underestimate Christine. She could very well be alive, somewhere in the Great Hall. And if so, my best bet is—she's not thinking about escape."

73

BEIJING

Xiang Chenglei entered the Politburo conference room, taking his seat at the head of the table. The lights were dim, matching the mood of the other seven Politburo members. Joining the Politburo today was General Cao Feng, head of the PLA's Fourth Department, responsible for China's cyber warfare, who was seated at the far end of the table. Also present—in electronic form—was Admiral Tsou, his grainy image displayed on the large monitor on the wall opposite Xiang.

It seemed impossible. Events this morning had unfolded at a whirlwind pace, quickly reaching a crisis level. Xiang found it difficult to believe the situation had deteriorated so drastically, and decided it was prudent to obtain the information firsthand. Surely, the data streaming into the Great Hall had been garbled. It was time to obtain an accurate update.

Xiang was about to address General Cao when the doors to the conference room opened and Huan, who had been unexpectedly absent all morning, entered. Wrapped around Huan's head was a white gauze bandage, a tinge of red seeping through the right side. Huan settled gingerly into a vacant chair at the end of the conference table. Xiang decided his questions about Huan's absence and physical condition could wait until after the meeting. He returned his attention to General Cao.

"What is the status of this American virus?"

General Cao cleared his voice. "A virus was uploaded into the main communications center here in the Great Hall, and it is spreading throughout the entire PLA command and control infrastructure, infecting all communication and tactical networks. The virus manifests itself in two ways. The first is that it corrupts the computer operating system, shutting down the computer and preventing start-up afterward. The second effect is that even when the computers are restarted from backup operating system discs, the virus corrupts the computer IP assignments, preventing the transfer of information between computers."

"How long will it take to clear the virus and restore our communication and tactical networks?"

There was a pained expression on the General's face as he answered. "It will take weeks to recover, Mr. President. All infected computers must be wiped clean—their hard drives erased, reformatted, and software reloaded. The IP links to other command centers and every unit in the field will have to be manually reentered."

"How did this happen? We made an enormous investment in cyber warfare, and it was the one area we had supremacy over the Americans."

"We *have* made an enormous investment," General Cao replied, "and our command and control networks are impervious to outside attacks. However, we did not consider an attack from within, from inside the Great Hall of the People. That was our shortcoming."

There was a momentary silence before Xiang turned to Admiral Tsou's image on the monitor. "What is the impact on the People's Liberation Army?"

Admiral Tsou replied, "All communication and tactical links are down, and the virus has also infected individual combat units, taking their IP voice circuits off-line. All of our newest, networked weapon systems are inoperative, leaving only legacy weapons, most of which have been destroyed by Tomahawk missiles and air strikes. As a result, America has control of the sky over Japan, protecting their Marine Expeditionary Forces, which are off-loading onto a beachhead on Honshu's eastern shore.

"Additionally, our submarine fleet has been devastated in only a few hours. It's hard to get a clear picture of what is occurring, but several of our submarines that have been sunk have relayed information via their emergency beacons on the surface. The American torpedoes can no longer be shut down by our submarine sonar pulse. It appears they are also now able to home on our submarines when they attempt to shut the torpedo down. The American fast attacks have sunk all of our submarines screening Honshu and have penetrated the Nansei Island chain, and they will soon cut off all reinforcements and supplies flowing onto the Japanese islands. If we don't react quickly, our troops on Japan will become stranded."

There was a long silence as Xiang and the other Politburo members absorbed Admiral Tsou's words. America had defeated them. And if they didn't act soon, hundreds of thousands of men would become prisoners of war.

China must retreat.

Xiang's eyes moved around the table, surveying each member of the Politburo. Without asking, he saw the consent in their eyes. Xiang was about to address Admiral Tsou when Huan interjected.

"What about the PLA Air Force? If we sink *Reagan* and her escorts, can we continue the campaign?" There was desperation in Huan's voice.

"Yes and no," Tsou answered. "The PLA Air Force has fared well thus far in our campaign against Taipei and Japan, but the main reason is because we have avoided engaging American aircraft and their carrier strike groups, attacking them with missiles instead. Our aircraft technology and pilot training are no match for that of the Americans. However, we have a significant numerical advantage, and if we commit the PLA Air Force to a direct assault on the *Reagan* Task Force, I believe we can overwhelm their defenses and destroy *Reagan* and her escorts, along with their amphibious ships. Unfortunately, we will suffer significant losses—several hundred aircraft—and only delay the inevitable.

"With American submarines controlling the water between China and Japan, we will be unable to ship adequate supplies to our forces in Japan; our airlift capacity is insufficient. Also, once the four Atlantic Fleet carriers arrive, we will lose control of the airspace again, since we can no longer prevent the carriers from approaching Japan. Our new missile systems and submarines that were supposed to keep the carriers away have been defeated.

"America's Marine combat units have already been transferred ashore, and although we can destroy their amphibious ships and whatever material remains aboard, we cannot dislodge the Marines from Honshu before the Atlantic Fleet carriers arrive. Once America has control of the airspace and is able to build an airfield for their Air Force to operate from and land Army units, it's over."

"We must make America pay," Huan replied, turning toward Xiang, "in every way possible. If we can sink yet another carrier strike group, then we should. It will help teach the Americans a lesson." Huan paused, then revealed the true intent of his recommendation. "There will be severe political implications once the people learn we have been defeated and so many lives lost for nothing. However, if we can claim we have destroyed the entire American Pacific Fleet, it will soften the blow. We can even retool the intent of our offensive, ending America's domination of the Pacific."

Xiang did not immediately respond, evaluating the situation and Huan's proposal. Finally, he sat up, his shoulders straight as he spoke to Admiral Tsou's image.

"Send orders to our PLA commanders through whatever communication circuits remain and begin their extraction from Japan. However, leave our units on Taipei. I will use our occupation of Taiwan as a bargaining chip during negotiations with the United States."

Xiang paused for a moment, then continued. "Commit the PLA Air Force. Destroy the *Reagan* Task Force."

Admiral Tsou acknowledged Xiang's order, then his image faded from the display. There was a painful silence in the conference room as the men around the table digested the sudden turn of events. Finally, Xiang stood to leave, as did the seven junior members and Huan. Xiang stepped into the hallway and Huan joined him at his side, the two men flanked by Cadre Department bodyguards, who had been waiting outside the conference room. As the four men headed down the corridor toward the president's office, Huan brought Xiang up to speed on what had occurred earlier that morning.

74

USS *RONALD REAGAN*

Off the eastern shore of Honshu, Captain CJ Berger leaned forward in his chair on the Bridge of USS *Ronald Reagan*. His eyes scanned the video screens mounted below the Bridge windows as he listened to *Reagan*'s strike controllers over the speaker by his chair. So far, things had been quiet in the air, and everything was proceeding smoothly ashore. The Marine Expeditionary Forces were incredibly efficient, rapidly off-loading their troops and equipment. All ground combat troops were ashore and their Harrier jets and Viper and Venom attack helicopters had been striking targets inland all morning. Within twenty-four hours, their remaining equipment would be off-loaded. In the meantime, it was the task force's job to protect the vulnerable amphibious ships. That responsibility fell largely on *Reagan*.

The Atlantic Fleet submarines had cleared a safe path to Honshu's shores, then expanded outward, preventing China's Navy from approaching close enough to become a threat. The PLA Air Force, however, was another matter. They fielded over one thousand fourth-generation fighters, while the *Reagan* Task Force, augmented by the Marine Joint Strike Fighters, mustered only ninety-six fighter aircraft, of which only half were on station. Three of *Reagan*'s fighter squadrons, along with one of the Marine squadrons, were flying CAP—Combat Air Patrol—with one squadron on its way out to relieve and another squadron on its way back for replacement pilots and refueling. On the Flight Deck, the sixth squadron of *Reagan*'s fighters were performing *hot-pump crew switch*—refueling with their jet engines still running, turning off an engine on one side of the aircraft long enough for the pilots to swap out.

Against potential Chinese air attack, the *Reagan* Task Force employed a layered defense. The aircraft were on the perimeter, with *Reagan*'s escorts—

only two cruisers and four destroyers—forming an inner ring, with *Reagan* and the amphibious ships in the center. The maximum range of Chinese air-to-surface missiles was debatable, but Intel's current estimate was that the range of the most capable missile variants was 150 miles. As a result, *Reagan* had established its Combat Air Patrol at 250 miles to allow time for their fighters to engage and destroy any inbound Chinese aircraft before they could launch their air-to-surface missiles.

Any Leakers—hostile aircraft that made it through *Reagan*'s Combat Air Patrol—would be shot down by Standard SM-2 and extended-range SM-6 missiles launched by the task force's cruisers and destroyers. Any missiles launched by the Chinese jets would also be engaged with Standard missiles. And finally, if Chinese missiles made it past the SM-2s and SM-6s, *Reagan* and the other ships would employ their close-in Ship Self-Defense Systems, which on *Reagan* consisted of the ESSM and RAM missiles and the CIWS Gatling guns.

Berger preferred to have his Combat Air Patrol farther out, but the Air Warfare Commander aboard the Aegis cruiser USS *Chosin* had made the decision to pull them closer in. Their aircraft were already stretched thin at 250 miles. Thankfully, half of the task force's fighters were the new Joint Strike Fighters. They were extremely capable aircraft—on paper. None had been tested in combat. But that might soon change.

Berger's attention shifted from the video screens on the bulkhead to the speaker by his chair. The strike controllers were directing the squadron of Joint Strike Fighters returning to *Reagan* to turn around and head back out.

In *Reagan*'s Combat Direction Center, Captain Debbie Kent watched airborne contacts populate her display. Their E-2C Hawkeyes, flying high above the task force, were transmitting tracks to the cruisers, destroyers, and carrier. Kent looked up from her console, examining one of the two eight-by-ten-foot displays on the Video Wall. It was littered with several hundred contacts streaming toward the *Reagan* Task Force from three directions—over Honshu and around the northern and southern ends of the island.

Kent waited as the E-2C Hawkeyes above queried the incoming aircraft using the IFF—Identification Friend or Foe—system. If they were friendly aircraft, the transponders aboard would transmit the correct response to the Hawkeyes' challenge.

The inbound icons began changing color, switching from yellow to red.

The aircraft were Hostile.

A few seconds later, the Air Warfare Commander's voice emanated from the speaker next to Kent. "Alpha Papa, this is Alpha Whiskey. Divide your CAP into three segments and engage incoming Hostiles. You are *Weapons Free.*"

Kent acknowledged the order, then relayed it to the Tactical Action Officer, who directed the strike controllers to begin vectoring their fighters toward the three streams of incoming aircraft. There were too many contacts for the strike controllers to individually assign to their aircraft, so targeting would be handed over to the pilots. This was going to turn into a free-for-all. She dropped her eyes to her Cooperative Engagement Capability display, reading the summary. There were over four hundred inbound aircraft: 4-to-1 odds.

This was not going to turn out well.

75

BEIJING

In the South Wing of the Great Hall, Christine leaned against the edge of the desk, checking her watch for the hundredth time. The last four hours had ticked by slowly, and she had spent the time alternately pacing the floor and leaning against the desk, periodically examining her captive to ensure she was still securely bound. The entire time, she worried the security guards would conduct another search. She had fumbled her way through the first one, but if they swung by again, she was done for. There was no way to hide her captive, taped to the chair. While she waited impatiently for lunchtime, her mind raced, reviewing her makeshift plan.

Earlier this morning, when she stepped from the communications center, she had pulled up the schematics of the Great Hall on the plasma panel, examining the locations of the security checkpoints, searching for an unguarded route out of the Great Hall. There were none. But in the process, she discovered there were no checkpoints between her and the Politburo's main offices in the heart of the South Wing. She couldn't make it *out* of the Great Hall.

But she could make it *in*.

She had a clear path to the president's office. She had no idea how effective the virus she had uploaded was, but she figured a pistol to the head of the right man could end this war. Even if it didn't, she could hold the man responsible for China's aggression accountable. It was a preposterous plan and at one point she almost laughed out loud. But she told herself repeatedly it could work. At the moment, her confidence was brittle but intact.

Glancing at her watch again, she decided it was time.

Christine examined her blouse, eyeing the woman's badge clipped to her lapel. There was no way the badge would pass close examination, but the picture on the badge was small and the hair color the same. As long as she kept moving at a decent pace, the dissimilarity between the picture on the badge and the woman wearing it shouldn't be noticeable. For good measure, however, she unfastened the highest button of her blouse, revealing the top of her ample, rounded breasts. Anything to keep people from comparing her face to her badge. She figured she had the men sufficiently distracted.

Retrieving the Glock from the top of the desk, she slid it into the woman's purse. She slung the purse over her left shoulder, leaving the top of the purse open so she could easily retrieve the pistol.

Badge. Purse. Glock.

She was ready.

After a final glance at her captive, Christine opened the door to the office, engaging the lock in the doorknob. Pulling the door shut behind her, she stepped into the corridor.

The hallway wasn't as crowded as she had hoped, but there were enough people traversing the corridors that she didn't stand out. The eighth person she passed was a Middle Eastern man, and a Caucasian woman passed by a few seconds later. Christine let out a silent sigh of relief. She wasn't sticking out like a sore thumb and there was actually a possibility she would reach the president's office unchallenged.

Her stomach tightened at the thought.

She had no idea what kind of security the president had. There weren't any checkpoints between them, but she doubted the president of China would traipse anywhere, even in the Great Hall, without the equivalent of the Secret Service nearby. Hopefully there would be only a few men, and with surprise on her side, she would break through.

During her last review of the Great Hall's schematics, she had memorized the path to the president's office. Left at the second intersection. Right at the next. Left again. As she traversed the corridors, the throng of personnel thickened, and her trek through the Great Hall was uneventful until she turned the second corner. Two uniformed security guards were heading toward her, glancing at the badges and faces of the men and women passing by. Christine hesitated momentarily, then forced herself to continue walking, hoping neither guard had noticed the slight pause in her gait when she spotted them. She felt her heart pounding in her chest as she continued down the corridor.

As she prepared to pass between the two guards, she decided to ignore them, giving the two men an opportunity to let their eyes wander toward the top of her blouse. Her eyes were set straight ahead, but she concentrated on the periphery of her vision, attempting to detect any indication the guards had become suspicious. She fingered the strap of the purse hanging from her left shoulder, ready at an instant to retrieve the Glock. The two guards were only a few paces away now, and she prepared herself for the worst.

As the two guards approached, they turned their attention to Christine, their eyes examining her face for a moment before shifting down toward her chest. The two guards passed by and Christine continued on, listening for any reaction behind her. There was no indication of anything unusual. As she put distance between herself and the two guards, her pulse began to slow and she suppressed a smile.

At the end of the long hallway, Christine turned again, stepping into a wider corridor, its floor constructed of marble instead of terrazzo, its walls decorated with large oil paintings on canvas stretched between elaborate, or-nately carved frames. She had entered the official Politburo spaces.

She was getting close.

Christine knew the corridor would T at the end, running into a perpen-dicular hallway containing the offices of the nine Politburo members.

Only a few hundred more feet.

Unfortunately, at the end of the corridor was a man wearing a business suit, standing behind a lectern, who would undoubtedly inquire about the purpose of her visit. She was confident she could get past him. What con-cerned her was what waited in the perpendicular hallway beyond.

One hurdle at a time.

As she approached the man at the lectern, she was thankful there was no one else in the corridor—it would make this part easier. When she was a few feet away, the man looked up from an appointment book, asking Chris-tine a question. She slipped her right hand into her purse, retrieving the Glock. The man's eyes widened, but before he could call out, Christine aimed and squeezed the trigger, putting a bullet in the man's forehead. The pistol re-coiled with a whisper and the man's body hit the floor with a dull thud. She

returned the pistol to her purse as she continued past the man without breaking stride, reaching the end of the hallway, turning right.

At the end of the corridor, just over fifty feet away, two men in black business suits stood outside a dark-stained wooden door, one man on each side.

Cadre Department bodyguards, no doubt.

These two wouldn't be so easy.

Christine continued toward them, hoping she would close at least half
the distance before she was challenged. She was a decent shot with a pistol
at close range, but that was without being nervous and while taking time to
aim carefully. Surprise would be on her side, but if she missed, she would
not get a second chance. Instead of aiming for their heads, she settled on
chest shots, increasing the odds she'd hit her mark.

When she was thirty feet from the door, the guard on the left called out.
Christine needed to buy a few more seconds to get close enough to ensure
she didn't miss, but didn't understand the question. She replied with a response that hopefully made sense.

"Good morning," she said in Mandarin.

The guard replied, but Christine again had no idea what he said.

She had to act before either man had an inkling of what was about to
occur. She'd rehearsed the sequence of events in her mind a hundred times,
and it was finally time to execute.

Christine reached into her purse again, extracting the Glock. As she
extended her arm toward the man on the left, she was shocked at how fast
the two men were reacting; both were already reaching into their suit
jackets.

She pulled the trigger and a bullet slammed into the man's chest. She
swung the pistol to the right and steadied up on the second man just as his
hand came out of his jacket, a pistol in his grip. She squeezed off another
round, the bullet also hitting him squarely in the chest.

She glanced back at the first man.

He was still standing. Something was wrong.

Things were occurring so fast they were blur, yet at the same time the
details were clear. There was a bullet hole in the man's shirt, but no blood.
The bullet had dazed him, knocking him back against the wall, but his clouded
expression cleared and he pulled his weapon from inside his suit jacket.

They were wearing bulletproof vests.

Christine swung her arm toward the first man again, this time aiming for his head. She halted her swing, raised her aim up slightly, and fired. Amazingly, the bullet hit the man between his eyes, jerking his head back. She watched him collapse onto the ground from the corner of her eye as she swung her arm back to the right, returning her attention to the second guard.

Like the other guard, he had been temporarily stunned. But he'd been faster than the first man, already pulling his pistol from inside his jacket before being shot in the chest. As Christine steadied up, she noticed he already had his arm extended and steady, his pistol aimed toward her.

She squeezed the trigger, praying she fired first and that her bullet hit its mark.

A gunshot echoed down the corridor, and her subconscious told her that was a bad sign. Her Glock had a silencer screwed into the end—it didn't make that kind of sound. That meant . . .

Christine's body jerked backward as white-hot pain tore through her left shoulder. The excruciating pain sapped the strength from her body and her legs gave way; she fell to her knees on the hard marble floor. She fought through the pain, trying to maintain her balance, trying to think clearly. She'd been shot, and if the second guard was still alive, another bullet was coming her way. She remembered squeezing the trigger of her pistol, but had no idea if she had fired or if the bullet found its target. She looked up, noticing the second man sprawled on the ground, a pool of blood spreading from beneath his head across the marble floor.

Warmth ran down her left arm, dangling by her side, and any attempt to move sent mind-numbing pain shooting through her shoulder. But despite her injury, her plan had been successful—she'd cleared the way to the president's office. Unfortunately, the guard's gunshot had announced her presence, and it wouldn't be long before someone arrived to determine what happened. She'd better get moving.

As Christine climbed to her feet, the door to the president's office opened. Xiang Chenglei, the president of China, appeared in the doorway.

Perfect.

Christine swung the pistol back up. "Don't move!"

Xiang could easily have slammed the door shut as she raised the pistol—it would have been an instinctive reaction. Instead, Xiang opened the door wider, stepping out into the corridor. He stood there, waiting for further direction as he took in the scene, his eyes examining first one bodyguard, then the other, finally coming to rest on Christine.

"You're injured," Xiang said. "Let me call for medical assistance."

"Not so fast. We're going to have a talk first." Christine moved toward him, her left arm dangling by her side, doing her best not to move her shoulder. She stopped a few feet away, pointing the pistol at Xiang's head. "Into your office, before *help* arrives."

"It would be best if we talked here."

"Into your office!" Pain shot through Christine's shoulder as she shouted. She clenched her teeth, waiting for the pain to subside. "Now," she added in a more controlled effort.

"As you wish," Xiang replied, then turned and stepped into his office.

Christine followed closely behind, her eyes set on his back, wary of any unexpected move. As she entered his office, she spotted another man from the corner of her right eye. Huan was standing by the door, his head wrapped in a white gauze bandage. His hand was high above him, holding something, and he swung it down toward her head.

She tried to duck out of the way but was too slow. A heavy object crushed into her skull and sharp pain sliced through her scalp. Her vision clouded in a yellow haze, the Glock falling from her hand as she crumpled to the floor.

76

USS *RONALD REAGAN* TASK FORCE

"Shrek, tally two bandits on your six!"

Marine Corps pilot Stan Borum, call sign Shrek, glanced at the glass touch-screen display that spanned the front of his F-35B cockpit, locating the two bandits behind him. A second later, the F-35's *Barracuda* electronic warfare system, which provided 360-degree surveillance, detected the targeting radar of the two aircraft, classifying them as J-11B Shenyang tactical fighters.

"I see 'em," Shrek replied as he recalled the capabilities of the Chinese aircraft. The twin-engine J-11B was a fourth-generation tactical fighter—an upgraded version of the Russian Su-27SK, able to fly almost fifty percent faster than Shrek's single-engine Joint Strike Fighter.

The voice of Shrek's wingman came across his helmet speaker again. "I can't help. I'm tied up with two of my own." Shrek didn't reply as he noted his wingman on his display, headed south with two bandits in trail.

With a six-foot, 230-pound barrel-chested body, Lieutenant Colonel Stan Borum had been awarded the call sign Shrek. He didn't resemble the animated ogre *that* much, he thought. His skin wasn't green. However, despite the connotation of his call sign, Shrek was secretly pleased. He was, after all, a Green Knight. He was the squadron leader of Marine Fighter Attack Squadron VMFA-121, the Green Knights, the first operational squadron of F-35 Lightning II stealth aircraft. Shrek felt fortunate this afternoon, seated in the cockpit of the most advanced fighter in the world. But even though he appreciated the technological advantage of his F-35B over the Chinese aircraft, Shrek figured he'd survived this far into the battle due to the most important ingredient in warfare.

Luck.

The first few minutes of combat had been overwhelming, the sky filled with a dizzying array of aircraft and missiles. Shrek had fired his wing-mounted ordnance as the two air forces approached each other, then evaded a barrage of incoming missiles. Moments later, the thirty-two U.S. fighters in this sector slammed into seventy Chinese aircraft. Who lived and died those first few minutes had been a crapshoot, each pilot dodging aircraft and missiles, dispensing chaff, and targeting enemy fighters while weaving through a sky lit up with exploding aircraft and streaking missiles.

The sky had thinned out now, with fifty Chinese fighters shot down along with twenty U.S. jets. Unfortunately, Shrek and the other American fighters were still on the wrong end of 2-to-1 odds; twenty Chinese aircraft against a dozen Americans. If that wasn't bad enough, there were another seventy Chinese jets approaching fast.

Shortly after engaging the incoming aircraft, Shrek had determined the Chinese wave was divided into two echelons. The leading group of seventy aircraft were air superiority fighters, predominately the J-10 Chengdu and J-11 Shenyang, followed by another seventy fighter-bombers, primarily the Xian JH-7 and 7A, armed with air-to-surface missiles. The leading Chinese fighters were attempting to clear a path for their fighter-bombers so they could approach within range of their air-to-surface missiles. That, of course, was what Shrek and the rest of *Reagan*'s Combat Air Patrol were attempting to prevent.

Shrek had done well, shooting down four J-10s, splashing the last one only a few seconds ago. Despite his success, Shrek and the other American pilots hadn't put a dent in the mass of JH-7 fighter-bombers rapidly approaching. Shrek needed to take out the two trailing J-11s quickly so he could focus on the JH-7s, which were the real threat to the *Reagan* Task Force. Unfortunately, he had only one missile left.

Shrek banked hard right to bring his F-35 around toward the incoming J-11s. Although the J-11s were much faster than his F-35, Shrek had the advantage when it came to weapon systems. He flicked a switch on his flight stick, then tapped his glass touch-screen display, selecting his remaining missile. The starboard weapon bay doors in the fuselage of the F-35 opened in preparation for firing. As Shrek's F-35 came around, he turned his head to the right and targeted the closest J-11 simply by looking at it, the sensors in his helmet visor locking on to the aircraft.

Even though his F-35 was still thirty degrees off-axis from the J-11, Shrek fired his last missile, an AIM-120 AMRAAM, and he guided the missile toward the J-11 by keeping his head pointed at the aircraft. As the AMRAAM completed its turn, its internal radar took over, locking on to the J-11.

The J-11 dispensed chaff and banked hard left, but the AMRAAM detected the aircraft speeding away from the chaff burst and adjusted course. Shrek turned his attention to the second J-11B as it launched one of its missiles, and a moment later Shrek's *Barracuda* classified it as a PL-12, an air-to-air missile similar in capability to the AMRAAM.

There was a bright burst of an explosion to Shrek's left. His AMRAAM had found its target, evidenced by the disappearance of both the AMRAAM and the J-11 from his touch-panel display. *Splash another one.* However, that still left the second J-11, along with the PL-12 missile, closing fast.

Shrek banked right and went inverted, turning his F-35 upside down. He pulled back on his flight stick, aiming his jet down toward the water, fifteen thousand feet below. He pushed the throttle past the détente, engaging his afterburner. As he rocketed toward the ocean's surface, he checked his touch-screen display. The PL-12 was chasing down after him. With a speed of Mach 4, the missile would reach Shrek in a few seconds. He had even less time before he hit the water. The F-35's *Bitching Betty* audio warning system activated, a woman's soothing voice informing Shrek of the impending danger. "Altitude. Altitude. Altitude."

"Shut up, Betty."

The F-35's voice recognition system turned off the alarm.

At five thousand feet, Shrek dispensed a round of chaff and yanked back on the stick. He eased off on the throttle as he monitored the g-force displayed on his touch screen, praying he didn't pass out as his F-35 hit eight g's. The legs of his G suit filled with air, helping to keep the blood in his head. He tightened his abdominal muscles and grunted through the turn, attempting to keep as much blood in his brain as possible.

Shrek leveled off at a thousand feet, then banked right to get a visual. The PL-12 missile had passed through the chaff, but the chaff had done its job. The missile had stayed focused on the reflective cloud of aluminum-coated fibers, allowing Shrek's F-35 to slip out of the missile radar's field of view. The missile continued downward, plowing into the ocean.

He turned his attention to the J-11. The pilot had followed Shrek down and was just now leveling off at a thousand feet, two miles behind him. Shrek didn't have much time to think about his next maneuver, because *Betty* came across his headset again.

"Missile inbound."

The J-11 had fired another missile, classified by Shrek's *Barracuda* as another PL-12. He had only one more burst of chaff left and wanted to save it, so he tapped the glass display again, activating the F-35's electronic jammer. He watched the missile closely to see what happened. The missile immediately adjusted course, aiming toward his jet. Shrek turned off the electronic jamming. This PL-12 variant had a home-on-jam feature.

He checked his display. A mass of forty JH-7s was approaching fast, and Shrek decided he couldn't afford to get tied up with this J-11 in a dogfight that could last who-knew-how long. He needed to shed this guy fast. The home-on-jam feature gave him an idea.

Shrek banked left again, returning to his original course, putting the missile and J-11 behind him. Just as the PL-12 closed the remaining distance, Shrek dispensed his last burst of chaff and went vertical, kicking in his afterburners. The missile stayed locked on the chaff and passed through the reflective cloud. With Shrek above the chaff and climbing, the missile lost contact. The missile turned left for a few seconds, searching for its target, then right for a few more seconds. Finding nothing, the missile turned skyward.

But Shrek had already gone inverted, turning back toward the incoming J-11. He rolled his F-35 back to a normal orientation, then checked the distance to the PL-12 and J-11. His adversary was staying close to the water, avoiding Shrek while his missile was still in play.

Shrek activated his electronic jammer again. The PL-12 missile immediately turned in Shrek's direction and increased speed. As the PL-12 gained on Shrek, he adjusted the trajectory of his F-35, angling down on an intercept course with the incoming J-11. The Chinese pilot realized what Shrek was doing and turned away. But Shrek adjusted course and passed barely a hundred feet above the J-11 as it continued its turn. Shrek turned his electronic jammer off as he passed above the Chinese fighter, and the PL-12 resumed using its radar-seeking head. The missile locked on to the larger radar signature of the Chinese fighter, slamming into the fuselage of the jet a second later. The J-11 morphed into a cloud of fire and shrapnel.

Checking his display again, Shrek located the group of JH-7 fighter-bombers. They were surging through a gap in *Reagan*'s Combat Air Patrol six thousand feet above. The Chinese fighter-bombers were headed in at Mach 1.7 and Shrek's F-35 was capable of only Mach 1.6. He wouldn't be able to run them down once they got past. Shrek kicked in his afterburner, climbing quickly toward the Chinese aircraft. His *Barracuda* alarmed again. Not far behind, two more J-11Bs were headed his way.

Now that Shrek was out of missiles, his only recourse was to fall in behind the JH-7s and shoot them down with his Equalizer four-barrel Gatling gun. To Shrek's left, another F-35 and two F/A-18 Super Hornets were also falling in behind the Chinese fighter-bombers. Apparently the three aircraft were also out of missiles, as they engaged the inbound JH-7s with their guns, the interspersed red tracer rounds streaming toward the fighter-bombers. The JH-7s weaved all over the sky to avoid the cannon fire, but maintained their overall inbound track.

Shrek checked the J-11s behind him. The two J-11s must also be out of missiles, because none were headed his way. But the J-11s were dangerously close now. He had only a few more seconds before they were a threat. Shrek steadied up behind the nearest JH-7, selected his Equalizer gun on his flight stick, then squeezed the trigger. The 25mm bullets and red tracer rounds streamed toward the Chinese aircraft, missing it just to the right. Before the pilot could react, Shrek tweaked his aim left and the tracers cut across the fuselage of the Chinese jet. The JH-7 began trailing orange flames and black smoke from its starboard engine, and seconds later the fuselage exploded. Shrek juked to the right to avoid the debris from the expanding fireball.

Red tracer rounds passed over his canopy. The nearest J-11B was firing. Shrek juked left and right at random intervals, hoping to prevent the Chinese pilot from getting a bead on him. Although the J-11Bs were his most pressing concern, Shrek had another problem. The inbound JH-7s were approaching the range at which *Reagan*'s cruisers and destroyers would engage incoming aircraft with Standard missiles. This was as far as he could follow the Chinese fighter-bombers. The other three U.S. planes disengaged and turned away from the JH-7s, met by a half-dozen J-10s and J-11s in pursuit. Shrek activated his radio, contacting his strike controller on *Reagan*.

"Alpha Papa, Knight One. Disengaging from incoming Hostiles. You've got thirty-five Leakers."

It was now up to the cruisers and destroyers.

Shrek banked hard right, looking through the cockpit window at the two J-11s. Both adjusted course, angling toward him.

Inside *Reagan*'s Combat Direction Center, Captain Debbie Kent stared at the displays on the Video Wall. She had watched their Combat Air Patrol almost disintegrate under the Chinese onslaught; less than a third of their fighters remained. They had performed admirably, shooting down an impressive number of Chinese aircraft, but a significant number of Chinese fighter-bombers made it through. As Kent counted the number of inbound aircraft on the display, she realized they weren't dealing with Leakers. It was a flood. Between the three streams of contacts headed toward *Reagan* and her escorts, there were over one hundred inbound Hostiles.

Now that the Chinese aircraft had penetrated *Reagan*'s Combat Air Patrol, the cruisers and destroyers would take over. Kent would be a bystander for this phase, watching as *Reagan*'s escorts engaged with Standard SM-2 and SM-6 missiles. There were so many contacts that they would have to turn things over to the computers aboard their ships. The Air Warfare Commander aboard USS *Chosin* reached the same conclusion.

"All units, this is Alpha Whiskey. Shift Aegis Warfare Systems to auto. You are *Weapons Free*."

Kent watched as the computers aboard the two cruisers and four destroyers began automatically "hooking" contacts, assigning them to missiles in the ships' vertical launchers. The Aegis computers worked together, communicating with each other so that no ship targeted the same contact. Missiles began streaking skyward from the six ships.

As the missiles headed toward the incoming Chinese aircraft, the number of contacts on Kent's display began to multiply. In a few seconds, the original one hundred contacts had morphed into over five hundred. The *Reagan* Task Force had engaged the Chinese fighter-bombers too late, and they had launched their air-to-surface missiles, which apparently had a longer range than expected. The Aegis computers continued to hook the incoming targets, now concentrating on the faster-moving group of four hundred contacts rapidly closing *Reagan* and her six escorts. Kent did the math. There were more incoming missiles than Standard missiles.

It was like watching a video game, streams of blue icons headed out in three directions, approaching the incoming red icons. The two waves of icons intercepted each other, and the Standard missiles intercepted the majority of inbound contacts. But not all. Over fifty missiles continued inbound, targeting *Reagan* and her escorts. It was time for the self-defense phase. Kent looked over at her Tactical Action Officer.

"Shift SSDS to auto."

The TAO acknowledged, then shifted *Reagan*'s SSDS—Ship Self-Defense System—to automatic. Like the Aegis Warfare Systems aboard the cruisers and destroyers, *Reagan*'s SSDS would automatically assign contacts to their RAM and ESSM missiles, then target any Leakers with their CIWS guns. It was out of Kent's hands now. All she could do was watch.

The TAO called out, "Inbound missiles. Brace for impact!"

Kent reached up and grabbed onto an I beam, watching as the SSDS automatically targeted the missiles streaking toward *Reagan*. It all happened in a matter of seconds. Two missiles made it through and Kent felt the ship shudder twice as the missiles impacted *Reagan*. On the Damage Control Status Board, red indications on the starboard side of the carrier marked the missile impact and damage radius. Thankfully, the Hangar Deck hadn't been penetrated, nor the carrier's Island superstructure damaged. *Reagan* had survived the Chinese missile onslaught relatively unscathed.

The surviving Chinese aircraft swept past the *Reagan* Task Force, their missiles expended, headed back to China. Kent examined the display in front of her, surveying the carnage. Only thirty of the ninety-six American fighters remained aloft. However, China had paid dearly. The American fighters and Standard missiles had shot down over three hundred Chinese aircraft. Kent let out a sigh of relief. *Reagan* had survived, as did the amphibs, which hadn't been targeted. The cruisers and destroyers, however, did not fare as well.

Several of the screens on the Video Wall in front of Kent switched to real-time video feeds. Black plumes rose from all six escorts, and USS *Chosin* was engulfed in flames, black smoke billowing upward. *Chosin* was their Air Warfare Commander and one of only two cruisers. They could ill afford to lose her.

Kent picked up the Navy Red phone next to her. "Alpha Whiskey, this is Alpha Papa. Report operational status, over."

There was no response. Only static on the line.

Kent repeated her request. "Alpha Whiskey, this is Alpha Papa. Report operational status, over."

A few seconds later, there was a response, but it was from the other cruiser, USS *Port Royal*. "Alpha Papa, This is Alpha Bravo. Alpha Whiskey has dropped off the grid. I am assuming duties of Air Warfare Commander."

"Alpha Bravo, this is Alpha Papa. Understand. What is the status of the destroyers and air-defense inventory?"

"Three destroyers are operational, but all units on the grid are Winchester on SM-2 and SM-6 missiles."

The last part of *Port Royal*'s report hit Kent in the gut. They were out of Standard missiles, leaving only close-in self-defense systems. They could now only target missiles approaching their own ship. *Reagan* and the amphibs were on their own. It was time to bring the remaining thirty F/A-18s and Joint Strike Fighters back for refueling and rearming.

As Kent turned her attention to the aircraft on the display, icons began populating the edges of her monitor. Three more streams of contacts were inbound, and the icons soon switched from Unknown to Hostile. It was a second wave of Chinese fighters—another four hundred.

Kent hung her head. With only thirty fighters aloft, their missile inventory and decoys no doubt expended, their CAP would be wiped out. With no Standard missiles to shoot down incoming fighter-bombers or their missiles, it was going to be a one-sided bloodbath. There was no way the *Reagan* Task Force would survive.

77

BEIJING

Christine had no idea how long she lay sprawled on the floor of Xiang's office; the room was spinning and she fought the urge to vomit. Blood was seeping into her right eye, and the side of her head throbbed with every heartbeat. She wiped the blood from her eye, and as her vision slowly cleared, she saw Huan standing above her, a one-foot bronze statue of Mao Zedong in his hand.

"Quid pro quo, my American friend."

She could hear the smugness in his voice.

Christine struggled to climb to her feet. She paused on her knees and right hand, waiting until the room stopped spinning.

Huan addressed her again, his voice agitated this time. "You will pay for what you've done." His right foot added an exclamation mark to his threat, connecting solidly with Christine's already-broken ribs.

Pain shot through her chest and the kick took the wind from her lungs, simultaneously knocking her onto her side. She heard Xiang's stern voice, but he was speaking Mandarin and she had no idea what he said. The only thing she could focus on was the pain coursing through her body. Every breath was pure agony, joining the pain shooting through her shoulder and head. Huan was bent on killing her, and death would be a blessed relief. But there was one thing that kept her going.

I'm gonna kill Huan if it's the last thing I do.

More easily thought than done, however. She glanced at the Glock, only a few feet away. If she ignored the pain, she could scramble for it. Huan caught her glance at the pistol and stooped down, grabbing it before Christine could make a dash for it.

Before she could focus on a new plan, Huan spoke. "On your knees, Christine."

Xiang spoke again, his words terse. Huan turned toward him, and Christine could hear the hatred in the younger man's voice as the two men exchanged heated words in Mandarin. Finally, Huan turned back to Christine as Xiang glared at him.

"On your knees," Huan repeated.

Christine eyed Huan's shoes warily as she pushed herself gingerly onto her right hand and knees again.

"Tell us how to disable the virus you injected into our command and control system," Huan said, "and I will let you live."

She looked up at Huan. "I have no idea if it can be disabled. But even if I knew how, I wouldn't tell you."

Huan studied her a moment before replying. "You lie." He raised the pistol, leveling it at her head. "Tell me how to disable the virus."

Christine stared at the pistol pointed at her head, then looked up at Huan. "Take a hike."

Huan's face clouded as he tried to decipher Christine's response.

There was a loud knock on the door, followed by a muffled question in Chinese. Christine could hear the concern in the man's voice, no doubt raised by the two dead bodyguards sprawled on the floor outside the president's office. Huan lowered his gun and opened the door, revealing two additional Cadre Department bodyguards.

After a brief exchange of words, one man took station outside the president's office, while the other headed down the corridor. Huan returned to his position in front of Christine, but this time left the gun at his side.

"If you don't know how to disable the virus, perhaps your friend does. We'll see how much he values your life."

There was another knock on Xiang's door a few minutes later. Huan opened the door to reveal Lieutenant Harrison standing in the doorway, his hands handcuffed behind his back, with a Cadre Department bodyguard behind him. Huan issued an order and Harrison was pushed into Xiang's office. Harrison looked pale and his face was bruised and swollen, and the left side of his rugby shirt was caked with dried blood. Despite his worn exterior, however, his eyes remained bright, shifting between Christine and the men in the room. He stopped beside Christine, while the Cadre bodyguard moved to the side of the room.

As she wondered what had happened to Harrison after she stepped onto the ledge, her subconscious gnawed at her, telling her there was something important she was overlooking. She examined Harrison again, then the Cadre Department bodyguard, and she suddenly recognized the guard. He was Yang Minsheng, head of Xiang's security detail.

The man who had set her free from the Great Hall and given her the flash drive.

Yang gave no indication he was willing to assist them, however. He stood with his hands at his sides, awaiting further orders. Still, there was a glimmer of hope.

"What is your friend's name, Christine?" Huan asked. "I'm afraid he hasn't been forthcoming with any useful information, including his name."

Christine refused to answer.

"Well," Huan said, "perhaps it's not necessary." He spoke to Harrison. "Tell us how to disable the virus and I will let Christine live. Refuse, and she dies."

Harrison said nothing, staring blankly across the room.

Huan raised his pistol, pointing it at Christine's head. "I'll give you one more chance. Talk or she dies."

Harrison stared at Huan dispassionately for a moment, then looked at Christine. "I'm sorry, Chris. You know I can't help them."

Even though she knew that would be Harrison's response, his words stung nonetheless. Deep down, she wanted Harrison to love her enough to do whatever it took to save her life.

"It's okay," Christine replied.

Looking at the pistol in Huan's hand, she focused on his index finger, wrapped around the trigger. As long as the flesh remained pink, there was hope. But when the flesh turned white, it would be over.

She glanced at Yang, but he remained as still as a statue. Christine then realized that Yang had killed the guard and given her the flash drive in secrecy—no one knew it was him. But to save her life, Yang would have to expose himself in front of Huan and Xiang. Would he? Or was his position within China's highest body of government more important than her and Harrison's lives?

As Christine prepared to meet her fate, Xiang interjected, speaking to Huan from behind his desk. The tone of his voice was unmistakable. A man in charge of an entire country, giving an order to a subordinate. Huan ignored Xiang's words, pushing the cold metal barrel of the Glock against Christine's forehead.

Huan turned his head toward Xiang as he spoke in English, apparently for Christine's benefit, maintaining the pistol pressed firmly into her forehead.

"I do not disobey you lightly, Chenglei, but I must take revenge for what she has done. She destroyed years of painstaking preparation, and China is humiliated again by an imperial power. The lives of many men will amount to nothing."

Xiang replied, also in English. "No one will obtain the revenge they deserve. Not me, for what was done to my mother, not America, for the lives lost in this conflict, and not you. Put down the gun."

Huan ignored Xiang's command. Turning back to Christine, he spoke in English.

"Time to die."

Terror tore through Christine's mind. Up to this second, she believed she would live; that she would somehow find a way out of her predicament. Her breathing turned shallow and her pulse began to race. She felt light-headed and she braced herself with her right hand, but that only caused her to lean forward, pressing her forehead more firmly into the pistol barrel.

Huan's finger turned from pink to white as he began squeezing the trigger.

There was a flash of movement along the side of the room. Yang pulled his pistol from its holster, leveling it at Huan as he shouted in Chinese. Huan's expression transitioned from surprise to malevolence, then he slowly lowered his gun and tossed it onto the floor.

The president's stern voice captured Christine's attention. He was yelling at Yang.

Yang ignored China's president, keeping his eyes fixed on Huan as he reached into his pocket and tossed Christine a key. "Unlock your friend's handcuffs. We're going to need his help getting out of here."

Christine pulled herself to her feet using Harrison's arm for assistance, as Huan verbally lambasted Yang. A torrent of Chinese streamed from his mouth, his face turning red as he no doubt cursed Yang for his treason. Christine unlocked Harrison's handcuffs, and he rubbed his wrists as he turned toward Christine and Huan. He was about to say something when a gunshot rang out.

Yang's body jerked backward. Christine's eyes went first to Yang. He'd been shot in the side. She looked across the room toward Xiang, still standing behind his desk, the top right drawer open. Xiang held a pistol in his hand, aimed at Yang.

Yang swiveled toward Xiang as China's president fired again, this time hitting Yang in the chest. Yang collapsed onto the floor, his gun falling from his hand.

As the second shot rang out from Xiang's pistol, Harrison was already moving. He took two steps toward Xiang, then launched himself headfirst over the president's desk. Xiang swung his arm toward Harrison as he crashed into Xiang with a flying tackle. The two men disappeared behind the desk as they fell to the floor, and Christine could hear them struggling. There would normally be no doubt as to who would prevail, but Harrison was injured, with a bullet in his shoulder.

Christine looked at Huan, only a few feet away from her. Their eyes locked for an instant, then Huan's eyes went to Yang's pistol on the floor. Christine suddenly realized her peril. He was closer to the gun and would reach it first. She glanced down, locating her Glock ten feet away where Huan had tossed it.

Huan ducked down, reaching for Yang's gun while Christine dove for hers. She landed on her stomach, sliding across the floor, ignoring the pain stabbing through her chest and left shoulder. Her outstretched right hand found the Glock, and she grabbed it. She slid her finger over the trigger as she twisted onto her back. Huan had Yang's gun and was swinging it up. Christine took aim as Huan's hand steadied, and both fired simultaneously. Huan's bullet tore into Christine's right thigh as her bullet hit him in the chest. He dropped to his knees, the gun tumbling from his hand.

As the sound of the gunshots faded, the door to Xiang's office burst open. In the doorway stood the Cadre Department bodyguard who had taken station outside the president's office. His gun was drawn and held extended with both hands. He surveyed the situation in Xiang's office—Huan, Christine, and Yang on the floor, with the sounds of a struggle coming from behind the president's desk. His eyes went back to Christine and the gun in her hand, and he took aim at her.

Christine swung the pistol toward the bodyguard and fired first. The bullet hit him in the chest, jerking his aim as he fired. The wood floor by Christine's head splintered as a bullet impacted an inch to the left of her ear.

The bodyguard stumbled backward a step, but remained standing. He regained his balance, showing no indication he'd been injured. Christine then remembered the two bodyguards outside Xiang's office had been wearing bulletproof vests. She raised her pistol, steadying up on the bodyguard's head and squeezed the trigger again.

The pistol hammer fell on an empty chamber.

She was out of bullets.

Christine glanced at Yang's pistol on the floor near Huan. He was still on his knees, supporting himself with both hands, oblivious to what was happening.

The Cadre Department Bodyguard adjusted the aim of his pistol. Christine knew there was no way she could reach Yang's gun in time. The bodyguard's hand steadied, his pistol pointed squarely at her head, and a shot rang out.

Christine flinched, but no bullet penetrated her body.

Instead, the bodyguard jolted backward again as two more shots were fired. Two bullets hit him in the chest, and a third in his forehead. His head snapped back and he fell to the ground.

Christine looked around and spotted Harrison standing behind Xiang's desk, the president's pistol in his hand. Behind him, Xiang was slowly pulling himself to his feet, his hand on the edge of his credenza along the back wall. Harrison moved quickly, heading toward the door to Xiang's office. He dragged the bodyguard inside, then closed the door and locked it. He turned to assess Christine and the two men on the floor.

Both Huan and Yang were alive. Huan was still on his knees, his head bowed and hands on the floor, blood spreading across his shirt from the bullet hole in his chest. Yang was trying to push himself into a sitting position. Harrison kicked the gun away from Huan, then after a quick glance at Christine's leg, hustled over to Yang, propping him against the wall. Harrison examined Yang's wounds, glancing occasionally at Huan and Xiang.

Christine stood, doing her best to ignore the pain shooting through her thigh, and retrieved Yang's pistol from the floor. She had unfinished business. She turned and leveled the gun at Xiang, who was standing behind his desk again.

"Order your military to stand down," Christine said. "End this war."

Xiang said nothing, glaring at Christine instead.

"Terminate all military operations," she said, "or I'll put a bullet in your head."

Xiang finally responded, "You would not kill an unarmed man in cold blood."

Christine studied Xiang, searching for a way to coerce him. She needed to convince Xiang she was serious about killing him—*in cold blood* as he described it. As she stood with the pistol aimed at China's president, pain from her broken ribs sliced through her chest with every breath, blood trickled down the side of her face from the laceration in her scalp, and blood from the bullet hole in her thigh soaked her pants leg. She glanced at Huan, the man responsible for all three injuries, still kneeling on his hands and knees a few feet away.

Christine swung the pistol toward Huan. He looked up at her, hatred burning in his eyes. She steadied her aim and squeezed the trigger. The back of Huan's head exploded outward and he slumped to the floor.

Harrison, who had been tending to Yang's wounds, stood and turned toward Christine, examining Huan's body. "What the hell are you doing, Chris?"

Christine ignored Harrison as she swung the pistol back toward Xiang. "Let's try this again. Order your military to stand down, or I'll put you down."

Xiang's eyes narrowed for a moment, then he reached for his phone.

"No funny business," Christine said. She glanced at Yang, sitting up against the wall. "Are you lucid enough to listen to what he's saying?"

Yang grimaced, then replied, "Yes."

Xiang lifted the receiver to his ear and punched one of the buttons on the phone. A few seconds later, he spoke into the mouthpiece in Chinese. After a short pause, he hung up the phone. Christine looked at Yang, who nodded his head.

Christine returned her attention to Xiang, keeping her gun pointed at him.

"Thank you, Chenglei. Now it's time for you to pay."

Harrison intervened. "He's done what you asked, Chris. There's no reason to kill him."

Christine replied, "This man is responsible for the death of tens of thousands. He needs to suffer the consequences for what he's done."

"You can't kill him. He's the president of China."

"He's the head of their army," Christine said. "He deserves to suffer the same fate many of them have."

"Put the gun down, Chris."

Christine didn't reply, focusing her attention on Xiang again. He stood there, stoically, giving no indication he feared for his life. "Give me one reason I shouldn't kill you," she said.

Xiang was silent for a moment, then replied, "Because if you kill me, you will not make it out of the Great Hall alive. You are not simply choosing between *my* life and death, you are deciding *yours*. Let me live, and I will ensure you and your friends receive medical care and a safe return home."

Christine considered Xiang's words. He had a point. By killing him, she'd be sentencing herself, Harrison, and Yang to death. There was no way they could fight their way out of the Great Hall of the People.

"How can we trust you?" Christine asked.

"Despite what you may think, I am an honorable man, Miss O'Connor. You have my word."

Christine's hand wavered as she evaluated her options. Finally, her hand steadied as she made her decision.

78

USS *RONALD REAGAN*

On the Bridge of USS *Reagan*, Captain CJ Berger examined the two displays on the bulkhead in front of him. One, connected to the ship's organic sensors, was void of enemy contacts, failing to display the danger headed toward them. The other monitor, however, told the real story. Connected to the Link 16 system, it recorded the location of every contact reported by the E-2C Hawkeyes above them, and well as every ship on the grid. Streaming in from three directions were another four hundred Chinese aircraft.

Despite the impending onslaught, it was eerily quiet on the aircraft carrier. The Air Boss on the Tower Deck had no incoming aircraft to direct, and the Flight Deck below was empty. All of *Reagan*'s aircraft were aloft, and there was no time to bring them back to refuel or rearm them.

Berger watched as the Chinese aircraft steadily closed the distance to the remaining thirty U.S. fighters. The Chinese would slice through the remnants of *Reagan*'s Combat Air Patrol like a hot knife through butter, then unleash a barrage of missiles that would overwhelm *Reagan*'s self-defense systems.

There was a slim chance the aircraft carrier would survive. She was a huge ship and could weather dozens of air-to-surface missile strikes, depending on where they hit. *Reagan*'s cruiser and destroyer escorts were not as fortunate. They were much smaller and would be devastated by even a few missiles. The amphibs were large but some of them had less capable self-defense systems.

The TAO's voice crackled across the speaker next to Berger. He could hear the desperation in the TAO's voice as he directed the strike controllers to engage all incoming Hostiles. As the orders went out from the strike controllers, Berger's eyes returned to the displays in front of him, surprised by what he saw. The red icons had halted their advance toward *Reagan*.

Berger picked up the microphone, selecting CDC, his eyes still fixed on the display. "OPSO, Captain. Report status of inbound Hostiles."

Captain Kent's voice came across the speaker. "Captain, OPSO. We're evaluating, but it appears all Hostiles have turned to an outbound course."

Berger studied the display. Sure enough, the icons began inching outward. It took a moment for him to process the information. He had no idea why, but the Chinese aircraft were heading home.

He watched the display a while longer, verifying that the Chinese aircraft were indeed returning to base, then he finally allowed himself to relax. He knew that down in CDC, they would be relieved as well. But there would be no cheering. They had lost too many good men and women today.

APRA HARBOR, GUAM

Under a clear blue sky, the air was still and the sun hot on Christine's shoulders as she stood on the wharf in Apra Harbor, the main port in the American territory of Guam. The small Western Pacific island was home to the only American submarine homeport, aside from Pearl Harbor, outside the continental United States. But today the port serviced more than submarines. Christine's eyes scanned the wharves, noting the dozen surface ships tied up, their superstructures blackened or their decks listing to one side. Except for *Ronald Reagan* and her escorts still at sea, this was all that remained of the once-powerful Pacific Fleet.

Next to her stood what remained of the five-man SEAL team inserted into China. Lieutenant Harrison had his left arm in a dark blue sling, matching the one Christine wore. Harrison's injury had not been serious, nor were her wounds. The bullets had been removed and her shoulder and thigh were now bandaged, and she leaned on a crutch under her right arm.

Standing in Xiang Chenglei's office six days ago, she had decided to spare his life, and he had kept his promise. After an overnight stay in Tiantan Hospital under the close supervision of Cadre Department personnel, she, Harrison, and Yang were transported to Beijing's Nanyuan Airport, where they embarked an American Air Force 747, which had arrived with a diplomatic entourage. They had headed east while negotiations between China and the West had begun.

After Xiang issued the cease-fire order in his office, the PLA Air Force had terminated its attack on the *Reagan* Task Force, and by the time she had confronted Xiang, Chinese troops had already begun their withdrawal from Japan. But not Taiwan. That was China's bargaining chip. Taiwan was firmly in communist Chinese control, and PLA troops had dug in and been well supplied. Even with the arrival of the Atlantic Fleet carrier strike groups, the PLA could not be dislodged from Taiwan easily. China would not leave Taiwan without concessions.

Although China had withdrawn its forces from Japan, a thinly veiled threat remained. The PLA Navy had been mostly destroyed, but the PLA Air Force, despite the losses inflicted by the *Reagan* Task Force, was still the most formidable air force in Asia, as was China's Army, still numbering near three million strong when fully mobilized. There were other natural resources in the region that China could wrest from its neighbors without reliance on its Navy. If the fundamental issue of affordable access to natural resources wasn't addressed . . .

It looked like China would achieve their objective after all. The negotiations were not yet complete, but China's military offensive—diplomacy through other means—had succeeded. The MAER Accord would be modified, restructuring the price calculations, allowing "equal" access to the region's natural resources. China would cede control of Taiwan in return.

As negotiations concerning one island—Taiwan—neared completion, Christine found herself on another. After boarding the 747 for its return flight to Washington, she had directed the pilot to proceed to Guam instead, informing the president she had unfinished business that required her presence on the small Pacific island.

Christine checked her watch; it was almost time. She shifted her gaze toward the entrance to Apra Harbor, searching for the silhouette of USS *Michigan*, spotting the black shape on the horizon. *Michigan* was pulling into port. Two tugs, *Goliath* and *Qupuha*, idling in the harbor up to now, began their outbound transit to mate with the inbound SSGN, guiding her final approach to the wharf. As Christine prepared to wait the remaining twenty minutes before *Michigan* tied up, her thoughts shifted from the submarine that was about to return to port to the thirty fast attacks that would not.

At least that was what everyone had initially thought. China had made the same strategic error that Japan made during World War II, attacking the Pacific Fleet in shallow water. On the evening of December 7, 1941, the Pacific Fleet lay in ruins in the shallows of Pearl Harbor. Yet in the following months, the Pearl Harbor shipyard raised every ship that had been sunk except for USS *Arizona*, returning every destroyer, cruiser, and battleship to service except for the *Arizona* and *Oklahoma*—the latter had capsized while being towed back to the mainland for repairs. China sank twenty-four of the American submarines in the shallow Taiwan Strait, where the water depth averaged only two hundred feet, well below a submarine's Crush Depth. As a result, if the submarines could be raised from the bottom, only the compartment that had been breached by the torpedo would need to be repaired.

Could it be done? The answer from NAVSEA engineers was—yes! The capability had already been demonstrated when the Russian submarine *Kursk* was raised from the bottom of the Barents Sea in 2001. The green light had already been given to the monumental project of raising the twenty-four fast attacks from the bottom of the Taiwan Strait, along with the first three submarines that were sunk in the shallow waters outside the South, East, and North Sea Fleet ports.

The four carriers sunk in the Strait would also be raised, although that feat would be significantly more challenging, since the carriers were hundred-thousand-ton behemoths. But hopefully enough of the carriers' compartments had been sealed during General Quarters that the carriers were lighter than their official tonnage. The major unknown was the status of their keels. If their keels were intact, the four Nimitz class carriers could be raised without breaking apart. All across the country, naval and private shipyards were gearing up for round-the-clock shiftwork, preparing for the arrival of the remnants of the Pacific Fleet. It would be expensive and take time, but it appeared that the Pacific Fleet could be restored in a matter of years, not decades.

A blast from one of the tugs brought Christine's attention to *Michigan*, gliding slowly toward the wharf. She spotted Captain Murray Wilson on the Bridge, supervising Lieutenant Herndon, who was on watch as Officer of the Deck and busy passing orders to the Helm. The eighteen-thousand-ton submarine coasted expertly to a halt alongside the wharf and a flurry of activity commenced, men passing lines across from the wharf to personnel on the Missile Deck, while others prepared to hook up shore power so the reactor could be shut down.

Wilson noticed Christine on the wharf and waved; she waved back. This was the second time America had relied on Captain Murray Wilson, and she felt obliged to offer her appreciation in person. A brow was soon in place and men began hustling across in both directions. Christine would wait for

Captain Wilson to debark, but Harrison would join his unit aboard the submarine.

During the days spent waiting on Guam, neither she nor Harrison had mentioned it. His passionate embrace before she stepped onto the ledge outside the Great Hall of the People had been nothing more than a good-luck kiss. At least that's what she told herself, each time her thoughts wandered. Harrison was a married man, and whatever feelings he had for her were irrelevant, as were her feelings for him. Still, she enjoyed spending time with him, and she went out of her way to arrange lunches and dinners together. She caught herself stealing glances at him, thinking about what might have been. But that was over twenty years ago. They had chosen separate paths, and there was no going back.

Speaking of going back, Christine had been debating whether to ask Harrison to return to Washington with her, purportedly to help debrief the president on the SEAL team mission. Up to now, she had opted against asking him. But with the arrival of *Michigan*—and Harrison's departure only minutes away, she finally gave in. She turned toward Harrison.

"Jake, I've been thinking, and I'd like you to join me at the White House to debrief the president. I think he'd appreciate the perspective of someone with a more tactical background."

Harrison was silent for a while, his eyes probing hers, and Christine hoped he hadn't seen through her thinly veiled plan. Finally, he replied, "Thanks for the offer, but I don't think that's necessary. You were with us the whole time, and you were the one who completed the mission. You're more than capable of debriefing the president without me. Plus, it's not my call. I belong with my unit, and Commander McNeil would be the one to authorize my absence. You'd have to ask him. But if it's all right with you, I'd rather just decline now and leave it at that."

Christine let out an inward sigh. It wasn't the answer she had hoped for. "All right, Jake. But if you change your mind, let me know."

Harrison said nothing for a while, then returned his attention to *Michigan*. There was a break in personnel crossing the brow, providing a path for him to board the submarine. He turned back to Christine.

"Any last words?"

Christine shook her head.

"Then I think this is where we say good-bye."

Christine smiled. "Again."

She resisted the urge to reach out and touch his arm, to give any indication of how she felt. He stared into her eyes for a long moment, and it looked as if there was something he wanted to say, but then he turned and headed toward the submarine without another word. Christine watched as he crossed the brow and disappeared down the Missile Compartment hatch.

COMPLETE CAST OF CHARACTERS

CHINESE CHARACTERS

WEDDING PARTY (PROLOGUE)

BAI JIAO, prime minister's daughter

HUANG FU, Bai Jiao's fiancé

FENG DAI, Bai Jiao's bodyguard

ADMINISTRATION

XIANG CHENGLEI, president and general secretary of the Party

HUAN ZHIXIN, chairman, Central Military Commission

BAI TAO, prime minister

SHEN YI, Politburo senior member (Huan Zhixin's uncle)

DENG CHUNG, Politburo junior member

WANG QUI, national security advisor

XIE HAI, President Xiang's executive assistant

YANG MINSHENG, head of President Xiang's security detail

MILITARY

TSOU DESHI (Fleet Admiral), Commander, People's Liberation Army (PLA) Navy

GUO JIAN (Admiral), Commander, East Sea Fleet

SHI CHEN (Admiral), Commander, North Sea Fleet

CAO FENG (General), Commander, Fourth Department

ZHANG ANGUO (General), Commander, Nanjing Military Region

SHAO JINHAI (Vice Admiral), Admiral challenging plan during operations brief

ZHOU PENGFEI (Captain), Commander, 34th *Hong Niao* Missile Battery

CHENG BO (Captain), Officer-in-Charge, East Sea Fleet Command Center

ZENG YONG (Commander), Commanding Officer, submarine CNS *Chang Cheng*

ZHAO WEI (Commander), Commanding Officer, submarine CNS *Jiaolong*

LIANG AIGUO (First Lieutenant), *Xian* H-6F bomber pilot

JIANG QUI, Chinese soldier landing on shore of Taiwan (Baishawan Beach)

XIULAN, Jiang Qui's girlfriend

FENG, Jian Qui's best friend

CIVILIAN

PENG YAOTING, CIA agent in Beijing

TIAN AIGUO, CIA agent in Beijing

YUAN GUI, driver who takes Christine and SEALs to the Great Hall of the People

PENG WEIJIE, Baishawan Beach grandmother

XIAOTIEN, Baishawan Beach granddaughter

"SCARFACE", Ringleader of teenagers stopping Christine O'Connor in hutong

CHRIS STEVENSON, Chinese agent in Panama

LIJUAN, President Xiang's mother (referenced only)

BOHAI, President Xiang's father (referenced only)

AMERICAN CHARACTERS

ADMINISTRATION

BOB TOMPKINS, vice president

KEVIN HARDISON, chief of staff

CHRISTINE O'CONNOR, national security advisor

NELSON JENNINGS, secretary of defense

LINDSAY ROSS, secretary of state

STEVE BRACKMAN (Captain), senior military aide

LARS SIKES, press secretary (referenced only)

JOINT CHIEFS OF STAFF

MARK HODSON (General), Chairman, Joint Chiefs of Staff

MEL GARRISON (General), Chief of Staff, Air Force

GRANT HEALEY (Admiral), Chief of Naval Operations

ELY WILLIAMS (General), Commandant of the Marine Corps

MAJOR MILITARY COMMANDS

VANCE GARBIN (Admiral), Commander, Pacific Command

CARL KRAE (Major General), Commander, Cyber Warfare Command

MICHAEL WALKER (Rear Admiral), Commander, Naval Special Warfare Command

TIM MOSS (Rear Admiral), Program Executive Officer (Submarines)

JOHN STANBURY (Rear Admiral), Commander, Submarine Force Pacific (referenced only)

USS *MICHIGAN* (GUIDED MISSILE SUBMARINE)

MURRAY WILSON (Captain), Commanding Officer

PAUL GREENWOOD (Lieutenant Commander), Executive Officer

KASEY FAUCHER (Lieutenant Commander), Engineering Officer

KELLY HAAS (Lieutenant Commander), Supply Officer

KARL STEWART (Lieutenant), Weapons Officer

STEVE CORDERO (Lieutenant), Junior Officer

KRIS HERNDON (Lieutenant), Junior Officer

ROBERTA CLARK (Lieutenant Junior Grade), Junior Officer

JOE ALEO (Commander), Medical Officer

JEFF WALKUP (Chief Electronics Technician), Radioman

SAM WALSH (Machinist Mate Second Class), Torpedoman

BILL COATES (Electronics Technician Second Class), Quartermaster

SAM MEADE (Mess Specialist First Class), Night Baker

USS *NIMITZ* [AIRCRAFT CARRIER]

ALEX HARROW (Captain), Commanding Officer

HELEN CORCORAN (Captain), Air Wing Commander

SUE LAYBOURN (Captain), Combat Direction Center (CDC) Operations Officer

MICHAEL BERESFORD (Lieutenant Commander), Officer of the Deck

NATHAN REYNOLDS (Lieutenant), Conning Officer

USS *RONALD REAGAN* [AIRCRAFT CARRIER]

CHARLES "CJ" BERGER (Captain), Commanding Officer

EMIL JONES (Captain), Air Wing Commander

TIM POWERS (Captain), Executive Officer

DEBBIE KENT (Captain), Combat Direction Center (CDC) Operations Officer

ANDREW FELLOWS (Commander), Chief Engineer

USS *ANNAPOLIS* [LOS ANGELES CLASS FAST ATTACK SUBMARINE]

RAMSEY HOOTMAN (Commander), Commanding Officer

TED WINSOR (Lieutenant Commander), Executive Officer

DON MILLER (Lieutenant), Weapons Officer

MIKE LAND (Lieutenant), Junior Officer

ARMANDO HOGARTH (Lieutenant), Junior Officer

USS *JACKSONVILLE* [LOS ANGELES CLASS FAST ATTACK SUBMARINE]

RANDY BAUGHMAN (Commander), Commanding Officer

BECK BURRELL (Lieutenant), Officer of the Deck

USS *TEXAS* [VIRGINIA CLASS FAST ATTACK SUBMARINE]

JIM LATHAM (Commander), Commanding Officer

JOHN MILLIGAN (Lieutenant Commander), Executive Officer

COLBY MARSHALL (Petty Officer First Class), Fire Control Technician

USS *LAKE ERIE* (TICONDEROGA CLASS GUIDED MISSILE CRUISER)

MARY CORDEIRO (Captain), Commanding Officer
SHVETA THAKRAR (Lieutenant Commander), Tactical Action Officer
MARIO CAITI (Senior Chief Fire Controlman), Combat Systems Coordinator

NAVY SEALS

JOHN MCNEIL (Commander), SEAL Team Commander
JAKE HARRISON (Lieutenant), SEAL Platoon Officer in Charge (OIC)
DAN O'HARA (Chief Special Warfare Operator), SEAL Platoon Chief
DREW GARRETSON (Special Warfare Operator First Class), Communicator
TRACEY MARTIN (Special Warfare Operator Second Class), Breacher
KELLY ANDREWS (Special Warfare Operator Second Class), Rappeller
MARLON CRANE (Special Warfare Operator Second Class), Replaced by
    Christine

OTHER CHARACTERS-MILITARY

LELAND GWENN, call sign Vandal (Lieutenant), F/A-18 Pilot
LIZ MICHALSKI, call sign Phoenix (Lieutenant), F/A-18 Pilot
STAN BORUM, call sign Shrek (Lieutenant Colonel), F-35B Pilot
JULIE AUSTIN (Lieutenant Commander), E-2C Combat Information Center
    Officer (CICO)
DEBRA DRIZA (Captain), Commander, Pearl Harbor Naval Shipyard

OTHER CHARACTERS-CIVILIAN

MICHAEL RICHARDSON, U.S. Ambassador to China
DANIEL DEVOR, Panama Canal Supervisor

CALEB MALCOM, Bluestone Security mercenary
ALICE LOWEECEY, Brandon County judge
TINA DILL, Shemya Island Radar Operator
DIMITRIOUS LOUPAS, Shemya Island Radar Supervisor
CINDY PON, Office of Naval Intelligence Analyst
JINA HONG, Office of Naval Intelligence Analyst (night shift) (referenced only)
JAY WOOD, Office of Naval Intelligence Cryptologist

JAPANESE CHARACTERS

MILITARY

SUZUKI KOKI, Japanese Army Major

AUTHOR'S NOTE

I hope you enjoyed reading *Empire Rising*!

This was a more difficult book for me to write than *The Trident Deception*, for two reasons. The first was that it covered areas where I was not a subject matter expert and I had to rely heavily on the expertise of others. The second reason was the scenario itself—war with China and the potential outcome. Some of you will no doubt take exception to the way the U.S. Navy responded, and are convinced there is no way China could destroy virtually all of the Pacific Fleet. I offer you this in my defense—I think you're right!

My personal opinion is that an all-out naval war between the United States and China would be one-sided in the United States' favor and resolved rather quickly. Unfortunately, this would result in a pretty short book. So I "tweaked" a few things so China could go toe-to-toe with the Pacific Fleet, which hopefully made for more exciting reading. Although I try to keep things as grounded in reality as possible, there is no secret Chinese base at Yin Bishou, no sonar pulse that will dud our MK 48 torpedoes, and no malware in our Aegis Warfare System software. (At least, I hope not!) Additionally, I am aware of our war plans with respect to China and therefore cannot replicate them in *Empire Rising*. Or maybe I did. (Gotta keep 'em guessing, right?) Whether our carrier strike groups would actually swing inside the Taiwan Strait, for example, I leave for you to decide.

Also, some of the tactics described were generic and not accurate. For example, torpedo employment and evasion tactics are classified and cannot be accurately represented in this novel. The dialogue isn't 100% accurate either. If it were, much of it would be unintelligible to the average reader, the book filled with Navy acronyms and terms that even I had a hard time following, particularly in the aircraft carrier scenes. (Command and control aboard aircraft carriers is incredibly complicated compared to submarines, with multiple spaces—Combat Direction Center, Air Ops, ID Ops, the Tactical Flag Communication Center, Bridge, Tower—and it would take several chapters just to explain who does what to whom.) To help the story move along without getting bogged down in acronyms, weapon systems, and other Navy jargon, I simplified the dialogue and description of shipboard operations and weapon systems. Those of you who are sticklers for everything being 100% correct will hopefully forgive me.

For all of the above, I apologize. I did my best to keep everything as close to real life as possible while developing a suspenseful, page-turning novel. Hopefully it all worked out, and you enjoyed reading *Empire Rising*.